A *New York Times* Notable Book of 2023 • A *New York Times* Editors' Choice • An Instant *New York Times* Bestseller • A Goodreads Choice Awards Finalist for Best Mystery & Thriller • An Edgar Award Fina**** **Best** Novel • A Libby Book Awards Winner f****

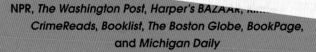

NAMED A BEST BO****
NPR, *The Washington Post*, *Harper's BAZAAR*, ****
CrimeReads, *Booklist*, *The Boston Globe*, *BookPage*,
and *Michigan Daily*

"Sharp, stinging . . . packed with moments when you feel the size of the deck stacked against any woman, young or old, who dares to be 'bright.' Knoll doesn't make Pamela's journey (or ours) an easy one, but it ends in a cathartic, long-bottled-up scream that more people need to hear."
—*The New York Times Book Review*

"A fearless and intoxicating ride into the aftershocks of a series of brutal murders. . . . It's a compelling, almost hypnotic read, and I loved it with a passion."
—Lisa Jewell, *New York Times* bestselling author of *None of This Is True*

"Jessica Knoll at her best—an unflinching and evocative novel about the tabloid fascination with evil and the dynamic and brilliant women who have the real stories to tell."
—Laura Dave, *New York Times* bestselling author of *The Last Thing He Told Me*

"*Bright Young Women* doesn't put its focus on the murderer. It's more interested in his victims—and the survivors who are on a mission to catch him before he kills again."
—*TIME*, The 36 Most Anticipated Books of Fall 2023

"A stunning, engaging subversion of the Bundy myth—and the true crime genre." —*Kirkus Reviews* (starred review), Best Fiction Books of the Year

"Stunning . . . The results are masterful."
—*Publishers Weekly* (starred review)

"PROPULSIVE" —OPRAH DAILY • "STUNNING" —PUBLISHERS WEEKLY

"Sharp, stinging . . . *Bright Young Women* is packed with moments when you feel the size of the deck stacked against any woman, young or old, who dares to be 'bright.' Knoll doesn't make Pamela's journey (or ours) an easy one, but it ends in a cathartic, long-bottled-up scream that more people need to hear. And, one hopes, the telling of this tale (and more like it) will shred the myth of the 'murderer/genius' one cut at a time."

—*The New York Times Book Review*

"*Bright Young Women* is a fearless and intoxicating ride into the aftershocks of a series of brutal murders. Knoll explores in vivid, pointillist prose the effects on the 'bright young women' of the title, both the victims snuffed out in their glorious prime and those left behind in their wake. It's a compelling, almost hypnotic read and I loved it with a passion."

—Lisa Jewell, *New York Times* bestselling author of
Then She Was Gone

"*Bright Young Women* is Jessica Knoll at her best—an unflinching and evocative novel about the tabloid fascination with evil and the dynamic and brilliant women who have the real stories to tell."

—Laura Dave, *New York Times* bestselling author of
The Last Thing He Told Me

"In her third and most assured novel, Knoll shifts readers' attention away from a notorious serial killer, Ted Bundy, and onto the lives—and deaths—of the women he killed. Perhaps for the first time in fiction, Knoll pooh-poohs Bundy's much ballyhooed intelligence, celebrating the promise and perspicacity of his victims instead."

—*The New York Times*, **100 Notable Books of 2023**

"*Bright Young Women* doesn't put its focus on the murderer. It's more interested in his victims—and the survivors who are on a mission to catch him before he kills again."

—*TIME*, **The 36 Most Anticipated Books of Fall 2023**

"A stunning, engaging subversion of the Bundy myth—and the true crime genre."

—*Kirkus Reviews* **(starred review),**
Best Fiction Books of the Year

"Stunning . . . By focusing on the women affected by her Ted Bundy stand-in instead of the nuances of his criminal psychology, Knoll movingly reframes an American obsession without stripping it of its intrigue. The results are masterful."

—*Publishers Weekly* **(starred review)**

"An utterly absorbing, disturbing, and absolutely essential read."

—*Booklist* **(starred review)**

"An unsettling and thrilling page-turner . . . Knoll's haunting, must-read account will captivate [readers] until the end."

—*Library Journal* **(starred review)**

"Blistering and powerful, *Bright Young Women* is an almost unbearably vivid story of sisterhood and survival. With razor-sharp skill, Jessica Knoll deconstructs the myth of a criminal mastermind, revealing the women he seeks to destroy as the truly brilliant ones."

—**Flynn Berry,** *New York Times* **bestselling author of**
Northern Spy* and *Under the Harrow

"In this fictionalized look at Ted Bundy and the fallout from his crime spree, the spotlight shifts away from the killer. Knoll, backed by research that's evident at every twist, compiles a riveting case study exposing how society mythologizes madmen at the expense of the women whose lives they end. Female rage has never felt more warranted—each word is intentional and revelatory, down to the restorative last line."

—*PEOPLE*

"In a world where an obsession with true crime tends to focus on the murderers, Knoll examines the lives of those impacted by heinous acts in a manner that is just as thrilling as any docuseries about a ruthless killer."

—*Entertainment Weekly*

"On one level, *Bright Young Women* is a breakneck thriller based on Ted Bundy's heinous crimes. It ties together the stories of two women with connections to the murders and their search for justice. On another, it functions as a sharp examination of our culture's obsession with serial killers and true crime."

—*Harper's BAZAAR*, **45 Best New Books of 2023 You Won't Put Down**

"With virtuosic pacing, Knoll flashes between perspectives and time-lines, constructing a chorus of women linked by one man's violence but not defined by it . . . Knoll's take down of true crime's misogyny is always razor-sharp. . . . The women have a far more compelling story to tell, one that is every bit as propulsive (and gruesome) as a *Dateline* special but infinitely more insightful."

—*Oprah Daily*

"Though fictionalized, this is a much-needed, deeply researched historical corrective to the strangely romanticized takes on Bundy we've consumed over several decades. Based on newspaper records and other documentary evidence, the beauty, vibrance, and stolen potential of the women who died, and those who survived the Talla-hassee attacks, are vividly rendered."

—*Boston Globe*, **Six Favorite Social Thrillers from 2023**

"After her success with books such as *Luckiest Girl Alive* (now a movie starring Mila Kunis) and *The Favorite Sister*, Jessica Knoll turns to history in her latest novel, specifically Ted Bundy. *Bright Young Women* opens with a powerful—and gory—scene evoking Bundy's killing spree at a sorority house in the late seventies, which left two young women dead and another two maimed. Rather than sensationalize violence against women, however, Knoll's provoc-ative novel focuses on the stories of those affected by the killer's rampages."

—*The Washington Post*, **The 12 Best Thrillers of 2023**

"All in all, it's safe to say this book earned a five-star rating among our readers."

—*Marie Claire*

"Part historical fiction—an old story told from a refreshingly new perspective—and part mystery. There are multiple voices and mul-tiple time periods, but it all gets woven together with a great payoff at the end. Read it for the great characters, lots of plot, and enough unanswered questions that you'll have trouble putting it down."

—**Elissa Nadworny, NPR, Books We Love**

"[An] electrifying thriller . . . This is a tale of courage and resilience, with evocative scenes and multidimensional characters. Knoll has written not only a propulsive crime novel that will keep readers riveted late into the night, but also a scathing indictment of the often-flawed justice system."

—*Shelf Awareness*

"*Bright Young Women* reads like a thriller, but it is so much more than that. It's about the misogyny of violence, sensationalism, sisterhood, the lessons we learn, and listening to our instincts. Above all, though, it's about survival and how we deal with the hand we are dealt."

—*Book Reporter*

"Inspired by the real-life case of the 'All-American Sex Killer,' the new novel from Jessica Knoll aims to flip the usual serial killer story upside down. Knoll's book focuses on the women involved—victims, survivors, and investigators—and turns a bright light on the banality of evil."

—*Goodreads*, **Readers' 55 Most Anticipated Books of Fall**

"Jessica Knoll is a careful writer, and this, her third novel, is a perfect match for her cold dissection of social mores and her fierce rage at misogyny. Knoll takes on the story of Ted Bundy, told from the perspective of a student who survives a horrific attack on a sorority house. . . . Some may claim that the crime genre is rift with misogyny; those people have not read Jessica Knoll. She tears apart the restrictive world of women's roles and lays bare the purpose of such hobbles: to keep women from making a scene, to keep them from seeking justice, and most of all, to keep them from seeking their own lives."

—*CrimeReads/Lit Hub*,
Most Anticipated Books of 2023

"*Bright Young Women* braids the stories of two survivors, Pamela and Tina, and their fervent bond forged through grief and a pursuit of justice."

—*Bustle*, **35 Best New Books of Fall 2023**

"Jessica Knoll's *Bright Young Women* is a primal scream for women past and present."

—*BookPage*

"Compelling . . . A smart, absorbing book."

—*Minneapolis Star Tribune*

"Something about fall weather begs for a thriller, and Jessica Knoll delivers with her latest."

—Country Living

"A serial killer thriller that grounds its fictional story in echoes of Ted Bundy's real-life crimes in order to explore complex themes of misogyny, survivor's guilt, and sensationalism, this is a true crime adjacent novel that thoughtfully deconstructs the genre at its center."

—Paste

MARYSUE
RUCCI
BOOKS

BRIGHT YOUNG WOMEN

JESSICA KNOLL

MARYSUE
RUCCI
BOOKS

New York London Toronto Sydney New Delhi

**MARYSUE
RUCCI
BOOKS**

Marysue Rucci Books
An Imprint of Simon & Schuster, LLC
1230 Avenue of the Americas
New York, NY 10020

First Marysue Rucci Books trade paperback edition August 2024

MARYSUE RUCCI BOOKS and colophon are trademarks of Simon & Schuster, LLC

Simon & Schuster: Celebrating 100 Years of Publishing in 2024

For information about special discounts for bulk purchases, please contact Simon & Schuster Special Sales at 1-866-506-1949 or business@simonandschuster.com.

The Simon & Schuster Speakers Bureau can bring authors to your live event. For more information or to book an event, contact the Simon & Schuster Speakers Bureau at 1-866-248-3049 or visit our website at www.simonspeakers.com.

Interior design by Jaime Putorti

Manufactured in the United States of America

1 3 5 7 9 10 8 6 4 2

Library of Congress Cataloging-in-Publication Data has been applied for.

ISBN 978-1-5011-5322-8
ISBN 978-1-5011-5323-5 (pbk)
ISBN 978-1-5011-5324-2 (ebook)

*For C—I couldn't have written
the last line without you.*

PAMELA

Montclair, New Jersey
Day 15,825

You may not remember me, but I have never forgotten you, begins the letter written in the kind of cursive they don't teach in schools anymore. I read the sentence twice in stinging astonishment. It's been forty-three years since my brush with the man even the most reputable papers called the All-American Sex Killer, and my name has long since fallen to a footnote in the story.

I'd given the return address only a cursory glance before sliding a nail beneath the envelope's gummed seam, but now I hold it at arm's length and say the sender's name out loud, emphatically, as though I've been asked to answer the same question twice by someone who definitely heard me the first time. The letter writer is wrong. I have never forgotten her either, though she is welded to a memory that I've often wished I could.

"You say something, hon?" My secretary has moonwalked her rolling chair away from her desk, and now she sits framed by my open office door with a solicitous tilt of her head. Janet calls me *hon* and sometimes *kiddo,* though she is only seven years older than I am. If anyone refers to her as my administrative assistant, she will press her lips together whitely. That's the sort of current-climate pretension Janet doesn't care for.

Janet watches me flip the navy-bordered note card, back to front, front to back, generating a slight wind that lifts my bangs from my forehead. I must look like I'm fanning myself, about to faint, because she hurries over and I feel her hand grazing my mid-back. She fumbles with her readers, which hang from her neck on a rhinestone-strung chain, then juts her sharp chin over my shoulder to read the outstanding summons.

"This is dated nearly three months ago," I say with a ripple of rage. That the women who should be the first to know were always the last was the reason my doctor made me cut out salt for the better part of the eighties. "Why am I just seeing it now?" *What if I'm too late?*

Janet mean-mugs the date. February 12, 2021. "Maybe security flagged it." She goes over to my desk and locates the envelope on top of my leather-looking-but-synthetically-priced desk pad. "Uh-huh." She underlines the return address in the upper-left corner with a square nail. "Because it's from Tallahassee. They would have flagged that for sure."

"Shit," I say insubstantially. I am standing there when, just like that night, my body begins to move without any conscious consent from my mind. I find that I am packing up for the day, though it's just after lunch and I have mediation at four. *"Shit,"* I say again, because this tyrannous part of me has decided that I will not only be canceling my afternoon but I will also incur a no-show fee for tomorrow's six a.m. spin class.

"What can I do for you?" Janet is regarding me with the combination of concern and resignation that I haven't seen in a long time—the look people give you when the very worst has happened, and really, there isn't anything anyone can do for you, for any of us, because some of us die early and inconveniently and there is no way to predict if it will be you next, and before you know it, mourner and comforter are staring dead-eyed into the abyss. The routine comes to me viscerally though it's been eight presidential administrations.

Three impeachments. One pandemic. The towers going down. Facebook. Tickle Me Elmo. Snapple iced tea. They never got to taste Snapple iced tea. But it didn't happen in some bygone era either. If they had lived, they'd be the same age as Michelle Pfeiffer.

"I think I'm going to Tallahassee," I say in disbelief.

Tallahassee, Florida

January 14, 1978

Seven hours before

On Saturday nights, we kept our doors open while we got ready. Girls went in one room wearing one thing and came out wearing something shorter. The hallways were as tight and restricted as the passageways on a navy ship, snarled with chatter about who was doing what and going where and with whom. Hair spray and nail polish fumed our personal ozone layer, the blast of blow-dryers raising the mercury four, sometimes five degrees on the analog thermometer mounted to the wall. We'd crack the windows for fresh air and mock the music coming from the bar next door; Saturday night was disco night, which was for old people. It was a statistical impossibility that something bad could happen with Barry Gibb cheeping in his far-reaching falsetto that we'd all live to see another day, but we are what mathematics models refer to as outliers.

A coy voice accompanied the patterning of knuckles on my door. "I think it might snow." I looked up from the volunteer schedules papering my hand-me-down secretary's desk to see Denise Andora standing on the threshold, hands clasped girlishly at her pelvis.

"Nice try." I laughed. Denise was angling to borrow my shearling coat. Though the winter of 1978 had brought a deep freeze to the Panhandle that killed the azalea trees along the Georgia border, it was never cold enough to snow.

"*Please,* Pamela!" Denise put her hands together in prayer, repeating her plea over red fingertips with crescendoing urgency. "Please. Please. *Please.* Nothing I have goes." She turned in place to prove her point. I only know the minute details of what she was wearing that night because later there was a description of her outfit in the paper: thin turtleneck tucked into snap-front jeans, suede belt and suede boots in matching chestnut brown, opal earrings, and a beloved silver charm bracelet. My best friend was approximately one hundred feet tall and weighed less than I did as a child, but by senior year I'd learned to manage my envy like a migraine. What triggered that star-seeing pain was looking too closely at Denise when she decided she needed attention from men.

"Don't make me beg." She stomped her foot a little. "Roger asked some of the girls if I was coming tonight."

I put my pencil down. "Denise," I admonished.

I'd long ago lost count of the number of times Denise and Roger had called it quits only to encounter each other out at night, however many warm beers and deep lovelorn glances it took to forgive the spiteful things they'd each said to and about the other, but this most recent split didn't feel so much like a split as it did a severing with a dirty kitchen knife, quite literally infecting Denise, who vomited everything she ate for nearly a week and had to be briefly admitted to the hospital for dehydration. When I picked her up at the curb, she swore Roger was out of her system for good. *I flushed twice for good measure,* she'd said, laughing feebly as I helped her out of the hospital-mandated wheelchair and into the passenger seat of the car.

Denise shrugged now with sudden, suspicious indifference, sauntering over to my window. "It's only a few blocks to Turq House. On the night they're calling for three inches of snow. I'll be a little cold but"—she swung the lock lever and pushed her palms against the glass, leaving behind prints that would soon have no living match—"maybe Roger will volunteer to warm me up." She faced me, shoulders thrust back in the frostbitten room. Unless her parents were coming to visit for the weekend, Denise's bra remained collecting pills in her top drawer.

I could feel my willpower eroding. "Do you *promise* to get it dry-cleaned after?"

"Yes, ma'am, Pam Perfect, ma'am." Denise clicked her heels with a militant clang. *Pam Perfect* was her not-entirely-affectionate nickname for me, cribbed from the popular prime-time commercials featuring the woman with the feathered bangs, talking about the pure vegetable spray that saves her time, money, *and* calories. *With PAM cooking,* she trumpets while sliding a silver-skinned fish from frying pan to plate, *dinner always turns out PAM perfect.*

Denise was the first friend I'd made at Florida State University, but recently we'd found ourselves at an impasse. The rot at the core of Panhellenic leadership had always been favoritism, with former presidents hewing close to the rule book for some of their sisters while allowing their friends to get away with murder. When I ran for the position and won, I knew Denise had expected leniency with my name at the top of the executive board. Instead, I was so determined to do better than those who had come before me, to be remembered as a fair and impartial leader, that Denise had more strikes against her than any other sister that quarter. Every time she blew off Monday's chapter meeting or postponed a service trip, it was like she was daring me to kick her out. The other girls watched us like two whitetail bucks who had put our heads down and locked antlers. Our treasurer, an auburn-haired Miss Florida finalist who'd grown up hunting in Franklin County, was always saying that one of us better submit before we got stuck and had to be sawed apart. She'd seen it happen in the wild.

"You can wear the coat," I relented.

Denise capered to my closet with childlike glee that made me feel like an awful shrew. Her eyes rolled back as she slipped her arms into the silk-lined coat. I had beautiful clothes that fit like a second, softer skin, thanks to a mother who devoted her life to caring about such things. Maybe I would care too if I wore half my wardrobe as well as Denise. As it was, I had a round Irish face that contradicted my figure. That's what I had—not a body but a figure. The disconnect between my freckled apple cheeks and pinup proportions was extreme enough that I often felt the need to apologize for it. I should be prettier or less, depending on who was looking and where.

"Can you shut my window before you go?" I slapped my desk with an open palm as a gust of wind blew into the room, threatening to spirit away my color-coordinated calendar pages.

Denise went over to the window and staged a hammy show, pressing down on the rail and grunting like she was giving it her all. "It's stuck," Denise said. "You better come with me so you don't freeze to death planning the thirty-third annual blood drive. What a way to go."

I sighed, not because I longed to attend a shouty fraternity party and couldn't because I did in fact have to organize the thirty-third annual blood drive; my sigh was because I did not know how to make Denise understand that I did not *want* to go, that I was never more content than I was sitting at my pencil-scratched desk on a Saturday night, my door open to the din and the drama of thirty-eight girls getting ready to go out, feeling like I'd done the job I was elected to do if, by the end of the week, everyone could put on music and mascara and taunt one another from across the hall. The things I heard from my room. The absolute hell we gave one another. Who needed to shave her big toes and who should never dance in public if she had any desire to eventually procreate.

"You'll have more fun without me," I demurred lamely.

"You know, one day," Denise said, turning to close the window for real this time, her long dark hair flapping behind her like a hero's cape, "those cans of yours are gonna be in your lap, and you're going to look back and wish—"

Denise broke off with a scream that my nervous system barely registered. We were twenty-one-year-old sorority girls; we screamed not because something was heinously, improbably wrong but because Saturday nights made us excitable and slaphappy. I have since come to loathe the day most people look forward to all week, its false sense of security, its disingenuous promise of freedom and fun.

———

Outside on the front lawn, two of our sorority sisters were huffing and hauling a blanketed parcel roughly the dimensions of a movie poster, their cheeks chapped pink with cold and exertion, their pupils dilated in a hunted, heart-pounding way.

"Help us," they were half-laughing, half-panting when Denise and I met them on our short stamp of lawn, edged with pink bursts of muhly grass to dissuade patrons of the bar next door from parking on our property when the lot filled up. It was such a successful trick of landscaping that none of the students crossing paths on the sidewalk, on their way to grab a bite at the Pop Stop before it closed, had stepped over to lend a hand.

I positioned myself in the middle, squatting and lifting the base in an underhand grip, but Denise just rounded her fingers and produced an earsplitting whistle that stopped cold two guys cutting through our alleyway. No amount of landscaping could deter people from pinching our shortcut, and I couldn't say I blamed them. Tallahassee blocks were as long as New York City avenues, and Denise loved that I knew that.

"We could use a hand." Denise tossed the dark hair she had spent hours coaxing into silken submission and popped a hip, every man's fantasy hitchhiker.

I saw bitten-down boy fingernails curl under the base of our illicit delivery, inches from my own, and I was relieved of the weight instantly. I moved to the head of the operation to direct the guys up the three front steps and then—*carefully, a little to the left, no, other left!*—through the double front doors. We'd just had them repainted cornflower blue to match the striations in the wallpaper in the foyer, where, at that moment, everyone congregated—the girls in the kitchen making popcorn, the girls who had bundled together on the rec room couch to catch up on weekday tapings of *As the World Turns,* the girls who were going out, hot rollers in their bangs and waving their wet nails dry. They wanted to see what all the commotion was about as much as they wanted to slyly assess our handlers off the street, older than we were by at least eight years but not any older than the professors who routinely asked us out to dinner.

There was some arguing about what to do next. Denise was insisting the guys continue up the stairs, but the only men allowed on the second floor were family members on move-in day and the houseboy when there was a repair to be made.

"Don't be like this, Pamela," Denise pleaded. "You know if we leave it here, they'll steal it back before we can make the trade." Though the cargo was draped in a bedsheet, we all knew that it was a framed composite from our sweetheart fraternity, every active member unsmiling in a suit and tie, their rattlesnake-and-double-sword coat of arms at the center. We'd been going back and forth for months, each house lifting one of the other's composites and leaving behind a sooty square that not even a heavy-duty ammonia solution would wipe away.

Denise was staring at me with glittering, kohl-rimmed *gotcha!* eyes. Over a decade later, when I finally became a mother, I would recognize this trick, this asking for something you knew you weren't allowed to have in front of a roomful of people who wanted you to have it. There was no saying no unless you didn't mind everyone thinking you were a mean old hag.

I produced a scoffing sound from the base of my throat. How dare she even ask.

Denise's lips parted, her features slackening in disappointment. I knew this look too. It was the look Denise got every time she encountered me as chapter president after so long of knowing me as her friend.

"Man on the floor!" I shouted, and Denise seized me by the shoulders, shaking me with playful contention. I'd *nearly* gotten her. We were swept up then by the other girls moving like a school of fish, one vibrant body thinned by the stairwell and reshaped on the landing, squeezed thin again by our tapered halls. The whole time we were singing "man on the floor," not in unison, but single voices in gravelly competition with one another. There had been that Paul McCartney song—"Band on the Run"—which to one of my sisters, no one could ever remember who, had always sounded like "*Man* on the Run," and with one more modification the inside joke of The House was born. It was so catchy that the next morning, sitting in our dining room in dazed compliance,

I heard the hum of the chorus. There were loads of men on the floor at that point, some in blue, some in white lab coats, the ones in charge in street clothes, and they were cutting bloody squares out of our carpets and tweezing back molars from the shag. And then someone else sang it full force—"man on the floor, maaaaan on the floor!"—and we started laughing, real deep-bellied laughs that made some of our uniformed house guests pause on the stairwell and look in at us, only traces of concern on their scowling, reproachful faces.

The composite was delivered to room four, the room of the girls who had pulled off the heist. Our handlers took in the limited quarters skeptically, before kicking the door shut with their heels and leaning the prized piece against the foot of one of the twin beds. If you wanted to get in that room, you had to turn sideways, and even then I don't think I could have slipped inside, not with my *figure*.

"You don't have an attic or anything?" one of the guys asked.

We did, but having the composite in your room was like hanging a pair of stag antlers on your wall, Denise explained to them. Already, some of the flatter-chested girls were squeezing through the cracked-open door with their cameras to take pictures of the hometown heroes in room four, who posed alongside their kill grinning, air guns drawn and hair tumbling down their backs like Charlie's Angels. In a few hours, he would try to enter this room but would be met with too much resistance owing to the composite of the 1948 class—I still remember that was the year the girls filched, can still see their oiled hair and horn-rimmed eyeglasses. Today Sharon Selva is an oral surgeon in Austin and Jackie Clurry a tenured professor in the history department of the very university held captive by terror that winter of 1978, all because of some silly Greek prank.

Denise went determinedly to the small amber-bodied lamp the girls kept on top of a stack of old magazines, screwing off the shade and stretching the cord as far as it would go so she could crouch before the picture and scan its surface with the bare bulb, not unlike a beachgoer with a handheld metal detector. She shook her head in awe. "Even their composites from the forties were mounted with museum quality!" she cried with deeply felt outrage.

For two years, we'd allowed the guys of Turq House—short for the shade their shutters and doors were painted—to think they were partaking in the classic friendly theft that had been occurring between sweetheart sororities and fraternities for generations. What they didn't know was that we'd been swapping out the high-quality glass from their composites for the acrylic plexiglass from ours before proffering the exchange. It was Denise who caught the discrepancy, back when we were sophomores.

This glass is gorgeous, she'd breathed, and the older girls had laughed, because Robert Redford was gorgeous, but glass? Little sophomore Denise had marched us down to our display wall and pointed out the differences—see how faded our composites had become? Turq House was using glass, expensive museum-grade glass that protected their photographs from damaging elements like the sun and dust mites. Denise was a fine art and modern languages double major—the former concentration had always been the plan, the latter added to the mix that past summer, after she read in the *Tallahassee Democrat* about the construction of a state-of-the-art Salvador Dalí museum down in St. Petersburg, Florida. Denise had immediately shifted to declare a double major in modern languages, concentration in Spanish, spending the summer after her twentieth birthday on campus, making up two years' worth of credits. Dalí himself would be flying in to interview prospective staff, and Denise intended to dazzle him in his native language. Hardly surprising, but when they eventually met, he was completely taken with her, hiring her as an assistant gallerist to start the Monday after graduation.

"I doubt they'd even notice . . ." Sophomore Denise had trailed off, smart enough to know that as a pledge, she couldn't be the one to propose it.

There were and continue to be plenty of disparities between fraternity and sorority living, but the big one that the chapter president at the time was always going on about was the level at which Greek alumni gave back to their organizations. Fraternity men had, for generations, gone on to become more economically sound than sorority women, and by and large their houses boasted newer furniture, top-of-the-line air-conditioning units, and, "As our eagle-eyed sister Denise Andora recently pointed out," she said at the top of the next chapter meeting, "even *clearer* glass than we do."

The ploy was condoned that evening, and I've heard rumblings that the girls are still at it today.

Denise tapped her long nails on that durable, reflection-controlled glass and groaned almost sexually. "God, that's good stuff," she said.

"Would you like us to leave you alone with the glass, Denise?" Sharon asked, deadpan.

"To hell with Roger." Denise planted a wet one on the limpid surface. "This glass and I are going to live a very long and happy life together."

Sometimes, when I get an unfavorable outcome in court, when I start thinking justice may be a fallacy after all, I remember that Salvador Dalí died six hours before Denise's killer went to the electric chair. January 23, 1989: look it up. The passing of one of the world's most celebrated and eccentric artists ensured that the execution of some lowlife in Central Florida was not the top news story of the day, and he would have dead-man-walked to the execution chamber bereft over that. More than his own freedom, more than the chance to make me sorry for what I did to him, what he wanted was a spectacle. On these bad days, I like to think that Denise is up there, wherever it is truly smashing women go when they die, and that she'd managed to pull a few strings. Overshadowed his death the way he did her fleeting time on this earth. Revenge is a dish best served cold. The vixens of *As the World Turns* taught us that.

"The future—she was looking forward to it very much."

—AUNT OF ONE OF THE FLORIDA STATE
UNIVERSITY VICTIMS, 1978

January 15, 1978

Five minutes before

||||t must have been more than hunger pains that roused me, but at the time all I wanted was to go downstairs and make myself a peanut butter sandwich and fall right back to sleep.

I rolled out of bed, stretching, groaning when I saw myself in the small oval mirror tacky-glued to the wall. I'd fallen asleep fully clothed, using my textbook for a pillow. After I'd posted the volunteer schedule to the bulletin board outside the bathrooms, I'd moved on to the reading for Monday morning's American Political Thought, and now my cheek bore a faint printing of the Equal Rights Amendment. I rubbed at it hard with the heel of my hand, but Alice Paul's words wouldn't so much as smudge.

Perks of chapter presidency started with living alone in the big balcony room off the front set of stairs and ended there. The bay window, the *privacy*, fooled some girls into thinking they wanted to run for the position, until they took the time to consider how much thankless work it was on top of your regular course load. It was the inverse for me. The meetings, budgeting, and managing, the litigating of the slights small and smaller—those were the draw. I fell into a depression with too much free time on my hands, and I dreaded going out, dating, guys, the whole scene. My figure had helped me secure a respectable boyfriend freshman year, and while kissing him didn't exactly set my heart on fire, I'd kept him around for expediency's sake.

The chandelier in the front hallway was set on a timer, switching off automatically at nine. But when I came out of my room a few minutes shy of three in the morning, the foyer was spit-shined in platinum light. They still don't know how this happened, but that chandelier saved my life. If I had turned right out of my bedroom, headed down the narrow hall for the back staircase designated for after-hours use, I never would have come back.

I descended the front set of stairs, hand grazing the wrought-iron railing, one of the oldest and prettiest parts of The House. In the foyer, I spent a minute or two fiddling with the light switch on the wall, to no avail. I added it to the morning's ever-expanding chore list: call the houseboy first thing, before the alumnae arrived for—

Don't just stand there, a woman cried. *Do something. Do something!*

A glass shattered somewhere in the back of The House. Then another. Another.

I looked down at my feet, in the corduroy slippers I'd wear for the last time, and found they were somehow moving toward the disturbance coming from the Jefferson Street side of The House. Even as I came around the bend to the rec room and saw that it was only the television, left on by one of my sisters to an old episode of *I Love Lucy,* the one where Lucy keeps offering Ricky objects to smash in lieu of her face, I knew something wasn't right.

Still, I went around, turning off all the lamps that had been left on in the room, collecting the plates littering the coffee table, sticky with the residue of Jerry's hot fudge cake. My eyes were burning with tears because I was someone who could cry only when she was angry. The alumnae Tea & Tour started at nine a.m. sharp, and *this* was how the girls left the place?

My ponytail had loosened in my sleep, and I kept having to shoulder my hair out of my eyes, and at some point, I realized it was because there was a freezing draft filtering through the room. I rocked back on my heels and squinted through the archway to see that the back door had been left open too. *Goddamn fucking children,* I thought, because that's what I would normally think if a part of me didn't also suspect that something unspeakable was unfolding, that moment, right above my head. *Drunk goddamn fucking children,* I thought again, performing for myself, clinging to the last seconds of normalcy before—

A thud. *The* thud.

I stopped. Stopped moving. Breathing. Thinking. All functions seem to shut down to divert resources to my eardrums. Overhead, there was a flurry of footsteps. Someone on the second floor was running at a nauseating, inhuman speed.

It was as though a magnet were attached to the soles of those feet, and the nickel in my scalp dragged me along for the ride—past the wall of our composites, under the poorly plastered crack in the ceiling, and finally, to the place between the coat closet and the lou-vered kitchen doors where the footsteps stopped and so did I. I was standing in the shadow of the main stairwell, facing the double front doors approximately thirteen feet and two inches in front of me. I guessed fifteen feet, but when the detective measured no more than an hour later, I found I'd ever so slightly overshot the distance be-tween us.

The crystal chandelier was undulating, disturbed but still unerr-ingly bright. When the man came down the stairs and darted across the foyer, he should have been very hard to see. Instead, the chan-delier acted as my archivist, logging a clear and unabridged shot of him as he paused, crouched down low, one hand on the doorknob. In his other hand he held what looked like a child's wooden base-ball bat, the end wrapped in a dark fabric that seemed to arch and writhe. Blood, my brain would not yet permit me to acknowledge. He wore a knit cap, pulled down over his brows. His nose was sharp and straight, his lips thin. He was young and trim and good-looking. I'm not here to dispute facts, even the ones that annoy me.

For a brief, blissful moment, I got to be angry. I recognized the man at the door. It was Roger Yul, Denise's on-again, off-again boyfriend. I could not *believe* she'd sneaked him upstairs. That was an orange-level violation of the code of conduct. Grounds for expulsion.

But then I watched as every muscle in the man's body tensed, as though he sensed he was being watched. With a slow swivel of his head, he focused like a raptor on a spot just beyond my shoulder. I was paralyzed by a hammering dread that still comes for me in my nightmares, locking my spine and vaporizing my scream in the sandpapered walls of my throat. We both stood there, alert and immobile, and I realized with a wrecking ball of relief he could not actually find me in the shadow of the stairwell, that while he was visible to me, I remained unwitnessed.

He was not Roger.

The man opened the door and went. The next time I saw him, he would be wearing a jacket and tie, he would have groupies and the *New York Times* on his side, and when he asked me where I was currently living, legally, I would have no choice but to give my home address to a man who murdered thirty-five women and escaped prison twice.

I found myself heading for Denise's room, planning on reading her the riot act. I would never be able to adequately explain this to the cops, the court, Denise's parents, or my own. That while I knew it was not Roger I'd seen at the front door, I had not picked up the phone and called the police but instead had gone back upstairs to reprimand Denise.

Halfway down the hall, the door to room number six opened, and a sophomore named Jill Hoffman staggered out, hunched over at the waist and headed for the bathroom down the hall. She was drunk and running to the toilet to be sick.

I called out her name and Jill turned fearfully, like she thought I might be mad about the flesh on the right side of her face, peeled back to reveal the very bone the fashion magazines told us to highlight with blush. She was trying to speak, but her tongue kept getting pushed under by thick currents of blood.

I took off down the hall, flapping my arms strangely and cawing for everyone to get up. One of the girls opened her door and asked blearily if The House was on fire. I guided Jill into the girl's arms and, in a moment of cogency, instructed her to close the door and lock it behind her. In my peripheral vision, someone else wandered into Jill's room and screamed that we needed a bucket. I thought we needed to start cleaning up the bloodstains Jill had left on the carpet before they set, and this made absolute sense to me at the time.

I went into room twelve on the right side of the hall and hollered for the girls in there to call the police. When they asked why, I had to stop and think for a moment. I do not remember saying this, but the author of one of the more ethical true-crime books wrote that I did. "Jill Hoffman has been slightly mutilated," I was alleged to have said, calmly, and then I walked at an unhurried pace to the bathroom, got a bucket from under the sink, and went into Jill's room, thinking I was going in there to scrub a stain out of the carpet.

Jill's room was wet, her sheets submerged in a dark, oily spill, the yellow curtains splashed with so much blood they strained on their hooks, heavier than they'd been seventeen minutes ago. Her room-mate, Eileen, was sitting up in her bed, holding her mangled face in her hands and moaning *mama* in her low country twang. Eileen was a loyal listener of Pastor Charles Swindoll's radio show, and though I was not at all religious, she'd gotten me hooked too. He was always saying that life is ten percent what happens to you and ninety percent how you react to it.

I shoved the bucket under Eileen's jaw and pried her hands away from her face. Blood and saliva hailed the metal base, indeed sounding so much thicker than water.

"Take this," I said to a junior who had followed me into the room. She turned her face away, gagging, but she held that bucket for Eileen until the ambulance arrived. "Don't let her cover her face or she'll choke."

I went left out of Jill and Eileen's room, toward my own. It was just like taking rounds at chapter on Monday evenings. The count started at the front.

Most of the girls were startled awake as I barged through their doors and hit the lights, raising the backs of their hands to their eyes, tonguing sleep crust from the corners of their mouths. Though their faces were scrunched up irritably, they were at least in one piece. Insanely, I started to wonder if Jill and Eileen had gotten into a fight with each other, if things had perhaps gotten out of hand. But then I got to room eight. A girl named Roberta Shepherd lived in room eight. Her roommate was away on a ski vacation that weekend, and unlike the others, Robbie did not moan and groan when I told her to wake up and turn on her light.

"Robbie," I repeated in the schoolmarm voice they all mocked me for behind my back. "I'm sorry, but you have to wake up." I was stepping into the room, my adrenaline performing the function of courage. But it turned out there wasn't a need to be brave. Robbie was asleep with the covers pulled up under her chin. I walked in and touched her shoulder and told her that Jill and Eileen had been in an accident and the police would be here any moment.

When she still refused to respond, I rolled her onto her back, and that's when I saw the thin scribble of red on the pillow. Nosebleed. I patted her on the shoulder assuredly, telling her I used to get them when I was upset too.

Out of nowhere there was a man in a uniform by my side, bellowing and blustering at me. *The medic! Get the medic!* I went out into the hallway, feeling at first wounded and then incensed. Who was he to yell at me in my own house?

The hallway seemed to have morphed in the brief time I'd spent in Robbie's room, into a crawl space of surrealism, crackling with the radios of pipsqueak campus officers not much older than we were. Girls wandered the halls wearing winter coats over their nightgowns. Someone said with total confidence that the Iranians had bombed us.

"There's a weird smell coming from Denise's room," reported Bernadette, our Miss Florida and, as treasurer, my second in command. Together we went around the curve in the hallway, sidestepping two slack-mouthed and useless officers. I wondered if maybe Denise had forgotten to wrap up her paint palette before going out for the evening. Sometimes she did that, and it emitted an odor like a gas leak.

Denise was someone who hated to be told what to do. She was bullheaded and talented and conceited and sensitive. Our friendship had not survived the role I had stepped into willingly, one where it was my mandate to make sure everyone followed the rules, no matter how pointless and archaic Denise thought they were. But still I loved her. Still I wanted her to have the big, swaggering life she was destined to have, though I had come to accept it would likely not involve me.

The moment I walked into her room, I knew. I *knew*. I'd only lost her sooner than I'd readied for. Denise was sleeping on her side with the covers pulled up over her shoulder. It had to be close to eighty degrees in the room, and the air was sick with a fetid bathroom smell.

Bernadette was physically restraining me, telling me to wait for the medic, but I wriggled free from her grasp. "She's a sound sleeper," I insisted in a strangled, furious voice. Whatever Bernadette was implying, whatever she was thinking—she was *mistaken*.

"I'll be right back," Bernadette said, and then she banged her elbow painfully on the doorframe as she turned to run down the hall.

As though she had been waiting for us to be alone, Denise's hand shot straight up into the air, a stiff-armed salute. "Denise!" My laugh sounded deranged, even to my own ears. "You have to get dressed," I told her. "It's a Code Bra. There are policemen everywhere."

I went over to her, and though I continued the ruse that she was only dreaming, I understood enough to cradle her in my arms. Her dark hair was studded with bits of bark, but unlike Jill's and Eileen's, it was dry and soft as I stroked it and told her again that she needed to dress. There was not a scratch on her face. It would have mattered to Denise that she left this earth unscathed.

I pushed the covers off her—she had to be hot—and found that although she still wore her favorite nightgown, her underwear was balled up on the floor, next to an overturned Clairol hair mist bottle. I did not understand how this was at all possible, but the nozzle top was gummed over with a dark substance and a clot of wiry dark hair, the kind of hair that gets stuck in your razor when you shave before going to the beach.

I felt a hand on my shoulder, nudging me out of the way, and that man was by my side again, the one who'd yelled at me. He dragged Denise out of the bed and onto the floor. I told him her name and that she had an allergy to latex. She had to be careful what paints she stored in the room because of it.

"That's good to know," he said, and I forgave him then, because he was so gentle with Denise as he pinched her nose and lowered his face over hers. She had fallen back asleep, but when she woke again, I would tell her that the man who'd saved her was handsome and not wearing a wedding ring. Was a medic the same thing as a doctor? Denise was the type to wind up with a doctor. Maybe this would be the story of how she met her husband, and someday soon I'd be telling it at her wedding.

January 15, 1978

3:39 a.m.

The police officer upstairs told us to go downstairs, and the police officer downstairs told us to go back upstairs. We encountered a different officer on the second floor, and this one told us in an exasperated voice that he really needed us to stay in one place and not disturb anything, and so I was the one to make the call. We'd sequester ourselves in my presidential palace.

My room had double floor-to-ceiling windows, directly above the white railing with the bronze Greek lettering. With the drapes buckled, the windows looked out over the white-bricked walkway where Denise had drawn our swirly Greek script in industrial chalk at the start of the semester.

Someone tugged on the drapery wand, and blue and red fulminated the room. "Another ambulance is here," she really didn't need to announce.

A few of the girls went over to the window to see for themselves. There must have been about thirty of us crammed in that room, and the smell—of night cream and beer breath—remains embedded in some primordial olfactory nerve of mine.

"*Three* ambulances."

"Seven cop cars."

"I count six."

"Six. I feel so much better now."

Bernadette and I fanned out, covering the room counter and clockwise, gathering as much information as we could. Who had seen something. Heard something. One of our pledges told me it was a burglary and we should check to see if the television was missing. Another insisted we'd been shot at by the Soviets, that the country was going to war. "I don't think that's what's going on," I said, giving her knee a little squeeze.

Bernadette and I huddled up to compare notes. Even in the mornings, in her bathrobe and single hair curler, she carefully margined her lips in glossy cherry lipstick. It was startling to see her pale mouth, and I could tell she was self-conscious to be without her signature color. She kept chewing on her bottom lip, flushing it momentarily with bright blood. She was still wearing the beaded blouse she'd started the night in. This turned out to be a crucial detail.

"I couldn't get this off," Bernadette said, indicating the button on her beaded blouse. I leaned in, pinching the fabric between my thumb and pointer finger. The crystal appliqué had gotten tangled in the buttonhole. "I knocked on Robbie's door for help. She has those fabric scissors." Robbie was a fashion merchandising major. "I remember her groaning that it was three in the morning. And I looked at her clock because I knew she was exaggerating. And I said it's two thirty-five, Robbie. And she said do you want my help or not?" Bernadette exhaled, incredulous. "When did this happen? How did I not hear anything? She was fine. When I left. She was *fine.*"

"We'll go see her at the hospital as soon as they let us out of here," I promised her. Everything I promised that morning seemed possible now that I'd had the chance to conduct reconnaissance. A stranger had come into The House, likely to steal from us, and he'd encountered some of the girls and panicked. Home invasions were not an uncommon event. No one had intended us harm, and though Jill and Eileen had been bruised and bloodied, it was one of those things that looked worse than it was. Like when you nick the back of your ankle in the shower and it gushes with the force of a main artery. It had to be like that; otherwise, like Bernadette had just pointed out, we would have *heard* something. I dusted my hands on my thighs, my concerns allayed for the time being.

It felt like we were in that room for hours, but it couldn't have been more than twenty or thirty minutes because the birds hadn't started up yet when a new officer opened the door. We'd fallen into a listless stupor, but the moment an outsider entered the room, everyone wiped their faces and sat at attention. We were used to gathering for meetings and announcements, and the officer seemed unprepared to have the floor so unanimously ceded. He stalled out for a long moment with something like stage fright.

"Do you have any news?" I prompted. He nodded at me, grateful for the reminder of what he was doing here. He was broad and barrel-chested, a local boy with a badge, but his voice didn't carry. We had to lean in to make out what he was saying.

"There's a lot of people on the second floor now, and they're gonna be here awhile. We're gonna move you downstairs."

I raised my hand, not to be called on but to announce that I was going to speak. That was how it worked in chapter too. If you had something to say, you signaled, but no one called on you. This wasn't class and we weren't students here. I was always saying that we were associates running the business of The House. "What's happening with the other girls?" I asked. "How are they doing?"

"The girls are at Tallahassee Memorial."

"All of them?"

He nodded, his face shiny and sincere.

The relief was stabilizing, not just because it was the answer I wanted but because it was an *answer*. In the month of uncertainty that was to follow, what I wanted, what we all wanted, was clarity. What had happened? Who had done it? What did we do now?

"When can we call our parents and let them know what's going on?" I asked.

The officer swished his mouth to the side, thinking. "Maybe

an hour? That's about how long it'll take to fingerprint a group this size."

The girls broke ranks then, their questions and objections unruly but reasonable. I allowed it, figuring everyone had earned a few moments of disorder. I stood and moved into the center of the circle, and everyone shushed one another. "We're being fingerprinted?" I asked in a calm but concerned spokeswoman's voice. "Why?"

"Everyone always gets fingerprinted."

"Who is everyone?" I snapped, losing patience.

"Anyone at a crime scene. Not just assailants."

"Assailants? Does that mean there were multiple?"

"What? No. Maybe. We don't know."

"So you haven't caught the person who did this?"

"We got a lotta guys out there looking."

I pinched the bridge of my nose in frustration. "Can everyone at least get back into their rooms to change before we go downstairs?"

"No," he said. And then, in response to a chorus of complaints about parading around without pants in front of all these men, the officer shrank into himself, retreating, and told us he would give us five minutes to get ourselves together.

"You can all borrow as much as you want from me," I said. I started for my closet, its contents so desired by the one person who was not there in the room with us, but I stopped at the knock on the door.

A different officer poked his head in this time. "Which one of you saw him?"

I turned. "I did."

"I need you to come with me right away," this new officer said.

"Can you take charge while I'm gone?" I asked Bernadette. She nodded, her naked lips pressed together resolutely.

I hurried out, eager to help, to get all this sorted so I could go and see Denise at the hospital and rush back here to tidy up before the alumnae arrived. I could call my boyfriend! Brian jumped at any opportunity to put his freshmen pledges to work, and they would get The House shipshape while the girls showered and dressed. The alumnae would no doubt be shaken when I explained we'd had an incident in the night—an attempted burglary, it seemed—but impressed that the tour still went off without a hitch. I imagined them reporting back to the governing council that the women of the FSU chapter showed extraordinary poise in the face of a harrowing ordeal. I followed the officer downstairs, fevered with hope.

Four a.m.

His nose. Really, it all came down to the nose. It was his most distinctive feature and the easiest to describe for the art major who volunteered to try her hand at that earliest forensic sketch. Straight and sharp, like the beak of some prehistoric killer bird. Thin lips. A small man. In seventeen months, I would relish repeating this description for a courtroom. I'd had about enough of hearing how handsome he was, and no man likes to be called small.

The hat he wore covered his ears and eyebrows. The art student, a sophomore named Cindy Young, struggled with the hat, taking the gray eraser to the page twice. The first try made him look like he was wearing a bathing cap, the second a helmet. "I'm usually better than this," she said, sweat on her furrowed brow. Like me, like all of us under that roof, she was a perfectionist whose hand was too shaky to meet her own exacting expectations.

"Let's see," Sheriff Cruso murmured, sitting down on the couch in the formal living room and hunching over Cindy's sketch. I was on the floor next to her for support, my legs straight out under the coffee table and my back against the couch's ruffled base. Sheriff Cruso's knee was right next to my face, and it was inappropriate how turned on I felt by the two of us sitting like that. I didn't even like sex. Denise said that wasn't a "me" problem but a Brian one.

Sheriff Cruso passed the sketch to Detective "pronounced like dill" Pickell, standing behind the couch. "Take a look at that, Pickell," he said. Pickell and Cruso appeared to be about the same age—younger than I thought a sheriff and detective should be—and while Cruso was Black, he was clearly the one in charge. This was highly unusual in the 1970s, not just in the Panhandle but anywhere. For generations, the Southern sheriff was white, middle-aged, and poorly educated, a defender of the status quo. But as crime increased in rural areas and racial attitudes shifted, voters trended toward younger, more educated candidates. Cruso had his criminology degree from Florida A&M and he was Leon County's first Black sheriff, which was a milestone New York City wouldn't achieve until 1995.

Detective Pickell held the drawing under one of the table lamps for a better look. "This is good, Cindy."

"Can I wash my hands now?" Cindy asked. She was sitting with her carbon-blackened palms turned up on the edge of the coffee table so she wouldn't stain the cream-colored furniture in the formal room. We were still worried about the nice couch in the nice room when, upstairs, Jill's blood had seeped through the mattress and would eventually rust the springs.

"Go ahead." Cruso tipped his head. Then, over his shoulder to Pickell, "Can you check to see if we're clear for Miss Schumacher here to take us through the house?"

Pickell headed for the foyer, arcing widely around the girls lined up to use the downstairs bathroom after being fingerprinted in the dining room. They were covering their faces so the police wouldn't see them cry, ruining the arms of my sweaters. The press would go on to write that you could hear our screams from outside, not their most offensive fabrication but one I took umbrage with nonetheless. We conducted ourselves with a restrained horror that I was proud of at the time. I thought if this had to happen to us, at least everyone would remember that we were strong and brave. Back then you were strong and brave if you didn't carry on about it. But people wrote whatever they wanted to about us with no regard for the truth. Looking back, I should have let everyone scream.

Sheriff Cruso gazed down at me and gave me an approachable smile. Now *he* was actually handsome, unlike The Defendant, who was just handsome for having done the vile things he'd done. Sheriff Cruso was well over six feet, with a defined, manly jawline but cherubic cheeks. I'd soon come to learn he wore cowboy boots with everything.

"So this Roger Yul. What's he like?"

I'd told Sheriff Cruso and Detective Pickell the truth. How at first I was so taken aback to see a man at the front door in the middle of the night that I'd thought it was Denise's ex-boyfriend, Roger. I was prelaw, the daughter of one of New York City's top corporate lawyers, and somewhere along the way I'd picked up a thing or two about the criminal investigation process. I knew law enforcement was trained to fixate on that first gut impression, but I wrongly assumed they possessed an appreciation for the nuance of a mind, for the ten-car pileup of neurons and chemical messaging that occurs in the moment your whole world goes sideways.

"Roger is a typical guy who can't make up his mind," I replied as patiently as I could. "But it wasn't Roger I saw at the door."

"What do you mean by that?" Sheriff Cruso asked, ignoring the second part of my answer entirely. "Can't make up his mind, that is."

I wanted to sigh. Kick my legs like a toddler having a terrible-twos tantrum. *You're wasting my time, your time, everyone's time! Go out there and find this guy with the pointy nose and the nice overcoat!*

But I kept my composure. "Sometimes he wants to be with Denise, and sometimes he wants to be single. But again, it was not Roger I saw at the front door."

"And right now?" Sheriff Cruso persisted. "Does he want to be with Denise or not be with Denise?" He smiled down at me in a *humor-me* way I did not at all buy. Most men couldn't stand me.

"She broke things off before the Christmas break, and now it's pretty obvious he wants to get back together with her again. Don't tell Denise I told you that, though. Her head's big enough." I rolled my eyes in a way that I hoped would make Sheriff Cruso see I wasn't trying to give him a hard time. People always felt like I was giving them a hard time, and I don't know, maybe I was. But Sheriff Cruso didn't laugh. He did this thing when I mentioned Denise. A sort of blink and a double take at the same time.

Detective Pickell returned to the room. "We can do the walk-through now. But first, Pamela, I need you to remove your slippers so that we can eliminate your footprints from those of the intruder."

I drew my foot into my lap and regarded the blood-cast rubber sole with an archaeologist's curiosity. I'd had no idea my arches were high until that moment.

I retraced my steps for them, starting at the back door. Where I heard the thud overhead, Pickell ripped off a strip of black tape and marked the carpet in the after-hours hall. He did it again at the edge of the foyer where I had seen the intruder come down the stairs and pause at the front door. We were told not to touch the tape until we were given the okay, but then no one ever gave us the okay or bothered to return our phone calls. Just before everyone went home for summer break, I ripped it up in a silent, towering rage.

Pickell told me to stand in the exact place where I saw the intruder and hold down the blade of the measuring tape with my big toe. At the front door, he looked down at the other end in his hand and declared, "Thirteen feet, two inches."

Sheriff Cruso nodded, satisfied, as though something inevitable had been confirmed. "That's pretty far in the dark."

"But it wasn't dark." I pointed at the chandelier, my grand seeing-eye glass.

"It's still not the best lighting in the middle of the night," Sheriff Cruso said, though objectively, he was wrong. We were both squinting, looking up at it. "And I don't want to be so quick to discount your initial instinct."

It is a guilty pleasure to be persuasive when you are wrong. That's what my father always used to say, to warn, really. Once you have the tools to win an argument, a good lawyer must use them not just wisely but ethically.

And yet, he would always add with a wink, *great lawyers know when to compromise.*

"Sheriff Cruso," I said slowly, as though something were just dawning on me. "One of my sisters, her name is Bernadette Daly— she's our treasurer, actually. Second in command." I wanted him to know she was a reliable source. "She went to Robbie's room at two thirty-five a.m. and stayed for a few minutes. She said Robbie was fine then. When I came down here, the TV was on. An *I Love Lucy* episode. And when I turned it off, the credits were rolling. They're half-hour episodes. So that must have been just three a.m. No more than a minute later, I heard the thud."

Pickell was feeding the blade of the measuring tape, closing the distance between the front door and where I stood, and his eyes were trained on his superior, as if to see whether Sheriff Cruso agreed that what I was saying was important.

"That means all this happened in about a twenty-minute span." It was seventeen minutes, according to the original crime scene report, oxidizing somewhere in the Florida Museum of Archives. "How could one man do what he did to four girls in a twenty-minute span? What if there were two of them? Roger and this other guy?" I held my breath. I did not at all believe what I was saying, and I had no idea the damage done in that moment, just trying to get them to listen to me.

"Interesting," Pickell said eventually, because Cruso wasn't biting. "Remind me the name of your sister who spoke to Robbie Shepherd?"

"Bernadette Daly," I said, drawing out her name, then spelling it for him too. He wrote it down, then leaned in and muttered something in Sheriff Cruso's ear, his face turned away from me so I couldn't read his lips.

Sheriff Cruso nodded grimly at whatever it was Pickell whispered, then said to me, "Thank you, Pamela. That's all for now. You can go call your parents if you'd like." He started up the stairs.

"Please use the phone in the kitchen," Detective Pickell added, following him.

It was clear I was being dismissed, and neither man was going to volunteer any more information about how the injured girls were doing. I'd have to ask. I walked backward so that I could keep Sheriff Cruso and Detective Pickell in my sightline as they ascended the stairs.

"I'll need to call the parents of the girls who went to the hospital," I said. "Let them know what happened and how they're doing. It's one of the guardian obligations under the oath you take when you become chapter president." I smiled while I said this, hoping to infuse my words with the peppy brand of helpfulness that I was all too often told I lacked. During my first year in The House, the former chapter president had reprimanded me for how I answered the phone: *Hello?* instead of *Hello!* It was the difference between *What do you want?* and *How can I be of service to you today?*

Sheriff Cruso was fiddling with the chandelier's switch on the second floor, strobing the foyer bright and dark, and I don't know why, but I thought of Studio 54, how Denise was always begging me to take her there, like I had any shot getting past that velvet rope when not even Warren Beatty could.

"What should I tell the parents?" I pressed with a wincing smile. *Sorry for being such a pest!* My eyes were itchy and dry from the lack of sleep, and if Sheriff Cruso didn't stop flashing the chandelier, I was afraid I was going to have a seizure.

He spoke without looking at me. "All the girls are at Tallahassee Memorial Hospital, Miss Schumacher."

Five a.m.

By the time I got to the phone in the kitchen, the number keys on the dial pad were smudged with ink. I added my own prints as I dialed home, brimming with a perverse kind of anticipation. My parents spent a lot of money to neglect me, and I was always fantasizing about something awful happening that would force them to take care of me in ways money cannot.

With each doleful ring, I devised for them a new excuse. It was so early, and they were sound sleepers. Maybe they couldn't hear the phone because someone in the neighborhood was having work done on their house. On a Sunday. At five a.m. Or maybe they were away. Sometimes they went on trips and assumed the other one would remember to tell me, though there was no precedent for this. We were a family of forgetters.

The answering machine picked up, and I considered leaving the terrible news in a message. But it was so rare to have what I had in my possession—a report of a cataclysmic event that would jump-start their dead parental batteries—that I decided to hold off until I got one of them on the line.

I slammed the phone into the receiver, hard, then picked it up and slammed it down again. Harder. Immediately I regretted it. What if someone had seen me lose my cool? But the industrial-sized kitchen was deserted and hospital-grade clean, which both pleased and agitated me. I'd abandoned those dirty plates in the rec room, where all the action was happening. I wondered if I should make up a reason for the police to come in here, to see that we were not, in fact, a bunch of messy and gum-chewing sorority girls, that we were responsible adults. That if I said it wasn't Roger at the front door, they could take me at my word.

I opened the sorority's directory and found the entry for Roberta Shepherd. I wanted to start with someone whose face wasn't viciously battered, but I didn't want to start with Denise. I was hoping that by the time I called the other girls' parents, more information would have come through about how she was doing.

"Shepherd residence," said a man who sounded like he had a phone on his nightstand, like gravity was pinning his voice to the back of his throat. Robbie's father.

"Mr. Shepherd?" I said.

He coughed up some morning phlegm. Then, formally, "Speaking."

I exhaled hard and led with the only thing that mattered to a parent. "First I want to say that Robbie is fine. My name is Pamela Schumacher, and I am the chapter president of The House. I'm calling because there has been an incident. An intruder broke in and some of the girls were hurt. They've been taken to Tallahassee Memorial Hospital to be looked at."

Mr. Shepherd aimed straight from the hip. "Are we talking about rape?"

"No," I replied, matching his tone, thinking it was some sign of maturity that I could discuss rape without so much as a wobble in my voice. I thought of Denise's underwear crumpled on the floor, even as I declared, proudly (proudly!), "No one was raped."

"Let me find a pen," Mr. Shepherd said.

Mr. Shepherd took down the address of the hospital and thanked me politely for the call. I thought, *Well, that wasn't so bad,* and in doing so placed a hex on myself.

Eileen's mother dropped the phone when I said Eileen had sustained some injuries to her face, and her younger brother picked it up and finished the conversation with me. Jill's parents demanded angrily that I let them speak to someone in charge. *I am in charge,* I said just as angrily.

I hung up and counted five deep breaths before punching in the phone number for the Andoras' home in Jacksonville. I didn't even need to flip the directory pages to the A's—I'd had Denise's number memorized since the first break of freshman year.

It was still early but, like Mr. Shepherd, Mrs. Andora answered on the second ring, even though I knew the Andoras didn't keep a phone in the bedroom. "Well?" she asked with a heavy sigh, suggesting she had been waiting for this call. "How is she?"

I wondered who had gotten to her first. Maybe the Shepherds. Denise and Robbie were both from Jacksonville. They were a year apart, but surely their parents had crossed paths over the years. "It's Pamela," I told her. "She's at the hospital, but she's going to be fine."

There was a long, bargaining pause, as though there was still time to take back what I'd just said. "Who is at the hospital?"

"Denise," I said, less sure of myself. "They took her a little bit ago."

"Denise?" Mrs. Andora sputtered. "Why? Why would she be at the hospital?"

"I thought you knew."

"Knew what?" When all language abandoned me, she repeated herself in a shrill tone that terrified me. "Knew what, Pamela?"

"You asked how she was, like you knew—"

"Knew what? Knew what?" Mrs. Andora was shouting by then. I wanted to tell her to stop, that she would startle the cats. She had four, and they were very skittish.

I came to, clinging to the edge of the counter with both hands, my chin in my chest, the phone spinning on the kitchen floor, wondering how the hell the phone had ended up spinning on the kitchen floor.

I picked it up and asserted bullishly, "There's been an incident." I thought that about summed it up, but then I realized Mrs. Andora was no longer listening to me. She had pulled the mouthpiece away and was hollering for Mr. Andora, something about Denise being in a car accident.

"No," I said, feeling unspeakably tired all of a sudden. I wished I could hang up the phone and walk away from this conversation, from the confusion, have someone else explain it to them as well as to me. Then I wanted to lie down and sleep for a week straight. "Not a car accident. It was a robbery. Maybe. We aren't sure."

"A robbery?" Mrs. Andora cried. "What are you saying, Pamela? Why don't you know? Where are you? Is Denise with you? Can I talk to her? It's Pamela, Richard. No, Richard. Stop—"

Denise's father came over the line and said furiously, "What in God's name is going on, Pamela?"

"Denise is fine," I insisted. "There was an incident at The House. An intruder. Some of the girls were injured and taken to the hospital to be looked at. Denise was lucky, really. Her injuries were the most minor."

"My God," Mr. Andora said while Mrs. Andora buzzed around him, telling him what to say, what to ask. "What hospital?"

I repeated the address of Tallahassee Memorial for the umpteenth time that morning: 1300 Miccosukee Road. Still with me after forty-three years.

I hung up with Mr. Andora, feeling drained but relieved. I'd done it. The hardest part, and I'd done it. But then the phone started up, jangling all through The House. I plugged an ear. Had our phone always sounded so piercing? I snatched it off the receiver, less interested in answering it than in making it *stop*.

"This is Linda Donnelly," said the voice on the other end of the line, the name sounding familiar but far too distant to grasp. "I'm a resident in training at Tallahassee Memorial. Who am I speaking to?"

"Pamela Schumacher," I said. "I'm the chapter president of The House."

"I know who you are," she said. "Do you remember me?"

I cast around for some kind of clue, but it was as if my memory had melted, like those clocks in the Dalí poster Denise had hung over her head.

"I'm your scholastic adviser. I was chapter of the 1967 class."

"I apologize," I said, mortified. I could not believe I'd blanked on the name of a member of our advisory board. I did not see how the evening, the morning, whatever we were in, could get any worse.

"Forgiven. You've had quite a night, from what I've gathered around here. Do you need anything? Can I help?"

"That is so kind, Dr. Donnelly," I said with extravagant deference, hoping to make up for my earlier gaffe. "I'm hoping they let us go see the girls soon. Actually, would you be able to share their room numbers with us?"

There was a half-second pause. "Eileen and Jill are both in surgery at the moment, but I can get you that information once they're out."

"Thank you," I said. "And what about Denise and Robbie?"

That pause again, but there was fear in it. I could sense it through the phone. "You mean for identification purposes?"

My hand, on the stainless-steel counter, was slick enough to slip. I buffed away the smudges I'd left behind with the switchblade of my elbow. "What do you mean, for identification purposes?"

"I mean identifying the bodies."

"I'm confused," I said testily, though I wasn't. I couldn't have been, otherwise I never would have taken a *tone* with an alumna. I must have understood enough that I knew I would be forgiven, that what had happened occupied the realm of the unforgivable.

"Robbie and Denise expired before they reached the hospital," Dr. Donnelly informed me clinically. "Did no one tell you this?"

There was a calendar on the wall. A circle around today's date. It was Super Bowl Sunday, I remembered. Denise was meant to make the dip for the party we'd been invited to later. I'd have to let them know, I thought, that they would be down a dish.

"I was told they were fine."

"Who told you that?" Dr. Donnelly demanded.

"The sheriff."

"Put him on the phone, right now," she said, sounding impatient and bossy. Sounding like me. "Do you have anyone else there to advocate for you? A school official or anything like that?"

I shook my head numbly, then remembered she couldn't see me. "No."

"I'll be there as soon as my shift ends. That's in one hour. Okay? Can you go and put the sheriff on the line now?"

"Yes," I said, and set down the phone. Realizing something, I picked it up again. "No, actually. I mean, not right now. I need to call Robbie's and Denise's parents."

"That's his job."

"No," I said. "You don't understand. I just told them Robbie and Denise were fine. I have to be the one to make it right."

"You called them and told them . . ." Dr. Donnelly trailed off as she absorbed the full impact of what I'd done. "Okay," she said softly. "I'll be there soon. I need you to hang in there for me, okay, Pamela? We're going to help you."

I was shaking my head *no*. Hanging in there was just not possible after what I'd done.

"Pamela?"

"Okay," I lied.

———

It is the moment that visits me in the middle of a meal at my favorite Italian restaurant, when the pedicurist sets the timer for the five-minute massage, or while I am decorating the house for Christmas. *You don't deserve to feel pleasure,* this moment reminds me, *not when you caused this level of pain.*

"Yes!" Mrs. Andora cried when she picked up the phone a second time. "We're on our way. We're running out the door!"

"Mrs. Andora," I said in a thick slab of a voice. "It's Pamela." I swallowed. "I have an update."

"We'll be there to speak to the doctor soon enough," Mrs. Andora said brusquely. She heard it in my voice, I could tell. She would not permit me to say it. "Are you there? At the hospital?"

"No."

"Then you don't know anything, Pamela."

"I do," I said. "I'm so sorry, but I do."

Mrs. Andora threw the phone against the wall. I know this because I saw the hole it left when I came for the funeral the following week. The sound that came out of her was manly, a guttural, bloodthirsty battle cry. It sent me staggering back, T-boning the edge of the kitchen counter. I whimpered because the corner was sharp and it had pierced my liver or a kidney, one of those important, tender organs. I listened to ladylike Mrs. Andora suffer in that grotesque, masculine way until Mr. Andora came on the line and choked out, like some kind of grief-programmed answering machine, "We can't come to the phone right now."

The line went dead, and then I was going through the louvered doors and into the bright foyer, asking for Sheriff Cruso in a twee little voice, as nonthreatening as could be, because he had already looked at me like I was the know-it-all beast of his nightmares. It was his job to know these things first, and yet I had found out two of the girls hadn't made it before he did. I was thinking, *I'll pull him aside. I'll tell him in private that Robbie and Denise are dead.* I didn't want to embarrass him in front of his subordinates. This was how my brain was wired back then. This is how I almost went on to live.

Eight a.m.

The decision to visit Florida State University had nothing to do with an interest in Florida State University and everything to do with getting a rise out of my mother.

In 1968, there were anti-war and anti-segregation protests staged along the campus's legacy walk. In the fall, students wore blue jeans in solidarity with the Tallahassee gay community. *Newsweek* called FSU "the Berkeley of the South." This was all according to the brochure that arrived in the mail my sophomore year of high school, addressed to my father, along with an invitation for him and his family to come for an all-expenses-paid campus visit. They were wooing him, hoping to lure him away from his cushy office on Park Avenue to join the department of the burgeoning law school.

Before my mother threw the invitation in the trash, she tore it up with a look on her face that I had seen only once before, when a neighbor brought over a carrot cake as a thank-you for some letter of recommendation she had written. As soon as the front door closed, my mother doused it in dish detergent, squeezing the bottle in both hands, like it was on fire. From that point on, Florida State University took on a flammable quality in my mind, something that set off my mother's alarm bells, made her sharp and attentive.

Two years later, when it came time to consider college, I mentioned FSU. "That's pretty far," she said, her voice jumping an octave. *Interesting*, I thought, and decided to press harder on this rickety key of parental concern, long out of tune.

"They offer something called an externship!" I exclaimed with legitimate enthusiasm, paging through the new brochure I'd requested. Even as a prelaw undergrad, you could earn credit by working in the courts at the Capitol Building, just a few blocks from campus.

"Why would you go to 'the Berkeley of the South' when you have the grades to go to Berkeley?" my mother pushed back. My mother never pushed back on me. Anything I wanted to do was fine by her.

It was a salient point, but I flicked my hair off my shoulder as if it weren't.

"You're too smart for a state school," my mother added a little desperately.

That got me to lower the brochure, examine my mother, wonder if she had been body snatched sometime in the night. I'd always considered myself an intuitive person, but you could be dull as a doornail and still see there was something about Florida that was deeply agitating to Marion Young. I might never have learned what, if Denise's death hadn't broken the proverbial seal on our vesicle of family secrets.

I arranged a visit to campus, using money I'd earned bookkeeping at my father's law firm, not because I needed to—my father made a lot of money, and my mother came from even more—but because my mother was so dead set against FSU that she refused to pay for the trip. I relished every second of fighting about my first choice for college with my beautiful, busy mother, who often seemed too wrapped up in her functions and hobbies and various women's clubs to pay attention to what was going on in my life. My sister was eight years older and moved out of the house for good when I was in the fourth grade. I was often alone and terminally bored, and I do not say that facetiously. Idle, my mind goes to places that scare me.

But when I saw the Gothic towers of the Westcott Building, when I stood in the damp shade of the moss-hung oaks older than the university itself, a funny thing happened, a sort of clarity of the senses. It was like someone had been twisting my radio dial all my life, trying to find reception, and all the fuzz cleared the moment we crossed the border into Leon County. I was simply in tune with this place. That may sound like the cozy sentiment of a painted wood kitchen sign a certain kind of woman impulse-buys at Home Goods, but the stillness of my mind felt eerie and unnatural, reminiscent of the way birds stop chattering in a forest when a predator is crouching in the brush. At the time, I chalked it up to nerves. Choosing where to spend the next four years of my life was a big decision, after all.

Choosing where to rush, less so. The House, we called it, as though it were the original artifact, had the reputation for being the smartest sorority on campus, and Denise and I showed up for rush week expecting Southern grandeur in the form of a Georgian colonial, white columns holding up the gabled roof, petticoat-shaped ghosts in the attic. But the L-shaped building on West Jefferson Street could have been an office space or a warehouse. Some drunk geezer was smoking outside the bar next door, swaying side to side and yelling belligerently at the girls to *be careful* as they filed into The House.

"Thank you, sir!" Denise called back. He shaded his eyes and smiled when he saw it was the prettiest girl who had finally acknowledged him.

"Don't encourage him!" hissed one of the girls walking ahead of us.

Denise held me back by the elbow. "Watch," she said, and like clockwork, the hissing girl miscalculated the height of the riser and stumbled gracelessly through the double front doors, propped open to welcome the class of '78. We'd later learn the front steps were installed improperly and varied in rise by a full inch. The drunk geezer had been watching freshman girls trip over their high heels all day and destroy their chances of getting a bid.

Despite its lack of curb appeal, I'd warmed to The House in-

stantly once I was inside. Other sororities had offered us lemon-
ade; here it was coffee so strong I left with lockjaw. The sisters wore
name tags affixed to their blouses with owl and skull pins, and they
were tactual, affectionate, out to change the world. They held hands
and sat on laps as they spoke about their experiences in The House,
the bonds they'd formed, the leadership and money management
skills they'd acquired, the community that would get them jobs and
admittance into competitive graduate programs, male-dominated
arenas that brave alumnae had started infiltrating in the fifties, weaving an intricate network for us to call on once we'd graduated too. I
could feel Denise trembling beside me as they spoke. I wanted it that
bad too.

They sent us away with reading material—an article called
"How to Discriminate Against Women Without Really Trying" by
a researcher named Jo Freeman. *Food for thought,* they called it. Denise and I went back to the dorms and devoured every word.

The author's argument was based on research collected from
graduate students at the University of Chicago, but I recognized
shades of my own experience in her conclusion, which was that
women who wish to advance in their career face an insidious kind
of discrimination, one that is not active, in-your-face sexism but,
rather, no response at all. It was subtle discouragement by neglect,
what the author called "motivational malnutrition."

I thought about that phrase—motivational malnutrition—as I
stared at the telephone, cradled in its receiver, for a good while after
I'd spoken to everyone else's parents, who had all picked up by the
second ring. After I tried my own again and still, there was no answer.

———

When that big, nervous officer came to my room and told us that
the girls had made it to the hospital, when Sheriff Cruso echoed
the statement to me, technically, neither man had lied. There was a
morgue in the basement of Tallahassee Memorial.

Robbie had died in her bed. Denise, on her way to the hospital.

I can't say that the police conspired to keep their deaths from us—a conspiracy by nature suggests malevolence, a coordinated effort at play. I can't even call what they did negligence, because how can something be negligent when it's not anyone's responsibility? It was not the job of the Tallahassee PD to tend to a bunch of mewling sorority girls in their jammies and winter coats. Their job was to find the person who'd done this before anyone else got hurt, and that's where, much like their predecessors back west, they dropped the ball, and instead of picking it up, they watched, whistling through the gaps in their two front teeth, while it rolled off the face of the earth. All of this should have stopped in the state of Colorado years earlier. But I was a long way from understanding any of that.

It was eight in the morning, the sun thawing the frost on the grass and the police rummaging through the upstairs rooms like mutant rats in the walls, when I stood at the head of one of the two long tables in the dining hall and told The House that Denise and Robbie were dead.

"Why?" someone asked straightaway, her eyes dry. It was a gritted-teeth *why,* the outraged kind that demands an answer.

I read about us in the paper, the way we hurled the word *why* around the church service we attended later that morning. The press made it sound like the question was rhetorical, as though we wailed it melodramatically. But it was always a serious question. Why did this happen? One day we would get our answer, and it's not the one you think. Right here, right now, I want you to forget two things: he was nothing special, and what happened was not random.

Still, it remained beyond comprehension that the ones who had survived were Eileen and Jill, with their pulpy faces, their ruptured eardrums, the pain in their jaws that would prove chronic. That Denise and Robbie had died when they were the ones who had just looked like they were sleeping. A few years later, the journalist Carl Wallace would publish his seminal true-crime bestseller and quote

Sheriff Cruso as saying that Jill and Eileen were alive today only because The Defendant was so tired from killing Robbie and Denise.
There's a diet for you. I lost five pounds in four days after reading
that.

"Do they expect us to keep living here?" Bernadette asked. Her
big beauty-queen eyes were swollen and shiny, as though she'd taken
a hit in a bar brawl.

"I don't think I can ever sleep here again."

"Who's going to clean it *up*? Do the police? Does the school?"

"Does the school know yet? I mean, what? Do we go to class
tomorrow?"

"Write your questions down," I said, producing a pen and paper,
"so that we don't forget them. I'm going to get them answered."

Answers. *Answers.* It was all we wanted. Even to be told that the
police had the same questions we did, that they were working to sort
it all out, would have been something. As the pen and paper made
their way around the table, someone raised her hand.

"We should go to church," she said. "Denise's church."

Privately, I knew Denise never went to church anymore, that
she only pretended like she did for her parents and anyone else who
asked. There were a few members of the press gathered outside, and
I thought it would protect our image if they reported we'd turned
to God in our time of need. That was what good Southern girls did.
I was afraid that if anyone looked hard enough, they would see we
were not good, not to the standard that a young woman is held. No
one is, not even today.

"Let's go to church," I said, so sure we would be the ones to game
the system.

Ten a.m.

oris Wren, head of campus safety, was waiting for us when we returned from the church service. He wore a wrinkled sack of a suit, and though his dark gray hair was gelled back, gluey pieces had gotten plastered in the damp of his temples like spindly-legged insects in amber.

There was little that was comforting about the slovenly head of campus security, but still I found myself wanting to crawl across the table and into his arms out of sheer gratitude. Here was a person with an impressive title and no doubt a plan who could tell us what the hell was going on, who could lay out what would happen next. My relief bordered on giddy.

"I wish I could say I am here to reassure you," Mr. Wren said, "but I am here to put the fear of God in you."

Someone moaned. Someone coughed. Someone dropped her dirty tissue on the floor and banged her head picking it up, muttering *ow* accusingly. Hadn't she endured enough?

"Last night," Mr. Wren continued, "about half an hour after this person fled your residence, he broke into an off-campus apartment on Dunwoody Street and beat another female student within an inch of her life."

I brought my hands to the back of my neck and dropped my

chin to my chest. *Protect your neck.* This is what you do when a bear attacks you. Denise taught me that, driving through Ocala National Forest on our way to her parents' house. Black bears denned in the sand pines, and there were safety signs posted everywhere. *What you do is you lie on your stomach and you spread your legs wide and you clasp your hands around the back of your neck and you don't fight, never fight, even if you're being torn limb from limb.*

"But she survived?" I heard myself ask.

"She's at the hospital with the others, but that's all I know for the moment."

Upstairs, one of the police officers slammed a door, and Bernadette grabbed my arm so hard she left half-moon indents in my skin.

"Whoever this person is"—Mr. Wren was speaking through his teeth, as though repulsed by his own fear—"he's a sick individual. He's depraved. He should have sought help for an illness a long time ago. And we cannot rule out that he specifically targeted this sorority, or the girls he attacked, or that he won't come back, or that he hasn't been planning this for God knows how long. The threat level is extremely high."

What I remember of that moment is the way we clutched at one another, desperately, the way we dug in our nails and held on for dear life. We were affectionate in The House, but this was about making sure we were all here, that we were hearing this, that we were *living* this. Overnight, we had fallen through the looking glass. Denise used to tell me how Salvador Dalí would deprive himself of sleep and stare at objects until he could reimagine them into something else, until their true nature revealed itself. I was shivering, delirious with fear, seeing The House for what it really was: a tank for waterfowl, open for the season.

"I recommend that you avoid anything that could identify you as a member of this house. No sweatshirts or pins. If you have stickers on your cars, remove them. Travel in groups of at least three. Do not travel alone with any men for the time being."

"Not even with our boyfriends?"

Mr. Wren gasped, making some of the girls gasp louder. "*Especially* not with your boyfriends." He looked so terrified at the prospect of us spending time alone with our boyfriends that I found myself wondering if my own shadow may be involved in the plot against our lives.

"But what are we supposed to do?" I asked. "Where are we supposed to stay tonight?"

"We've put in an order for extra locks, though they won't arrive for a few days," Mr. Wren said. Locks. That's what they did for us. Locks. "Some of the other sororities are having fraternity members stand guard through the night."

"But you just told us not to see our boyfriends," Bernadette said.

"I said not to see them alone. In groups is different."

"There's nowhere we can stay?" I asked, insulted, already knowing the answer was no, or it would have been the first thing he'd offered. I had a hard time imagining that the Stepford wives in training at Alpha Delta Pi, in their grand brick mansion, wouldn't be rescued on white horses. "Empty dorm rooms, or a hotel?"

"I may be able to fit a few of you into alumni housing. But we don't have the budget to pay for a hotel for all of you. If you're able to stay with family and friends who live nearby, I'd strongly recommend that you do so."

"Tomorrow's Monday," I pointed out, wringing my hands nervously. "Do our professors know what happened? Will we be penalized for not attending class?" Grades were never not a concern of mine, even at a time like this.

"I can make sure of that," Mr. Wren said in an offhand way that sent me spinning. Not something he had already done, or was planning to do, or would absolutely do. Where was everyone's sense of urgency? I felt stark raving mad with urgency.

"And what about all of them?" I gestured in the direction of the front window, though the press had accumulated not just there but at the side door, descending on us when we left for the church service. Any illusions that they would handle us gently were shattered the moment they followed us inside the chapel and *yelled* at us as we walked back to the house. "Are they allowed to be here? Are they allowed to bother us like this?"

Mr. Wren asked me to bring him the pad of paper with all our written questions and concerns; he would take them to the president and sort it out as best he could. I never heard from Mr. Wren again, but over the next year of my life, one of my questions was answered time and time again. Yes, the press was allowed to be there. They were allowed to be anywhere I was. And yes, they were allowed to bother me like that.

———

Dr. Linda Donnelly called back later that morning.

"I couldn't even get down the street," she said breathlessly. "It's a scene over there. Don't talk to any members of the press. You know that, right?"

"Of course," I said, though I didn't. "Right now I'm trying to find us a place to stay." I explained the situation to her.

"Let me make some calls," she said.

I lifted the kitchen curtain with the side of my hand, monitoring the scene out the window, my lips pursing in distaste. There were multiple cruisers bending the Bermuda grass, media vans making a hatched pattern behind the wooden police barrier, newscasters clutching various-colored microphone boxes, looking cold and ready. For a moment, I was lulled into thinking it was just an ordinary Saturday night since that new bar had opened next door. When the parking lot filled up, there were always spillovers tearing up our front yard. *I should call the police*, I thought, which is what I normally did. Then I realized I would be calling the police *on* the police, and a sound came out of me that I supposed was a laugh. The phone rang.

"Dr. Donnelly?"

"Pamela!" It was a man's voice, a voice I'd heard a hundred times before and yet still could not place. "I've been trying to get through all morning!" And I remembered I had a boyfriend, someone who loved me and was as worried about me as the other girls' parents.

"Brian," I croaked, beginning to cry.

"Are you okay? Are you hurt?"

"No. No. I'm fine. But Denise—"

"I heard."

"How?" I looked around for something to use to wipe my nose, and all I could come up with were the plaid pot holders the cooks used to handle our food. I cringed as I plugged a nostril and blew into one.

"The police are here. They took Roger away in handcuffs." Roger lived in Turq House, down the hall from Brian.

"Handcuffs!" I cried. "I told them it wasn't Roger. I told them I was just surprised to see a man at the front door, and they sort of looked alike, and—"

"You *saw* him?"

"Right before he ran out the door."

"Did he see you? Did he . . . do anything to you?"

"What? No! I just told you. I'm not hurt."

"Thank God," Brian said, and I could tell in that moment that a real weight had been lifted off his shoulders. What had happened was bad, but it was removed enough from me, and therefore from him, that nothing would really need to change for us. I imagined him closing his eyes and sinking down on the cushioned banquette in the alcove where they kept the phone. The cord was oddly short, and his fraternity brothers joked that he was the only one tall enough to sit and talk at the same time. I liked how tall he was, sure, but I liked more that it was a quality others valued. I liked that he wore needlepoint belts bearing the crest of his Alabama country club but kept his dark blond hair on the shaggy side. I liked people to know I was with someone physically imposing, someone who was not too straight-edged but not a strung-out beatnik either. I know this sounds strange, but I liked that next to Brian, I was not only safe but could pass for normal. If you saw me back then, you would understand how little sense any of this made, because I was normal-looking to the point of parody.

"Listen," I said to him, "I have to go. I don't want to tie up the phone line. I'm trying to find a place for all of us to stay."

"Call me and let me know," Brian said. "I'm going with you. I love you."

"I love you too," I said, and it felt so good to say that to someone, to hear that from anyone.

————

Dr. Donnelly connected me to an alumna named Catherine Mc-Call, class of '37, a retired government statistician who lived out in Red Hills with her publisher husband, about twenty miles from the center of Tallahassee. Mrs. McCall was happy to take in as many of us as she could and helped to arrange accommodations for the rest.

It was around five in the evening when the pattering overhead began to recede and those of us whose rooms had been cleared were allowed upstairs to collect our things. As I stuffed a suitcase full of sweaters and underpants, the sun was slipping behind the West-cott Building's twin brick towers. I imagined its rays clinging to the Gothic guardrail, trying to hold on just for me. I did not know how anyone expected me to survive nightfall.

All day, I'd felt wretched at the thought of Sherriff Cruso in our rooms, touching our things, going through our drawers. But then, when his men did leave a week later, I had to suppress the urge to chase them down the street and beg them to come back. *Don't leave me in charge. Please. I can't do this alone.*

I pulled back the drapes in my bedroom, donated to us by an alumna who married the owner of Florida's top fabric chain; I was checking for Brian's denim-blue Bronco. He and a few of the Turq House guys were going to bus us out to Mrs. McCall's house in Red Hills. Two armed guards were supposed to meet us there, but in the end we got only one.

"Brian is here," I called out to the girls who were coming with me.

Downstairs, Bernadette glanced out the windows uncertainly. "How are we going to get past them?" She was talking about the cancerous mass of press, multiplying by the minute outside our back door.

I gave my coat a shake and drew up the hood. "We just have to make a run for it. Cover your head and pretend it's pouring rain. At least we have practice with that." At FSU, you could walk to class in the sunshine and come home drenched to the bone.

The patrolman stationed at the back opened the door for us, and we ran out into the storm, the flash of the bulbs invoking the same panicked plea as lightning—*please, just don't strike* me. The group shifted so that our hands were on one another's shoulders, trying to push through the kicked wasp's nest in a wedding conga line. I heard a woman shouting to back *the fuck* up! For a moment, I feared it was me. When I got my bid for The House freshman year, it came with the caveat to smile more, roll my eyes less, and introduce some color to my wardrobe. I peered around Bernadette's head and was relieved to identify the true offender, a woman in a camel mohair coat, pin-straight blond hair sticking out of a newsboy cap like the ones Jane Birkin wore. She was waving a lit cigarette, and cameramen and reporters were jumping back to avoid a slashing by the cherry.

Bernadette leaped into the back seat of Brian's car, but before I could follow, someone grabbed my elbow and yanked me back, saying excitedly, "It's *her*." A flash went off inches from my face, stunning me senseless. I couldn't see; I couldn't move. I only heard—I only smelled—what happened next.

There was a man's high-pitched screech, one acrid inhale, and I was released. I stumbled, trying to wave away the colorful spots before my eyes like a cloud of gnats.

"Watch it with that thing, lady!" a man shouted.

"Go," the hatted woman whispered, close to my ear. Though the flash had blinded me, I knew it was her because I could smell the cigarette smoke on her breath. She gave me a boost up into the back seat of the car, and the door slammed shut, and Brian's voice was asking me frantically if I was hurt. I rubbed my eyes, blinking away the constellation of spots, and saw the guy I was planning on marrying, how badly he needed to hear that I wasn't.

Seven p.m.

Mrs. McCall opened the door wearing a belted shirtdress, her shoulder-length white hair immovably curled. She sighed at the state of us standing on her porch, between the Corinthian columns, the boys loaded down with overnight bags and the girls with limp, uncombed hair.

"What an absolute ordeal you've all had," she said, her sigh fatalist, as though the events of the last twenty-four hours were both atrocious and completely inevitable in the world in which we lived. She narrowed her eyes at something over my shoulder. "Are we expecting anyone else this evening?"

We all turned to see she was speaking to the police guard who had trailed us through the velvety dark of the canopy roads. "Just me, ma'am," he said. He was clean-shaven and all arms and legs, no more than twenty-five. The needle palms clattered in a sudden wind, and his hand shot to his holster, eyes sweeping the remote landscape with a petrified vigilance I wished I hadn't seen.

Mrs. McCall frowned. "How do you take your coffee?"

In the dome-shaped entrance hall, we were told to set down our bags. I never saw anyone else in the house other than Mr. and Mrs. McCall, but someone took our things upstairs and into the rooms where we would sleep. In the dining room, we were fed oily bowls of beef and barley soup beneath a bronze crucifix, agony stretching the mouth of Jesus diagonal.

I traced letters in the fatty foam of my supper while everyone sat around talking about everything except what had happened. The cold, the new grading system that was making it harder to earn A's, the cold, the ugly new Capitol Building. Denise had called it a brutalist scourge on Tallahassee, too tall and too gray, a man's idea of modernity.

I looked down and realized my plate had been cleared, that Mr. McCall had downed the last of his sherry and moved on to something in a darker shade of brown that had turned his nose scalded and bulbous.

"You let me know if your fraternity brother needs a lawyer," he said to Brian. "I've got a good one."

Brian nodded dutifully. "Yes, sir. I'll let Roger know."

I felt capable of violence in that moment. Not against anyone in that room—but my crystal water glass, the marble bust of some slave-owning relative regarding me from a pedestal between the windows, those I wanted to blast to pieces.

"I can't believe they took him away in handcuffs," I fumed. "I told Sheriff Cruso it *wasn't* Roger."

"Sheriff has the election to think about," Mr. McCall said in his defense.

"Might actually turn his prospects around if he gets this guy," Brian added with a wry laugh. Brian's father was a congressman in Orlando. He knew all about campaign strategy.

"I'll tell ya what," Mr. McCall said, lips slick with beef marrow, "I wouldn't mind taking a crack at the animal once they catch him." This man was a Christian.

Mrs. McCall stood with a trained smile. "Who wants coffee with dessert?"

"Give me twenty minutes alone in a room with him," Brian agreed, in a ravenous, juicy way that churned my stomach. This became something of a Rorschach test over the years. There were men who cracked their knuckles while divulging to me what they would do to The Defendant if they got the chance, thinking this was somehow reassuring for me to hear. But all it did was make me realize that there wasn't so big a difference between the man who'd brutalized Denise and half the men I passed every day on the street.

Mrs. McCall went into the kitchen. I could hear slices of her conversation through the swinging door, with someone whose only contribution was a series of *yes ma'am*s and *no ma'am*s.

She soon returned with coffees in hand-painted porcelain cups on hand-painted porcelain saucers, spiked for the girls, virgin for Brian and Mr. McCall, who were planning on staying up all night guarding the various entry points of the house.

"To help you sleep," Mrs. McCall said as she served mine.

At some point during dinner, a striking clock had chimed in the house. Seven times. I did the math. Denise had been dead for sixteen hours, and still I had not told my mother. I gulped down the stiff coffee with the ease of someone drinking a beer on a hot day.

"Could I use the phone?" I asked, and Mrs. McCall got up and led the way to the informal parlor, a more comfortable place to conduct my business than the formal one, she assured me.

———

I was, at that point, aching to speak to my parents and weighted with despair at the thought of picking up the phone and trying again. If they did not answer a third time, I was sure I would disintegrate into thin air. It did not matter that they were in New Jersey and had no way of knowing what had happened—the news wouldn't hit the *Tallahassee Democrat* until Monday morning—what mattered was that people who really loved their children were acutely attuned to their distress signals, and I would have to accept that my parents' antennae would never arc in my direction.

And yet if they did pick up, what a rush it would be to regale them with what I'd *survived*. Sometimes, while crossing a busy intersection or standing at the top of a stairwell, I wondered how they might react if I were struck by a car or lost my footing. I pictured myself in a hospital room, my mother kneeling at my bedside sobbing and begging me for forgiveness. She should have been there. She should have been paying attention. I was deeply ashamed to admit that this is what I yearned for in my most private moments. I thought it pointed to something about me that was innately invisible.

"You finished with the phone?" It was Brian, hunching in the recessed doorway to the parlor. My tiny coffee cup was empty, my breaths slow and shallow. No telling how long I'd been sitting there, staring at all of Mrs. McCall's various degrees. She was a mathematician who had worked as a government statistician for many years, assigning numerical value to local trends so that public officials could decide how to best allocate funds, the only woman in the Capitol Building whose phone had a direct line to the governor.

"Not yet."

"I wanted you to talk to my dad," Brian said, ducking to enter the room; he was one of those tall guys who had learned to do so in old Southern mansions like this, with their vaulted foyers and sloping doorways. Brian had grown up in Orlando but was descended from serious Birmingham stock, where his family still belonged to the shooting club his great-grandparents helped found. He had been courteous to an obsequious degree all night after seeing the way Mr. and Mrs. McCall had eyed his long hair, his bare feet in peeling leather thongs. *I'm a good ole boy in a hitchhiker's clothing,* he was saying every time he stood when a woman got up from the table.

"Your dad?" I looked at him like he'd suggested I get in touch with John Lennon.

"There's something called a crime victims' assistance program. I guess Florida has one of the best in the country? It just started here a few years ago. But you can apply and request compensation for any damages done to the house."

I nodded. Yeah, sure. That seemed like something I should do. On the downswing of my chin, my whole world fell apart again.

There was a long black hair snaked in the weave of my sweater. I was a blonde.

"Are you worried about how your mom might take it?" Brian asked in a gentler voice. He'd met my mother once. He thought she was beautiful; she called him Byron, then Brad.

"Something like that," I whispered, tears blurring that last piece of Denise stuck to my sweater.

"I know y'all aren't close," Brian said harmlessly.

That set me straight. No one could ever know how little interest my parents had in me. It was not even something I discussed with Denise. "We're playing phone tag," I said with an edge.

In truth, I had been sitting in there wondering if I should wait until Monday, when the news hit the papers. When my parents had some sense of the enormity of the tragedy and would be waiting by the phone for my call. Maybe they would even pick up on the second ring, like Denise's mother had. But I couldn't stand the pitying way Brian was looking at me, like he knew something I'd worked so hard to conceal. I reached for the phone.

———

My father was a small, smiling man with a shiny red face like Santa Claus's. I'd seen him angry maybe twice in my life, both times at inanimate objects. The corner of a bureau where he repeatedly stubbed his toe had taken some abuse.

I was about to hang up when he answered, and I was so stunned to have him on the line that I was temporarily at a loss for how to begin.

"Hello?" he said for the second time.

"You're home."

"Did you leave something behind?" He sounded confused.

"*Dad,*" I said sharply. "It's me."

"Sweetheart!" He laughed at the mix-up. "I thought you were Wanda." Wanda was our cleaning woman.

"I've been calling," I said, heat in my voice. "Where have you been?"

Brian made some sort of gesture—a silent hush, a lowering of his hands—that amounted to *stay calm.*

"We've been here."

"Even in the morning?"

"What time did you call?"

"I tried you around five."

"That was you?" my father said, then raised his voice. "Marion! It was Pammy calling this morning!"

They'd heard the phone ring. They'd heard the phone ring before the sun came up and they hadn't gotten out of bed to answer it, though they had two daughters who no longer lived under their roof. I'd soon learn my mother had her reasons for keeping me at arm's length, and while I'd go on to forge an unexpected connection with my father, I would never shake the image of them lying in bed with the covers over their heads when I needed them most.

I looked over at Brian and he nodded at me—a vote of confidence. I would not be taking his advice to sound smart and sure and capable, which was how he'd coached me as I'd dialed the number for home. It was good advice for a girl with normal parents, but I was wounded, and I needed my parents to tend to me for once. I would make what had happened sound as bad as I could, as bad as it was, really.

"Something awful has happened, Dad," I said.

There was an anxious pause that I savored. "Should I get your mother?"

I refused to let him off the hook. "Someone broke into our house last night and attacked a bunch of the girls. Denise is dead."

"Pamela!" my father cried, and the load on my heart lightened. "Are you hurt?"

"I'm not hurt. But I saw him. I'm the only one who saw him, Dad."

"Thank God you've never needed glasses," he said, and at the time I thought it was a funny comment to make, but later, I'd realize that was his lawyer brain at work. No one on the defense team could suggest that my vision was spotty and therefore my identification unreliable. "Let me go get your mother."

I heard him say my mother's name, the shuffling of his feet as he moved toward wherever she was in the house. The wait for her to come to the phone was much shorter than it felt. I was bursting with things I'd wanted to say to her since I was a child.

"Remember to let them know about the precautions you're taking," Brian whispered while I waited for my mother to come to the phone so I could tell her about everything but the precautions I was taking.

"Pamela," she said, sounding nervous. Like I was the authority figure, she was in big trouble, and she would not even need to ask *why*. "What's happened?"

"Mom," I said, and just the word on my lips brought me to tears. "Where have you been?"

"We were—"

"Where have you been? Where have you been?" I kept repeating it, my voice a ferocious roar, husky with hurt. "You are my mother! You are my mother and you answer the phone! You answer the fucking phone!" I looked over at Brian, who was staring at the floor respectfully, like I was changing and he was trying to give me privacy. Though we'd had sex, he'd never really seen me naked.

On the other end of the phone, I heard my mother weeping. We had been performing the same dance all our lives—one in which I asked for little and received even less—but that was the moment I changed the steps on her. She never quite caught up, but she did try.

———

That night, sleep tackled me from behind, pinned my shoulders down, and released me at 2:59 on the nose. I did not yet understand the significance of that minute, nor the hours it would go on to collect from me over the next forty-three years. I knew only that it was late, it was dark, the wind was rattling the shutters, and Bernadette didn't sound like she was breathing. I jammed my elbow into her side, and she yelped softly.

"Why did you do that?"

"You're awake?"

"Of course I'm awake."

I sprang up, my pulse pummeling the bridge of my nose. "Why? Did you hear something?"

"No. But I didn't hear anything last night, did I?"

I groped around wildly, trying to find the lamp, nearly knocking it over and scratching the walnut nightstand before managing to turn it on. I scrambled out of bed and pushed the curtain aside, same blue-and-white chinoiserie pattern as the rug, same blue-and-white chinoiserie as the seat of the very small chair in the corner, checking to make sure the skinny, scared police guard wasn't splayed out on the front steps with his throat cut. But his scalp gleamed pink as he scanned the fields from left to right and right to left. The land was too vast for one man to monitor, and yet what had happened had happened in a full house with neighbors on all sides. Maybe what felt unsafe was safe. Maybe I should never sleep through the night again.

I tripped over one of Bernadette's shoes and splintered my shin on the baseboard of the bed. I face-planted onto the sheets and curled up in the fetal position, moaning in pain. Denise was not a neat freak, but she seemed to understand that my penchant for order and organization was about something deeper, so she did the best she could to honor it. If Denise were here with me in this room, her shoes would be in the closet and not strewn all over the floor. If Denise were here, she would ask what the hell was wrong with that very small chair in the corner, too small for an adult and too fancy for a child. If Denise were here, she would have made me laugh with her opinions, her observations, the remarkable lens through which she saw the world.

"What if it is Roger?" Bernadette whispered.

For a moment, I felt like I was swallowing glass. Then I remembered. "It can't be," I said, rolling over to face her. On the wall adjacent, there was a painting of Mother Mary, wearing blue and praying with her eyes upcast. "I saw him, remember?"

Bernadette picked at the scratchy, expensive fabric of the comforter. She opened her mouth, and half a vowel came out. She pressed her lips together, tight.

"Bernadette?" I asked, apprehension pooling in my bowels.

She shook her head. *No.* She wouldn't say it. *No.*

I sat up, scooting closer to the foot of the bed and placing my hands on top of her knees. She turned her face away from me.

"You know whatever you tell me is in confidence until you give me permission to talk about it, right?" I had started to say this once I took office, like I was some kind of priest. But I found it worked. It was something about the part "until you give me permission." It was a sharing of power.

"There was this time." Bernadette closed her eyes. "With Roger."

It happened in his car, parked right outside The House, on their way home from a movie. His hand on the back of her neck as they kissed, gently at first, then not. He pushed her face down into his lap. Held it there. He thrust until she sobbed. Her nose stuffed up and she could not breathe. She was sure he was going to accidentally kill her.

"It was last year," Bernadette said, her face still turned away from me but smeared with tears now. "He and Denise had that huge fight in the middle of Winter Gala, remember? And they didn't talk for a whole month?"

Oh, I remembered.

"Anyway," Bernadette said, swiping at her face with the back of her hand, "he asked me out a little bit after that. I didn't want to advertise it. They were broken up, sure, but you could tell she wanted to be back together with him. And I didn't want to deal with that, you know?"

That. Denise's bruised ego; her wrath. I did know.

"We don't have to tell the police, do we?" Bernadette faced me finally, desperation in her bloated eyes. "I would lose my title if this got out."

I caught myself about to say I didn't think we needed to. I didn't want to give Sheriff Cruso one more reason to suspect Roger. But keeping something like this from the authorities felt unethical, like we were vaguely conspiring to protect a person who didn't totally deserve it. "Would you be okay if I spoke to my father about it? He's an attorney. A good one."

Bernadette replied without taking the time to consider it. "Can I let you know in the morning?"

We stared at each other with honest, exhausted faces. If the answer wasn't yes now, it certainly wouldn't be yes with clearer heads.

"Of course," I told her. The thing about what I said to them— about speaking to me in confidence, about needing their permission to share—it worked because I always kept my word.

Jacksonville, Florida, 2021

Day 15,826

The Jacksonville airport is much newer and nicer than Newark's. They don't just have better food options and bathrooms where all the toilet sensors actually work; the floors are gleaming white terrazzo as far as the eye can see, not so much as a swatch of carpet to slow me down as I speed-roll my suitcase alongside me, trying to beat the other business-class passengers to the front of the Hertz line.

It is after midnight by the time I am buckled into my sanitized-smelling midsize SUV. The parking attendant scans my reservation barcode and tells me to enjoy my trip with a genuine smile. She is drinking from a coffee tumbler that says *Life with Christ is a wonderful adventure*, written in the same loopy cursive as the letter that brought me here. The boom barrier lifts.

From Jacksonville, it is a long, mind-numbing drive on a wide highway that slants imperceptibly north to Tallahassee. I listen to Blue Öyster Cult and drum the steering wheel to the beat, feeling painfully wired. There are hardly any other cars on the road at this hour, and the pine trees fur together thickly outside my window. I realize with a jolt of panic that I need to pee. There are signs every twenty miles or so for interstate rest areas, but no way am I trapping myself in a public bathroom in the middle of the night, out in the middle of nowhere, where gators and bears would find my body sooner than a park ranger. No fucking way.

I pull over onto the shoulder of the road and hurriedly unbutton my wool suiting pants. It is early spring, damp and mild, but the backs of my knees are sweating as I drop trou and squat in the grass. I've left the driver-side door open for cover, not that I need it. The night is solid black, the highway quiet save for the harsh pulse of the insects in the trees.

I don't hear the car or even see the headlights, and at first I think he's come out of the woods.

"Excuse me?"

I shoot to my feet, snatching up my pants and looking right and left and up and down, trying to find the man attached to the voice. I spot him over the hood of my car, standing at the passenger-side door, a faceless silhouette. He could be nineteen or ninety; I have no sense of his age or his stature, where he materialized from, and if the passenger-side door is locked. I think about just diving behind the wheel, but what would stop him from diving in right alongside me, weapon of choice against my cheek. *Drive, bitch. Do exactly as I tell you.*

"You startled me," I say stupidly into the dark. There is urine dribbling down my thigh.

"Do you need help?" he asks me in a sugared voice that I just know is fake. "With your car? I'm a mechanic."

"I'm fine. Thank you." I realize I am thanking the man who might kill me, and I am ablaze suddenly at this indignity. I think about what you're supposed to do if a shark attacks you, something I read up on a long time ago, worried I might need it. I almost lived in the coastal town that boasts the second-highest rate of deadly attacks against humans. If you're bitten, you're supposed to dig your nails into its eyes, its gills. You're supposed to fight back and prove you're not prey.

"Go away," I tell this fuzzy stranger. "I'm calling the police." I hold up my phone and show him that I've pressed send on the 911 call.

The man laughs. "That won't never go through out here."

I look at the screen and see that the call is indeed stuck.

"That's why I offered to help," he says in this singsong way that knots up my throat. But then he turns and begins to cross the highway, and I see that he was coming from the other direction and parked along the center strip, and that's why I didn't see or hear him approach. Maybe he really did think I was having car trouble. Maybe he really was a mechanic. Or maybe he was a bull shark and I just managed to fight him off.

I get behind the wheel and burn rubber getting back onto the road. I slap at the media deck of the rental car until the music finally shuts off. I need to concentrate. I drive the rest of the way in silence, and my hands don't stop shaking, not even when I arrive safely in Tallahassee. Janet emailed right before takeoff to tell me that she'd called down to let them know I was coming, and that the man who is threatening to kill me is still very much alive.

Day 1

In the morning, I carried one of those delicate porcelain cups out to the screened porch and listened to the frogs and shorebirds, singing Disney-like in the cold. The reason I knew what a shorebird sounded like still depresses me, but I'll get to that in time.

Though I was clearheaded for the first time in twenty-eight hours, the problem was the sheer volume of my thoughts. I was making a mental list of the things I needed to pick up at the Northwood Mall before we went to see Jill and Eileen at Tallahassee Memorial. Flowers, maybe a soft blanket for the hard hospital bed. Yellow for Eileen, blue for Jill. I'd noticed they wore a lot of those respective colors. I was thinking about what Bernadette had told me with her face turned away in shame, and I was thinking about Denise and all the people she encountered in her daily life. The woman who sold Denise the multivitamin that made her hair healthy and strong and the family with the dog Denise sometimes walked for a little extra cash and the saleswoman at Denise's favorite clothing store in Tallahassee who always set things aside she thought Denise would like. I was wondering who would tell all these people that Denise was dead and if it should be me.

"May I join you?"

Mrs. McCall stood at the threshold, wearing a cream-colored

sweater over a blue collared shirt, pearl bulbs in her ears. She carried a slender book in one hand and a large Styrofoam tumbler of coffee in the other, the handle of a spoon poking out. I would have given anything to trade her my dainty porcelain cup, which had one last cold sip remaining.

I stood formally. "Good morning, Mrs. McCall."

She flapped the book at me. *Sit.* "Did you sleep?"

"I did," I said, though my head was pounding with the distinct lack of it. "The room is very comfortable. Thank you for your hospitality."

"You're good at that." She lowered herself into the rocking chair. "Instilling confidence in people that what you are saying is true even when it's not. Some people call that lying."

I held my breath, wondering if I was about to get my wrist slapped in the very singular way Southern women have. With a wink and a lash.

"Those people ought to examine their diction." She stirred her coffee with the spoon, arched an eyebrow—didn't I agree?

I exhaled. "You asked if I had slept, not if I slept well."

Mrs. McCall raised her Styrofoam cup to that. For a moment, we listened to the song of a shorebird we could not see.

"I thought about you all last night," she said, gazing out at the sun-blanched scrubland. "About what advice I have to offer you." She handed me the book. *A Statistician's Guide to Black Swan Events.* "Do you know what that is?" she asked while I traced the simple font with my thumb.

I had only ever heard of the term *black swan* in connection with the ballet. I shook my head.

"A black swan event is a highly improbable event but also one that, upon closer examination, was predictable. The sinking of the *Titanic* is an example of one; so is World War One. These are outcomes that are referred to as outliers on an economist's model."

I studied the cover of the book sadly and remembered Mrs. Mc-Call's sigh from the night before, when she first saw us on her front stoop. I'd thought I detected a measure of inevitability. That something was happening out there in the world, a force hurtling with Newtonian aim toward the object of us.

"But not all black swan events are bad," Mrs. McCall added. "Some people use the models to play the stock market and get filthy rich." She blew the surface of her coffee with pursed peach lips, took a slow, careful sip. "The point is that nothing can be predicted, really, and so you want to be sure to expose yourself to luck too. Things can go catastrophically wrong, but they can also go so right as to be profoundly transformative."

I thanked her for the book and told her I couldn't wait to read it, though I couldn't think of anything I wanted less than more profound transformation.

———

Tallahassee Memorial Hospital didn't look like a place where sick people went. The exterior facade was edged in aquatic shades, and a new neurological wing led the way in treating traumatic brain injuries and dementia. It gutted me to think about Denise, blue-lipped in the basement of a building that already looked like the future.

"That's Mrs. Neilson," I said to Bernadette and the other girls as we approached a prim woman wringing the silk scarf around her neck. Her timid, hopeful smile made my heart twist in my chest. I knew Eileen had always felt like a bit of a misfit in The House, that her mother had likely advised her to put herself out there more.

"Eileen's favorite color," Mrs. Neilson said, a hand cupping her cheek. We had come bearing a yellow blanket and yellow tulips. She hugged us, smelling of cigarettes and all the perfume she had used to try and cover them up. Then she lowered her voice to a conspiratorial register. "I need to chat with all of you before you see Eileen." She gestured for us to follow her a little ways down the hall, so that Eileen wouldn't hear what we'd be asked to do.

"I told Eileen you were all coming today, and she's very excited to see you," Mrs. Neilson said. "She's a little embarrassed about her hair, so please don't stare or comment on it."

"Of course, Mrs. Neilson," I said.

"But that's not all. See—" Mrs. Neilson paused to center the knot in her scarf and collect her thoughts. She was a more angular, anxious version of her daughter. More than once I'd heard Eileen on the phone with her, insisting that she stop worrying already. She was making friends, going on dates. She was having fun living in The House. "Eileen doesn't have any memory of Saturday night. She thinks she's been in a car accident."

I found my composure as quickly as I could, and still I stuttered. "So, uh," I began, "should we not mention . . . or does that mean she thinks she's the only one who's been hurt?"

"She thinks Jill was driving, and so she knows Jill is recovering in the hospital as well."

"But are you ever going to tell her?" I asked in amazement. I imagined Eileen going her whole life without ever knowing what had happened in The House on Seminole Street. I felt faint, wondering what it would take to sustain this fiction.

Mrs. Neilson sawed at her neck with her scarf. The skin there was a scuffed shade of pink. I had to resist the urge to reach out and pull her hand away. I couldn't stand to witness any more suffering. "Eventually, I'm sure. Yes. We are trying not to upset her for the time being. Her jaw is wired shut, and she can't scream."

————

When I'm interviewed about this, which isn't often, the reporter always wants to know about Eileen's mouth, fastened into a grimace with metal wires, her broken teeth bared. I'm encouraged to talk about the puckered red incision horseshoeing her left ear, slathered in Vaseline, and how the windows were double-locked for her safety so that the small white room reeked of blood and saliva, like a dentist's office after wisdom teeth surgery.

But what I want to talk about is the way Eileen looked at us when we came into the room, with a desperate remorse that haunts me to this day. If she could speak, I knew she would be apologizing that we had to see her like this.

Eileen's older brother stood protectively at the head of the bed, eating a bran muffin without a napkin. I recognized the shopping bag folded in the small wastebasket at his feet. Someone had brought them muffins from Swanee's, the fancy French bakery on Main Street with the *Bonjour!* sign on the door. I kicked myself for not thinking of doing that.

"Look who's come to see you, Eileen," her brother said. Eileen whinnied a greeting.

Bernadette perched on the edge of the bed, delicately, so counter to the coarse physicality we showed each other at The House that I discovered a new loss to mourn. We were always piling into beds, feet in faces, accusing someone of smelling or having crusty toes. Never before did we have to worry about hurting anyone.

"We miss you at The House, Eileen," Bernadette said. She shot me a look. *You're president. Say something.* I was standing there, recalibrating, like I had blown a fuse.

"We brought you something to perk up the room!" I said at a tinny pitch that made my own ears ring. I tried to untie the yellow ribbon binding the yellow blanket—three places I had to go to find it—but my fingers would not cooperate with what my brain was telling them to do. Eileen's brother stepped forward to help, but it wasn't his job to help. It was mine. I hadn't even brought him anything to eat. I raised the bundle to my mouth and gnashed at the ribbon with my teeth until it tore. Eileen's hands fluttered at her sides nervously while I shook out the blanket and tucked it into the lower corners of the bed with aggressive precision.

"Better already," I declared, and Eileen gazed fondly at the blanket for my sake.

"Is there anything else we can bring y'all?" Bernadette asked. "Magazines? Or maybe a puzzle?"

"A puzzle." Mrs. Neilson gasped as though it were a new invention. "Now, that sounds fun."

There was some commotion out in the hallway, a woman's voice raised in alarm. My pulse blew out my ears, and my vision clotted. He had found me.

"It's okay," Mrs. Neilson was saying to the guard, who had occupied a wide stance at the door. "You can let her through."

In walked the woman who had shooed the press out of our way with her lit cigarette, the one in the newsboy cap, although that day she had her yellow-blond hair tucked under a beret, pinned at a traditional Parisian tilt. She would be a part of my life forever, but at that moment, I didn't even know her name.

"Sorry that took so long," she said to Mrs. Neilson, passing her a brown paper bag rolled tightly shut. "I got a little turned around trying to find my way back here." The woman noticed the blanket on the bed. "How pretty," she commented. "You girls should help yourself to some muffins. I got too many."

"I'm just going to pop out a moment." Mrs. Neilson left the room, the brown paper bag pinned under her arm like an evening clutch.

The woman went over to Eileen's bed, stooped down, and examined her face. "What do you think? More Vaseline?"

Eileen nodded eagerly. At the foot of the bed, the yellow blanket lifted and lowered as the woman swathed Eileen's lips with a Q-tip. Eileen was curling her toes.

"Are you members of Eileen's sorority?" The woman capped the jar of Vaseline and tossed the Q-tip in the trash, which was filled with used cotton balls and gauze dressings, the grayish white of bodily fluids exposed to air. Though I was certain my face was the same sickly shade, I dug deep to lift my chin and extend my hand.

"I'm Pamela Schumacher, chapter president." I tried to smile, but I was still wincing. No one tells you how painful it is to be afraid, like a bee sting to the entirety of your central nervous system.

"Martina Cannon," the woman said, giving my hand one taut tug. "Most people call me Tina." She was nearly as tall as Denise, and she smiled down at me with something that felt like reverence, but all these years later, I know it wasn't that. It was optimism dueling fear. When Tina saw me, she saw her last hope.

"Are you family of Eileen's?" I asked, wanting to know everything about this beautiful woman with the rotating selection of stylish hats. She looked to be in her early thirties. Maybe a cousin or a young aunt.

"I'm not." Tina noticed that the sun was hitting Eileen directly in the eyes, and she went over to the window and adjusted the blinds.

I frowned at her. "Are you a nurse?"

"Just helping the families out," Tina said with an evasive smile that infuriated me.

Eileen lifted her hands, miming the act of writing something down. Her brother handed her a pen and a pad, on which I read dispatches from her new one-word world. *Socks. No. Yes. Day?* We all waited while she scribbled her note, then handed it to her brother to read out loud. His eyes traveled the message, and his face tightened.

"Eileen wants to know if Denise and Roger got back together last night, Pamela."

I must have looked horrified. We all must have, because I realized we were frightening Eileen.

"Tell her, Pamela," Bernadette said, shooting me a panicked look.

I remembered what Mrs. McCall had said about diction. "He regrets breaking up with her for sure," I told Eileen.

Eileen couldn't smile, but she looked pleased.

I smelled Mrs. Neilson before I saw her. Another cigarette, another lung-wrenching layer of perfume. "How's it going in here?"

I coughed into the crook of my elbow. Eileen's shoulder blades tensed, released, and tensed again. I realized she was trying to cough herself but couldn't, not with her mouth armored shut. Her eyes watered, and soupy bile dribbled out of one cracked corner of her mouth, pooling in the depression of her collarbone. Mrs. Neilson looked around for something to wipe it up, considered the yellow blanket we'd brought, and ultimately removed the silk scarf from her neck.

"I think it's time for Eileen to rest," Mrs. Neilson said in this awful, broken voice. She was dabbing at poor Eileen's chin like she must have done when she was a baby. But I want you to know something about Eileen, which is that after she got out of the hospital and the hair on the left side of her head grew back, she realized she looked better with it short, tougher and cooler. She moved to Tampa for business school, and to get over her fear of strange men she began driving taxicabs at night. She met her husband while shuttling him home from the airport—he could only see her from the back and he called her "sir"—she turned around and they had a good laugh about it. Eileen could have chosen to view the world as an ugly and hostile place, but instead she was nimble in her life in a way that most everyday people can't manage. Next month, it will be twenty-four years she's been married to her soul mate.

"We'll see you soon, Eileen!" I said with that strange jangly cheer, and I went out in the hallway and bent over, putting my hands on my knees. For a moment, I couldn't tell if I was going to cry or throw up. Then I did both.

———

I was in such poor shape that I couldn't remember where I'd parked the car Mrs. McCall had lent us. Bernadette and the others were of no help. Upon arrival, I'd dropped them off at the entrance to the hospital, like men do when their wives wear heels.

We were going to catch a ride back to The House with my police escort when Tina appeared and insisted on being the one to take us, though she had to transfer a bunch of stuff into her trunk to make room—loose bottles of shampoo and soda, old newspapers, and half-eaten bags of pretzels. To my surprise she drove slowly, like someone much older or, more likely, someone who didn't know her way around town.

"Fuck you," Tina said to the third red light we hit on Miccosukee Road.

"If you don't mind," I protested weakly. The girls had given me the front seat, and I was slumped over with my forehead pressed up against the glass, breathing hotly through my mouth. Some electrifying wartime president I was.

"Why are there so many red lights on this road?" Tina demanded. "And why do they look like that?" In Florida, the traffic lights are mounted horizontally. I'd always thought it gave them a sentient quality, like squat little robots, winking and blinking at you. *They're sort of adorable,* Denise said once, and I'd laughed admiringly and told her that was such an artist's thing to say.

"Hurricanes," explained Bernadette, ever Miss Florida. "The winds."

The little robot opened his green eye, and we continued on our way.

"It was really nice of you girls to visit Eileen and play along with everything," Tina said. "I don't agree with the family's decision not to tell her, by the way. It's infantilizing."

This new, exotic word rolled off Tina's tongue and activated the part of me that sought out the attention of bawdy, glamorous women, women like Denise and Tina, who, in their own ways, reminded me of my mother.

"What is"—Bernadette paused a moment, playing back the pronunciation in her head—"in-fan-til-iz-ing?"

"It's when people treat perfectly capable adults like children," Tina said, "and they tend to do it to young women."

"They just don't want her to get hysterical," I said in the family's defense. I had to speak with my eyes closed, licking my dry lips between words. I flailed a hand aimlessly. "You saw what just happened."

Tina scoffed. "And so? What's wrong with being hysterical? It's a hysterical thing that happened."

"We have more dignity than that," I said, lifting my head with enormous effort. *Never let them see you sweat,* I was always saying, except I could see the filmy residue my glands had deposited on the window.

"I'll tell you something from experience," Tina said, flexing her fingers on the wheel. "They will call you hysterical no matter how much dignity you have. So you might as well do whatever the hell you want."

"Right," I told her at the four-way stop on Copeland, because she was clearly not from around here.

Tina approached the back entrance to The House at a respectful crawl, though the street was mostly deserted. Low, heavy clouds had overtaken the sun, and there was no one to crunch over the dead leaves and pine cones on any of the paths that cut between Seminole Street and the south gates of the university. Someone's father was hurriedly throwing her suitcase into the trunk of a station wagon parked outside the Delta house, rushing around to the driver's side and yelling at his daughter that they needed to get on the road. The back of my neck prickled. On that block alone were three sororities, a cheeseburger joint, a popular bar, and an even more popular church. It was always bustling with activity, and yet at the moment, it felt fled and war-torn, under siege. Everyone getting out while they had the chance.

Tina parked at the curb, parallel to the metal police barricade that fenced off the back lot of The House. The officer on duty crouched down low to observe us. He straightened, appeased, seeing it was only a car full of women.

"Do you girls feel safe here at night?" Tina asked us. There were police and crime scene technicians all over The House, but they would be gone by dinnertime, their fingernails scrubbed of blood and their minds numbed with cold beer. I envied them, that this was merely a part of their life and not their life. "Because if you don't, I might be able to help you."

"We're not staying," I said. "We just have to pick up some more things before we go back to Mrs. McCall's house. She's an alumna of the sorority."

"How will you get there, though?"

"The police will take us." I opened the car door. "Thank you for the ride."

Tina stamped her hand on my knee. "Pamela? Can you hang back a moment?" I had no fight left in me, so I gave my sisters a half wave. *Go ahead. I'll meet you inside.*

Tina and I sat in silence, watching Bernadette and the others link arms and approach the guard at the next barricade, who was asking for IDs. The girls rooted around inside their purses for their wallets.

"Is the school providing you with any kind of support?" Tina asked, regarding me with what felt like parental concern. "Professionals to talk to about this?"

"You mean like a shrink?"

Tina smiled at the way I said *shrink*. "I mean like a shrink, yes."

"No. I don't know. It's barely been two days."

"Okay, well. I have names of people, if you or anyone you know needs them."

"Is that what you wanted to talk to me about?"

"It's not, but I do want you to know that." She let the offer stand as she drew her mohair coat tighter against the creeping cold. It was an expensive-looking piece, the material burnished of lint and pills. Denise would have offered to take it from her so she could peep at the label and see who she was up against.

"You're the one who saw him, right? That's what the paper said."

I swallowed queasily. "I can't believe the *Democrat* printed that." At that point in time, I thought I was only local news.

"Pamela," Tina said starkly, "it's in the *New York Times*."

I was poleaxed. I imagined the paper—I imagined my picture—on every stoop in our neighborhood, just thirty minutes south of the city. "They can do that? They're allowed to just do that?"

"It's unethical but not illegal." Tina reached for the pack of menthols she kept on her dashboard at all times. One in the car and one in her purse, I'd soon learn.

"You burned that guy," I said, remembering his yelp, the smell of singed body hair.

"I branded him," Tina corrected me, jiggling loose a cigarette and offering the pack to me. I shook my head and she shrugged. *Suit yourself.* "Make anyone who wants to interview you roll up his sleeve first. Do not give that guy a quote, whatever you do. You should have heard the way he was talking about you and your friends before you came outside." There was the catch of her lighter, and she went cross-eyed as she tried to match the flame to the tip of her cigarette.

"What was he saying?"

"That you shouldn't have made yourselves so known."

"Known," I repeated, confused. "What does that mean?"

"That if you'd been tucked in bed at ten p.m., none of this would have happened to you."

That touched a live wire in me. "Every last one of us was tucked into bed," I snarled.

"Can you tell me what he looked like?" Tina faced me with worried, bloodshot eyes. "I promise to explain myself. I just need to hear what he looked like from you."

I'd been asked to go over it so many times already that I was starting to feel like certain aspects of my story were more hindrance than help, that I ought to simplify it, either leave out the half second when I'd thought it was Roger or make a full-throated accusation. No one tells you that the truest stories are the messy, unwieldy ones, that you will be tempted to trim in the places that make people scratch their heads and pad the parts where they lean in closer. It takes fortitude to remain a true and constant witness, and I did.

"I mistook him for this guy, Roger," I told Tina. "He dated Denise. Used to. Not just her either. He had a thing with a few of the girls, I'm learning." I shook my head; I didn't have the energy to get into all of it. "But I realized pretty quickly it wasn't Roger. The man I saw was a lot smaller than Roger."

Tina drew quickly on her cigarette with bulging, *I'm-choking* eyes. "What else? Do you remember anything else?"

"His nose." I brought my fingertips to my own, demonstrating. "It was like a beak. Really sharp and straight. And he had thin lips."

Tina seemed to need a moment with this. She closed her eyes. The corners of her mouth lifted into a not-quite-smile. "I knew it," she whispered to herself, almost happy.

Tina opened her eyes and leaned across me, cigarette balanced between her teeth. I held my cough in my chest until my eyes watered. I liked being in that car with her, and I didn't want to give her any indication that I couldn't handle who she was and what she was telling me.

"This is why I came," Tina said. "I got on a plane immediately when I heard what happened here. Because I *knew* it."

She unfolded a piece of paper, smoothing out the creases with the heel of her hand. I was reminded of the flyers the fraternities would post for their charity parties until she offered it to me. No. Not a flyer for a party.

I read his rather prosaic-sounding name for the first time in that moment, but some years ago I vowed to stop using it. This is no symbolic abstinence on my part—*his name has been said enough and ours forgotten, yada yada*. I mean, sure, fine, that can be a part of it, but who I want you to remember, every time I say *The Defendant*, is not him but the twenty-two-year-old court reporter dressed for success in a pussy-bow blouse. She was the one who recorded him in the official transcripts not by his government name, like the licensed attorneys on the case, but by the two most honest letter combinations her sensitive ear and flying fingers could produce: The Defendant.

What people forget, or rather what the media decided muddied the narrative, is that although The Defendant would go on to represent himself at his murder trial, he was never a lawyer. Any Joe off the street can fly pro se, litigate their own case, without graduating from law school or passing the bar. But it made for a more salable story if he was portrayed as someone who did not have to kill to get his kicks, who had prospects in his romantic life and his career. To this day, I revere that scrubbed-faced court reporter, younger than me by only a year, because she is one of the sacred few who did her job without so much as a sliver of an agenda. The truth of what happened lies in those transcripts, where he is The Defendant and he is full of bullshit.

On the Wanted poster I held in my hands that dingy afternoon in Tina's rental car, The Defendant peered back at me with black vacant eyes. They are scary eyes, don't get me wrong, but what frightens me, what infuriates me, is that there *isn't* anything exceptionally clever going on behind them. A series of national ineptitudes and a parsimonious attitude toward crimes against women created a kind of secret tunnel through which a college dropout with severe emotional disturbances moved with impunity for the better part of the seventies. Law enforcement would rather we remember a dull man as brilliant than take a good hard look at the role they played in this absolute sideshow, and I am sick to death of watching them in their pressed shirts and cowboy boots, in their comfortable leather interview chairs, in hugely successful and critically acclaimed crime documentaries, talking about the intelligence and charm and wiliness of an ordinary misogynist. This story is not that. *The* story is not that.

"That's the man you saw," Tina said. "Four years ago, he killed my friend Ruth."

RUTH

Issaquah, Washington

Winter 1974

don't like the idea of you going to a stranger's house," my mother said when I pointed out the advertisement in the post office. The Complex Grief Group met every Thursday evening, six to eight, out of a counselor's home in the Squak Mountain neighborhood of Issaquah. *No Men* was underlined twice in red ink.

"It's all women, though," I said somewhat longingly.

"That girl was living in a house with all women too," my mother reminded me, hitching the strap of her purse higher on her shoulder and starting for the door. "Let's go, Ruth. I need to get to the dry cleaner before it closes."

I started to follow her out, then doubled back and tore off the tab with the counselor's phone number, just in case.

"What if you drove me," I suggested on the way home from the dry cleaner. We'd made it before closing, and the tailor was in that day. Things were going her way, which (according to my mother) was rare, which, rarer still, made her pliable. "We could check it out together. Make sure it is what the flyer says it is."

"What is complex grief, exactly?" she wanted to know, sounding dubious that such a thing could exist.

I shrugged. "I guess they tell you once you get there.".

"But what if it turns out you don't have it? Then you went all the way over there for nothing."

I couldn't tell you what complex grief was, only that I was sure I was suffering from it.

Squak Mountain was mere minutes from my parents' house in Issaquah, where I'd been living since my father passed away the previous summer. Issaquah itself is located about twenty miles from downtown Seattle, tucked into the base of three mountains that make up the Cascade foothills. Evergreens umbrella the neighborhood, insulating each home and forming a natural sound barrier. Even on the populated streets with smaller lots, there is a hushed sense of isolation that I guess is part of the appeal.

"You never know what you're going to get over here," my mother commented as she navigated a tight, steep right. Squak is supposedly one of the hardest neighborhoods to price because there are so many kinds of homes, everything from ticky-tacky ranches to Queen Anne mansions, properties with steely gray views of Lake Sammamish and ones that don't even have yards. The counselor's home was somewhere in the middle: a traditional Northwest Regional offering a forest panorama. There were several cars parked in the driveway and young women waving and hugging one another on the front porch. I'd had to miss the first two sessions because my mother needed more time to think about whether I could be trusted to attend a complex grief group without a chaperone, and now I felt like a girl who had transferred to a new school in the middle of the year. If I wanted to make any friends, I had my work cut out for me.

"Do you want to come inside and check it out before it starts?" I held my breath, praying she wouldn't take me up on the offer.

My mother surveyed the women on the front patio. "I don't see any ax murderers."

My mother didn't usually make jokes, and I knew what she was doing. Ingratiating herself to me in case I was tempted to betray her. I laughed reassuringly, and she seemed to relax some.

But as I got out of the car, my mother told me to be careful. "And smart," she added, which was what she really needed me to be. "Please, Ruth. Be smart."

———

The counselor's name was Frances. She was about my mother's age, with a manly wedge of brown curly hair. She wore no makeup and no jewelry but a pinkie ring, which I noticed only because as the other women eventually started to talk and cry, she supported her chin in her hand while she listened to them. My mother always shooed my hand away from my face when I did that. Maybe my skin would clear up if I could just stop touching it.

"Help yourself," Frances said, gesturing to the cookies and coffee she'd set out on a tray in the entryway. I had expected more rustic decor to match the stained-wood-and-river-stone exterior of the house, but inside I felt like I was in Morocco. (All those times I've been to Morocco, I should know.) There were real and fake plants tucked into corners, clay pot vases, brightly knit afghans draped over brightly patterned chairs, so much art on the walls I couldn't tell you what color they were.

I reached for a cookie. "Are these pignolis?"

Frances beamed. "You must be Italian."

"Polish through and through," I replied. "But I have a good recipe for them. Haven't made them in a while, though." I took a bite and closed my eyes in ecstasy.

"Good?"

"Oh my God." I laughed a little. "I have to start making these again. I forgot how much I like them." My mother didn't see the point of nuts in a cookie, and why were pine nuts so expensive, anyway?

Frances smiled and tapped the corner of her mouth, where I must have had a crumb. I wiped it away, blushing, but Frances only waved off my embarassment. "I'm wearing my breakfast most days. Come and meet the others."

———————

About ten women were clustered together in the corner of the living room, on their knees, heads bowed. *Praying,* I realized, and I felt my shoulders slump with disappointment. My Catholic high school had more or less expelled me.

Hearing us enter, the group broke apart to reveal the leader of their congregation—a woman in a beanbag chair, splaying open the lapels of her blouse to exhibit three thin gashes in her sternum. A black cat perched on the windowsill, licking clean his weapons.

"Nixon is an asshole," the injured woman told Frances. She had long lemony hair parted down the middle, dark eyebrows, and dark brown eyes, like there was a protest going on inside her about whether or not she was truly a blonde. With her shirt pulled open like that, it was easy to see that she was small-breasted enough to not need a bra.

"There's Neosporin under the sink in the kitchen," Frances said. "Everyone, this is Ruth."

The injured woman quipped, "Welcome to the party, Ruth," then got up and went into the kitchen. She was tall, with a sporty, windburned quality about her, as though she had just stepped off the slopes after a long run. Like a complete idiot, I thanked her as she walked by. I could hear her low laugh from across the hall.

The other women got settled around the coffee table on floral pillows, chatting animatedly, in surprisingly chipper moods for having recently lost people they loved. A chalkboard on an easel bore a numbered list, the first two items already crossed out.

1. One thing you did that always made me laugh . . .

2. One thing you did that always made me angry . . .

Frances gestured for me to find a seat and took her place at the head of the coffee table. Everyone quieted down without needing to be asked.

"I want to briefly reintroduce myself and talk about what it is we do here," Frances said. The other women glanced over at me and gave me polite, encouraging smiles. "My name is Frances Dunnmeyer, and I started the Complex Grief Group over ten years ago, after my husband died and I found myself feeling like no one else could possibly understand what I was going through. My late husband was not a bad person, but we were not in a good marriage, and the conflicting emotions that came up around his death were difficult to manage, even for me, and I've been a licensed therapist for twenty-five years. I started this group to help other women like me, women who are struggling to reconcile mourning the loss of someone you loved, who may have also been someone who hurt you, or treated you poorly, or held you back from realizing your full potential."

Frances spoke directly to me now. "This is only the third time the group is meeting, so you aren't far behind in our work. Each session, we concentrate on a prompt." She indicated the chalkboard behind her. "The goal of the group is to tackle every prompt on the list, one for each week of the year, fifty-two in total. I say that you aren't far behind in our work, because processing grief is some of the hardest work you'll ever do. Time does not heal all wounds. Grief is just like a sink full of dirty dishes or a pile of soiled laundry. Grief is a chore you have to do, and it's a messy one, at that."

I read the crossed-out prompts with renewed interest. I had been upset to miss the first two weeks, but I had to admit I was relieved that I didn't need to discuss my answer to the second one with the group. My father, whom I loved more than anything in this world, had made me very angry right before he died.

Then Frances said, "Ruth, I'd like you to answer the first two prompts in a journal entry, and we can discuss them privately over the next few weeks."

Homework. Great.

The prompt for that evening read: *My support system includes . . .* Frances asked the woman to her left to start it off. She had big white teeth and a small, pointy nose, mere slits for nostrils. I found myself feeling concerned for her. How did she breathe through nostrils that narrow? She was already clutching a tissue in her hand as she started to talk about her sister, who had lost a baby in her sixth month of pregnancy and admitted to her recently that she was relieved because it meant she could continue with nursing school unencumbered.

At seventeen weeks, a baby is the size of a turnip. My sister-in-law told me this; personally, I couldn't care less about pregnancy. The woman with the whittled nostrils had lost a turnip and I had lost my dad, who took me to see the debut of women's speed skating at the Winter Olympics in Squaw Valley when I was nine. Helga Haase of Germany had won, and she was signing programs after the competition in the parking lot at the same time as the men's alpine ski racing event, and even though my brother whined and begged and called me a Nazi for wanting to meet her, my father waited with me in the parking lot to get her autograph. *This is important to your sister,* he had said in that way of his that was authoritative but also persuasive at your most empathetic level. *All right,* my brother had said, sighing, and then he'd waited without complaint.

I thought I was going to meet women who had lost wonderful, terrible people, not turnips. But then the woman with the claw marks returned to the room with two Band-Aids on her chest and declared, "Your sister is a real piece of work, Margaret." She plopped back down in the beanbag and continued with effusive familiarity, "You've got to stop minimizing your pain in service of her! She lost a fetus, and you lost a three-year-old with special needs who required your undivided attention at all hours. You should not have to deny the magnitude of your loss to make her feel seen."

I realized my misunderstanding with a sharp intake of breath. The woman with the big teeth and narrow nostrils—Margaret—wasn't there because her sister had miscarried a turnip. Margaret had lost a three-year-old and not died herself. I took her in again, this time with awe and extreme hope, remembering she had been laughing just before we started.

"Tina brings up a good point," Frances said, giving the injured woman a name and such a smile that it was instantly clear Tina was her favorite. "Which is that members of our support team don't need to understand every dark corner of our grief in order to provide us support."

Tina caught me looking at her and smirked, as if to say, *I was right*. I looked away quickly, the tips of my ears hot.

Frances talked more about doing the work of building a support system. We talked about work so much in that room. Healing was work, a job, something to dread and grouse about but necessary in order to put food on the table and a roof over our heads. Frances said that a good support system included people who were willing to listen to you and who would not judge you for anything you were feeling, even if your feelings were provocative. I couldn't be sure, because I was too afraid to get caught looking again, but I sensed Tina staring at me when Frances said that part.

"I had complicated feelings about my husband's passing," Tina piped in. "Unlike Frances's husband, mine was not a good man. But he was beloved by the community, and so there weren't a whole lot of people who wanted to hear me talk about what he was really like behind closed doors. I had to do the work of going out and finding the people who wouldn't try and convince me that I was to blame."

Tina had been in a bad marriage, and so had I. I was divorced. This seemed to matter somehow.

When it was my turn to talk about my support system, I led with my ex-husband. I didn't want the women to get the wrong idea about me. I was having a bad breakout, but I didn't always look like this. Someone had married me and had sex with me. "We had a lot of problems in our marriage," I said, leaving out the part that my ex-husband was having an affair. I didn't need them thinking, *Well, of course he did, can you imagine waking up to that face without makeup in the morning?* "But we still care about each other.

He's still a part of my life. He's helping me out with something that's important to me right now."

From Tina, a loud *huh*.

My pulse quickened in a way that was not unwelcome. Tina had this way of staring at you while you spoke, like she wasn't at all listening to what you were saying and instead was trying to figure out what you weren't saying. It had to have been why every woman who spoke to her came away with cheeks flaming, feeling unbelievably exposed.

But when I met her eye, Tina only nodded firmly, showing her approval. "I think it's all very modern."

———

The session came to a close, and everyone pitched in, bringing empty mugs and leftover cookies into the kitchen, where there was more art. I'd never seen art in a kitchen before, or a pink-and-purple rug. The offending black cat was curled up on a stack of *New Yorkers* on the kitchen table, and the women fawned over him, cooing. *Why'd you scratch Tina, Nixon?*

Frances touched me on the shoulder. "Don't go yet, Ruth. I have something for you."

The other women started to disperse, but Tina stuck around, scratching Nixon under his chin, telling him she forgave him for what he'd done to her.

"He got his name because he's a thief," Tina explained. "He steals socks and panties from the laundry bin." At this charge, Nixon yawned. Tina purred, "You're a panty crook, aren't you, Nixon?"

I felt tongue-tied and hideous in the abominable kitchen lighting. If I could see Tina so clearly as to count the freckles on her nose, then surely she could see the peach-hued scales of my foundation, the mounds of pus that throbbed like sore muscles. Something I did in those situations was raise my eyebrows and frown at the same time. I'd practiced many an expression in the mirror, turning my face from side to side, trying to land on one that hid the bumps on my forehead and the ditches in my chin. This combination was the most effective, but it made me look insane. Tina glanced back at me, saw me making that face, and nodded as though that were exactly the right way to look.

"It's weird because you think you're going to come here and you're going to get advice, and then if you just follow that advice, it will get better. Instead, what you learn is how to take responsibility for it."

I had no idea what she was talking about. "Take responsibility for what?"

"Your own feelings."

I was annoyed with her fresh California-girl face then, her slender fingers on Nixon's soft fur. "But what do I have to take responsibility for, exactly?"

"Talk to me in a year," Tina said in a cloying voice that was meant for the cat. "Right, Nixon?" She kissed him on the head. She turned her face and looked up at me, her cheek resting on Nixon's cheek. "You'll see what I mean then. This is my second cycle. I'm infatuated with the process. I'm studying to get my license. This counts as my work experience."

Frances reappeared holding a leather diary in her hand. "Oh, Nixon!" she cried when she saw Tina cheek to cheek with him. "You're lucky Tina has such a generous heart." She handed me the diary. "I wrote down the first two prompts for you so that you remember them. Try and respond to the first one between now and next week."

I opened it to the first page. *One thing you did that always made me laugh . . .*

" 'Misty watercolored memories,' " Tina sang to me, that Barbra Streisand song, and laughed. I realized she was dismissing me so she could speak to Frances privately. I felt I needed to assert myself, to offer something before I left. I pointed at the plate of cookies.

"Pignolis go stale fast. It's the oils in the nuts. If you store them with a slice of bread, they'll stay chewy longer."

Frances looked at me, even more impressed than I'd privately hoped she would be. "What a valuable tip, Ruth."

————————

Outside, my mother was waiting in the car with the interior light on, reading one of her romance paperbacks. She jumped when I opened the door, which was understandable. A college girl had disappeared from her bed in the middle of the night, her roommate right next door. Everyone was on a razor's edge.

"Was it fine?" my mother asked as we wove down the rain-slicked mountain at a walker's pace.

"I didn't say much. Mostly listened."

"That's good, Ruth."

She waited until we hit Rainier Boulevard, the stretch where there are no streetlights, giving her just enough time to say what she wanted to say without having to remain in the car long enough to endure my response.

"You don't need to talk about all the decisions you've made in there. It wouldn't be fair to your father. I don't even want to tell your brother you're going to this thing. He'd probably want to know why I'm not the one in there talking about my grief. He was *my* husband, after all."

We pulled into the driveway. My mother always did this. Trapped me in the car with her wishes, her martyrdom.

"I'm not there to talk about all that," I said.

My mother opened the door, and the interior light illuminated. She put one foot on the pavement but then looked back at me concernedly, and for a second I thought she might apologize for the part that was her fault, or at the very least thank me for my continued discretion. I was twenty-five, so that made it nine years.

"Ruth, honey, stop picking." She swatted my hand away from my face, a little harder than she needed to. "You're going to scar."

PAMELA

Tallahassee, 1978

Day 2

'd passed the campus police station countless times on my walk to and from the Longmire Building, but I'd never before been inside. It was a compact space, crowded with filing cabinets and storage boxes stacked as tall as the frosted glass partitions between a dozen or so desks. Here and there, a black push-button phone rang, but on the whole, it was much quieter than I'd expected it to be, given the circumstances.

"My name is Pamela Schumacher, and I'm here to see Sheriff Cruso," I said to the guard behind the crescent moon–shaped desk. "I have urgent information."

"The sheriff works out of the Sheriff's Department."

"But I called and they said he was here."

"He happens to be," the guard said snottily. "You got lucky."

But I hadn't gotten lucky. I'd called. It took everything in my power not to say as much to his lazy pink face. "Can you let him know I'm here?"

Somewhere behind one of those privacy panels came Sheriff Cruso's extended sigh. "I'm aware, Miss Schumacher."

"This interview beginning Tuesday, the seventeenth of January, 1978, at approximately eleven-oh-five a.m. Present at the interview are Detective Ron L. Pickell, Sheriff Anthony Cruso, and Pamela Ann Schumacher. Miss Schumacher, will you confirm your name for the record."

As briskly as I could, I identified myself. Then: "I need to show you something." I reached for my purse.

Pickell held up a hand, stopping me. "Can you first state your school year and address?"

"It's all standard procedure," Sheriff Cruso said when he saw the flash of impatience on my face. "You just happened to show up several hours before your scheduled procedural interview." He and Pickell shared a weary smile I'd seen men make around me a million times before. It was the smile that agreed *She's a handful, huh?*

I rattled off the answers to their standard procedural questions, one knee bouncing.

"Okay, then."

I opened my purse and handed Sheriff Cruso the Wanted poster. "That's him. That's the man I saw at the front door."

I sat on my hands while they reviewed it. I was wired to within an inch of my life. I'd been trying to track down Sheriff Cruso since yesterday afternoon, when Tina drove me home from the hospital. I'd caught one or two hours of sleep alongside Bernadette at Mrs. McCall's house, before showering and dressing and waiting for the sun to rise. Then I'd taken off for campus, checking at every red light that I'd remembered to fold the Wanted poster and slip it into my purse.

"Have you been speaking to Martina Cannon?" Sheriff Cruso asked in an exhausted way that stunned me. I'd just *handed* him his suspect—ignite the manhunt!

"I only met her at the hospital yesterday."

Sheriff Cruso shot Pickell the look of an angry boss. "We had security," Pickell told him, a note of defensiveness in his voice. "The family told him to let her through."

"The security was for her?" I asked, trying to keep up.

Sheriff Cruso drew one cowboy boot to one knee and reclined in his seat, slowly shaking his head in annoyance. "The security was to protect Eileen and her family from anyone who may want to hurt or harass them, a banner under which Martina Cannon falls."

"What has she done?"

"She's interfering with an active police investigation, for one thing." Sheriff Cruso put a finger on The Defendant's face and slid it back my way. "This is not our guy."

I wanted to put my finger in the same spot and slide it back toward him, but I doubted that would go over well. "That is the man I saw at the front door," I said as calmly as I could. "I am positive."

"Not so positive that you didn't name Roger Yul in your initial statement." Pickell smiled at me almost sadly. He wasn't trying to be antagonistic, just stating an unfortunate fact.

Sheriff Cruso picked up the thread. "How well do you know Roger, would you say?"

"Very well," I answered with far too much confidence. "He was Denise's boyfriend for three years."

"And yet they broke up a number of times."

"Yes, but he's a member of the same fraternity as my boyfriend. Even when Denise wasn't dating him, he was always around."

"Since you know him so well, I'm curious if you know how old he is."

What an odd question. "He's twenty-two," I said. "His birthday is in April, so he'll be twenty-three soon. He was held back a year in high school."

"We are not trying to make you feel bad here," Pickell said. "But your answer demonstrates some of our deepest concerns about Roger."

I blinked between the two of them, furious and confused. What weren't they saying? What didn't I know that, as chapter president, as Denise's best friend, I should have known?

"Roger Yul is twenty-eight years old," Sheriff Cruso said.

I laughed coarsely. "He is not."

"Yes, Pamela," Pickell said gently, "he is. He served in the Vietnam War from 1968 to 1970 before being discharged for 'mental abnormalities.' He spent the following year in an institution in Alabama before going off the grid completely. In 1973, he falsified high school records and applied to Florida State University."

I thought about what Bernadette had told me just two nights ago, in Mrs. McCall's chinoiserie-covered guest bedroom. What he had done to her. How she'd seen spots. She'd been sure she was about to die. I found that, like her, I'd opened my mouth and allowed half a vowel before remembering. She hadn't given me permission.

"Were you about to say something?" Pickell asked. He was watching me closely.

"I was just about to say, isn't it possible that Roger is . . . disturbed and also that this is the person who did it? Could they have been working together?"

"You're going to law school in the fall, aren't you, Pamela?" That was Sheriff Cruso. I must have mentioned my plans during our initial interview, though I couldn't remember doing so. Or maybe he knew because his position made him privy to such things. Confidential things. Maybe I should respect that. Just let him do his job. Focus on doing mine. I remembered the victims' assistance fund Brian had told me about. Apparently, you had to apply within seven days of the event in order to qualify. I needed to get on top of that. I wondered if there were applications right here in the station. I should ask.

"Columbia, right?" Pickell said. "Very impressive."

A bolt of shock struck my tailbone. That wasn't true. Why in God's name had I told him that?

"I'm going to Shorebird College of Law. Down in Fort Lauderdale." Brian and I were going together. He wanted to specialize in campaign finance law, just like his father, and I wanted to specialize in corporate, just like mine.

Pickell frowned. "Oh. I see."

"Regardless," Sheriff Cruso said, "you are someone who understands that we never say nothing is impossible. It's impossible—it's irresponsible—to make official determinations at this point in the investigation. We follow the trail that the evidence cuts. And right now the preponderance of evidence cuts to Roger."

I could find no objection to that.

"What happened to Martina Cannon's friend back in Seattle was a terrible thing, and I have no doubt that this is the man who did it." We both looked down at The Defendant's honed, carnivorous features. "It's a total mystery how he pulled it off, to be honest with you. I feel for Martina, and I feel for the families of the girls who went missing. But it has absolutely nothing to do with what happened here."

I nodded numbly.

"And one more thing," Sheriff Cruso said in a firm tone that wasn't unkind. He was looking at me with worried, pitying eyes. He was in his midthirties, but there was a baby-faced softness to his cheeks that telegraphed a sort of *Leave It to Beaver* wholesomeness. I could picture him drinking a glass of milk at the breakfast table, his wife removing the mustache left behind with her thumb and a smile. "I have to watch what I say here, because Martina Cannon has deep pockets and friends in high places, but I'll leave you with this." He leaned forward, elbows on his knees, and clasped his hands together, pointing conjoined index fingers at my chest. "I'd advise you not to spend time alone with the woman, Pamela. I'd advise you not to spend any time with her at all, for your own safety."

RUTH

Issaquah, Washington

Winter 1974

After the second girl went missing, the Seattle police chief warned women live on Channel 5 not to venture out after dark. It was March in the Northwest, the sky blue-black by four in the afternoon. That the call to stay at home for three-quarters of the day coincided with the height of the women's lib movement in downtown Seattle did not seem to me like any coincidence.

I trailed my mother through the stationery store, checking my watch only when she wasn't looking. The grief group was meeting in thirty minutes, but if she felt hassled, she would spite me by dawdling. She'd already changed her mind twice on the calligrapher as we worked out the invitation wording for my father's garden-naming ceremony at Issaquah Catholic, where he'd been the high school history teacher for eighteen years before he died last summer.

For the one-year anniversary of his death, Issaquah Catholic had planted hydrangea bushes in the front yard of the old clergy house, which for a time had served as a rehabilitation station for fugitive slaves who had escaped the South. It was an important piece of the school's history, and my father had made up his lesson plan in such a way that the unit about the Underground Railroad fell in the springtime, when it was warm enough to conduct his class in the unkempt yard outside the sagging white cottage. The new history teacher planned on continuing this tradition, and the school had sprung to clean up the grounds and install a plaque dedicating the space to my father. This sounded more like landscaping than a garden, but I was trying to hurry my mother along and kept that observation to myself. Besides, I hated to remember the clergy house and all the abasement that occurred under its rotten roof.

"Have you spoken to CJ about it yet?" my mother asked when we were finally in the car on the way to Frances's house.

CJ was my ex-husband. He'd been in my older brother's class at Issaquah Catholic. It was of the utmost importance to my mother that CJ attend the ceremony so that all the nuns would think we were still happily married.

"I haven't," I admitted, squinting like a bad dog caught tearing up a couch cushion. "But I will."

My mother pulled into a Chevron station abruptly, failing to signal, and someone smacked a horn, a short burst of indignation. My mother put her hand up in the rearview mirror and waved apologetically. "Can you please take care of it this week, Ruth? I've been asking for months. It's not like you are so busy."

My mother had a way of making me feel like I was both too old to behave the way I did and also too young to be trusted out of her sight. "I promise."

"And please apologize to Martha on our behalf and tell her we are so sorry about this."

Martha. My ex-husband's *new* wife. I nodded dutifully, my eye on the time. The grief group was meeting in seven minutes, and we had half a tank of gas. There really was no reason we had to stop at that moment. In a small, penitent voice, I asked, "Is there any way you could fill up after you drop me off?"

My mother turned off the engine and heaved her door open. "I completely forgot that I told your brother I'd take the kids to the winter sale at Frederick's tonight. Your nephew desperately needs a new coat."

She was blushing violently when she got out of the car. Funny, for all the lies my mother expected me to tell, she could hardly stand to tell one herself.

I looked down at the container of meatballs in my lap. I'd wanted to cook the girls something sophisticated, something that wouldn't be served by a cafeteria lady in a hairnet. *Good Housekeeping* had a recipe for salmon mousse canapés in last year's holiday entertaining issue, but my mother had wrinkled her nose and said *yuck* when I told her what went in them. *I'm not spending nine dollars on a nice piece of salmon just so you can turn it into mush.* There was a pound of chuck in the freezer left over from Christmas; I was welcome to that. I'd sealed the meatballs in one container and some chopped parsley in another. I could at least impress the women by sprinkling fresh herbs over the dish. My father had taught me to finish a dish with something green. He'd happily moonlighted as the home ec instructor every time Mrs. Paulson had another baby. Cooking was one of my favorite hobbies, but it had died along with the only other person in my family who appreciated good food.

I sighed, full of pity for myself. Maybe I could freeze them for next week. The parsley wouldn't keep, so I'd have to buy some more, but parsley was cheap. And I *was* sporting an especially vile blemish on my chin. I'd just started on a new medication, Acnotabs, that I'd seen advertised in that same issue of *Good Housekeeping*. "Now stop acne where it starts . . . inside your body." I was supposed to start seeing an improvement in two to three weeks. Maybe by next week I could attend the grief group and not have to worry about finding a seat in the shadows. And certainly by the time my father's ceremony rolled around, I'd be a brand-spanking-new version of myself. Everyone would see that I'd come a long way over the last few years, and maybe they'd stop looking at me like that. Like I was fragile but also frightening.

I started at the knock on the car window. Someone was speaking my name. "Ruth, right? Ruth?"

There was fog on the glass, and I wiped it away to see Tina, waving and smiling and talking, though I couldn't hear most of what she was saying through the pane. I rolled down the window.

"I ran out of windshield wiper fluid!" She smacked her forehead with the heel of her hand. "I'm always running out of windshield wiper fluid here! I'm from Texas," she said, as though that might explain it, "trying to get used to all this *rain*."

At this I brightened. "Actually," I informed her, "it rains more in New Hampshire and Florida than it does in Washington State."

Tina put her hand on her hip with an *I'll-be-damned* laugh. "Is that true?"

I nodded earnestly. "We have a reputation for rain, but actually what we don't have is good water pressure. Think of it like a shower. The rain mists out, so it feels like it's raining all the time. With the exception of June through August, of course, when it's the most beautiful place you'll ever visit."

"Fascinating," Tina agreed, and we smiled at one another.

My mother exited the gas station. She had her head down, counting out her change, and when she looked up to see me smiling at a woman she didn't know, she picked up her pace. "Ruth?" she ventured shakily, once she was within earshot.

Tina turned around. "Oh, hi. I'm Martina Cannon. Tina, if you want. I'm in the grief group with Ruth."

My mother raised her chin imperiously and accepted Tina's outstretched hand as if it were Tina's great honor to meet her. "I'm Shirley Wachowsky. Ruth's mother."

"I'm so sorry for your loss," Tina said, and my mother braved her condolences with a fatigued exhale.

"Thank you. I keep telling my daughter that I'm the one who needs this group, but with two grandchildren, who has the time?" Her laugh was absurdly modest. There was nothing at all taxing about having two grandchildren.

"Oh!" Tina said. "I didn't realize you had a difficult relationship with your husband."

Well, no shit. I clapped my hand over my mouth, trapping my surprised laugh in my throat. No one had ever leveled my mother so breezily before.

My mother gathered herself to her full height, not very tall. "I'm not sure what that means, exactly, but we need to get going." She stepped around Tina and hoisted her purse higher up on her shoulder, holding it tight to her person as though Tina were a hoodlum who may try and swipe it.

Tina gave me a little wave over her shoulder. "See you in a few," she said, and then she *winked* at me.

My mother shot me a scathing, wordless warning through the windshield, but I did it anyway. "Actually," I called after Tina, "would you mind giving me a ride?"

Tina drove a beige Cadillac that stunk of cigarettes. She moved aside a stack of textbooks in the front seat, and I sat clutching the bowl of meatballs in my lap as she took the turns on Squak Mountain too fast in the rain, marveling at whatever forces were at play in the world that she and I could be headed to the same place, only with her in the driver's seat. Tina had clearly suffered a great tragedy in her life, but here she was with her car, her books, her freedom. Sometimes it all seemed so simple—I had moved home after my divorce to get back on my feet and to help my mother get back on hers after my father died. But it had been eight months now, and I knew I should go back to school, get a good job, and move out. I was a grown woman, and so was my mother. She would get on fine without me and I without her. But if it was that simple, why couldn't I bring myself to do it?

"Your mother is exactly what I pictured," Tina said.

There was a sensation I preferred not to identify, low in my stomach. Tina had been thinking about me. "You pictured her?"

"You make me sound like a creep." I caught one side of Tina's grin. No matter how the light struck her, she didn't have to worry about how she looked. People with good skin have no idea the agony the rest of us live with. I was grateful for the long shadows of the evergreens as we wound our way to the house, but it was no way to live, seeking out the darkest corner in a room, counting down the minutes until the daylight traded shifts with the friendless night. "It's just, you talked all about your ex with that prompt, and you never mentioned your own family. I knew right then and there your mother must be a witch like mine. We haven't spoken in two years."

I couldn't conceive of not speaking to my mother for two years. It would destroy her. "Oh," I said, backtracking a little. "It's not like that."

"Not like what?"

"We argue sometimes, but we love each other."

Tina's silence seemed dubious.

"It's not like she's abusive to me or anything."

"Ha!" Tina barked. "That is exactly what I said at one point too. You and I are so much alike."

I wasn't sure, but I didn't want to argue. We hardly knew each other. "What about when your husband passed away? Didn't you speak then?"

"That was why we stopped speaking." Tina rolled through the stop sign at the turn for Frances's street. "It's a long story. I'm sure I'll tell it to you sometime. I tell everyone." She laughed at herself. "I'm not ashamed of it anymore, thanks to Frances."

"What about your dad?"

"Oh, he talks to me," Tina said, "but he has to hide it from my mother, or he'll be sorry. So it's sporadic. He's not really someone I can call at three in the morning when I feel like I'm so sad I might—"

Tina slammed on the brakes as a fox dashed across the road. I chose to save the meatballs, and my purse tipped over, its contents spilling all over the textbooks at my feet.

"Are you okay?" Tina gasped, setting her hand on my wrist. I adjusted the bowl of meatballs in such a way that I shook her off without having to actually shake her off.

"Fine."

"Sorry," Tina said, whether for slamming on the brakes or for touching me, I couldn't be sure.

We parked at the curb to Frances's house and Tina shut off the engine, staring as the others hurried from their cars to the front door, jackets drawn over their heads against that infinite *mist*. "Thank God for Frances and Irene. They're really all I have."

"Irene?" I repeated, confused. "Who is Irene?"

Instead of answering, Tina turned to survey me as she unfastened her seat belt. Whatever test was administered, I failed, because Tina's tone suddenly turned vague. "Just another friend of mine."

———

That night, the chalkboard read *I wish someone would say . . .*

Tina added an amendment before anyone could answer. "Remember too that you can also say what you wish people would *stop* saying."

Frances smiled in a way that suggested she and Tina had argued about how to phrase the prompt. "The prompts are meant to get you thinking about your loved one and your grief in a dynamic way," Frances said, "but they aren't ever meant to be prescriptive." She turned to a woman in an old UCLA sweatshirt who was on her third meatball. They'd been a huge hit. "Sharon, would you like to start us off tonight?"

Around the circle we went. Sharon wished people would stop reminding her that she was still young enough to have another baby. "Maybe I don't feel like having another baby. I already did it twice. It's not exactly a day at the spa."

I realized how eager I was to get to Tina, the one whose idea it was to adjust the night's prompt. She was hugging her shins to her chest, chin on her knees, observing these angry women with obvious pleasure. At her turn, she didn't adjust her position. Her chin kept scraping the tops of her jeans as she stared dreamily at the art on the wall and spoke in a serene voice. "I'm with Sharon a little. I wish people would stop telling me it's time to move on. It's the way they say it that I wish would stop, really. Almost like . . . congratulatory. It reminds me of the time I lost a lot of weight, and even the doctor was like, *Good job, Tina, but enough is enough now. You don't want to take it too far*. But he was smiling. He approved. The first year after

Ed died, I didn't date. I didn't put on lipstick. I didn't show any interest in anyone. People were so damn proud of me. *Look at Tina, who is so devastated by Ed's death that she's gotten ugly."* Tina paused so some of the women could laugh at the hilarious suggestion that she could ever be considered ugly. Tina frequently made references to how beautiful she was, but always in a way that suggested it was a defect, the way some women did when they'd gained weight. They were aware there was a problem, and they wanted you to know they were working to overcome it.

"Now we're coming up on the second anniversary, and people are starting to say this to me," Tina continued. *"It's time to move on.* It's the same way the doctor spoke to me. Like I've done a really pure job at grieving. And I wish they would stop, because it hasn't felt like a job or like work at all, really. I have no interest in replacing Ed. I never want to be married again."

"You don't want children, then?" someone asked, and maybe it was just me, but I detected a note of envy, or at least longing.

"The more I understand, psychoanalytically, about my own life, the clearer I am about what its true purpose is. I can't say for sure, because I'm not a mother myself, but all of you mean as much to me as I think a child would. Helping other women view their lives in a liberated way, so that they can make choices that make them happy instead of worrying about making all the people around them happy, *that* fulfills me."

There was a long, poignant silence, and I wondered if everyone else was sitting there as ablaze with awe and yearning as I was. I couldn't imagine a greater satisfaction than knowing you were doing exactly what you were put on this earth to do. I didn't know what that thing was for me, only that I was fairly certain it had nothing to do with the life I would have had if I'd stayed married to CJ.

———

That night, when my mother picked me up, I was cool to her. The invitation for my father's garden-naming ceremony was sitting in the passenger seat, as though my parents had been driving around together, discussing my problems and how to fix them. My mother would have been telling him that they'd tried it his way—the nice way—and look where it had gotten me.

"Your friend was quite nosy," she said to me, breaking what was starting to feel like a standoff. Usually, I was the one to do it—I couldn't stand her being upset with me—and it felt almost too easy to turn the tables on her. I couldn't believe I hadn't tried it before. "Martina, right?"

"She goes by Tina."

"What happened to her? Why does she go?"

For a moment, I was tempted not to tell her. I didn't think I could stomach her reaction. "Her husband died."

My mother did that thing I'd known she would do, a sort of tsk-sigh, scolding the cruel web of the universe while resigning herself to being trapped in its sticky silk net. We hit the pothole that the city council had voted to fill in last winter, and I held on to the empty bowl. The women had gobbled up the meatballs within minutes and then demanded to know my secret. I'd swelled with pride when I told them. *Yogurt?* they'd repeated back, as if they never would have guessed.

"Well." My mother sniffed. "She's a looker. Knows it too. That part's not attractive, but men don't care about that." My mother, the exact opposite of a looker, cleared her throat of some persistent winter phlegm.

"She offered to drive me to the sessions from now on," I blurted out before I lost my nerve. "She lives in Clyde Hill, and we're on her way."

"Don't inconvenience the woman, Ruth. Doesn't she have children?"

"No. She's studying to become a therapist."

"Ah," my mother said, her voice full of understanding. When I looked over at her, she was nodding, placated.

"What?"

"Well, therapists need clients, don't they? That's how they earn their living."

The implication was a blazing backhand across the face. I thought about what Tina had said at the meeting—how helping other women was her true purpose in life, what fulfilled her. What a fool I was. Tina didn't want to be my friend; she wanted to shrink me. My mother was just sensitive enough not to say the rest of it out loud, the part we were both thinking as we pulled into the driveway I'd salted before we left.

I needed her too.

PAMELA

Jacksonville, Florida

Day 6

On a map, it is an all-but-straight line east from Tallahassee to Jacksonville. In real time, the drive felt just as flat. Sometimes the pines looked like Christmas trees, sometimes they were skinny and bare, only their tops decorous, strangely reminiscent of the palm trees in the next county over. The day of Denise's funeral, they flew by outside the window of Brian's Bronco, densely plotted in their own segregated communities.

Neil Young was on the eight-track. "Old Man," breaking my heart while I copied the law enforcement report, word for word, onto the proof-of-crime section of the victims' compensation claim form. It had taken fourteen phone calls and three *Just popping by!* trips to the Sheriff's Department to get my hands on a copy, and if it wasn't postmarked by midnight, I'd miss the deadline.

My pen lurched across the page. I looked up to find Brian crossing the wide, empty lanes to catch the exit coming up.

"I gotta take a leak," he said.

I sighed. "Can't you hold it?" I'd promised Mrs. Andora I'd be at her door at nine a.m. sharp to help clean and set up the house for the funeral reception.

"No, actually!" Brian said with a laugh as he parked in the ranger's lot of the Wildlife Management Area. He glanced around;

there was one other car parked a few spaces away from us. "You okay by yourself a minute?"

I had to go too, but I could hold it. "Hurry," I told him, and turned to the next page of the report. I knew I could get a lot more written when we weren't moving.

Section nine was the referral source information. I put down Brian's dad. Under relationship, I paused. He would be my father-in-law, someday not too soon. The plan was to get engaged right after graduation so that we could live in the newly married dorms at Shorebird Law come fall. For the time being, I wrote *Family friend.*

"One section left!" I told Brian when he climbed into the car.

"Cutting it close," he commented.

"They should really give you more time with these," I said.

"It's sort of like cashing a check, though," Brian said, merging back onto the highway. "If you wait too long, the person hasn't budgeted for the amount to come out. Without a deadline, they can't properly manage the fund."

Fair enough.

" 'Section ten,' " I read out loud. " 'Type of victim compensation requested.' " I scanned the options. Disability. Wage loss. Property damage. Sexual battery relocation assistance. Sexual battery recompense assistance.

I drew an X through the box for property damage and paused, tapping the bulbous end of my ballpoint pen against my lips. "Do you think I can also check off the relocation assistance? It says sexual battery, but we are out of pocket for everyone who flew home and stayed at hotels."

Brian scrunched up his face. "To be safe, I'd say no. You don't want to give them a reason to deny you."

My pen was tracing a phantom check mark, just above the page. "True," I wavered.

"I mean, no one was raped, right?"

"Right," I said quickly. "But I think it can also apply if there was, like, a sexual nature to the crime."

"But there wasn't really that either."

I saw Denise's underwear on the floor. "Right," I said again. I left the box unchecked.

A car sped past, the driver cheerfully slapping the horn. Brian raised his hand in the rearview mirror. "Steve," he told me. Steve was one of his fraternity brothers, presumably on the way to the funeral too. "That was his car in the ranger's lot."

I nodded, signing the form with a flourish, not really listening.

"He said Roger tried to come with him this morning."

That I heard. "Are you for real?"

Brian grimaced. *Afraid so.* Upon the revelation of Roger's troubled past in the papers, FSU had expelled him, and his fraternity brothers had packed up his things and left them on the curb. Though Roger had been questioned for close to forty-eight hours, Sheriff Cruso had no choice but to release him. There wasn't any evidence to keep him behind bars. I'd heard he'd gone to stay with a cousin in Pensacola for the time being.

"You don't think he'd just show up, do you?" I chewed my lip, thinking how awful it would be for the Andoras if there was a scene. Thinking how awful it would be for Bernadette.

"Honestly?" Brian ducked away from me as I went to smooth down a flyaway in his hair. I'd asked him to trim it for the funeral, to which he'd said, *How about we meet in the middle?* Which meant combing it off his face. "He just might. He's taken all this really hard. Losing Denise."

"Mmm," I murmured neutrally. I didn't feel like arguing with Brian, but I was about to see Mr. and Mrs. Andora for the first time since they'd lost their only daughter. The people who weren't just taking this hard but couldn't take it at all. Who had shattered.

"I know he lied," Brian said. "I know he's done a lot of bad things, and maybe he even did this, but I can't help feeling sorry for the guy."

"Brian," I said, appalled.

"I can't help it, Pamela!"

I didn't care that Brian felt bad for Roger. I felt bad for everyone, always, especially the people who had done something they should feel bad about but for some reason didn't.

What I did care about was Brian still thinking there was a possibility Roger had done this. That I was confused about whom I'd seen at the front door. "Roger has done a lot of bad things, and you don't even know the half of it," I said sharply, "but this, he didn't do."

"Agree to disagree," Brian said with a shrug, as though we were arguing over the ref's polarizing call at last weekend's Super Bowl that allowed the Cowboys to take home the win.

Denise's home in Jacksonville was pale yellow with upper and lower wraparound porches and a short fat palm tree in the front yard still strung with Christmas lights.

"I'll wait for you in the car," Brian said when he saw those lights. They'd knocked the wind out of me too. Mrs. Andora took great pride in appearances, and yet she hadn't had the energy to take down the Christmas lights before one hundred people showed up at her house that day.

Inside, Denise was everywhere. Her parents had her sit for professional photographs before the school year started, every August since kindergarten. Denise and I used to laugh about how she'd be hobbling into a Sears portrait studio with a cane when she was ninety years old, but instead she died decades before she could count her first gray hair.

Denise's aunt Trish put me to work for the next few hours, vacuuming the curtains, moving every chair in the house into the living room, salting a fruit salad, something I had no idea anyone did before I went to school in the South. She appeared here and there to tell me what I was doing wrong and what I needed to do next. Every time I heard her footsteps, I held my breath, thinking it was Mrs. Andora. But I spent all morning in the pretty yellow house, mopping and mixing, and the only evidence that Mrs. Andora was even under the same roof was the blast of the hair dryer upstairs. I remember

thinking if Mrs. Andora had the strength to blow-dry her hair, I had
no excuse not to get out of bed that morning.

The phone rang and Aunt Trish answered. "Andora residence."
She held out a canister and gestured for me to keep salting the can-
taloupe in her stead. "No, this is *not* she. May I ask who is calling?"

I went to take the canister but found that Aunt Trish's knuckles
had calcified around it. We stood there, awkwardly holding the tube
of table salt like some kind of baton, while Aunt Trish spoke to the
person on the other end of the phone in a pleasant tone she never
used with me. "If you call here again," Aunt Trish said through her
country-club smile, "I will have you arrested. Goodbye, now." She
swung the phone at the receiver, but at the very last minute caught
herself, placing it into the cradle with a trembling delicacy.

I was dying to ask who that was, what that was all about, but I
knew Aunt Trish well enough to know she would only tell me to
mind my own business.

"Was it him?"

Aunt Trish and I reached for one another at the sound of
Mrs. Andora's voice, at the state of her in the doorway of the kitchen.
She had always been thin, but on the morning of Denise's funeral,
she was skeletal. Her skin was gray and loose, and a dirty bra strap
hung limply off her shoulder.

Aunt Trish arranged her expression into one of pure capability.
"He won't be calling here again." She went over and tucked Mrs. Andora's undergarments back into her clothing.

"Did you read it?" Mrs. Andora was looking at me over her
sister-in-law's shoulder with provoked animal eyes.

I nodded, petrified. Sheriff Cruso's interview had been devastating.

"We think the killer planned the attack, picking Denise Andora as
his first victim, and keeping her under his surveillance," he'd told the
reporter at the *Tampa Bay Times*. "The design of the sorority house
on Seminole Street, where four of the five victims lived, allows an
observer to learn which room a girl lives in. Each second-story room

has a large window. Any person watching the girls enter the house at night could see the lights in the room come on a few seconds later."

When asked why he thought Denise had been targeted, Sheriff Cruso had reportedly run a hand down his face. "I hate to make the Andora family feel bad," he'd answered, "but Denise knew a lot of people. We think it was probably someone known to her, and the other girls were collateral damage."

Denise knew a lot of people. The polite language was what gave the appearance of impropriety. Denise was gorgeous and got asked out a lot, and she knew how to enjoy sex, which was a quality I admire about her to this day. It was the dancing around the truth that made it seem like she had something to be ashamed of, that gave others license to blame, and you better believe they used it.

"Remember," Aunt Trish said, patting Mrs. Andora's bare upper arm, "we are setting the record straight today."

"Can I help?" I asked.

Aunt Trish glanced at Mrs. Andora, who nodded. "There's a reporter from the *Tallahassee Democrat* doing a piece about Denise," began Aunt Trish. "We've invited him back to the house after the burial. He's looking forward to speaking to you about Denise. Who she really was, from her best friend and the president of the smartest sorority on campus."

I clasped my hands at my pelvis and said with regret, "I was told not to speak to the press."

"Who told you that?" Aunt Trish laughed brashly. Whomever had said such a thing was sorely mistaken.

"An alumna. Her name is—"

"You're the president. I thought you decided."

"Certain things I can."

"People are looking at us like it's our fault, Pamela," Mrs. Andora said in a pleading voice that didn't sound right coming from her. Mrs. Andora was someone who lived life with élan. She was a prankster who seemed to have an inside joke with everyone she knew. I've always thought there was something quietly seditious about a funny woman, but he took her humor when he took Denise. "The Shepherds asked us not to attend Robbie's funeral." Mrs. Andora stared at the floor as she said this, and I remembered that public humiliation was still a judicially sanctioned practice in some countries.

"You saw the person." Aunt Trish did not have to remind me. "You are the only one who can reliably say that he wasn't anyone Denise knew."

I bit down on the inside of my cheek, feeling torn in two.

"Put that in a nice bowl," Aunt Trish said of the fruit salad, as though the issue had been settled, then huffed away, in search of more of my work to rectify. The old Mrs. Andora would have rolled her eyes, whispered a clever remark, shared a laugh with me. This Mrs. Andora gazed around her house like she hated every square inch of it.

"What would Denise make of all this?" she asked with an ugly sneer. I followed her eyeline. The flowers, the food, the rented plastic chairs we'd set out in the den for extra seating.

"She'd still be upstairs doing her hair and wouldn't have seen any of it yet." I was reassured when Mrs. Andora nodded, agreeing. I'd said the right thing, the thing that showed I knew Denise the way she knew Denise.

"Do you know I told everyone no lilacs, because Denise is allergic to lilacs?" Mrs. Andora laughed, squeezing and releasing her long, thin neck with one hand, over and over, like it was a second-by-second decision to allow herself to keep breathing. "In case she walks through the door, I don't want her sneezing. That's how much I still don't believe it."

I cast around desperately for another right thing to say, but all I could come up with was what she was prepared to hear so many times that day that it had already been rendered meaningless. "I'm so sorry, Mrs. Andora." I stepped forward, timidly, wondering if I should offer her a hug. But Mrs. Andora put up her hand. *Stop. Don't come any closer.*

"You were there," Mrs. Andora said, amazed, as though just real-

izing this for herself, as though she hadn't heard my worthless plat-
itude at all. "She got to be with someone she loved at the end of her
life. Someone who didn't care about the smell or the sound of it."
She looked right at me, and I saw that the light was indeed on in her
eyes. That she had heard me say I was sorry, and she was doing her
best to forgive me. "It should have been me. But at least it was you.
So it's okay, Pamela."

———

Most people don't know that Denise and Robbie are buried in the
same graveyard, that their funerals took place just one cool, muggy
day apart in Jacksonville, Florida. The new round-shaped Holiday
Inn in San Marco offered the press a promotional deal—two nights
for the price of one. I tripped over a camera cord as I left Denise
behind, her steel casket kept dry under a thorny layer of single roses.

"At least the rain held off until the last few minutes," Brian said as
we made our way back to the car.

"At least," I agreed flatly. Some parts of her funeral were easier
than I'd imagined, but the ones that were worse had left me pulver-
ized. The members of The House had gathered around Denise and
sang to her as she was lowered into the ground, a song Denise had
learned as a pledge, the song we were all meant to sing at graduation
and at one another's weddings. I couldn't stop thinking about the day
our pledge class met in one of the rehearsal rooms at the new Ruby
Diamond Concert Hall to practice. The song opened and ended
with a solo, and Denise had volunteered herself for the job, boast-
ing about her beautiful singing voice. We all readied for a moving
performance and then we practically fell to our knees with laughter
when Denise opened her mouth and brayed the opening verse. *Who
told you that you could sing?* We were gasping, tears streaming down
our faces, while Denise stared at us, confused. *Everyone!* she'd cried,
at which we became inconsolable. *Well, they lied,* someone managed
to choke out, and Denise flipped her the bird, but she was laughing
too. And I was realizing that any time I wanted to visit Denise in my

mind, I would be looking at her and thinking, *You're going to die soon,* and I wouldn't want to see her anymore. My memories of Denise made me feel like I was keeping a terrible secret from her.

I heard my name, and Brian grabbed my hand protectively, his eye on the reporters who had broken away from their camera crews at the gravesite, pretending to head back to their cars when, really, they were eavesdropping, encroaching, paring their vicious angles.

"Pamela," Tina wheezed. She'd had to run to catch up to me. Peripherally, I noticed she was carrying a thick stack of the funeral programs, which I did think was odd.

"I didn't realize you were here," I said stiffly. I was acutely aware of the way Brian was looking at Tina, then at me, then back at Tina, like he was owed an explanation about who she was and how I knew her. Anything I said would only invite some kind of patronizing reminder that it wasn't my job to investigate a double homicide; that I needed to sit back and relax and trust the police would find the person who'd put Denise into the ground seventy years too soon. Whenever he said some version of this to me, Brian always sounded a touch irritated. Why did I have to insist on making everything so much more difficult than it needed to be?

"You haven't returned any of my calls," she said, matching my stride so that I was stuck between her and Brian, whose neck had assumed an ostrich-like quality. His face bowed toward Tina with an expression I can only describe as territorial. How dare this beautiful woman in the hat (that day a black fedora, bordering on a gag at that point) speak to me like we'd known each other ten years and not ten seconds?

"I've had a lot on my plate," I said, eyes straight ahead. Later, there would be a picture in one of the newspapers of the crowd departing the funeral, and I would see that both Tina and Brian were turned toward me expectantly, like I was the deciding vote on a polarizing issue, which in some ways I was.

I was wary of Tina after my conversation with Sheriff Cruso. *I'd advise you not to spend time alone with the woman, Pamela. I'd advise you not to spend any time with her at all, for your own safety.*

"I'm leaving for Colorado on Friday," Tina announced, "and I want you to come with me."

It was such an absurd request that I laughed impatiently. "Excuse me?"

"Did she say Colorado?" Brian asked me, pointedly ignoring Tina, who pointedly ignored him right back.

We overtook a group of Denise's high school friends, and Tina offered them one of the funeral programs. "This man is very dangerous," she said to them as we passed. "Please keep your eye out for him."

I looked at the stack in her hands and realized it wasn't funeral programs she was hoarding. Tina had made a flyer using The Defendant's mug shot. Large bold font blared the question she'd been asking since 1974: *Have You Seen This Man?* Tina had come to the funeral not to honor Denise but to implement her own version of a neighborhood watch. How tacky.

"What the hell is in Colorado?" Brian asked, addressing Tina for the first time.

"The prison where he escaped," Tina said, exasperated. She didn't have time to explain it again, especially not to him.

"The prison where *who* escaped?" Brian pumped my hand, hard. *Hello. Answer me.* "What is she talking about?"

Tina leaned close to me and said, "I'm staying at the Days Inn in Tallahassee. Practically roughing it. Come talk to me when you're back."

"You are clearly disturbed, and I'm going to kindly ask you to leave us alone now," Brian said in the genteel twang that had surfaced here and there over the years when it served him, which is to say when he wanted something he wasn't getting. Respect, namely. With his easy, loping pace and hippie hair frizzing in the humidity, he was suddenly repugnant to me. As hypocritical as a Christian lawmaker in a strip club.

"Well," Tina said, "since you asked *kindly.*" She bumped my shoulder with her own. "Room two-oh-three." With that, she did leave us alone.

Brian threw an arm around my shoulders and glued me to his side possessively. "All the crazies are out today, huh?"

I felt squeezed all over, like my skin was too tight for my body and I needed the seams let out. We were coming up on Aunt Trish helping Mrs. Andora into the limousine, and I saw my out: I ducked under Brian's arm and reached Mrs. Andora just in time to cup the back of her head in my hand, the way cops do to suspects right before they put them into the metal cage of their cruiser, so that even if they fight the inevitable, they don't hurt themselves.

———

I was putting out the second bowl of potato salad when Aunt Trish came up behind me.

"He's ready for you, Pamela." I turned to see she'd pressed too hard when she'd applied a fresh coat of lipstick, pruning the tangerine tip with her front two teeth.

"Remember to talk about Denise's faith," Aunt Trish coached me as we made our way into Denise's childhood bedroom with the lilac walls and butterfly bedspread. A strange man was examining a piece Denise had hung in the space between the window and the chest of drawers.

"This one of Denise's?" he asked, turning to me. He had a pencil tucked behind one ear, dark green eyes and thick black eyelashes, prominent horse teeth. His clothes were bad, his pants too short and his shirt too long. I couldn't stop the terrible, snobbish thought from forming—he looked like he had dug his clothes out of a bin at the Salvation Army.

"That's a weaving," I said.

"Is that different from what Denise did?" It was the sort of soft question you ask a child, right down to the feigned wide eyes.

"Denise painted for some of her classes, but that wasn't her real talent."

The man slid the pencil out from behind his ear, releasing a lock of sandy brown hair. "Oh?" he said with what actually sounded like genuine interest this time. "What was that?"

"Curation. Denise had a keen eye."

Aunt Trish averted her eyes as the man reached into the waistband of his pants and retrieved a notebook, revealing a flash of stomach, the disappearing trail of dark body hair. "Keen eye," he repeated, balancing the notebook on his thigh so he could write it down.

"This is *Carl Wallace*," Aunt Trish said, emphasizing the name the way you would an important client at a business dinner. "He's the senior staff writer for the *Tallahassee Democrat*."

Carl looked up from his notebook, blinking the hair out of his eyes. "Thank you for speaking to me, Pamela. I'm just looking for some background from the president of what I'm told is the smartest sorority on campus"—he flashed those big teeth at Aunt Trish, who was no doubt his most dogged source—"and Denise's best friend."

I shrugged gamely, though an unease was pooling in the pit of my stomach. "Of course. Happy to help."

"I would love it if you could tell me a little bit about Denise."

I found the cue lazy and impossible to answer. "Anything?"

Carl brought a hand to the back of his neck and looked up at me with a chagrined half smile. His hands were sprawling, calloused things. *He's not as tall as Brian,* I thought, almost as a rebuttal to the other thought that was forming, which was that Brian sometimes reminded me of a middle school boy who had hit a sudden growth spurt, hunching and hairless in his gawky new body.

"Fair enough." Carl tapped his pencil on his notebook, thinking of a way to rephrase. "I've gathered Denise loved clothes. Maybe you could speak a little on that. I always like to start by giving the reader a good visual."

"She was a fastidious dresser," I said.

Carl seemed delighted. "*Fastidious*." He jotted that down. "Great word. Are you an English major?"

"Political science."

"Pamela is planning on attending law school," Aunt Trish said grandly.

"My parents certainly would have preferred that to J-school," Carl said self-effacingly, so that he was in the clear to ask the million-dollar question. "And what about boys and dating?"

"Denise didn't have time for dating," Aunt Trish interjected.

"A beautiful girl like Denise?" Carl looked at me long enough that I could pick out feline-like flashes of yellow in his eyes. "I don't believe it."

"Denise was asked out a lot," I said carefully, "but she was picky about who she went with."

Momentarily, both Aunt Trish and Carl were appeased. Carl moved on. "And what did Denise want to do with her life? I hear she had plans to work at the new Dalí Museum."

"She did," Aunt Trish said. "We have a photograph of her and Dalí. He was her *biggest* fan."

"I'd love to see that," Carl said. "And any other photographs of Denise that the family might want included in the piece."

Aunt Trish shot me a look before she left. *Do us proud.*

Alone, Carl put his hands on his knees, leveling with me. "Gestapo's gone," he whispered, and laughed a little.

My stomach pitched. The reporter working on a piece about Denise could see right through the duress I was under to portray her in a positive light. I had better think fast.

"How old are you?" I asked.

Carl leaned back in surprise. "Why?"

I took my shot. "You look young enough to have graduated from J-school this decade. Which means you're a student of new journalism."

Carl closed his notebook and wrapped his forearms around his rib cage, lips curling into a small smile, as though I'd said something devastatingly cute. "And what do you know about new journalism?"

"One of my sisters is studying to be a journalist, and she said it's not as objective as traditional journalism."

"That's subjective," he teased.

"You're asking me about Denise's romantic life," I said, hoping I sounded as imposing as my bigwig father, "instead of focusing on the quality evidence." *Quality evidence*, how I loved that term. It made me feel like I knew what I was talking about.

"Being?"

"That I saw him. And it wasn't someone she knew. That any of us knew."

"The attack has all the markings of something personal," Carl pointed out, "given that Denise's injuries were particularly brutal."

I thought about Denise's peaceful sleeping face. "You didn't see the other girls."

Carl gave me a strange look. "The fact-checker at the *Democrat* isn't even sure if I can use the word *rape* to describe what he did to her. Is it technically rape? You probably know how the law defines it better than I."

I felt my face go slack. I swayed, made woozy by that word. Not *rape*; that I could handle. *Technically*, I could not. "Sheriff Cruso doesn't like to upset me, apparently."

Carl told me then what was done to Denise with the Clairol hair mist bottle she'd purchased just the week before. In the beauty aisle at Walgreens, Denise had hand-selected the object that punctured the lining of her bladder and caused a fatal internal bleed, saying, *I heard Clairol holds up better in the humidity than White Rain.* I covered my face with my hands, thinking about what Denise looked like when she was in pain. The year before, she'd stepped on a nail in the basement on her way to pull out the Christmas decorations. It went through her shoe, and one of our sisters, premed, had propped Denise's leg on an overturned milk crate and told her to turn her face away. I remembered the way Denise had clasped my hand and looked up at me, still wearing the Santa Claus hat she'd discovered among the ornaments and fake pine garlands. Her lower lip was quivering, and I saw what she must have looked like as a little girl when she fell off her bike. I stifled a sob now, seeing that face, imagining how much more this would have hurt.

"He should fry," Carl said, real hatred in his voice, "for what he put her through."

I hiccupped once, loudly and excruciatingly, and swallowed the bile that came up with it. It was indigestible, all the methods humans had devised to inflict more suffering.

"Are you planning on putting that in your story?" I asked. "What he did to Denise?" I imagined Mrs. Andora reading what I'd just been told, her hand taloned to her throat as though stoppering some fatal wound.

"Not in the level of detail I just shared with you, but the public is frightened, and they are looking for answers. And I need to address the fact that Roger's name did not come out of nowhere. You said it first."

I freed the leather flap of my purse. "Can I show you something?" I fished around until I found the copy of the Wanted poster that Tina had shown me in her car. I watched Carl read it, running his tongue along those big teeth, perplexed at first, then intrigued.

Wanted by the FBI
Born November 24, 1945, in Burlington, Vermont, 5'11" to 6'.
Build, slender. Complexion, sallow, law student, occasionally
stutters when upset.
CAUTION.
  The Suspect is a college-educated physical fitness enthusiast
with a prior history of escape, is being sought as a prison escapee
after being convicted of kidnapping and while awaiting trial for
a brutal sex slaying of a woman at a ski resort in Colorado. He
should be considered armed, dangerous, and an escape risk.

The man in the picture was unshaven and in need of a haircut. His jaw was tilted down and to the side, his mouth not so much open as closing, as though he had just finished speaking when the camera clicked. His eyebrows were unruly and raised, bunching his forehead into three distinct lines.

"Where did you get this?" Carl wanted to know, and I told him about Tina, how I believed her but I still didn't trust her.

"I could hold on to this," Carl offered. "Do some research. Look into him, and her. See if there's anything there."

I hesitated. That sounded very close to teaming up, and I wasn't sure that was prudent.

"You said this guy saw you, right?"

I shook my head. "He looked in my direction, and that's when I saw his face. But he didn't see me."

"How can you be sure?"

"Because he ran out right after."

"Maybe he thought you had already called the police. Maybe he thought he didn't have time."

A shudder went down my spine as I thought about the idea of time. How you would need a certain amount of it to do what he would have wanted to do to me.

"Can I have that?" I motioned. The flyer. Carl hesitated before giving it back to me. But I wasn't taking it back; I only wanted to tear off a tab at the bottom. "Write your number down," I told him, and immediately flushed, hearing myself tell a man I had just met to give me his number. "I don't want you calling The House," I added professionally. "I'm not really supposed to talk to press, but I'd be interested to know what you find out."

Carl scribbled his number down, eyebrows raised amusedly. I pocketed the scrap.

"Denise beat out one thousand candidates for the job at the Dalí Museum," I said, and waited for him to realize I was giving him material for his story, to flip open his notebook and write all this down, the things about Denise that I never wanted anyone to forget. "She did it by telling Dalí she thought he should object to the chronological order of the gallery, which has been the way modern art has been displayed for the better part of the last century. She called it a postmodern time warp, which appealed to a physics nut like Dalí immensely. She did all of this in Spanish. She practiced in the mirror for weeks. When the public is allowed into the space later this year, it will be the first anti-chronological exhibition ever, and it's because of Denise. Denise may not have lived long"—I swallowed and tasted the salty fruit salad languishing in my gut—"but she still managed to leave her mark on the world."

The next day, when Carl ran my beautiful quote alongside a beautiful photograph of Denise, Mrs. Andora made a bouquet out of the funeral flowers and attached a handwritten note that said, *With my deepest gratitude*. Carl wrote about Denise like she was a human, and that was when I knew I could trust him.

PAMELA

Tallahassee, 2021

Day 15,826

I wake early in my hotel room and walk to campus, dragonflies skirting my feet, phosphorescent flashes in the pale spring sun. There is a campus tour happening and I tag along, learning things I probably should have already known about my alma mater. That the big red circus tent was built in 1947 and offered classes like trapeze flying and juggling in an attempt to integrate men and women when FSU became a coed institution. When we reach the dining hall, I nearly fall over when I hear the student tour guide say that the cafeteria employee known for doling out hugs to all her "babies" still works in customer service for the school and has been written about in *Forbes*.

I break off from the group at the Pop Stop, still located in the same bungalow with the overhanging eaves catty-corner to The House. The front patio is hedged with potted plants, and two college girls are discussing the hair color of their future children at a table beneath the ceiling fan. It's busy inside, cooler but steamy from the open kitchen. I order a mushroom-and-cheese omelet and an orange juice. While I wait, I wander over to the whiteboard-painted walls to read the things kids have written in black marker since the fifties, their names and dates, who rocks and who sucks, whom they love and will be with forever. I squint, trying to find curls of

Denise's handwriting in a high corner above the back booth where she used to drink black coffee and practice her Spanish with one of the cooks. Over the years students have scribbled over her Dalí quote—something about genius and death, if I remember correctly.

I hear my order number and carry my tray outside, where I can see the girls coming and going from The House half a block away. I thought about knocking on the door, letting them know I was here, and just . . . what? Warn them? It seems bordering on hysterical. It's me he's after. But if he can't find me, would he settle for them?

I eat half the omelet and drink all the juice and throw away the grease-sopped paper plate. My appointment is at eleven, and I know from plenty of experience that it's only a twelve-minute drive. I plug the address into Waze as I walk to my rental car, in case there is more traffic now, or maybe a shortcut, but amazingly, the automated voice suggests I do everything the same.

RUTH

Issaquah

Winter 1974

My brother brought over one of his kids. A boy. Seven or eight. He had small wet eyes, like he was sick or crying. I think they were blue. His skin was pulled tight against the fragile bones in his face, so that you could see the blood thrumming the green veins in his temples. Like all children, he was too young to take care of himself but capable of extreme emotional destruction. I had offered to watch him while my brother and sister-in-law took the baby to some special doctor's appointment and my mother picked out the shade of hydrangeas for my father's garden ahead of the last frost, but once we were alone in the house, I regretted it. Allen terrified me.

"How come you're old but you live with Grandmom?" Allen asked after I'd gotten him situated at the kitchen table with paper and crayons.

I checked my watch. Hardly thirty minutes had passed since my brother dropped him off. The special doctor was located somewhere in Utah. Something about a cleft, surgery, a mouth? The baby looked fine to me. I wished they had left her with me instead of Allen. I actually liked babies, even the fussy ones, which apparently my niece was. I thought it was adorable when she puffed out her lower lip and jammed her fat fists in her eyes. *Allen was the best baby,*

my sister-in-law was always saying with a loose strand of hair stuck
to her lip.

"Grandmom needs my help right now." I opened the door to
the refrigerator. It was almost lunchtime. "Do you want a ham sandwich?"

"Sure," Allen said in the same breath as his rough laugh. Was he
saying *sure* to a ham sandwich? Or *sure* in the sarcastic sense, to the
first thing I'd said? *Grandmom needs my help right now.*

"My dad says you like detention," Allen said, gouging harder
at the paper with a pink crayon. He'd used up the red crayon completely. I'd seen him hesitate before picking up the pink, as if touching it may make him less of a man.

I put ham and mayonnaise on the counter. "That doesn't make
any sense, Allen."

"Yes, it does."

I got out the plate with the crack down the middle, deep enough
to trap the kind of bacteria that was known to cause a gnarly case
of diarrhea. "Do you know what detention is? It's when you have
to stay after school because you've done something wrong. Nobody
likes detention."

"He says you do things so that everyone will look at you more."

I got out a knife. Not detention. Attention. Don't kids hate mayonnaise? I slathered it on nice and thick for Allen, then grabbed an
onion and started chopping that up too.

"He says you hurt Grandpop's feelings so bad he died from it."

We had cheese, but I wasn't giving Allen any cheese. I hid the
onions between slices of ham and squished the sandwich flat. "You
want to know a funny story about your dad, Allen?"

Allen didn't answer. He was busy running the pink crayon down
to a nub. "Your father was the worst player on the school baseball
team, but Grandpop felt bad for him, so he begged the coach to let
him play in a game that they were sure to win anyway. He was about
to strike out, and he was so embarrassed he wet himself, Allen. All
the kids on the opposing team laughed at him."

"You're mean," Allen said. "And ugly. Look how ugly." He held up his drawing. It was a portrait of me, my face spackled in red and pink marks. I understood completely why people hit their children.

I walked over to Allen and slammed the plate down on the table. "Eat your sandwich."

On my way to the bathroom, I heard Allen yelp and sputter in disgust. He'd gotten a taste of the onions.

———

When I wanted to despair over my reflection, there was no better place than my mother's bathroom, where the light was so bright you could hear it fritzing in your skull. Sometimes I played a sick game with myself in the mirror. Would I rather have a million dollars to run away with or perfect skin? Still married to CJ or not a mark on me? I had yet to come up with a scenario in which I did not choose my own skin. What did that say about me?

It's just that, without acne, I was sure I could handle it. Whatever crippling remarks my family made about me. I could stop twisting myself into unnatural configurations, trying to hide whichever side of my face offended most that day, at angles that were starting to give me chronic muscle aches. My family may be less disgusted with me if I were beautiful, or maybe their disgust wouldn't sting so much if I didn't feel so ugly all the time.

I twisted the tap and let the water run until it steamed. There was a pimple that had come to a head over the course of the morning. All the magazines tell you not to pick. Picking causes scarring. Picking doubles the length of time it takes for the blemish to heal. These are lies told by women with occasionally imperfect skin. Pimples leave marks behind whether you touch them or not, and they clear up in one or two days if you wait until they're at their ripest to release them. Only rookies pick when the blemish is freshly forming, and this I *can* confirm will extend the life of the bump. I should write a story for *Cosmopolitan*. "How to Deal with Pimples by Someone Who Actually Has Pimples."

I was blotting away a mixture of goo and blood when I heard a knock at the door. The only indication that Allen had gone to answer it was the sound of his chair scraping the linoleum floor in the kitchen. Allen was light as a feather, just like my sister-in-law, who was pint-sized and adorable and looked up at me through her blond eyelashes as if I were a gruesome spinster, though she hadn't always seen me that way.

"Aunt Ruth!" Allen shouted.

I blotted my chin one last time for whomever was at the front door. Probably a Bible salesman, and maybe I would buy one. I could never say no to anyone so desperate. And a family of so-called Catholics should probably have at least one Bible in the house.

Only pick when you have at least thirty minutes of free time, I thought about adding to my article as I made my way to the stairs. That's how long it takes for the crater to stop oozing, so you can spackle it in foundation and powder and get on with your day.

"Aunt Ruuu-uthhhh!" Allen said again, this time in a sort of teasing, *come and find me* way. Like we were playing hide-and-seek.

"Comiiing!" I called back, matching him.

Halfway down the stairs, I stopped and brought my hand to my chin in a panic. Had I been seen, or was there still time to run back and slap on some emergency cover-up?

"There she is," Allen said to Tina, outing me.

Tina had been crouched down, speaking to Allen eye to eye. She stood and tucked her straight yellow hair behind her ear, a pantomime of a shy schoolgirl, down to the neat cashmere coat buttoned to the neck. "Ruth!" She waved as though we were in a large crowd and she had spotted me first. "Hi! Sorry to drop by unannounced like this. But I found this under the passenger seat." She was pinching something between her two fingers, a bell about to ring. Reluctantly, I descended another stair to get a better look and realized it was the bottle of my favorite foundation, the expensive one I'd had to special-order from a store in New Orleans when they stopped carrying my shade at Frederick & Nelson.

"Oh, wow, thank you," I said, and I meant it. That stuff had been seven dollars an ounce and worth every penny. I had backups, of course, which I used on days I wasn't planning to leave the house. I'd gone nowhere since Tina had dropped me off last and hadn't realized it was missing.

"What is it?" Allen had to ask.

"It's makeup," Tina said, and I braced myself for whatever debilitating comment Allen would make in front of her. *My aunt Ruth needs it,* probably. But before he could, Tina pretended to paint it on his face, and Allen squealed in delight.

"Well, thanks," I said. I was still standing halfway up the stairs. I didn't want to get too close, not with a seeping abscess on my face.

"We're eating ham sandwiches," Allen said. "Do you want mine? It's disgusting."

Tina looked up at me deferentially. She did want to stay, I could tell, but not unless I wanted her to. "I should really get going," she said.

Regret lumped in my throat, but I simply couldn't look Tina in the eye with an open sore on my chin, with a nephew like this, who would thrill in pointing out my every flaw to her. "The least I can do is make you lunch," I offered weakly.

"I don't really like ham," Tina said. The pair of us, unable to say what we really wanted, would have been comical if it weren't so sad.

"There's cheese," Allen said. He grabbed her hand and tugged her inside. "The yellow and white kind." He dragged her into the kitchen, eager to impress our beautiful visitor. When you look like Tina, children like Allen are just children. They can't hurt you.

———

Allen insisted on being the one to make the cheese sandwich for Tina. I was a terrible cook, he told her, and I argued that I was actually an excellent cook, and he said no, I wasn't, and I knew it would go on and on if I didn't put an end to it, so I forced myself to do the adult thing. Tina laughed and said, "More women should be terrible cooks, actually." I laughed with her, and Allen glowered, too young to understand but old enough to feel left out.

"I'll be right back," I said to the two of them, and then I dashed upstairs to pat the good makeup on my chin. For a moment, in the more humane lighting of my own bathroom, I wondered if those Acnotabs were actually starting to work. I didn't look half as hideous in the mirror as I did in my mind.

When I came downstairs, Tina was standing in the wallpapered dining room before a photograph on the mahogany chest that had belonged to my grandmother.

"Allen wanted me to eat in here," she explained without turning around. She pointed. "Is this your dad?"

The picture had been taken at my brother's wedding eight years ago. When the photographer had said, *Just the groom's side now,* my father had clapped his hand on CJ's shoulder and stayed him in place. My sister-in-law had cast me a sympathetic look from behind her lace veil, acknowledging what had taken me years to recognize: my father was giving me an out. Quite literally an out—at the time that photograph was taken, I was living in a hospital, working through a severe emotional disturbance. Just like Elizabeth Taylor in *Suddenly Last Summer,* I would tell myself on my darker days.

CJ was married to another woman on the day that picture was taken, but no doubt my father had viewed this as a mitigating factor. CJ's wife was a pathetic woman four years his senior. They had gotten together in high school when he was just a freshman. CJ had always looked older than he was; he was short and stocky and entered Issaquah Catholic Upper sporting a full beard, a man's beard. The older girls went after him like it was a blood sport—students placed bets, money was won and lost.

In that photograph, CJ was still young, but his twenty-five-year-old wife was getting old. She was a heavy drinker, a nasty drunk who had to be escorted out of bars, stumbling and slurring obscenities. She had shown up to the church reeking of gin, and by the time we'd reached the reception, she had removed her shoes and lost her purse. My father had to break up an argument between her and CJ, and he was the one who called a cab for her and asked one of our cousins to escort her home. He insisted CJ stay, that he was like a member of the family and he could not miss the wedding reception of one of his oldest friends.

I knew CJ had feelings for me. Everyone in my family did. He was my protector when we were kids—he punched a neighborhood boy in the mouth after he threw a snowball that accidentally struck me and knocked me off my bike. I sensed it growing into something else, at least on his side, once I hit high school. I never thought it would amount to anything, though, not only because CJ was married by then but because he knew the reason for my hospitalization.

He shouldn't have wanted anything to do with me, but on my brother's wedding day, liberated from his angry, aging wife, his old longing surfaced again. I'm sure my father thought he was doing both of us a favor by moving CJ to our table, by spinning me into CJ's arms on the dance floor when the music slowed and couples swayed. But now I think we might have been the ones performing a service for my father.

I'm seventeen years old in the picture, my skin institutionally dull but clear—the acne cropped up after I married CJ, like protective warts. I look very agreeable and lovely in my blue bridesmaid's dress, but my shoulders are slumped, like I'd just released a heavy sigh, realizing what I'd gotten myself into.

"That's my dad," I told Tina.

Tina stroked her chin like some sort of British detective puzzling over a clue. Then she made a noise, the sort of *hmmm!* you make when someone has a good point, a point you'd never considered before.

I stepped up alongside Tina and looked again at the picture, at my father's lips parted in a laugh while the rest of us wore our polite picture smiles. If you had never met my father, you might imagine from his expression that he produced a booming laugh from deep within his low-hanging Buddha belly. My father appeared beefier in pictures than he was—in person he was tall and pear-shaped, with a girlish giggle, an impish *heeheehee* that he seemed to serve on his tongue, the sort of laugh that made everyone else laugh too.

"And that's my ex-husband," I said, indicating CJ.

Tina seized the photo in both hands and brought it close to her face, examining every hair in CJ's red beard. "For how long?"

CJ and I had sneaked around for years, but our marriage had lasted far less. "Not long," I said with a short laugh.

Tina turned the picture around and showed it to me as though it were my first time seeing it. "I mean, no wonder. Look what a knockout you are."

I blushed, wondering if I was still a knockout.

Tina set the picture back on the mahogany chest. "But your posture." She copied me by rounding her shoulders. "I hunch like that too when I'm depressed."

I felt like she'd dumped a bucket of ice water over my head. Immediately sobered, I saw Tina clear-eyed, the way my mother had all along. *Well, therapists need clients, don't they? That's how they earn their living.* How pitiful of me to think she had stopped by for any other reason than to fish, to try and get me to open up and realize that I needed her help.

"That picture was taken after a long day," I said defensively. "Partly I was just tired." Tina was reading too much into things, looking for some kind of psychological underpinning in places where, yes, it *was*, but only coincidentally.

Tina pursed her lips and nodded. She wouldn't argue with me, but she didn't believe me either. "What's the rest?"

"Huh?"

"You said partly. What else is there?"

"I wish you'd knock it off," I said, to my own absolute shock. I never spoke to people like that. I hated to hurt people's feelings, to make anyone feel bad even when they deserved to feel bad. I started to apologize, but Tina shook her head vehemently. *No. No. No.*

"I'm the one who should be apologizing. You are so right. Frances is always warning me not to do this to people. Analyze their every breath when I don't have all the information. Plus, who wants to feel like they're being studied? It's annoying. *I'm* annoying." She could laugh because she knew it wasn't true. Still, I was amazed that she'd taken my outburst in stride. It wasn't like I had never been critical of someone, but I was used to seeing that person crumple in agony and realizing it just wasn't worth it to be so honest. People were too easily destroyed.

"It's just," Tina continued, "I'm studying this stuff, you know? Why people are the way they are and how I can help them, and it's like I've seen the light, or I'm seeing it, at least, and it's helped me so much, and I want to help everyone around me too."

Allen came into the room then, carrying a place mat, napkin, fork, and knife. He went about setting a place for Tina at the head of the table. "She doesn't need a fork and knife for a sandwich," I snapped at him. I knew he knew she didn't, that he was only doting on her, and I wanted him to feel as stupid as I did for thinking Tina was here for any reason other than to psychoanalyze my mind. I walked over and collected the silverware, and that's when I realized—he had set down the crude portrait he'd drawn of me as the place mat.

"You are in big trouble," I hissed.

"I couldn't find the place mats!" Allen cried. He sounded sincere, but I was too mortified to give him the benefit of the doubt. "Here, I'll turn it over if it bothers you so—"

I snatched the drawing off the table and tore it to shreds, right in front of Allen's veined, anemic face. He screamed like I used to, right before the nurse stuck the rubber bite block between my lips. "I hate you!" he cried. "I hate you so much!"

"Good!" I shouted.

Allen started to sob. "I'm telling my dad! He hates you too! Everyone hates you! Grandpop hated you!"

I raised my hand and experienced the almost erotic pleasure of

Allen cowering. But before I could deliver the blow, Tina grabbed my wrist, the pads of her fingers pressed into the flare of my pulse. I hadn't even heard her come up alongside me, and a strange, thrilling second passed, one in which I allowed her to restrain me.

"You're better than they are," she said into my ear. I had no idea who *they* were, but somehow I knew she was right.

Allen turned to her, tears running down his face and snot puddled in the bow of his lip, and he spit on her. He *spit* on her. Tina looked down at the glob of saliva on her soft cashmere sweater, then back at me, aghast. *What the hell are you doing here?* I swore her expression said.

"I don't know what's gotten into you," I growled at Allen, seizing him by the back of the neck and forcing him up the stairs. "You are going to take a time-out until you calm down."

Allen was inconsolable, wailing that he hated me, he hated Tina, he was going to tell, and I would be sorry. I shoved him in my bedroom and slammed the door. When I came back downstairs, the scraps of Allen's drawing had been thrown in the trash, and Tina had left without me.

PAMELA

Tallahassee, 1978

Day 8

Two days after Denise's funeral, a few of the Turq House guys came over to clean up the blood. One of the officers recommended a solution of two parts bleach, one part water, with a wink, as though he were letting us in on the secret ingredient in an old family recipe.

The room that Eileen and Jill shared was a nightmare. I never got over it. How the girls in the bloodiest room were the ones who survived.

There wasn't much to do in Denise's room, though I spent the longest in there, hiding anything that might embarrass her in front of all the cute shaggy-haired boys who would have jumped at the chance to take her out, open the car door for her, buy her dinner, go home and tell their friends—I kissed *Denise Patrick Andora*. Guys included her middle name when they talked about her, like *she* was the serial killer.

The tube of hair lightener that she used on Abbott and Costello— right sideburn was Abbott, left Costello, and don't you dare mix them up—went in a drawer, along with the pair of pantyhose that had seen better days, left to dry on the inside knob of the door. The photographs of friends and prints of surrealist masterpieces I left hanging above her bed, but I took down the astral page she'd torn out of that month's *Cosmopolitan*, from the comprehensive booklet the editors put together every January to help readers plan "the best year of their lives." I removed the tack and sat cross-legged on Denise's bed to read her horoscope. In June, Denise was supposed to *reorganize office procedures, slipping into her boss's shoes as if they belonged to her (which soon they would)*. According to her planetary prophecy, she would find herself in Lisbon or Madrid come September. Her most dynamic day of the year was still ten months away. I began to vibrate, inwardly, a buzzing under my skin that I can only describe as the instinct to kill. There was something about Denise's excitement for a future she would never get to experience that made me murderous with grief. I couldn't stand the idea of anyone coming into her room and pitying her, or, worse, judging her for having the audacity to make plans when she should have known God would laugh. That was a real thing people said down here, but fuck God for laughing and fuck *Cosmopolitan* too. I was a Virgo, and nowhere in my horoscope did it foretell any of this.

The last thing I did for Denise: I got down on the floor and I put my nose to the carpet where the hair mist bottle had been cast aside. The officers had long since removed it, put it in a box with all the other evidence, but I wanted to make sure it hadn't left a stain, that innermost private smell. There was a lot that others would expect of me over the next year and a half of my life, but this was the only thing I knew Denise would ask if she had the chance: to do what little I could to allow her to hold her head high, even in death.

There was no stain and no smell, but I cracked the window anyway, and then I went outside and jogged three and a half blocks in the cold drizzle to the iron university gate, where I pulled up some of the purple cornflowers planted at the base of the brick pier. Sophomore spring, a Seminole flute player performed on Landis Green, telling sunbathers that at one time, this land was nothing but a field of purple cornflowers, which the Muscogee relied on to pack the wounds of their warriors.

Back at The House, I arranged the flowers in a water glass and placed it on the windowsill. I practiced walking in, taking exaggerated inhales at the moment I crossed the threshold, checking to make sure the hallway didn't smell any different than the room. When all I could detect was the damp mulch of the flower beds and my own hair spray, some chemical activated by the rain, I told the boys to come upstairs.

————

Bernadette accompanied me to the hardware store for new combination locks, to the Northwood department store for new linens, and finally to Hartford Appliances for new mattresses, carpet swatches, and a used air-conditioning unit if they had one. It was going to take some cajoling to get anyone to move into Jill and Eileen's room, potentially for years to come. I had the next generation of The House to think about, my successors, their chapters. I was under enormous pressure to set them up for success, and rooms with their own personal air-conditioning unit were currency back then, especially in the Panhandle, where October may as well have been July.

"Here's one for only sixty-five dollars," Bernadette said, turning over a price ticket with a red slash-through line.

I crossed the warehouse floor to examine the unit. It was a GE Slumberline with wood paneling. It should have cost a lot more. "Does it worry you that it's on sale at that price?" I ran a finger through a grate, inspecting it for grime. "Something's got to be wrong with it."

"The next cheapest one is ninety-five dollars," Bernadette said.

I grimaced. We'd nearly drained the semester budget that morning, though I had assurances that it would be replenished imminently. Brian's dad had received the compensation claim form and was fast-tracking it through the approval process. Still, I felt an acute sense of anxiety every time I handed over the Panhellenic credit card, like I was a corrupt politician misappropriating community funds.

"Let's go with the Slumberline," I said after the salesman told us about the ten-day return policy. It came out to nearly eighty dollars, with tax and tip. The thing was compact but brick-dense, and it took two salesguys to maneuver it outside and into my lap in the passenger seat, where I held on to it in a bear hug.

"Whoops," Bernadette said, unbuckling her seat belt. "I left the carpet swatches."

She ran back inside, head bowed to the rain. It was a dreary Monday, everyone bundled in scarves and hats, toes wet in their boots. Braid weather, Denise called it. She would have sat at my feet that morning, underlining passages in her physics and art textbooks, while I laced her bushy hair tight. She had been dead eight days.

The driver's-side door opened. *That was fast,* I turned to say, until I saw it wasn't Bernadette climbing behind the wheel but a man in a green-and-yellow baseball cap pulled down low. Bernadette had left the engine running, the keys in the ignition. The man put the car in drive, and I watched Hartford Appliances slip away in a stupefied, wordless freeze.

"You're gonna talk to me now," he slurred, and we started to drift into a lane of oncoming traffic.

His voice, the silhouette of his chin and lips beneath the brim of the Oakland A's cap. It was Roger. Drunk Roger. The very worst kind.

"Yeah, fuck you too," Roger heckled when a car in the fast lane laid on the horn. He overcorrected, and we dipped off the edge of the pavement. *We are going to flip,* I was thinking when Roger jerked us back onto the road and my temple cracked against the window. I moaned in pain.

"Oh, shut up," Roger said in a whiny way, like he'd had about enough of me. We were approaching a yellow light from too far away at too high a speed.

"Roger!" I cried, stabbing my finger frantically at the road.

Roger stomped the brakes, and there was a movie sound effect skidding in my ears, but we weren't stopping, we were sliding for the light on a jagged lightning-bolt course, the rear end of the car lashing like the tail of a stinging scorpion. I held on to the Slumberline for dear life and screwed my eyes shut, bracing for impact as we blew through a compass of caterwauling.

"I told you!" Roger was yelling at me, sour-breathed and belligerent. "Just shut the fuck *up,* Pamela. I can't focus with your annoying fucking voice in my ear." He cowered, doing a vicious impersonation of my terrified face, my clenched body language. *"Roger! Roger!"* He mimicked a nagging female cry.

I was shaking violently, more afraid than I was the night I found Denise, when shock blitzed my system, blunting the severity of the situation. In that moment I was acutely aware of how much more danger I was in with someone who knew me, who had constructed a world in his head where I was his antagonist. Roger was sparking with righteous hatred for me. If he didn't kill us on the road, he would take me somewhere and relish in making me suffer. I had very little time to get out of this alive. I directed all my energy into coming up with something I could give him, some crucial piece of information that would support the choice to spare me. "I have a meeting with the sheriff this afternoon," I lied. "I know the name of the person who did it, and it's right here in my purse . . ." I strained to reach my handbag at my feet, but I couldn't, not with the bulk in my lap. "Come with me and we'll tell him together."

"To the sheriff's office?" Roger's laugh was ugly, and he sounded genuinely insulted. "You really are a dumb bitch, aren't you?" He shook his head in disgust, and the seat belt sliced at my skin as we took a hard left onto County Road, which led onto Route 319, which led to the Apalachicola National Forest, where last year a student's body was found one week after he wandered off the trail. "You sure get off on telling people what to do, Pamela. Denise was so sick of you. You know that? So goddamn sick of you."

I knew she was. I saw it in the petulant set of her jaw every time I asked her to turn down Fleetwood Mac on a school night, or reprimanded her for touching the thermostat because inflation was through the roof and I was trying to keep the electricity bill down. *What happened to you?* she muttered just a week before she died, when I caught her adding more than the allotted two tablespoons of milk to her coffee. Denise had made no secret of being sick of me, but still, it hurt to hear it from someone who had treated her so poorly.

"I loved her," Roger said in a broken voice. "I never would have done it to her. That? *That?*" He looked over at me, eyes webbed with burst blood vessels. "A hair spray bottle? A hair spray bottle . . ." He put his forehead on the wheel and let out an agonized wail. We crossed the solid line into the lane of oncoming traffic, their head-lights picking out pellets of rain in the sooty afternoon.

"Roger," I begged, "please!"

He jerked the wheel and the Slumberline crushed my hand against the door. I bit down on my lip so I wouldn't cry out. I had to think. *Think.*

"There's someone you need to meet," I said. Then, with urgency, because I'd figured it out: I had to make him feel a part of the solution to this unfortunate misunderstanding. "I really need you to meet this woman. She has proof that you didn't do it. She's staying at the new Days Inn. She has a *lot* of proof, Roger. We need to look at it. Together."

Roger didn't say anything. Just kept driving, strangely at the speed limit, like we had someplace to be and we'd left on time. "Don't trick me," he warned quietly. I was nodding, but I realized I should be shaking my head. *No, no. I would never.*

"It is outrageous," I said, trying to muster up some authentic-sounding indignity, "that no one will listen to me. I need your help. We need to get all our facts straight and then go and talk to Sheriff Cruso together. Show him that we're friends. That you never would have hurt Denise. I need you and you need me. We have to set our differences aside."

In profile, I caught one side of Roger's odious smile. At the no-tion that we were friends. That he would never hurt Denise.

———

We parked in the lot of the new Days Inn and engaged in a blackly comic struggle trying to free me from the Slumberline. I weighed 115 pounds back then, and Roger had the motor functions of a toddler doped with cough syrup. In the end he wrapped his arms around the unit and pulled it off my lap with gritted teeth, scrap-ing skin from my thighs and stepping back to let the air conditioner splash in a scummy puddle. I'd have bruises for days, but all I could think was: *Eighty dollars, down the fucking drain.*

The Days Inn was one of those exterior-corridor motels, no lobby, no front-desk attendant to whom I could slip a note: "Call the police. This man is dangerous." Room 203 was right next to the sign for the heated pool, taped over with another sign apologizing for its closure for the season. This was the reason my mother always gave for never coming to visit—Tallahassee's dearth of five-star accommodations.

The door opened mid-rap, like Tina had been standing there, waiting for me since the moment she got back from Denise's funeral. She was wearing a silk turban and I could smell that she'd just washed and set her hair. She glanced at Roger and snorted. "This your bodyguard?"

"This is my friend Roger Yul," I said pleasantly. Before knocking, Roger had wrapped his fingers around my elbow, right at the funny bone joint, and pinched hard while he reminded me of how much he didn't like me. My arm was numb above the wrist and I was terrified of doing anything that might set him off. "I wanted to show him the mug shot you gave me, but I think I misplaced it."

I was hoping the name Roger Yul might mean something to Tina, that she had heard Denise's ex-boyfriend was a person of interest in the investigation, but I saw no sign of recognition on her face. She opened the door wider and invited us inside.

There were two queen beds, one made, one slept in, and a standing television in the corner, on but the volume low. The room stank of stale smoke and chlorine. "I'm surprised Tallahassee doesn't have nicer hotels," Tina said, responding to the wrinkle in my nose. She gestured to the two chairs at the small round table, where a dirty glass acted like a paperweight for the headlines of the day. *Sit.* Roger landed only one ass cheek and made a wild grab for the edges of the table before he went over.

"I guess I need to catch up," Tina said with a wry laugh.

I had hoped to flash her a look as she reached between us for the glass, ringed a crusty maroon at the base, but Roger was watching me with pure malice in his eyes. "Mug shots in that pile." Tina indicated a stack on the windowsill before she went into the bathroom to wash out the glass.

Roger picked up a copy and held it out at a long angle, trying to bring The Defendant's image into focus.

"That's the man I saw at the front door," I told him.

"Why's it say he's from Colorado?" Roger asked angrily, like we were wasting his time.

"Washington, actually," Tina said, returning from the bathroom, drying out the glass with a hand towel. "His first victim was a woman named Lynda Ann Healy. She was a senior at the University of Washington who reported on ski conditions for a local radio station. When her alarm went off at five a.m. and she didn't turn it off, her roommates checked on her and found that her bed had been made and her nightgown hung in the closet. The police discovered a small drop of blood left on the pillowcase and determined that she got a nosebleed and went to the hospital in the middle of the night without telling anyone or taking her car, purse, or shoes. They found her body six months later off a hiking trail on Taylor Mountain. Who wants wine?"

"I'd rather a beer," Roger said.

"I'm not a bar," Tina said. She poured him a glass of red and set it in front of him, looked at me.

"None for me," I said. "Thank you." Roger mimicked me again. *Thank you.* I sounded like a stuck-up bitch you wouldn't hesitate to smack around.

Tina poured herself a hearty glass and lit a cigarette. "After Lynda, he developed a pattern. He struck once a month for six months. Mostly he kept to the Seattle area, though the year prior he had been in Aspen, where he abducted a woman named Caryn Campbell from a hotel that was hosting a medical conference. She was there with her fiancé, a physician. She went to her room to grab a magazine one evening and never came back. They found her body along a rural dirt road a month later, when the snow finally melted." Tina went over to the nightstand, switched on the gooseneck lamp, and emptied the ashtray into the waste bin. She set it on the table and offered Roger a cigarette.

"In June 1974," she went on, striking a match for him, "another University of Washington senior named Georgeann Hawkins left a fraternity party early to go home and study for her Spanish final. She lived in an area of campus known as Greek Row, a bunch of fraternities and sororities all right next door to one another along a brightly lit street. It was a warm night, and everyone had their windows open. She stopped to talk to a friend through his window on her way. He estimated she had about twenty steps to go to the back door, and yet she never made it."

"Were me," Roger said, with stained merlot lips, "I woulda walked her home."

"He'd just have found someone else," Tina said, unmoved by this bogus claim to chivalry.

I counted on my fingers. "You said he struck once a month for six months. June is five months."

Tina sank down on the edge of the bed she hadn't been sleeping in, drawing a pillow into her lap. She rested her elbows on it, massaging her temples with her cigarette still burning between two fingers. I kept thinking about her freshly washed hair under that turban, how it would need to be washed again.

"In July," she said, "we got unusual weather. Eighty-seven degrees on a Sunday. I know that's not breaking any records down here, but the hardware store sold out of coolers. There's this beach in Issaquah. Lake Sammamish. Lake Sam, everyone calls it. Ruth and I had plans to go and lay out all day. But then . . ." Tina studied Roger a moment before continuing, cryptically. "There was a change of plans. I went alone. I guess she came later and tried to find me, but they estimated there were thirty thousand people at the beach that day." She pulled contemplatively on her cigarette. "Thirty thousand people," she marveled through a lacework of her own exhaust, "and he killed two girls, precisely two hours apart in broad daylight, and no one saw a thing."

My eyes slid nervously to the window, the hairs on the back of my neck prickling like I was being watched. "Do the police have any sort of theory? About how he pulled that off?" I started scratching at my arms, my scalp, every part of me feeling suddenly infested with bugs.

"They only know that Ruth went first." Tina had a foul smile on her face that I could understand, that something so preposterous could be true. "Just like Denise. And, just like Denise, she wasn't enough for him."

We stared at each other, and a moment of raw understanding passed between us.

"What does Ruth think?" came Roger's contribution, in his dumb gargled voice. He had to tilt his head back to see through the heavying hoods of his eyelids, and his cigarette had burned down to a precarious line of ash. Gingerly, I removed it from between his fingers and stubbed it out in the ashtray. His fingers stayed stuck in a V-shape.

"Hey, man," Tina said, patting the bed, "you wanna lay down?"

Roger's head bobbed around on his neck, a nod in the affirmative, it appeared, but he did not get up. Tina shot me a look—*what's his deal?*—before continuing on.

"Then it was like . . . it all stopped. Or it seemed like it did. We know now that he moved to Utah to attend law school, a good one that he had to scam his way into. Despite hundreds of hours of preparation, his Law School Aptitude Test results were mediocre and his performance on the grammar part of the exam below high school level. So he forged his recommendation letters and moved to Utah, and that was when women in the Salt Lake City area began to disappear. One after another, until an eighteen-year-old named Anne Biers managed to escape and identify him. He was arrested, sentenced to fifteen years for kidnapping, and then they found in his compounded car a strand of Caryn Campbell's hair. He was extradited to Colorado to stand trial for her murder, and that was when law enforcement shit the bed."

Roger's chin touched his chest and his head snapped up. "I didn't do it," he insisted.

Tina ignored him. "In Colorado, he filed a pro se motion to represent himself, arguing that it was a violation of his constitutional right to a fair trial to be restrained while using the law library at the Aspen courthouse." Tina's upper lip curled to indicate what she thought about The Defendant's *rights*. "The judge agreed, with the condition that he must be supervised at all times. Only, the guards took one look at the guy and decided he didn't pose a real threat, and it wasn't long before they were leaving him to do his research in the library while they popped out for a smoke break. One of those times, he opened the window, jumped two stories, and took off. A week later, he was apprehended in the mountains. The public was understandably outraged, and so the sheriff moved him to a higher-security prison, about an hour outside of Aspen, and put him on a twenty-four-hour watch. Within six months, he escaped a second time. What the hell kind of incompetence happened there, God only knows. In any case, that was December. Exactly one month before you saw him at your front door."

Roger's head landed on his forearm with a final-sounding whump. I poked him, to be sure he was really out, before whispering, "Can you call the police? I think he was trying to hurt me."

Tina went over to him, shoving her hand down the waistband of his jeans. It was only then I noticed that fresh blood was streaking his upper thighs. When had he started bleeding?

Tina extracted what appeared to be a small Swiss Army knife, partially unlatched.

I gaped at the blade. "How did he not feel that?"

"I'm a licensed therapist," Tina said. "Everything in my toiletry kit is legal."

I glanced at the open bathroom door, the leather kit on the sink, where Tina had stood a few minutes ago, washing out the glass she gave Roger.

Tina went over to the nightstand and lifted the phone from the receiver, dialing the police. "Please don't tell the sheriff that part," she said to me. "He already thinks I'm some kind of black widow." Her laugh was gravelly, like it wasn't all that ludicrous a thing to think.

I waited while she explained our situation to the operator. "It's the Days Inn on West Tennessee Road. Room two-oh-three."

"Why did the sheriff tell me not to spend any time alone with you?" I asked when she hung up.

Tina groaned—*this again?* "I was married to a rich old dinosaur who died of natural causes, and I got almost everything even though he had five adult children who are all nearly twice my age."

"So he thinks you had something to do with his death?"

"Yes."

"Did you?"

"Even if I did," came Tina's non-answer, "I have no reason to want to hurt you."

"My family has money," I said. "Maybe you're somehow after that."

Tina smirked. "I'm scraping by, all right." She started tidying the room—fluffing the pillow she'd held in her lap and propping it against the headboard. "Come to Colorado with me," she said, moving on to make the other bed. I got up to help her. It mattered to me too that when the police arrived they found a tidy room. "I've been in touch with The Defendant's old cellmate. He's agreed to put me on his visitors' list." In unison, we drew up the top sheet and gave it a half-foot fold.

"What is talking to him supposed to accomplish?" I asked as I lifted my side of the mattress and tucked in the corners of the comforter.

"Think about it," Tina said while we straightened the pleated bed skirt. "You're stuck in a six-by-six cement box all day, nothing to do, no one else to talk to in the world but your cellmate. You get to sharing things. About your plans. About friends, family, places where you can hunker down, and people who will help you go undetected."

"Isn't talking to him the sort of thing the sheriff should do?" I shook out the pillow, then gave it a good pounding with my fist. Tina held out her arms. I tossed it to her.

"It's good policework," she said, catching the pillow with a little bend at her knees. "So, no. Not your sheriff. Not any sheriff I've come across in all this."

I stood staring at the freshly made bed, thinking about how much of my life I'd spent feeling simultaneously like a child and the only adult in the room. Why couldn't people just do their jobs? Why was it that I could rely only on myself?

"I can't just take off," I said. "We're moving back into The House in a few days. I have to show everyone there is no reason to be afraid. I have to be the example."

"Well"—Tina laughed, collecting the dirty glasses and taking them to the bathroom for a rinse—"there is plenty to be afraid of. The Defendant is here in Tallahassee, and it's in the papers that there was an eyewitness. You're not safe as long as he's out there." The water went on, and Tina raised her voice to be heard over the stream. "Look at what just happened to you!"

"So this is about keeping me safe?" I fired back.

The tap went off. "It is as inhuman to be totally good as it is to be totally evil."

I'd read *A Clockwork Orange* twice the summer I turned fifteen. "I can quote Anthony Burgess too, but I'd prefer an answer that doesn't evade the question."

Tina turned off the light in the bathroom and went over to the window, checking to see if the police had arrived yet. "Ruth deserves a proper burial. There are *rituals* around dying. They're not for the dead, they're for those of us who are left behind. I think I deserve that. And I think you deserve better too. Has anyone even acknowledged what you've done, Pamela?"

The room spun suddenly and silently with red and blue lights. The police hadn't even bothered to turn on the siren. "What is it I've done?"

Tina went over and unlocked the door for the officers. "You ran toward him. Don't you see that? Anyone else, if they'd heard what you heard, they'd have run away. They'd have saved their own skin. You heard his footsteps overhead, and you *pursued* him. That takes a set of steel, Pamela. Everyone should be calling you a hero, but I have a feeling I'm the only one."

"Afternoon, girls," said the responding officer, taking off his hat and cupping it against his chest in a mannerly way as he came through the door. He saw Roger, passed out at the table, and clicked his tongue, chuckling. "Heard we're having some boy trouble."

RUTH

Issaquah

Winter 1974

When Tina called to tell me that a pipe had burst at Frances's house and the grief group would be meeting at her place, her voice was sweet to the point of cloying. It was how we'd been speaking to one another ever since she came by my house and watched me make my nephew cry. Bubbly and impersonal.

"I don't mind picking you up," Tina said. "I know Clyde Hill is sort of a far drive for your mother."

"Actually, I can ride my bike over." I'd salvaged my childhood Schwinn from the junk pile in the garage and spent the weekend scrubbing at patches of rust with a kitchen sponge. My mother had barely spoken to me since I'd told her that CJ had sent his best but wouldn't be able to attend the ceremony for my father, except to tell me that a more considerate person would have gone to the store and replaced the ham they'd gone through on Saturday.

"Are you sure, Ruth? It's pretty far in the dark. And they still don't know what happened to that U Dub girl."

"I heard she ran off," I told her.

Tina gave me her address, and I did a double take. I knew her house. I knew exactly who she was.

I left early for the session, after my mother picked another petty fight with me. I'd forgotten to bring in the mail, and if I wanted to live at home for free, a twenty-five-year-old adult *woman*, then I needed to remember the arrangement. I was there to step in where my father had stepped up, to help her ease into her new life as a grief-stricken widow.

"It's right here," I had the immense pleasure of saying after allowing her to prattle on and on, the most she'd spoken to me in nearly a week. I led her into the laundry room. It had sleeted overnight, but the day had been warm and the mail soggy and full of grit. I had spread it out on a dish towel to dry.

"Were you planning on telling me it was there, or were you waiting for me to ask where it was?" She didn't give me a half second to answer before moving on to my next offense. "And you need to find another place to park that bike if you're going to be using it again. I can't get to anything I need with where you have it in the garage now."

That was when I started snapping up my coat. I didn't have to leave for another hour, but it was time to go.

Tina lived in the Spanish-style mansion in Clyde Hill. Everybody knew the house. A few years back, some old Texas millionaire blew into town and built a six-bedroom behemoth with a red barrel-tiled roof and a grand central courtyard. On either side, two ranch-style homes squatted like the estate's ugly stepsisters. People had been up in arms, and I learned a lot of new words then: *gaudy, ostentatious, arrogant*. I knew what *arrogant* meant because I had a sister-in-law. I just hadn't realized it was something a house could be too.

I'd never actually laid eyes on the Texas millionaire. He was rarely in town, and when he was, he remained in his fortress. The Spanish mansion was not his main residence, and it was a mystery as to what he was doing in the Seattle area. Rumors flew—he was there to buy out Dixon Group, to run for mayor. But he never did any-

thing except build a gaudy, ostentatious, arrogant eyesore too close
to the neighbors, and then he died. I saw his picture in the paper
and barely registered the news. He looked like someone who would
die. He was at least eighty years old. I could not believe *that* was
Tina's late husband. I imagined sharing a bed with him, his scabby
legs sanding mine in the night. I was a little bit disgusted with her, a
little bit impressed.

I approached the house, taking small, demure steps, the way
I had when I walked down the aisle to CJ. I was never one to be
self-conscious or intimidated by people with money. Quite the
opposite—their privilege triggered a sort of serenity within me, *ums*
and *uhs* lifted from my speech, and my ankles wound like those of
a noblewoman taking her seat in a European court. The etiquette
came so naturally that I almost believed in reincarnation. In another
life, I'm sure I was a wealthy woman.

No one came to the door for a while, but I could hear voices inside.
Angry voices. Two women, fighting. There was another car in the
driveway, next to Tina's, but I had just assumed that was hers as well.
If she'd had to have sex with that old man, I hoped she'd at least gotten a second car out of it.

When the door finally opened, I could tell Tina had been crying.
She'd made a poor attempt to cover it up. Her bloodshot eyes were
ringed with a foundation much too pink for her skin tone. "You're
early," she said, "but come on in." She held the door open resentfully.

Whatever was going on, this felt fair to me. She had witnessed
an ugly scene inside my house, and now it was her turn under the
microscope.

The house was spectacular and freezing cold. I must have shivered, because Tina said with rancor, "The heat is on. It's just always
cold in this fucking ghost house." The weighty wood door clobbered
closed behind me, rattling a glass vase on a table.

"I was just about to set out some coffee and snacks," Tina said, walking in the direction of the kitchen, I supposed. "You can help if you want."

I was dying to check out the rest of the house. I followed Tina with my head tipped back, admiring the wood beams on the ceilings. The walls were pure white stucco, absolutely nothing painted or wallpapered. There were no photos or art hanging up; there was no need. The wrought-iron grillwork on the windows and the bronze candle-style chandeliers were decoration enough. I wished everyone who had called this place gaudy could see the inside. Tina knew what not to do with money, and I approved. My approval probably didn't matter to Tina, but I felt she should know it was not easily earned.

On the kitchen table there was a dead flower in a clay pot. Nothing on the countertops—no sugar or sponges or cooking utensils. Tina opened the refrigerator and removed a tray of vegetables and dip that she had bought preassembled from the grocery store. My mother was always pointing to it and saying what a rip-off it was. You could buy three bags of carrots and a bottle of ranch for a dollar less.

Tina placed the platter on the counter and stared at it. "I guess I need napkins," she said, and then she burst into tears.

I was staring at her, stunned, when another woman entered the kitchen. She was older than we were, midthirties, striking but not beautiful, and wearing pounds of silver jewelry. She jangled and glinted as she put her arms around Tina, who was sobbing by then.

I had no idea what to do. I stood there, still as a statue, as Tina wept into the crook of the woman's neck. "Why don't you go upstairs and pull yourself together before your guests arrive?" the woman suggested to Tina. "I can set up for you."

"Okay," Tina agreed in a wobbly voice. "Oh"—she gestured at me as if I were a feature of the house a new homeowner needed to know about—"that's Ruth, by the way. She came early."

I was tongue-tied a moment. "Sorry," I ended up saying.

Tina shrugged miserably as she started for the stairs in the kitchen. The house had two sets of stairs.

The woman picked up the platter. "I'm Janelle. Grab those plates. The den is on the left at the end of the hallway."

The den was dim and warm, a fire dwindling in the hearth. Janelle picked up the poker and nudged one of the logs; it hissed at her, serpent-like, and reared back up again. I stationed myself in front of a sideboard cluttered with pictures of Tina from over the years. I wondered if this was how she'd felt when she discovered the photograph from my brother's wedding in my dining room. *Tell me what I don't already know about you.*

There was no nice way to say it—Tina had looked wrong as a child. Standing between her parents, she was a runty girl scowling in a dress, a proper towhead with jet-black eyebrows, her extremes even more pronounced back then than they were today.

On her wedding day, Tina was beautiful and stoic next to her happy groom. Some women might have said that at his age, he was still a handsome man, but those women would have been much older than we were. All I could think about, looking at the two of them together on their wedding day, was the two of them on their wedding night. My stomach made a sickly sound in protest.

Then there was Tina at her college graduation, holding her cap to her head and laughing against the breeze that threatened to blow it away. It was the only picture without men and the only one where Tina was smiling. I'm not saying the two are related.

I looked closer at the other women in the picture and gasped, realizing one was Frances. I didn't recognize the woman on Tina's other side; she was nearly six feet tall, with waist-length silver hair.

"Who is the other woman in this picture?" I asked Janelle.

Janelle tilted her head to see around the glare set off by the fire. "Oh. That's Irene."

Irene. Tina had mentioned an Irene that day in her car. When I'd asked who she was, I could tell Tina had withheld something from me.

Janelle leaned the poker against the wall, saying, "Can you let Tina know I'm going? I know everyone is arriving soon, and I don't want to get blocked in."

"Do you think I should check on her?" I asked, realizing how much I wished she would give me her blessing to go upstairs.

"Frances will be here soon," Janelle said, tucking her shiny hair into the collar of her raincoat. "Nice meeting you. Good luck."

I wondered if she meant with Tina or with the complex grieving.

———

Tina still hadn't come downstairs by the time the other women started to arrive. They all seemed excited to see me answer the door. With me, they could widen their eyes as if to ask, *Can you believe it?* Their families had talked about this house around the dinner table too. When Frances walked in—like it wasn't a Hollywood estate, like she'd been here before—I told her that Tina was upstairs and that she was upset. I don't know what came over me, but when Frances started for the stairs, I barged past her, saying, "I don't mind!"

At the top of the stairs, the hallway went left and right. But there was only one door that was expressly closed.

"Tina?" I knocked gently. "Everyone's here."

"You can come in," I heard her mumble on the other side. Or maybe it was *You can't come in*? I was already opening the door.

Tina was curled up on one of those fainting sofas under a trio of bay windows. The room was big; too big. It was clover-shaped, the canopy bed in the center surrounded by nooks for office, dressing, and living areas. In just this one bedroom, there was more furniture than we had on the first floor of my house. I don't have a problem pitying rich people. There are a lot of sad things in this world, and getting everything you want only to realize you are still empty inside is certainly one of them.

"Oh," Tina said, a little sullenly, when she saw me. "I thought you were Frances."

I stepped back. "I can get her."

Tina considered. "No. Don't. She always takes Janelle's side, anyway. Can you close the door? I don't want anyone to hear us."

I shut the door, bursting with importance. Tina had chosen me as a confidante. She shifted over, making room for me on the sofa. The windows looked down on the back of the property, where Tina and her late husband must have been building a pool before he died.

"I don't know what I'm going to do," Tina said tearfully.

"About what? What's happened, Tina?"

Tina picked at a loose thread in her sweater. She didn't seem to want to answer. "I have to attend this conference in Aspen this weekend. I'm supposed to do a mock therapy session. It's all part of my work experience. Janelle was supposed to come with me and help me practice and just be there for me." Tina covered her face and wailed, "She promised me."

I was glad Tina was covering her face so she couldn't see the bafflement on mine. That was what she was so upset about? "Can't you go without her?"

"I have to speak in front of a bunch of people who will be judging me, and I'm terrified. And . . . and there's just a lot about this trip that will be hard for me." Tina used the cuff of her sweater to wipe away her tears. "It's a long story. But she knows it. And she's just abandoning me anyway."

I was still confused. "Why isn't she going anymore?"

"Because she's married."

"Won't her husband let her go?"

Tina gazed down at the ragged hole in her backyard with a bitter laugh. "He doesn't even know about me." She drew her thighs to her chest and made herself into a tight little ball. "We loved each other, Ruth." She glanced at me over the ledge of knees bashfully, waiting to see how I would react.

I was thunderstruck. I was elated. I was devastated, and I was angry. My face took her along for the ride, so I could tell she had no idea what was going through my mind. *But you're not sick,* is what I was thinking. *You're young and beautiful, wealthy and educated, loved, respected by Frances, a therapist for twenty-five years. Is it possible to be* that *and not be sick?*

"I'll go with you," I declared boldly. I pictured telling my mother that I was going away with the woman who lived in the Spanish mansion: payback for picking on me earlier. She would be oozing with nosy questions, but she would have too much pride to ask any of them. It was the perfect revenge.

"We have to fly," Tina said cautiously. "It's far."

"I know." I rolled my eyes as if I'd been to Aspen a thousand times.

"Company would be nice," Tina said to herself, cheering some as she gave my offer serious thought. "You really don't mind?"

I grinned. "I'm due for an adventure."

PAMELA

Aspen, 1978

Day 12

I asked Carl to come with us to Colorado, telling myself it had everything to do with getting justice for Denise and nothing at all to do with the way he had looked up at me from the corner of her bed. Like what I had to say was not just interesting but important.

It was four years before the release of the Meryl Streep movie *Sophie's Choice*, before the title took root in the public consciousness, but when the police asked me if I wanted to press charges against Roger, that was very much my predicament. A prosecutor could easily argue that the presence of a weapon—the Swiss Army knife—met the criteria for aggravated kidnapping, a felony charge that could carry a life sentence.

Though it would be a service to the women of Tallahassee to put him away for life, a felony charge was sure to only bolster the police's theory that this was their guy. And what would happen when the press got ahold of the news? When the public heard about it? A twenty-eight-year-old man who had spent a year in an institution, falsified his transcript to pose as a college freshman, and dated the girl who was murdered first. Roger looked so good for it that I sometimes wanted to believe it. I'd have to remind myself: *But you saw him. And yes, for a second you thought it was him. So maybe it was him.* No. Stop this. *You saw him and it wasn't.* That was the obstacle course my mind laid out every time my head hit the pillow. Sleep, the unreachable finish line.

I asked Sheriff Cruso for the weekend to think about what I wanted to do. When I called Carl, it was my attempt to have it both ways—Roger prosecuted at the felony level and the media on my side.

"I have a story for you," I told Carl.

Carl listened while I spelled it out. Police incompetence, at a criminal level, that had led to two deaths and three beatings here in Florida.

"He escaped *twice* under Colorado's watch," I stressed. "We know how it happened in Aspen, but how do they move him to a so-called higher-security prison and let it happen again? It's malfeasance, and you could be the one to expose it."

Carl put his hand over the mouthpiece and spoke to someone in the background, asking for a pen so he could write down my flight information. I found myself straining to make out if the voice that responded *Here you go* was female. *You are engaged,* I reminded myself. *Practically.*

———

"This is a fashion statement," Carl said as we buckled our seat belts for takeoff.

I looked down at what I was wearing. I'd come straight from my externship at the Capitol Building in my page uniform—navy wool skirt, tights, starched white button-down, loafers swapped out for white sneakers. I'd known I'd have to race back to The House to grab my bags and make the flight. Only a few years later, this look would become popular among professional women with a commute, immortalized in the movie *Working Girl,* but on that January afternoon in 1978, I suppose I just looked weird.

"My externship is Wednesday and Friday mornings," I explained.

"It's not even been two weeks. You're already back at that?"

I gave him a sideways look. "I never left."

Carl did a double take. "Not even the week it happened?"

"That was a Saturday night," I said.

Carl was staring at me, his eyes roving back and forth, like he was waiting for me to break. Surely I had to be pulling his leg.

"So by Wednesday . . ." I trailed off, figuring the point had been made. So by Wednesday, things had settled enough for me to get back to work.

Carl rested his head on the back of the airplane seat, closing his eyes. "You're pretty incredible, Pamela. All you girls are." His voice was sincere but immeasurably sad.

Tina was seated across the aisle from us, her head bowed over a marked-up map of Colorado, but at this she looked up, cocking her head curiously at me. Carl sounded like he was about to cry.

"Oh," I said unsteadily. "I guess. I mean, we're just doing what anyone would do in our situation."

"No," Carl said forcibly, "not what anyone would do." He exhaled hard, his nostrils flaring like he was remembering something unpleasant, and opened his eyes. "I served. And when I came back, I wasn't okay for a long time."

The airplane was gaining speed, bumping and skidding along. I always hated this part. It never felt like we were moving fast enough, for long enough, to actually lift into the air. We hit a pocket of something as the plane nosed into the sky, and Carl's hand flew to my wrist.

"Sorry," he said, giving the back of my hand an apologetic pat.

Across the aisle, Tina was studying the map again, but she was also chewing her lower lip like she was trying not to smile.

On the way to Glenwood Springs, the site of The Defendant's second escape, we drove by the Pitkin County Courthouse, the site of his first. We wanted to see for ourselves the window from which he leaped during a recess in his pretrial hearing for the murder of Caryn Campbell. Over the years, I've read accounts that claim it was the third floor from which he daringly absconded. But I was there, and it was the second floor. People always want to make him more than he was.

"It's nine? Ten feet?" Carl estimated as he wrote it down.

"I would have fucking jumped too if I got the chance," Tina said. "What were they *thinking,* leaving him alone in there?"

In just a few months I'd be in law school, where I would be warned against exploiting my knowledge to make the weaker argument strong, taught that was a technique only sophists employ. From that introductory course of civil procedure onward, I've nurtured a slow-burning contempt against every member of law enforcement and the legal profession who went on to suggest that The Defendant's move to represent himself was all a part of his master plan. That he had worked out his argument to the judge—free rein at the law library as a constitutional right—ahead of filing the pro se motion. That he was always ten steps ahead.

There is substantive evidence that points to no plan at all, points to nothing but *ego* as his predominant guiding force. Representing himself was always about the appearance of education, of calibrated, strategic thinking. The opportunity to escape arose as a by-product of the status-obsessed actions of a man who failed out of the only third-rate law school that would take him, and then, instead of working harder, he cheated and lied his way back into the classroom, taking a spot from someone who actually deserved it.

And yet the myth of his mastermind persists, though a few Google searches is all it takes to corroborate the truth.

When my daughter was young, I found myself telling her what my mother had told me—that she had to wait at least an hour to swim after eating. *Why?* she would argue, tiny fists on tiny hips, chocolate ice cream ringing her frowny mouth. *Because you'll get a cramp and drown.* Recently, my daughter forwarded me an article debunking some of the most common old wives' tales. Waiting to swim after eating was first on the list. The Red Cross Scientific Advisory Council had come out and said there was not a single reported case of eating contributing to drowning. We laughed about it; it was one of those rules that had led to some of our most legendary fights.

Sometimes I think The Defendant is just another old wives' tale. That law enforcement backed up his self-purported claims of brilliance to cover up their own incompetence—in interviews they gave the media, in testimonies they made before the judge—and it all cemented from there, hardening into a generational truth passed down from mother to daughter. Consider this my own warning: The man was no diabolical genius. He was your run-of-the-mill incel whom I caught picking his nose in the courtroom. More than once.

Glenwood Springs was a blink-and-you'll-miss-it kind of town, population 4,993—*4,994, congratulations to the O'Toole family*, read a handwritten amendment affixed to the welcome sign off the exit. We stopped for lunch at a place called The Stew Pot. Skis propped against the log cabin exterior, water trapper mats at the front door, and college guys in duct-taped down jackets.

The waitress came bounding over with the energy of someone who spent all her free time outdoors, her face freckled and tanned by the winter sun. "What can I get you folks today?"

I ordered the chicken club. Carl, the chili.

"Which one do you prefer," Tina asked the waitress, "the prime rib or the filet?"

"Depends what you're in the mood for," she said. "The filet is my favorite, but on the smaller size. Prime rib has more marbling, and it's"—she demonstrated with her hands, big, heavy slab of *meat*—"so it really depends on how hungry you are."

"I'll have the filet," Tina said, "and the prime rib to go. With a side of carrots and mashed potatoes. Where's the bathroom?"

The waitress pointed, and Tina balled up the paper napkin on her lap and left it in a wrinkled wad on the table.

"Good conditions this weekend," the waitress said to us as she collected our menus. "You came at the right time. March is our busiest month, but I've gotten my best runs in January."

"Actually," Carl said, "I'm from the *Tallahassee Democrat*. Do you mind if I ask you your name?"

"The *Tallahassee Democrat*?" The waitress's demeanor turned instantly guarded. "Is this about the election?"

Carl glanced at me curiously. "It's the name of a newspaper in Florida."

The waitress looked down at us with a long sigh. "Uh-huh" was all she said.

"We don't know anything about an election," I promised her.

"Well, you should," she said sharply, "if you're here to do a story about all of it."

"Would you be willing to speak to me?" Carl asked. "On or off the record, your choice."

"You're free to use my name," she said, shifting the tall menus onto her hip and tapping the name badge on her blouse. *Lisa.* "I'm disgusted by what's going on here, and I don't care who knows it." Lisa nodded at another group of diners, over our heads, who were signaling her for the check. "Come back tomorrow around this same time. I'm off after breakfast service."

We were scheduled to fly back later that evening.

"I'll be here," Carl said before I could explain that we'd be gone by then. Lisa nodded and hurried off.

"I can't stay," I said when she'd gone. "I have to get back tonight."

"But it's the weekend," Carl said, tearing open a dinner roll and stuffing a cold pat of butter inside. "What does it matter?"

"We're moving back into The House on Sunday, and I need tomorrow to get everything in order."

"Is that really a good idea?" Carl sank his large teeth into the hard outer crust of the roll, sending crumbs flying everywhere.

I reached across the table for Tina's napkin, sweeping golden flakes into an open palm. "I actually can't imagine a safer place for us to be. Everyone's eyes are on The House right now. He'd be a fool to come back."

This was the argument I'd put forth to the rest of the girls, the one I wholeheartedly and foolishly believed.

The Sheriff's Department in Glenwood Springs contained nine jail cells, and one of them had been repurposed into a visitors' room. There was a lumpy old love seat and a bistro dining set that not only looked like something someone had donated when they decided to pull the trigger on new furniture but, Tina pointed out, sported whittled metal legs that were not even bolted into the floor. The three of us sat at the table and waited an hour past our scheduled appointment. Apparently, Gerald had been assigned to do some yardwork at one of the national parks, and the job had to be completed before the sun set. At long last, a man wearing a prison-issued parka and knit cap appeared, a stone-faced guard at his heels. The prisoner smirked at his captor, who unlocked the door to the visitors' cell and gestured for him to step in first.

"Always the gentleman, Sammy," said the prisoner, and he had to raise both his hands to mime tipping the brim of his hat because they were cuffed. This was Gerald Stevens. "I'm starving," he said, drumming his belly demonstrably, and Tina popped the lid on the take-out container.

"It *was* hot," she said.

Gerald didn't seem to mind. He went over to the love seat and tore apart his cold prime rib with his bare hands; at least they didn't give him a knife.

"And the rest?" Gerald asked, sucking grease off a finger. Tina got up, hooking her finger through the handle of a small shopping bag and going over to dangle it before Gerald: a carton of Marlboro Reds, a six-pack of Coke, and a tin of chocolate chip cookies. That's what he'd asked for, in exchange for answering any questions we had about his 107 days as The Defendant's cellmate.

Gerald pulled the tab on a can of soda, chugging the whole thing in four long gulps. Blink, and I could have been at Brian's fraternity house on a Tuesday night. He drew an arm across his upper lip and sat waiting with watery eyes to burp. He was an average, angry-looking man. Light brown hair, dark brown eyes, normal height, normal weight. On Christmas morning 1976, he'd walked into a home in Aspen high and drunk and held up a family at gunpoint, making off with the woman's jewelry and the family station wagon. He'd never killed anyone, that he could remember.

"I got everything you asked for," Tina reminded him. *We made a deal.*

Gerald dotted the corners of his lips with a paper napkin, in no great rush to keep up his end of the bargain.

I checked my watch anxiously. At this rate, there was no way we were making the red-eye back to Tallahassee.

"We're hoping you can perhaps shed some light on where The Defendant's head was at right before he escaped," Carl prompted.

"What's he gone and done now?" Gerald bit into the cigarette carton's wrap and spit a sliver of plastic out of the corner of his mouth like chewing tobacco.

"We're not sure he's done anything yet," Carl said.

"What's it you suspect him of doing, then?" Gerald gestured for someone to light him up. Tina reached into her purse, obliging.

"Did he ever talk about where he might go if he got the chance to escape again?" Tina rolled the lighter's wheel with her thumb and offered the flame to Gerald, who leaned in to meet it. I was impressed that Tina hadn't mentioned Florida, which could have easily led Gerald into giving her the answer she wanted. That although she had an agenda, she could show restraint.

"I'm no snitch." Gerald's nostrils pulsed with smoke. He considered that declaration while the air between the love seat and bistro table dispersed in various directions. "Not opposed to it on principle. Just not my line of work, you see." He shot a gummy grin at the guard, who stared straight ahead at the wall, expressionless.

Tina nudged me with her elbow and made eyes. *Now. Now is the time.* I reached into my purse. "These are my friends," I said, bringing out the photographs of Denise and Robbie. I'd stuffed an envelope full of options that Tina had reviewed on the flight. We'd gone with the ones from field day, the girls on home plate wearing red shorts and red baseball caps, posing with bats and tough faces. I was worried it was too much leg, but Tina had said to bring photographs that wouldn't appear in the newspaper. The flat, soulless yearbook style, which made the subjects look like it was their born destiny to have their untimely deaths reported in the paper, didn't pull at anyone's heartstrings.

"Denise is the one with the paint on her face," I said while Carl brought the images over to the love seat where Gerald sat. "And Robbie is the one wearing kneepads. They were both killed two weeks ago, and we just"—I inhaled shakily—"we just don't want anyone else to get hurt."

Gerald's eyes flicked over Robbie and Denise emptily. He pulled the tab on his second can of soda and said, "You're asking the wrong guy."

"Who do we ask, then?" Carl said.

"The right guy." Gerald's smile was toothless.

There was a metallic clang then, like the heavy steel door had been thrown open with too much force and collided with the bars of the jail cell behind it. Someone muttered, "*Dang it,*" and I heard that traditional wood heel striking the cement floor, a man whistling a leisurely tune. The guard reacted as though the fire alarm had gone off. He came toward Gerald and slipped a hand beneath his armpit, hauling him to his feet, telling him his time was up.

"But we've barely been here ten minutes!" Tina cried.

"Visiting hours are from nine to four," a new voice said, and we turned to see a grandfatherly man outfitted in all khaki and, yes, cowboy boots, the walking kind with the slight slant, fitting his key into the door of the visitors' cell. "You can come back tomorrow."

"I sure hope they do, Sheriff," Gerald said agreeably. "Bring me the filet next time," he told Tina, sucking on his lips lewdly as the guard led him out.

"We're leaving tonight, sir," I told the Glenwood Springs sheriff. I dreaded having to address anyone as *sir* or *ma'am*. That wasn't how I was raised, and no matter how hard I tried, I always sounded like I was mocking the person to whom I was supposed to be showing respect.

"You should have come earlier, then," he said unsympathetically, and motioned for us to follow him, wriggling his meaty fingers like he was tickling something from the underside. I felt an extreme revulsion rise up in me.

"We did get here earlier," I couldn't stop myself from saying as I got up and followed him into the prison's reception area. "On time. You were the ones who were late, sir."

"Our sincerest apologies, ma'am," the sheriff said, about as insincere as I'd ever heard a person, "but the prison transport van had to go to the shop for a little tune-up, and the guys got a late start at the park."

"How convenient," Tina remarked.

"You need me to look at it, sir?" Carl offered in an obsequious voice. When the sheriff glanced back at him, he added, "I was an airplane mechanic in the army."

The sheriff swung the door wide with the side of his forearm. "Thank you for your service, but we go to the automobile mechanic when there's a problem with our automobiles. You folks have a nice evening." It wasn't enough to allow the door to swing shut behind him; the sheriff pulled it closed with two hands on the knob, then tugged down the security shade for good measure.

Outside, the sun had dipped beneath the snowcaps, but the sky remained a soft, stained blue. Tina looked up, then back down at the hunk of gold on her wrist. It was a Rolex with the jubilee bracelet and jade mosaic dial, the same one my father wore.

"It's three fifty-one," Tina said. The three of us stood there, forming a small ring and passing between us a look weighted with understanding. We'd had nine minutes left with Gerald, enough time for him to tell us whatever it was they did not want him to tell. We'd stumbled onto something here in Colorado, and possibly it was the truth.

RUTH

Aspen

Winter 1974

saw the kitchen curtains flutter furtively as Tina reversed out of the driveway. My mother had been opening and shutting drawers with deep, woeful sighs when I'd told her I was leaving, like finding anything she needed was impossible now that I'd organized the kitchen for her. It was as good a goodbye as I was going to get. My fifty-two-year-old mother turned into a sullen teenager when she didn't get her way, giving her oppressor flat, monosyllabic answers when a shrug or nod wouldn't do. Normally, when she iced me out like this, I spiraled into a state of unparalleled terror. I'd become convinced that not only did everyone hate me but I had cancer and I was going to die. But on the day Tina and I left for Aspen, I was too in love with my face to care. In the bathroom mirror, I tilted my chin down and up, turned my head left and right. The only bump on my face was my nose, and I had always liked my nose.

Aspen. I felt so worldly saying it: *I'm headed to Ah-spin for the weekend.* Tina was wearing not an outfit but an ensemble—knit hat with a cute pom-pom on top, a fuzzy white jacket, suede and fur snow boots that made her legs look miles long. I wouldn't have been able to stand looking at her if I didn't feel so beautiful myself. People could finally see my bright eyes, my pale skin, and my pitch-black hair. Earlier that week, a little girl in the grocery store had tugged her mother's sleeve and asked her what Snow White was doing in the cereal aisle.

"Have you ever been?" Tina asked once we were at the airport, waiting to board the flight.

"Just drove through once when I was a kid," I said.

"It's totally plush. There's this place on the mountain. It's all glass, and it feels like you're drinking champagne outside." Tina smiled longingly. "I always wanted to go back and actually enjoy myself."

"You didn't have a good time before?"

Tina's smile faded. "Oh. I came with Ed. We spent most of our time in the room."

I giggled. "Ooh la la."

Crossly, Tina said, "Because he was eighty-three years old and not feeling well."

The hotel was swankier than the place CJ had taken me on our honeymoon. In the lobby, a fire danced on the hearth's stage, green apples gleamed in bowls, and uniformed staff milled about, refusing to let you touch your bags or press the button to the elevator. Tina tipped every last bellhop, even the one who did nothing but hold the door for us. Alone in the hotel room, which was smaller than I think we'd both anticipated, I awkwardly asked how much I owed her for the weekend. I didn't have a ton of money to throw around, but I had a small amount saved from the time I worked as a cashier at the pharmacy during the last few months of my dying marriage, enough to pick up dinner one night.

"The conference is paying for the hotel room," Tina said. "Let me get the rest. It's the least I can do. I would be miserable if I were here alone. You're really helping me out, Ruth. You have no idea." I might have thought she was laying it on a little thick, doing that thing rich people do where they act like *they* owe *you* so as not to make you feel like some pitiful charity case. But Tina was wringing her hands, suddenly seeming very young and unsure of herself. "Let's go down and get some dinner," she said before I could refuse her offer. "I could use about ten drinks."

We ordered steak and split a bottle of red wine and a slice of cheesecake for dessert. I ate my half, but Tina only scored the custardy surface with the tines of her fork, distractedly, while she nursed a nightcap of whiskey. Up until dessert, she'd been in a great mood. She was loud and pally with the waitress, cracking jokes about the biceps the girl must have developed while ferrying the huge silver trays from the other side of the hotel, where, stupidly, the kitchen operated.

"Let's go upstairs and get a good night's sleep," I told Tina after she signed the check. When the waitress collected the billfold and saw her tip, her eyebrows shot way up.

In the room, Tina tried on different outfits for me. She'd packed five options, everything brand-new, tags dangling from the care labels. I wanted to be annoyed—she must know she looked spectacular in everything, did she really need me to say it?—but objectively, the woman was a wreck.

"Do you think we can practice?" she asked me after we decided on a slim-fitted black wool sweater and tweed pencil skirt with a thick belt that made her waist look slimmer than it already was. "I'm too worked up to go to bed."

"What do you need me to do?"

Tina went over to the desk area and dragged out the chair so that it was facing the foot of the bed. "You sit here," she said. She perched on the edge of the bed and crossed her legs, hooking her hands around her knee. She was barefoot, wearing the tweed skirt and a lacy silk camisole. She'd packed the third floor of Frederick & Nelson but no bra. "So I'm the therapist and you're the patient," she explained. "And this is just pretend. I mean, you can say real stuff if you want, but you can also make it up."

"Got it."

"But also, just go along with what I say."

I nodded, trying to keep a straight face. Tina was blushing, and it was very sweet.

"It's stupid, but I have to introduce myself."

I laughed. "Just go already!"

Tina seemed to hear herself at last, and she laughed a little too. She closed her eyes, inhaled deep, and dropped her shoulders on her long exhale. Her eyes opened, revealing a composed and capable woman. "Hi, Ruth. I'm Dr. Cannon. It's nice to meet you."

Dr. Cannon. How thrilling for her. I smiled widely. "It's nice to meet you too, Dr. Cannon."

"I understand you have been referred to me by your physician because you've been feeling depressed recently."

"I have been feeling a bit down, yes."

Tina nodded approvingly, as if to say, *Good job playing along.* "And how long have you been feeling like that?"

"Oh." I worried my face with a hand, thinking. "Do you mean this time or last?"

"So you've had spells before?"

"I guess you could call them that."

"Let's talk about the first time."

The room seemed to darken as I thought about the first time. "I was in high school."

"Did anything happen to trigger it?"

I saw my sister-in-law's face—her real face, features slack and helpless—and then I saw my father's, his heartbroken horror. "I got in some trouble."

"What sort of trouble?"

Tina had positioned the chair too close to the bed. I scooted back before our knees grazed. "It was on school grounds. My dad was a teacher there, and he tried to stick up for me, but, well . . . in the end it was best for everyone if I left."

"That must have been devastating for you."

"I guess," I said disagreeably. I didn't care for the word *devastating.* It implied a sort of wartime destruction, a razing to the ground, and I was made of stronger stuff than that. "I had a problem, and it was better for me to be someplace where I could get help, anyway."

Tina didn't bat an eye at that. "So you received professional care after that first spell?"

I realized I was sitting on my hands and that they were going numb. *Here is where I should probably make something up,* I thought, but my mind went blank with everything except the truth about the nine months I'd spent at Eastern State. I sat, tolerating the pins and needles in my fingertips and saying nothing for a long stretch of time.

"It's okay to stop here for now," Tina said. "Sometimes the only way to talk about a difficult event is to give ourselves permission to stop when it gets to be too much. Each time you go into it, the hope is that you push yourself a little further."

I nodded, my eyes downcast, feeling exposed and a little resentful. Tina stretched her arms over her head with an extravagant yawn. "I'm finally tired now. Thanks, Ruth. You've saved me again."

In the middle of the night, I awoke to the sound of Tina crying. She was on her side, facing away from me and trying to be quiet about it, but the sound was unmissable. I'd gone to bed regretting having shared so much with Tina, but a balance had been restored once again, both of us unmasked in our misery. Feeling something like kinship, I was lulled back to sleep.

I woke again from a disgusting dream. I was having sex with my brother, and I knew it was wrong, but I couldn't help feeling aroused. When I opened my eyes, I found that I was curled into Tina's back, my knees in the crook of Tina's knees, her backside nestled into my swollen pelvis. I'd been sleeping with my hands on either side of my face, squeezed into fists, my forehead pressed between Tina's shoulder blades, like I was cold or ducking behind Tina for cover.

In the morning we were both serious and stiff. We showered and got ready in near silence. Tina wore a different outfit than the one we'd picked out the night before, a blue dress that was gorgeous but big in the bust. On the bed, she'd left the wool sweater and tweed pencil skirt, the thick black belt that had made a disappearing act of her waist.

"Black doesn't wash you out the way it does most blondes," Tina said with a wink, suggesting she was, of course, the exception to that rule. I was encouraged to catch a glimpse of her old cocky self, and while I wanted nothing more than to cloak myself in that heavy, heady tweed, I hesitated.

"You're spending a lot of money on me," I said.

Tina clasped a string of pearls around her neck. "The way I see it, we both deserve to be treated with value and respect. And people treat you like that when you look like you have money. Wear the fucking skirt, Ruth."

———

The elevator doors opened, and an older man and a younger woman stepped back against the mirrored wall to make room. He was wearing a suit and tie, she a pair of bulky ski pants and a weatherproof coat. The man took us in and remarked to the woman, harmlessly enough, "I think we're all a little jealous."

The woman turned to him quizzically. "How do you mean?"

He indicated her outdoor clothing. "I was hoping to catch a run or two while I was here. But the schedule this year." He groaned. "I'll be lucky if they let me use the bathroom."

"I'm here for the conference too," the woman said in a prickly tone. "With the Forensic Anthropology Group."

In the elevator's front mirror paneling, she and I made eye contact. She rolled her eyes and mouthed two words. *Of course.* Of course he would assume she wasn't one of them, she meant, though it seemed to me an honest enough mistake, since she was outfitted to go skiing.

The doors opened to a lobby roaming with men yoked with lanyards. I followed Tina to the large poster board that read *Welcome, Healthcare Professionals of America!* Tina ran a finger down the day's schedule until she found the listing and location for her breakout session. Offhandedly, I noticed that members of the Forensic Anthropology Group had been instructed to meet at the valet station. Their bus was departing promptly at nine a.m. It struck me as curious then—a forensic anthropology group. Was that something to do with horticulture? But what would that have to do with a medical conference?

"We have ten minutes," Tina said, twisting and slapping the face on her clunky man's watch, as though the battery had gone out.

"Do you want any coffee before we head in?" I asked her.

Tina shook her hands out, like a runner loosening up before a race. "Nuh-uh. I'm too jittery already. If you want to go grab some, I'll wait here for you."

The man from the elevator was blocking the table. "Excuse me," I said. He took an exaggerated, almost scornful step to the side, but then he got a better look at me, and I felt a distinct shift in his energy.

"Not sure how you take it, but they're out of milk," he told me. "Someone is bringing out a fresh pitcher."

"I burn my tongue without milk," I said.

He held up his mug in solidarity. "Are you here with the psychiatric group?"

I could feel the weight of the tweed skirt on my legs, its warm, important swaddle. "I'm with my friend. She's getting her license."

"I did think, what are the odds that all three women on the elevator are here for the conference?" he mused, and I retracted the generous thought that he had made an honest mistake. "Smart move to include the shrinks this year. Healthy mind, healthy body, and that's coming from a cardiologist." He patted his ticker with a laugh. "Ah, here is the milk." He reached for the pitcher, the fabric of his jacket setting off a spark as it brushed the wool of my sweater. "I asked for low-fat. Better for the figure and the heart."

I'd envisioned an auditorium with a stage, velvet curtain drawn, prop couch on which the mock patient would lie, prop chair on which Tina would psychoanalyze her. Of course, Tina's patient would be a woman. Women generally had more troubles than men, and it was the men, generally, who were trained to treat them. It was the way

of things at Eastern State, and it was the way of things in that narrow
banquet room painted to resemble a European chalet, no stage and
no women but the two of us, that smelled of morning breath and
aftershave.

At the check-in table, the moderator introduced himself as
Dr. Harold Bradbar and gave Tina a name tag to fill out, along with
copies of her patient's medical transcripts to study. He indicated my
coffee mug and asked if I'd like a refill, lifting a hammered silver carafe. I was wondering when Folgers became the official sponsor of
libidinous old men when he said to Tina, "Could you run this back
to the lobby and get us some more before we start?"

"I'm so sorry," Tina said with a winning smile, "but I need to
study this."

I reached for the handle. "I can do it," I volunteered.

Tina grabbed my arm and tugged me away. "You can't either,
remember?" As she muscled me to the back row, she said under her
breath, "Frances warned me they would do that."

"Do what?"

"Ask you to get coffee. Take minutes. Secretarial stuff. You have
to say no, or they'll never see you as one of them. But do it nicely, or
you're a lib bitch."

"Oh," I said, feeling thick.

"It's okay," Tina said as we took our seats. "I would have happily
trotted back to the lobby if no one had warned me first. Helping is a
bad habit I'm trying to break."

"Helping people is a bad habit?"

"Feeding the hungry is helping people," Tina said. "Getting their
coffee is servitude." She bowed her head over the transcript. "I really
do have to study this now."

When it was Tina's turn, an amused hush fell over the room, as
though the polar bear had climbed out of the water at the zoo
and we were all waiting to see what it would do. It was so quiet

you could hear the silky fabric of Tina's blue dress swishing between her thighs as she made her way to the front of the room;
there was something faintly vulgar about that sound and where
it was coming from, and Tina was pink-cheeked by the time she
took her seat.

Tina adjusted her skirt so that it covered her knees as Dr. Bradbar introduced her patient, a forty-three-year-old woman who had
been receiving electroshock therapy for rage attacks. Two men in
front of me looked at each other and, without needing to say a word,
shared a low laugh. I cleared my throat audaciously, and one of them
shot me a withering look over his shoulder. I panicked and cleared
it again, mouthing *sorry* as I pointed to my throat to signal there was
really something stuck in there and that I was not in fact a lib bitch.

Then the floor was Tina's, and for a moment, I wanted to run
straight out of the room. It was nightmarishly quiet, and there was
a scarlet rash mottling Tina's neck and chest, poison red against the
blue of her dress. Suddenly, she rose from her chair and dragged it
closer to her patient. They had been placed rather far apart, I realized. When she sat down again, the chair cushion emitted a juvenile
puff of air that drew muffled laughter.

"I hear you're struggling to control your anger," Tina began in
a loud voice that shook, and gestured for her patient to enumerate.

The anger experienced by Tina's client was directed at her husband and children. She was studying for her real estate license, and
none of them could be bothered to pitch in just a little bit around the
house. She would rant and rave when she came home from class to
find dirty dishes left in the den and laundry molding in the washing
machine. Things came to a head the night she shattered one of those
dirty dishes and threatened her teenage son with a shard of porcelain. Her husband called the police, and the police referred them to a
local psychiatrist who diagnosed her with rage attacks. Electroshock
therapy hadn't been helping.

Maybe I was imagining it, but Tina's rash seemed to recede as
the patient described her condition. My shoulders dropped, and

the urge to flee from what seemed like Tina's imminent humiliation vanished.

"Tell me," Tina said in a commanding voice that still trembled on certain words, "do you ever feel anger toward people who are not your husband or children?"

"Oh, I'm angry all the time," the woman said, which elicited plenty of laughs.

Tina looked out at the crowd and indulged them with a rueful smile. "Give me an example," she said.

The patient mulled it over. "At the grocery store, for instance, when someone takes too long at the deli counter. Show some common courtesy. You can see all these people are waiting. You couldn't have made up your mind about what you wanted before your number was called?"

"And do you ever yell and scream at those people?"

"Of course not. Never."

"How come?"

The answer was so obvious the patient laughed. "Because they would think I was crazy."

"And you don't want them to think you're crazy."

"I do not."

Tina stared off into the middle distance, organizing her thoughts. Someone coughed impatiently. I blushed on Tina's behalf.

Tina focused her sights on the patient. "If you had to weigh your feelings of anger toward those people in the grocery store against those you have toward your children and husband, would you say that the anger you feel in the deli line is more or less intense than it is at home?"

"More," the woman said without hesitation.

"And why is that?"

"Because the people at the grocery store are strangers to me. I don't know any of their good qualities. I feel nothing toward them but anger."

"And yet," Tina pointed out, "you are able to control your anger with them, even though you experience it more intensely at the grocery store than you do at home."

At this I dared a look around. Surely others must be as impressed as I was. I could see where this was going, and Tina's logic was undeniably sound. But either people were listening with snide half smiles or they were dozing off.

The patient pursed her lower lip in concentration. "Yes. Clearly, I can keep ahold of myself if I want to."

"So it's actually inaccurate to say that you can't control your anger."

"I suppose it is, and I'll give you that, I never stopped to think of it that way. But I don't want to just control my anger. I want to get rid of it."

"What if I told you that would not be my recommendation?"

"I don't follow."

Tina's gaze swept the room as she delivered the diagnosis—not for the patient but for her audience. "I'd like to propose that anger in women is treated as a character disorder, as a problem to be solved, when oftentimes it is entirely appropriate, given the circumstances that trigger it."

That incited a mild mutiny, everyone in the room crossing and recrossing their legs, adjusting pants legs and crotch seams, clearing contempt from their chests.

The patient scanned the crowd a little desperately, as though searching for a real doctor to come and save her. "You think breaking a dish in my child's face is appropriate?"

Tina answered with a tolerant smile. "We don't want you doing that. But I wouldn't label that as excessive. You're fed up and you're exhausted, and no one is listening to your pleas for help. Anger in that case is very much appropriate."

The patient sighed begrudgingly. "I don't know that I agree, but say it's true. I still don't want to go around breaking things."

"No," Tina agreed, "that's not a productive outlet for your anger, though it is one less dish to wash." The patient let out a yip of involuntary laughter, and the man in front of me turned to his friend and inquired casually about lunch.

"I've heard The Stew Pot is good," the other replied, so that I could only grasp pieces of Tina's treatment plan. Something about shifting, accepting, but it was impossible to hear, not just over the two men discussing their lunch options but because the rest of the room had resumed conversation as well, at an insouciant, punishing volume.

"Shush," I said, too timidly for anyone to mind me, as Tina returned to her seat. There were sweat stains beneath the seams of her bust and before she sat I could see them all down the length of her back too.

"That was about what I expected," Tina muttered dryly. She lifted the hair at the nape of her neck, fanning her damp skin, and shot me a covert smile. "Let's get very drunk after this."

PAMELA

Aspen, 1978

Day 12

We missed our flight by ten minutes. Carl was planning on taking the next available one anyway so he could interview the waitress from The Stew Pot after her Saturday breakfast shift, but I was beside myself to learn that it wouldn't depart until the following evening, with a three-hour layover in Denver. I'd arrive in Tallahassee at 5:19 Sunday morning, wearing the same shirt I'd been wearing since Friday morning, smelling like *jail*. I held back furious tears as the airline attendant took us through the rebooking process; I was thinking about everything I'd meant to do on Saturday to get The House ready for Sunday. Buy the ingredients for the cupcakes and have them in the oven by noon, which was when the locksmith was scheduled to arrive and fit the doors with the new combination locks. Brian had a brief window of free time in the afternoon during which he'd promised to come over and help me move around the furniture in the rec room so I could transform the space into a nest. I'd asked the alumna whose family ran the sporting goods warehouse on the outskirts of town if they would give me a discount on a bulk supply of sleeping bags. I wanted the first night back to feel like one big sleepover party, everyone burrowed in a warm puppy pile, eating junk food and staying up too late watching classic black-and-white movies. I wanted us to have fun again.

"It's Friday night, so it's not like you're missing class," Tina consoled me, when she saw how distraught I was about missing our flight. "Plus, I know a nice hotel. My treat, everyone." Carl looked pretty relieved to hear that.

I put on a brave smile. Maybe Brian could meet the locksmith, and I could just buy the cupcakes. I was getting in early enough on Sunday to pull it off. I'd be wiped, but that was the easiest part to cheat.

The hotel was nicer than nice, the sort of place my mother would book. The staff wore smart navy uniforms with white piping, and the clientele was the sort who came to be seen in the latest skiwear fashions more than they did to take a run in them. Neon and fur, no duct tape holding their jackets together.

"Good evening, Ms. Cannon," said the front-desk clerk. "Is this your first time staying with us?"

"It is not," Tina said.

"Welcome back!"

Tina's smile was thin. My stomach churned with unease. "Is this the hotel where—"

"Yes," Tina said hastily.

Carl and I glanced at the lobby area where Caryn Campbell had sat five years ago, playing board games and combing through the magazines in the honeyed leather rack, finding none that interested her. Where she had sighed irritably, wondered aloud why there wasn't any reading material for women, and told her fiancé she'd be gone only a minute.

"Lightning doesn't strike twice," Tina said.

That had been my rationale as well—to my sisters, to their parents and my parents, to the Panhellenic council based in Cleveland, who I knew were pleased with me for setting a date to move back into The House, for circling the Sunday in January on which we would ostensibly move on. The council did not want a couple of salacious headlines to overshadow a storied seventy-five-year history, and some people have perverted that over the years, as though our governing body cared more about our reputation than they did our safety. But wanting us to return to normal as quickly as possible came from a well-meaning place. In their minds, if a woman didn't get back on the horse immediately after she was thrown, she stayed down.

At the end of the day, I did believe what I was parroting to everyone. That there was no safer place for all of us than The House. The odds of another bloody attack under our roof, with everyone's eyes on the L-shaped property between Seminole and West Jefferson Street—well, they seemed more in our favor than they did anywhere else in the state of Florida.

In the elevator, Carl's stomach grumbled loudly. He brought his hand to his abdomen with a laugh.

"I'm starving too," I realized.

"Let's meet back downstairs in ten," Tina said as we headed for the elevator with our individual room keys in hand. I'd told Tina not to spend money on a room for me, that I was fine to share with her, but she got very flustered and insisted we each have our own space.

In my room, I found my small duffel bag already unzipped and splayed open on the luggage stand. I always traveled with a toothbrush and floss. To this day I am that person whom you'll find flossing in the firm's bathroom after lunch, though since 2001 the firm has been mine, so anyone who has a problem with that isn't exactly in the position to take it up with management.

Without really looking, I took the toiletry kit into the bathroom and unzipped it. Inside I found men's shaving cream and a battered box of Band-Aids. I went back out into the room and saw that the canvas duffel was a beaten army green, hysterically masculine, and when I went to return the toiletry kit, I noticed Carl had packed a copy of *Helter Skelter*, the firsthand account of the Charles Manson murders written by the lead prosecutor. My father had devoured that book too, wondered with a laugh if he should go the way of Vincent Bugliosi—prosecute a diabolical criminal and sell the story for a fat check. Spend the rest of his days on the golf course.

I called down to the front desk and explained they'd put Carl's bag in my room by accident. While I waited for them to deliver my things, I dialed the number for Turq House. The cook answered and I asked for Brian.

"We're spending the night now," I told him.

"Spending the night?" I could hear the concern in Brian's voice. "That wasn't the plan, was it?"

"No, but we missed our flight."

Brian laughed. "*You* missed a flight?"

"Please," I moaned, "I already feel horrible enough about it. The interview didn't start on time. I swear the sheriff did it on purpose. It's clear he doesn't want us speaking to the cellmate."

"Did he manage to tell you anything worthwhile?"

The right guy. That had been Gerald's response when Carl asked who might have information about The Defendant's whereabouts. Something about it was knocking around my brain belligerently.

"No," I admitted. "But one of the locals might." I told him about the encounter with the waitress.

"I wouldn't put too much stock in town gossip," Brian said.

"We don't even know what she's going to say," I snapped. There was a long pause, and I knew Brian felt like he was owed an apology. "Sorry," I added reluctantly.

"Forgiven," he said, and I surprised myself by rolling my eyes. "Speaking of gossip . . ." He trailed off tantalizingly.

I pressed the phone closer to my ear, intrigued. "What about it?"

"One of the guys here—John Davis. Freshman. He's from Dallas."

"Okay."

"That woman—Martina, Tina, whatever—that's where she's originally from. He told me something. Pretty alarming. Makes me a little worried you're there alone with her, actually."

"I'm not alone with her," I said. "I have my own hotel room, and the reporter is with us, the one who wrote that nice piece about Denise."

"Hey," Brian protested, an edge to his voice. "I thought you weren't allowed to talk to the press."

"That was a suggestion," I replied tersely, "not a hard-and-fast rule."

There was a crackling silence between us.

"Anyway," I said, "I can guess what you're going to tell me. I know all about the husband and how he died and left his kids out of the will. Tina told me herself."

"Did she also tell you about Ruth?" Brian asked.

"Her friend who went missing?"

Another pause, this one worrisome. "Actually, Pamela," Brian said, "it seems you don't know what I was going to say."

———

Tina was spearing a plate of salad when I came downstairs. "You two were taking forever," she complained as I slid into the red leather booth across from her. The restaurant had stone walls and timber beams, wild game on the menu, and a rowdy, dispersing crowd. It was nine thirty on a Friday night, and the group at the bar was readying to move on to a popular line-dancing club down the block.

"There was a mix-up with our bags," I said, glancing at the untouched place setting. I wondered if I had enough time to have this conversation before Carl joined us, if I should hold off until I knew we wouldn't be interrupted. "I need to ask you something," I ended up saying in a spontaneous burst. "About Ruth."

"Shoot," Tina said, fitting a fat wedge of tomato in her mouth.

"Was Ruth . . ." I found I didn't know what word to use. "Your lover?"

Tina's fork clattered to her plate, and her hand went to her mouth. For a moment, I thought I had offended her, and I almost apologized. Then I noticed her shoulders quivering. She was laughing. Silently, her eyes in slits. It turned into such an ordeal that she had to spit out the unchewed piece of tomato into her dinner napkin.

"Sorry," she managed, bundling up its pulpy remains. "But *lover*?" She made a puke face, caught the giggles again. "Is Brian your *lover*?"

"Excuse me," I objected. "No. He's my steady boyfriend. Fiancé, actually."

Tina did something approximating a seated curtsy. *Fiancé. How noble.* "Congratulations are in order then," she said mordantly, re-trieving her salad fork and wiping the handle clean. "Ruth and I had a romantic relationship, sure." She went back to lancing the bed of lettuce before her. "It's not a secret or anything I'm ashamed of."

"Except it was a secret."

The fork struck the plate in a caustic way that made me grind my back molars.

"You called her a friend," I said stridently. I was angry, I realized. I felt lied to, taken advantage of. "And I'm sitting there wondering why her family aren't the ones chasing answers for her. Or why the police don't seem to like you or want to work with you. And it turns out it's because you haven't been forthcoming about your relation-ship with the victim. I'm prelaw—"

"So you've mentioned—"

"And people who omit key information," I boomed over her, "people like you, you aren't considered credible. You left out an im-portant piece of the puzzle in order to convince me to be in cahoots with you, and now I look like I've been manipulated. Now my repu-tation could be in question."

Tina had amassed quite the collection of spinach leaves while I spoke, none of which she showed any intention of eating. "Maybe I prefer to prove myself a credible person first." She sniffed, disgusted, like she'd caught a whiff of a foul odor. "Since the world isn't all that understanding of *people like me.*"

"What you do in your personal life is none of my business."

Tina laughed abrasively. "Right back at you, Pamela."

"What's that supposed to mean?"

Infuriatingly, Tina said nothing. She kept stabbing away at her salad. I couldn't take it one more second. I snatched the plate away from her. She froze with her fork raised mid-blow.

"What have I done that could possibly invite criticism from any-one?" I demanded. "I do everything by the rule book."

"By whose rule book? That sexist cult they let you think you run?"

I sent the plate spinning back in her direction. "*That's* sexism, actually."

Tina picked spinach off her blouse; flicked it onto the table. Coolly, she asked, "Does the council tell you to say that?"

"No one tells me to say anything," I fumed. "I've been a member of this organization going on four years, and I've seen it with my own eyes. The chapter exists to support like-minded women in their goals and values."

"Is going to Shoreline College of Law your one goal and value in life?"

How dare she. "It's Shorebird, and you're a terrible snob."

Tina laid down her fork with a surrendering sigh. Almost sadly, she said, "I know you got into Columbia."

Even though I was furious with her, my chest expanded, full and proud, at the mention of Columbia. Of course I was dying to know how she knew about Columbia, but I had too much pride to ask.

"Despite what you may think," Tina obliged me without my having to ask, "not every member of law enforcement considers me a nuisance. Some of them actually think I'm onto something. Some of them talked to me about the items retrieved from the scene, and one of them told me they found your acceptance letter in Denise's nightstand. She kept that for you. In case she succeeded in getting you to change your mind." Tina folded her hands on the table contritely. Her dark eyebrows relaxed, her whole face smoothing out in a display of genuine remorse. "So now I would like to apologize, because it sounds like Denise was your most avid supporter. And I really have no room to talk." She laughed tiredly. "Psychiatry is one of the patriarchy's favored tools to control women. They're still committing *people like me* for doing what I do *in my personal life.*"

I was breathing like a bull, tears spilling down my cheeks, thinking about Denise holding on to my acceptance letter. I was remembering the remarks Detective Pickell had made during my police interview. About being impressed I'd gotten into Columbia. At the time I assumed I'd told him about it in the immediate aftermath of the attack, that I'd been so out of it I'd forgotten. But that wasn't where he'd heard it. He'd heard it from Denise. He'd heard it from beyond the grave.

"Wild guess here," Tina continued plaintively. "Your fiancé wasn't Ivy material. So you're going to the school you both got into, the one with a goofy name that is criminally beneath you."

I could not bear to meet her eye. Nothing she'd said was so wild at all. "Shorebird has good placement in the job market," I said pathetically to the stone wall. "Better than you would think."

"If he had gotten into Columbia and you hadn't, would he be going to Columbia?"

"Yes, but it isn't the same thing," I rushed to say. "I'm from up there. I'd have friends. Family. Other options."

Tina just looked sorry for me.

"He's not like that," I insisted. "Whatever you're thinking, he's not. Between school and running the chapter and my volunteer hours and my externship, I'm constantly, you know, go, go, go, and he never gives me a hard time. He lets me do whatever I want. Most guys don't do that. And I despise dating. I'd rather stick hot pins in my eyes. Brian is . . . one less thing I have to do." I could hear that I'd lost control of the conversation, that I was losing at this, whatever *this* was.

"He lets you," Tina repeated damningly.

"No!" I cried. "No. I don't mean it like that. You're twisting it. Anything I say, you'll find a way to twist it, because it's not what you think I should be doing. I did struggle with the choice. I did. But in the end. This is . . ." I stopped, picturing my well-bred boyfriend, his needlepoint belts and stringy hair, remembering what it felt like when he threw his arm around me at Denise's funeral, carrying me along at his own sovereign pace. Brian's gait was one that was both sure and easy, as though he had places to be but there was no rush to get there. For him, people would wait. Marrying Brian was something I *should* want, and it made me feel diseased, how little I seemed to want the things that other women my age did without complication.

"This is a good option for me," I concluded.

Tina nodded with profuse empathy. Like everything I said made perfect sense. For a moment, I felt light and unburdened. All I'd had to do was explain it, get that off my chest, and now even Tina had to admit that just because a relationship was complicated, it didn't have to be disposable.

"The hardest part of my job," Tina began in a heartsick voice, "is allowing patients to make their own choices. I cannot tell them what to do or what not to do, even when the right choice is clear as day to me. My role as a shrink is to provide people with a framework to understand what drives them and informs their behavior. A person's childhood shapes everything about that framework. I don't know you well enough to know what happened to you young, why you must always be *going, going, going,* why your life is so tightly scheduled and controlled"—she was making a fist and speaking through a clenched jaw, animating what I supposed she thought was my ironclad attitude toward life—"why you are so distressed by the thought of dating that you'd rather just marry Freddy Frat Boy than face the discomfort and explore what it is all really about. Anyway"—Tina placed her palms on the table and pressed her weight on them, leaning forward like she wanted her words to physically reach me— "you're not my patient, and I'm not your therapist. Which means I can tell you exactly what I think you should do."

The last of the diners were making their way out the door, yelping in the frigid night, on their way to kick up their heels, and I felt myself edging into the corner of my booth, unreasonably frightened about whatever it was Tina was gearing up to say.

"Being back here," Tina said wistfully, watching the happy brigade set off down the powdered street, "I'm reminded of how short life is for some people. Ruth had gotten some really exciting news just before she died. She'd had a difficult few years, but she was finally turning her life around. Look at Denise. About to go off and apprentice with one of the last of the living masters. The two of them break the pattern. Almost all of them do, actually. Enough to establish a *new* pattern."

The beaded sconce above my head flickered malevolently like some sort of paid actor. I knew nothing of patterns, then. Of intelligence, data, the psychology of the offender and his interactions with his victims and society. But in the years since, I've thought about what Tina said to me in that cracked leather banquette every time the story flared like pain in an arthritic joint, waiting for a time when people would realize how wrong they'd gotten things in the sepia-tinted seventies. But those closest to the case have continued to stick to the dog-eared theory that he leaned on his fine patrician bone structure and his magnetism to trick women into going off with him, so I'm done waiting now. I'm done with the defamation of Denise, of all of them. Soon I would learn that there was a group of high school girls within earshot of Ruth on the day he approached her, that they reported to the police that she clearly found him "annoying" though she still agreed to leave the beach with him. Another would-be victim grumbled to her friend she was pretty sure she was about to dance with a felon as she begrudgingly accepted his request for a dance at the night club next door to The House, the same night of the murders. Women got that feeling about him, that funny one we all get when we know something isn't right, but we don't know how to politely extricate ourselves from the situation without escalating the threat of violence or harassment. That is not a skill women are taught, the same way men are not taught that it is okay to leave a woman alone if what she wants is to be left alone.

"No one was lost or struggling or unhappy, all the things that predators usually seek out in their victims because it makes them vulnerable, and vulnerable people are easier to subdue. I've thought about this for so long." Tina brought a fist to her mouth, scraping the thin skin of her knuckles with her two front teeth, the way you do when you want to scream but you can't. "I've tried to make sense of how someone who didn't stalk his victims in advance ended up going after the best and the brightest. And I think that's it, the thing they all had in common—a light that outshone his. He targets college campuses and sorority houses because he's looking for the cream of the crop. He wants to extinguish us—we are the ones who remind him that he's not that smart, not that good-looking, that there's nothing particularly special about him." Tina removed her napkin from her lap and folded it, arranged her silverware upside down on the plate, the way you do to indicate to the waitress that you're finished with your meal. "Because I am not your shrink, I get to say that you do a disservice to them, to every woman who was interrupted in the middle of something good, if you don't tell this fiancé who lets you do what you want to go to hell, because you're going to Columbia."

RUTH

Aspen

Winter 1974

We went to that glass bar, the one Tina told me about at the airport, and we ordered the most expensive bottle of champagne on the menu, celebrating . . . what, exactly? No one had clapped for Tina as she took her seat, not even me. I'd been too intimidated by the stony reception. Even the patient seemed disgruntled, like she wished she'd gotten a different doctor, one who'd written her a prescription and recommended more rest.

We sat by the window, though I suppose everywhere was a window. The floor, the walls, the bar, constructed in heavy double-paned glass. Between my rain boots, skiers cut a course of moguls, looking like astronauts on wooden runners with their orbed helmets and cylindrical goggles. The sun shattered the snow into white-hot shards, winnowing our pupils to specks of dirt in our bright eyes, and soon I was drunk and thinking about Julia Child, whose show my father and I watched religiously, and whose first cookbook was rejected by twenty-one male publishers before going on to sell hundreds of thousands of copies. I felt energized and quickly reframed the whole humiliating morning as the sort of anachronistic anecdote all pioneering women eventually tell at dinner parties thrown in their honor.

We finished our first glasses with giddy speed, and in no time the waiter was by our side, topping us off, excitedly asking what else he could bring us. At the table next to ours, two couples were politely picking through a three-tiered seafood platter heaped with lobster and crab and oysters. My mouth watered.

"We want that," Tina said, indicating with a jut of her chin.

The waiter glanced behind him. "That's the large. For your party size, I'd recommend the small."

"I'm not that hungry," I added, though I hadn't eaten breakfast. I had no idea how much a large seafood platter cost, but it had to be a lot.

Tina ignored us both. "Large, please."

The waiter dipped his head deferentially and returned the deep emerald bottle of champagne to the ice bucket.

"My husband was allergic to seafood," Tina said when we were alone again. "Sometimes I thought about getting a bunch of shrimp"—she mimed mincing them up— "and making a paste. Stirring it into his morning oatmeal."

I stared at her. She was laughing, but she wasn't kidding.

"I know you heard me crying last night," Tina said. "You curled into me after." She was wearing big diamond posts in her ears, and every time she tucked her hair behind her ears, as she did now, her lobes shot laser beams that forced me to turn away from her. "It was sweet," I heard her say. Then, a little shyly, "Don't you want to know why I was crying?"

I did, but still my stomach roiled with fear. Whatever Tina was about to tell me, I sensed it would change something between us. In my cowardice, I hedged, "I know you were nervous about today."

Tina let her hair fall over her ears so that I could look at her painlessly. "I don't cry when I'm nervous."

———

Tina grew up outside of Dallas, in an affluent neighborhood called Highland Park. Her family had money—not oil or real estate money, but enough to send Tina to private schools and pay for horseback riding lessons. Tina had a natural seat, and on weekends she competed in local shows, counting the strides between jumps on Anda-lusians with braided manes, wearing starched white button-downs pinned with blue ribbons. She was ten years old the first time Ed noticed her in the ring.

Ed's daughter was the lead instructor at the barn, and Ed owned the barn. He was the most successful industrial and office builder in the state, and he'd bought the sixty-acre horse farm as a high school graduation gift for his daughter, who competed professionally for a few years before retiring in her late twenties and opening the sta-bles to the public. Her name was Deborah, and she was the meanest person Tina had ever known. She once made Tina take her horse out back and beat his hind leg with a switch after he refused a brush fence and got Tina disqualified from her class.

Ed would drop by the barn with bags of carrots for the horses and cigarettes for the instructors. All that hay and wood everywhere, the animals trapped in their stalls, and horse people smoked like you wouldn't believe. Tina never saw Deb eat, only smoke and drink whiskey that she kept out on the barn's kitchen sink, next to the bot-tle of leather polish.

Tina welcomed Ed's visits because Deb held her tongue around her father. Ed would sit on a bench outside the ring and watch Tina warm up with a long rein in canter, and Deb would refrain from shouting at her *Lean back before you fall off and break your neck and can never brush your pretty blond hair again* as Tina approached the fence. Tina rode for seven years and never once took a fall. You were not considered a real rider until you were thrown, and Deb might have respected Tina more if she'd just let it happen, and no doubt Tina would have been a better rider if she weren't always choking up on the reins to avoid the inevitable, but Tina could never bring herself to let go. It drove Deb crazy. She called Tina a princess, a pampered baby who was afraid of getting dirty and getting hurt.

One day, after a tense hour in the ring, Ed approached Tina as she was hosing down her horse. *I hope you don't mind that I've been coming around so often,* he said, patting the horse's neck, *but I don't want to see you take a spill.* Ed chucked her chin with a knuckle, the gesture brief but establishing—a commencement of something. *Gotta protect that face of yours.* Tina focused hard on guiding a white stripe of sweat from the horse's flank to his hoof. Later, after she quit riding, she learned it was a sign of excessive labor when the horse's sweat foamed white, and she cried for all those times she'd unwittingly rode a living creature so close to collapse.

Ed started bringing little gifts for Tina after that—a horse-shaped Christmas tree ornament, lemon-scented oil for her saddle. For her mother, pouches of French potpourri to hang in her car. *I know how that barn smell lingers,* he'd say, and they'd share a laugh as the unlucky parents of horse children. Tina's mother was thrilled by the attention. She was the type of woman who went around saying she'd met Tina's father "at the office," allowing everyone to assume she was the receptionist. In truth, Tina's mother was the cleaning girl for the building, the daughter of a married white man and an unmarried Mexican teenager, and Edward Eubanks's interest in her daughter, in *her*, subsidized all the gaps in her newly minted Highland Park pedigree.

Ed was a figure in the community, obscenely charitable and well connected. Tina's family found themselves invited into smaller and smaller social circles, on island vacations in smaller and smaller planes. Sometimes her parents weren't invited at all, and it was just Tina and Ed on those islands. Ed was in his seventies and twice divorced. Tina was the same age as most of his grandchildren, and wasn't it fun for Tina, as an only child, to go on vacation and pretend like she had siblings? From the top deck of his beachfront compound in Maui, a cowboy-hatted Ed would watch Tina and his grandkids try to surf. With the Pacific dissolving the orange fireball on the horizon, Ed would call to Tina that it was time to get ready for dinner.

Ed would bathe her in his bathroom, lapping soapy water over her nascent breasts and between her legs. The house was full of people, and no one acted like there was anything inappropriate about this. Tina's body was developing, but she was only eleven years old, very much a child. But then she was twelve, and fifteen, and still Ed was the one to give her a bath. Complicity was reshaped—from the faultlessness of a loving grandfather taking a vested interest in a promising pupil of his daughter's to the faultlessness of a red-blooded man taking a vested interest in a beautiful young lady he intended to marry.

Ed came to the house the day after Tina's seventeenth birthday and proposed marriage to the whole family. He was nearing his final act in life, and he did not want to be alone at the end. In turn, he would offer Tina what no man her age could. With tears in his eyes, he told Tina and her family that he would see to it that she could do whatever she wanted with her life. Go to Radcliffe, if it called to her, and live anywhere in the world. Tina thought about the barn that Ed bought Deb right after high school, and she felt ill because she understood how it was that Deb was so miserable doing whatever she wanted with her life too.

Ed left Tina and her family to think it over for a few days. *You'll never have to worry about any of this,* her mother said the next morning at the breakfast table, the electric bill splayed alongside the plate of bacon. *You'll never know this kind of tired,* her father bookended when he came home from work that evening. On Tina's wedding day, her mother pulled her great-grandmother's veil over her daughter's face and compared the whole thing to punching in at an undesirable job for a solid retirement package.

Tina quit riding soon after, but just before that happened, the barn hosted a group of women from a halfway house in South Dallas. They arrived on a school bus with a female psychiatrist who explained to Tina and Deb that horses were often used for therapeutic purposes, to help people feel connected to their bodies again after trauma. Deb stayed glued to the side of the counselor all day, and later, Tina discovered a scrap of paper in the office with the counselor's name, address, and an appointment time. In the weeks that followed, she began to notice a distinct change in Deb—the whiskey bottle disappeared from the kitchen sink, and she spent less and less time with the family, and, consequently, with Ed. She seemed gentler, more introspective, and Tina was both impressed and intrigued. She wanted to know what sorts of things went on in these sessions, and a not yet awakened part of her wanted to know how to distance herself from Ed too.

Tina enrolled at the University of Dallas, majoring in organizational psychology, and met Frances when she came to deliver a lecture on a technique she had developed, known as the Strange Situation Assessment, which demonstrated the importance of healthy childhood attachments. Tina approached Frances after the lecture, and they hit it off. When Frances went back to Seattle, they remained in touch through letters and phone calls. Though, later, Frances admitted that her goal was always to extricate Tina from what she saw as a blatantly abusive and disturbing marriage.

After graduation, Frances talked Tina into moving up to Seattle. In Texas, marriage and family therapists needed to complete two thousand supervised hours before getting a license. In Washington, it was half, and Frances agreed to take Tina on as an apprentice, which would account for many of those hours. One of the age spots on Ed's head had turned out to be cancerous, and his doctors endorsed a move farther from the equator. He built the Spanish-style mansion in Clyde Hill as an ode to the architecture of his hometown.

Tina and Frances lived close and grew even closer. Ed liked Frances too, or rather, Frances allowed Ed to like her. He was in his eighties by then, and growing frail. He never even touched Tina anymore. All he asked for was companionship, and Tina didn't see how she could refuse him that, not after everything he'd done for her.

For their seven-year anniversary, Frances invited Tina and Ed over for dinner. Ed was a stickler for Frances's steak frites with peppercorn sauce. He could go through three ramekins of the stuff, and Frances always set out extra for him.

That night, after the first few bites, Ed started licking his lips, clearing his throat. "More peppercorns in the sauce this evening," he remarked, not yet afraid.

"I'm experimenting with Chinese hot mustard instead of Dijon," Frances said.

Ed coughed. "What's in that?"

"Just mustard powder and water," Frances said, as Ed rubbed his lips together and wondered why they were going numb.

Tina dropped her fork as Ed started to claw at his throat, wheezing through a windpipe that had constricted to the diameter of a cocktail straw. "We need to call an ambulance!" she cried, pushing back her chair.

Frances stood up too. "The phone is in the living room," she said. She put her arm around Tina and led her to the kitchen, where there was a container of shellfish stock, open next to the saucepan. She held Tina firmly by the shoulders and quizzed her on Piaget's stages of moral development to drown out the sounds coming from the next room, uncannily like those of a baby first learning to burble.

He was an old man who lived a long, prosperous life and died surrounded by a dear friend and his beloved wife, eating his favorite meal. *As peaceful a death as one could hope for,* seemed the presiding sentiment at the funeral back in Dallas. Though every time Tina looked over at Deb, she found her staring back with watery black eyes.

The plan, after the funeral, was to gather at Ed's Highland Park home and make some decisions about what to do with his various properties. But when Tina arrived, she found the doors barricaded and the locks changed, all five of Ed's children wandering the perimeter of the house in their funeral attire, trying to figure out how to get inside. Tina counted again, more carefully this time. No. Not all five, actually.

A window on the second floor cracked open, and Deb's hard voice ricocheted against the grounds. "I need to speak to Tina."

The two of them sat in the grand room, where, at Christmastime, hundreds of presents ringed the base of a fourteen-foot Douglas fir like an impassable moat. Underprivileged children from underprivileged neighborhoods were invited into the Highland Park grand room and given their pick—Tina's mother was one of them once. Now Deb was there to offer Tina another kind of gift.

Ed had noticed Deb's withdrawal from the family several years prior, and had tried to buy back her affections by modifying his will to make Deb the executor, saying in the codicil that only his first-born could see to dividing his assets fairly. To that effect, Tina would inherit the Maui house, retain the Seattle residence, and receive a small but substantial portion of the proceeds from the sale of the real estate company. Everything else belonged to Deb, and if any of her siblings tried to fight her on this, she would go to the press and destroy the memory of their father.

The offer was good on one condition—Tina was never to step foot in Highland Park again, because Deb couldn't stand to look at Tina. In Tina, she saw only what her father had done to her when she was young too. She had been asked to divide the assets fairly, and this, she had decided, was fair.

Tina thought about her mother and what she had said through the scrim of antique lace, whitened with lemon juice and salt for her wedding day. Rising from the couch, hand extended in Deb's direction, she punched out.

PAMELA

Aspen, 1978

Day 13

I woke in the hotel room in Aspen seconds shy of three a.m., only, instead of lying pancaked to the bed in fear, I bolted straight up as if I had overslept for class. Something had resolved for me with those few hours of sleep, something so important that it could not wait until the morning.

I reached over and switched on the tableside lamp. Immediately, my eyes went to Carl's duffel. The hotel had promised to send someone up to take my bag to Carl's room and Carl's bag to mine, but they must have knocked on the door when I was downstairs talking to Tina. I knew he was staying in room 607 because I'd noted the engraved brass numbers on the key fob when Tina had passed them out. I dressed in the previous day's clothes and ran my fingers through my hair, brushed my teeth, and pinched life into my cheeks. I looked as good as I could, given the circumstances. Anyhow, I was engaged.

I went down the hallway toward the elevator, glancing over my shoulder every few steps. The carpet under my feet was orange and gold, a trippy diamond pattern that made my vision swirl and shapes loom menacingly in the shadows. I was out of breath by the time I reached Carl's room, beady-eyed as a fox in a hunt. It took all my restraint not to pound on the door and scream for Carl to let me in. I knocked, a rapid, soft rhythm, whispering as loudly as I dared, "Carl? It's Pamela."

Carl came to the door sooner than I expected him to, his expression zombie-like and movements heavy and uncoordinated. He stumbled, trying to see around me out into the hallway, as though someone really had been chasing me, and I lost the last dregs of my composure. I practically lunged into the room and slammed the door behind us, drawing the lock chain tight on the track.

"I have your bag," I said ludicrously. I patted the army-issue duffel resting against my outer thigh.

With sleep-slugged eyes, Carl looked me over. I'd noticed, of course, that although he'd fallen asleep in his pants, he wasn't wearing a shirt, but with the door closed behind us, it was an oppressive fact. Carl was half-naked. I stared at my feet, over his shoulder, anywhere but his narrow, woolly torso. I was pleased to find that Carl's room was remarkably neat. The covers were peeled back just where he'd been sleeping, and a bath towel was folded in half and left to dry on a hanging rack in the bathroom. My small weekender bag was hooked to the back of the desk chair. I crossed the room and went to swap them, and that was when I noticed two empty airplane-sized whiskey bottles in the trash can. I averted my eyes, not wanting Carl to know I'd seen that.

"What time is it?" Carl asked in a froggy voice, his throat sounding ragged and dried out from the whiskey. He put a fist to his mouth, coughing, and went into the bathroom for water.

"I realized something important," I said, reddening, rather than answer that it was three a.m., "and I couldn't get back to sleep."

The tap went off and Carl appeared in the bathroom doorway, gulping from a glass. He drew a forearm across his mouth and motioned for me to go on.

"Gerald said he was the wrong guy to ask for information, and that we had to talk to the *right* one. It was like he was toying with us, giving us a riddle to solve. But maybe that's because he had to, because he's not free to say what he knows. And then I remembered—the sheriff's plaque on his door. His name is Sheriff Dennis Wright."

"The *Wright* guy," Carl said, instantly revived and alert.

"I think the police in Colorado know something about where The Defendant was headed," I said. "What if they saw what happened down in Florida and are purposely staying out of it? It's bad enough that they let him get away again, but if he went and committed another horrible crime and it comes back to them? God"—I realized something truly upsetting—"they probably don't even want him caught. This is blood on their hands."

Carl leaned against the bathroom doorframe, arms strapped across his bare chest and a distant kind of excitement on his face. "If it's true, it's a career-making story."

"How do we prove it, though?"

Carl brought a hand to his jawline, mottled with scruff, and thought a moment. "Tina has money, doesn't she?"

"She does," I said, and felt a stab of something, not quite anger, thinking about the adversarial conversation we'd had at dinner.

"I can't be a part of anything like that," Carl said. "But I'm speaking to the waitress tomorrow. Maybe you can drop me off, head back over to the jail . . ." He raised an eyebrow at me.

"And what?" I laughed. "Bribe the sheriff?"

"No. Stay away from the sheriff. But maybe a guard or someone would be willing to talk to you."

I furrowed my brow, trying to picture myself doing something like that. "I don't know that I have it in me to bribe someone."

"Stop saying *bribe,* Pamela," Carl said in a passionate way that made my toes curl in my ugly white sneakers. "It's reward money for the truth."

I felt an unexpected thrill rise up in me—reward money, I could see myself offering that to someone. "And whatever we bring you," I said, "you'll write about it?"

"I'd have to corroborate it myself," Carl said. "But I could guarantee anonymity to anyone who spoke to me on the record."

I nodded, working it through. "So, best-case scenario. We find out tomorrow that Colorado does know something about what happened in Florida. How long does it take to corroborate it with other sources, then actually write the piece?" I chewed on my thumbnail, knowing whatever the answer might be, it would not be soon enough to solve my predicament.

"A few weeks, probably."

My stomach was twisting painfully, just thinking about the impossibility of the position I was in with Roger. Press charges against him and risk people thinking they were safe, that the coed killer was behind bars where he belonged, or let Roger off the hook so he would be free to hurt someone else.

"Pamela," Carl said, eyes soft with concern, "what is it? You look like you have the weight of the world on your shoulders."

"That's because I do," I said, my chin abruptly puckering. I steepled my hands over my nose so Carl wouldn't see. My mother was always telling me that not even Mia Farrow looked beautiful when she cried.

I felt Carl come nearer. "I want to help."

I shook my head hopelessly. "You *can't*."

"Try me, Pamela." He pulled my hands away from my face and crouched at the knees so that we were eye to eye. I stared at him, horrified, our faces inches apart. I was completely infatuated with him and completely unprepared to act on it. I blurted it out because I was afraid he was going to kiss me. "Roger did something to my sister Bernadette," I said. "He forced her to do things . . ." I looked away, embarrassed and unsure of how to put it. "*To* him. And she couldn't breathe. She thought she was going to die. Do you understand what I'm saying?" I glanced back at him to find him nodding, this heartbroken look on his face.

"And now," I rambled on, tearfully, "the police need to know if I plan on pressing charges for what he did to *me*. If I don't, I'm scared of what might happen, what he might do next. And if I do . . ."

"It's only further proof that he's capable of murder, and they're even less inclined to look at anybody else," Carl said with a heavy sigh, as though he felt every last leaden ounce of my dilemma.

I nodded wretchedly.

Carl pressed my palms together, prayer-like, and said to me: "I will do everything in my power to make sure this guy doesn't hurt anyone else."

"That's why I asked you to come," I said, a half-truth.

Carl clutched my hands to his chest. His skin was warm and slightly damp, like he'd exerted himself in making me this promise, and some long-coiled tail of desire unfurled from my throat to my inner thighs. "We should really get some sleep," I said before I acted on it.

Carl nodded, a look on his face that told me he understood what I hadn't said. He went over to the closet and thrust his arms into the only shirt he'd brought, hooked the strap of my bag over his shoulder, and then escorted me back to my room.

———

The next morning, we piled into the car and headed for the bank. Tina was more than game to wave a brick of bills at one of the prison employees, entice them to tell us what they knew. Before dropping Carl off at The Stew Pot, we strategized an approach—we'd go in and ask to speak to Sheriff Wright, who would no doubt keep us waiting out of spite, providing ample opportunity to slip a note to one of the guards.

"What do we do if the sheriff agrees to speak to us, though?" I asked.

"I very much doubt that will happen," Tina scoffed.

"No, but it's good to be prepared, just in case." Carl had glanced back at me and smiled supportively. It was a clear, cold day, the bracing morning sun turning his hazel eyes jewel-toned. I smiled back and quickly looked away before Tina picked up on anything.

"My advice?" Carl said. "I'd appeal to the sheriff's narrative that The Defendant was a force beyond anyone's control."

In the years that followed, I would locate back editions of the

Aspen Star Bulletin and read Sheriff Wright's gun-strapping, cigar-chomping interview, and realize how right Carl had been. How good he was at all of this.

He's one slippery snake, the sheriff had said, thumbs hooked in his suspenders, a hint of a smile on his face, *but I'm the gardening shovel that'll chop him off at the head.*

Sometimes I think it was machismo that killed Denise.

————

As we made the turn into the prison's muddy drive, Tina slammed on the brakes.

"Did you see who that was?" she said excitedly, spinning the wheel while the seat belt cut into my throat. She stepped on the gas and peeled up alongside the truck that was exiting as we were pulling in; she tapped on the horn and motioned for the driver to roll down his window and told me to roll mine down too. I poked my head out to see that the driver was the blond guard who had schlepped Gerald out of the makeshift visitors' room yesterday. I vaguely remembered Gerald calling him Sammy.

Sammy regarded us through his open window with an impatient scowl. *What?* he looked like he wanted to groan. *What do you want?*

"We were here yesterday," Tina said, unbuckling her seat belt and leaning across me. "Visiting Gerald Stevens?"

Sammy sighed in a beleaguered way. He had purple shadows beneath his eyes. Perhaps he had just come off the night shift.

"We were hoping," Tina said, wearing her most feminine and helpless expression, "that we could buy you a coffee and talk to you, just for a few minutes."

Sammy's eyes slid toward the low stone station in his rearview mirror. "What about?"

"We want to know the details of The Defendant's escape," Tina said. "From someone who was there."

"I can't help you," he said, and began to roll up his window.

"I think he killed my friend," I called out at the same time Tina said, "I'll pay you three thousand in cash."

Sammy froze, the window just below nose level. He glanced at the station in his rearview mirror once more. Then, robotically stiff, as though someone inside could possibly read his lips, "Wait five minutes. Then meet me at Dinah's on Eighty-two."

———

Dinah's was one of those diners with a rotating pie display. When we walked in, the guard was sitting at a booth polishing off a slice of cherry.

"If this comes back to me," he said when we sat, "I'll tell the sheriff you stole something from the jail and set it up to make it look real bad for you."

"Understood," Tina said. The deal was struck, simple as that.

Sammy thumbed a crumb from the corner of his mouth and looked out over the parking lot, inspecting a Toyota pickup as it chewed up the slush and the grit. He waited until the driver climbed out before deciding he didn't know him.

"You have to understand," Sammy said, continuing to monitor the comings and goings of the parking lot, "that the guy never should have been in Colorado to begin with." He sighed and went all the way back to the beginning.

In March 1976, The Defendant was in Utah, serving a fifteen-year sentence for the kidnapping of Anne Biers from a shopping mall. Prosecutors there were working to tie him to the murder of another Utah woman, a girl, really—seventeen-year-old Barbara Kent, who disappeared after leaving a high school play to pick up her younger brother, mere hours after Anne Biers had escaped her abductor. Investigators had discovered a key in the school parking lot where Kent was last seen that fit the handcuffs used on Biers. The case was strong, but the Colorado DA couldn't be bothered with anything approaching justice. His name was Frank Tucker, but Sammy told us that everyone around here had taken to calling him Tucker the Fucker after what happened.

Sammy pushed his cleaned plate to the side so that he could periodically jab the table with his pointer finger to punctuate the more outrageous parts of his story. "So the guy escapes again, and everyone is in an uproar, wanting to know how we could have let this happen. The sheriff points the finger at Tucker, saying it's his fault, that Colorado wasn't ready for him. And we weren't."

"What would you have done differently?" Tina asked.

"There is a *protocol* you follow around high-profile prisoners," Sammy said. "So I wouldn't have acted like I was above the goddamn law. I woulda followed it."

"Why not just follow it?" I asked, confused.

He flung his hand, miming the act of throwing something carelessly out the window. "Because Tucker had a special election coming up that he knew he was gonna lose." Sammy smirked. *Ready for this?*

According to Sammy, Tucker the Fucker had billed two counties to finance the abortion of his eighteen-year-old mistress—grossly hypocritical behavior coming from the elected official whose job it was to prosecute criminal violations of the law, the kind of shit you can't make up, and I haven't. In a few years Tucker would be prosecuted on two charges of embezzlement of public funds, but in March 1976 he was in the throes of a heated reelection campaign. So he did what all politicians do when they need to rehabilitate their image— he found a straw man. For Tucker, The Defendant was a godsend.

It happened to be true that Colorado investigators had strong evidence to connect The Defendant to the murder of Caryn Campbell—a strand of her hair was discovered in his car, and the use of his gasoline credit card put him near the scene at the time she disappeared from her Aspen hotel. But it was no stronger than the evidence Utah had for the murder of seventeen-year-old Barbara Kent. Colorado should have waited its turn to prosecute, but Frank Tucker didn't have time to do things by the book. He wanted to be able to say at his campaign rallies that he was the hero for catching Caryn Campbell's killer. He needed that, if he had any hope of remaining in office and dodging his own criminal charges.

"The last straw," Sammy continued with seething contempt, "was when Tucker blamed the county commissioners for his escape, saying if they'd properly funded the prison, it never woulda happened. Well, of course they didn't have any money to keep up the place! Because Tucker stole it to pay for his mistress's hotel rooms and dinners and clothes and jewelry. Even an abortion." Sammy's nostrils flared scornfully. He wore a long gold chain tucked into his collar, and maybe it was my imagination, but I was certain I could make out the pious shape of a cross beneath his white cotton undershirt.

The Defendant was extradited to Aspen in early 1977, and by June, he'd pulled off his first escape. Just before dawn on the sixth day of the statewide manhunt, two sheriff's deputies came upon a stolen 1966 Cadillac and found The Defendant slumped behind the wheel, severely dehydrated and fatigued, frostbite on three of his toes. He was less than a mile outside Aspen county lines and taken into custody under the jurisdiction of Glenwood Springs, where he was questioned without a lawyer for several hours before the sheriff back in Aspen got wind of it. A pissing match ensued—with Aspen demanding The Defendant's return and Glenwood Springs refusing. The Defendant was captured on *their* turf. Aspen had their shot with him, and they'd blown it. A judge ruled in favor of Glenwood Springs: a reckless ruling, not another word for it.

"Glenwood's supposedly the more secure facility," Sammy said. "We're smaller, better equipped to keep an eye on him. But from the start, we were out of our depth."

Sammy eyed both of us to see if we understood what that meant. I glanced at Tina; she shook her head.

"With prisoners who have a history of escape, Marshals Service is supposed to get involved, come and inspect the facility. But that never happened. There wasn't even a mention of a previous escape on his intake screening form."

"You're sure of that," I said, feeling winded.

"I read the form myself. Every guard in my unit did. That form's supposed to list what the prisoner's in for. He was down for theft."

"Theft," Tina repeated incredulously.

Sammy jabbed his thumbs into his eyes and clenched his jaw angrily. "None of us had any idea of who we were dealing with. Enough time passed between when he was caught and when the judge sent him back to Glenwood that we didn't even know he was the same guy from the manhunt. Plus, he seemed normal. Easy to talk to. The guy they caught looked feral in the pictures in the paper, but by the time we got him, he'd cleaned himself up again. Then"—Sammy turned his eyes up to the ceiling—"he started going up there."

Tina and I looked up at the ceiling in a coordinated motion.

"There was a loose tile in his cell," Sammy said. "The sheriff knew he'd been up there once or twice. But he just said not to worry. Don't go nowhere anyway. I told him he was getting real thin. I'd collect his dinner plate, and he'd hardly have touched anything on it. Sheriff just laughed and said he wouldn't touch that shit with a ten-foot pole neither."

By December 1977, four weeks before I saw him at our front door holding a bloody log from our own cord of firewood, The Defendant had dropped twenty pounds from his already lean frame, enough to shimmy through the narrowest part of the ducting, exit into the empty apartment of a prison worker, change his clothes, and escape Colorado for good. It took them six hours to realize he was gone—he'd pulled the covers over his law textbooks and various documents and piles of letters, arranged to pass for a sleeping body.

"People say he's living off the land in the mountains," Sammy said. "There are sightings all the time. Like Bigfoot."

"Well, he's not," Tina said. "He's gone to Florida State University."

Sammy looked at her square in the face with an alarming urgency.

"What is it?" I asked, my heart pounding.

Sammy folded his hands and bowed his head, lines deepening in his brow, thinking hard.

"What?"

"Give me a second!" Sammy clenched his eyes shut. "I'm trying to *remember.*"

Tina and I sat there, not breathing, not wanting to do or say anything that may ruin his concentration.

"There was a university brochure," Sammy said. His eyes were still closed, but his lids were moving rapidly, as though he was scanning the scene in his memory. "In with the other items that he'd put under the covers. One of them"—Sammy opened his eyes—"it had palm trees. And I remember thinking he must have gone to California. But you all got palm trees down there too, right?"

I could see the Florida State University brochure that came in the mail my sophomore year of high school, the fat ancient oaks and the leggy palms, up and down like waves on a heart monitor.

"What happened to all that stuff?" I asked, thinking if we could produce a Florida State brochure, then we'd have our smoking gun.

"It all went to Seattle," Sammy said.

"You're sure of that," Tina said, a tremor of hope in her voice.

"Positive. When he got caught that first time, he refused to talk unless it was to one of the Seattle PDs. Guy who'd been working those missing girl cases for years. I remember Sheriff Wright was real pissed to have to bring them in. And then when he escaped, they came back, and they left with boxes."

I swore I could hear Tina's heart pounding with recognition at the mention of the missing girls in Seattle.

Sammy signaled for the check. "That's all I know. What did he do down in Florida?"

"He broke into my sorority house," I said. "He murdered two girls, and he severely beat and disfigured two others. Then he went down the street and attacked one more. I heard a noise, and I went to investigate. I saw him, clearly, before he fled."

Sammy grunted his sympathy. "That shouldn't have happened." His hands drummed out an anxious rhythm on top of the Formica table, and he looked out over the parking lot once more. Then he lifted his butt and dug around in his back pocket, retrieving his wallet. He licked a finger and counted three ones, enough for the pie and a tip. Fanning them out on the table, he said to Tina, "Prefer to do this in the car."

Tina seemed confused. "Do what?"

"The money," Sammy reminded her. "You said you had some."

When we picked Carl up from The Stew Pot, he was sparking with as much excitement as we were. We compared notes and found that we had heard more or less the same story about Frank Tucker. But Carl hadn't known about Seattle PD coming here and taking evidence back with them to Washington. That part we gave him.

Carl was pinching his lips contemplatively as we approached the signs for the airport. "Should I go to Seattle?" he wondered.

Tina looked at him in the rearview mirror. "Now?"

"Why not? I'm already halfway there."

Tina and I glanced at each other. It was true.

"It just feels like this story is so much bigger than I first realized. I mean, he's up to ten, twelve victims? Spanning multiple states? And if it started in Seattle, and Seattle has evidence of a cover-up happening in Colorado, maybe they'd cooperate with me. Maybe they'd want everyone to know it was Colorado that screwed things up, not them."

"I can give you the names of the detectives you'll want to try and talk to," Tina said. "*Don't* mention that you know me." She laughed the way you do when something is distinctly unfunny.

I raised my hand. "So does this mean I should move ahead with pressing charges against Roger?"

"Yes," Tina and Carl said at the same time.

That weekend, that moment, is something I've thought about every day for the last forty-three years. It was my responsibility to protect the girls, The House, Denise's and Robbie's reputations and their memories. I went with my instincts, and my instincts were wrong. That rattled me. *Still* rattles me.

PAMELA

Tallahassee, 2021

Day 15,826

The twentysomething security guard glances away from a game of Candy Crush long enough to see me place my bag on the belt, then goes right back to the game. I set the metal detector off, and he sulks at this second interruption. He peels his eyes away from the screen and jerks his chin at my feet. "Haveta take those off."

I try not to think about how many things this underpaid and uninterested guard doesn't catch as I remove my boots and shuffle through on the sides of my feet. I'm cleared.

I am met in the waiting room by an attendant who asks me to sign a waiver before getting on the bus. I sign without reading any of it. Once I hit the stage in life where biopsies and scans and anesthesia became a once-or-twice-a-year occurrence, I learned to spare myself the fine print. There are risks involved with everything, and needing to know all of them is a surefire way to drive yourself nuts. What I came here to do may as well be an emergency surgery, a tumor that has to be removed immediately if I want to live with myself.

It's a short, bumpy bus ride to the recreational yard, where there is an herb and vegetable garden walled with wire. He's gotten into gardening over the years, and this is how he spends his outdoor hours. No shovels or pointed tools, I am assured by the attendant who had me sign the waiver. *Obviously,* he adds with a chummy laugh, and I want to tell him it's not actually obvious. You would be amazed how easy this country makes it to hurt someone if that is your goal.

When I spot him, he's wearing a wide-brimmed hat in tanned canvas, watering bouquets of dark dinosaur kale with a garden hose, and I am appalled. Not just because the hose could be repurposed into a garotte, but because he looks so peaceful on this sunny spring day, and I am running on two hours of jagged sleep. We both know the clock is running out, and yet I am the only one with something to lose when it does.

He sees me and shuts off the water. At first he approaches slowly, poking higher the underside of his hat's brim so that he can see if it's really me. He begins to move faster—he is charging me, actually—and I'm thinking about all the fine print I refused to read in the waiver I signed, how I cannot hold anyone but myself accountable for bodily injury or even my death, when I taste blood.

RUTH

Aspen

Winter 1974

Evening descended on the walk back to the hotel. Tina and I were up against a shiv-like wind that chapped our faces and stripped the branches of their iced sleeves. But under my wool coat and Tina's wool sweater, I was burning up, agitated, and thirsty. The champagne had hit my system like a live wire, startling dormant sensations from their slumber. I was tormented by the image of that old man lathering Tina's pubic hair while his family set the table for dinner downstairs. It wasn't late enough for bed, and we had decided to hang out in the lobby for a little while longer, but I was working up the courage to lie to Tina. I needed to escape from her, just for a little while, to sedate the wild animal clawing at my skin from the inside.

We entered the lobby, stomping and scraping our wet boots on the carpet runner, to find a few guests warming up before the molten fireplace. From the other side of the room, a stocky woman with a blunt haircut called out to Tina.

"Marlene!" Tina waved. She leaned into me. "That's Frances's cowriter on the book."

I seized my opportunity. "Go say hi. I want to run upstairs and change out of these wet socks." I wrapped my arms around myself and shivered for show.

I made my way to the elevator with short quick strides, the way you do when your stomach is upset and you need a bathroom now but you don't want anyone to know you need a bathroom now.

I punched the button and squeezed my eyes shut. I couldn't stand to see if anyone else joined me while I waited for the elevator to arrive. There were fifteen floors, and we were on the twelfth. If we had to stop on the way, I would have a conniption. I heard the brake release with a dull clank, and I opened my eyes, relieved to find that I had the car to myself. I pulsed the button for twelve with my thumb, over and over, though I knew it wouldn't make the thing move any faster.

Someone slipped inside just before the doors clasped. It was the same woman I'd ridden the elevator with that morning, the one who had mouthed *of course* at me in the mirror when the cardiologist assumed she was there to ski. She pressed the button for fourteen; at least I wouldn't have to stop for her.

"I hate when people do that to me," she apologized. "But we're better off riding together."

I turned to her with a blank look. She gave it to me right back.

"You do know about the woman who went missing here last year?" She arched an eyebrow expectantly, sure my memory could be jogged. But I had no idea what she was talking about. The woman filled me in. "Her name was Caryn Campbell. She was here with her fiancé. For the conference. They came back from dinner and were going to sit and read in the lobby by the fire for a bit. She went to grab a magazine from her room. She got on the elevator, and that's the last time anyone saw her alive."

The floor felt like it was pushing against my feet, insisting it was there, as the elevator's brass arm began its count. "Was she ever found?" I heard myself ask.

The woman shook her head grimly. "Not alive. No."

The elevator clutch released at my floor, but my head still felt pressurized and heavy. The doors opened.

"Let me walk you," the woman offered. "My name's Gail, by the way. Gail Strafford."

"Ruth Wachowsky," I told her. We stepped off the elevator and went left down the orange-and-yellow diamond-patterned runner. "Did the police catch the person who killed her?"

Again Gail shook her head. "That's why I'm here."

"How does"—I paused, trying to recall the name of her department—"forensic anthropology come in?"

"We can perform certain tests that can help determine the most accurate time of death."

"But you said she was killed a year ago," I said, pulling out my room key.

"She went *missing* a year ago. Her body was found a month later, a little ways off a rural trucking lane. But even though it's been a while, the soil in the area holds clues as to when she was put there. That at least helps answer a few outstanding questions the police have. Was she killed here in the hotel? Was she kidnapped and held for a period of time? All of this can help create a profile of the type of person who would do this. Help the police catch him, whoever he is."

We'd stopped in front of my door. The gold numbering above the peephole seemed too bright, like some sort of calling card. "You can tell all that from the soil?"

Gail nodded cheerfully. "The decomposition of a body can actually change the phenotype of the local vegetation. In some cases, even decades after human remains are found, plants that should grow green foliage can grow bright red. It has to do with the nitrogen released in the cadaveric process and the leaf's response to the integration of these nutrients."

"Wow," I said, doubting my every last contribution to the world.

Gail fell silent a moment. "It's kind of comforting, if you think about it. It's like, even though she lost her life, she still gets to be a part of the world, in her own way."

We smiled at each other, quick and sad. I'd come up here to splash water on my face, to get ahold of myself. Square off with my reflection in the bathroom mirror and ask again where all my perversion came from. But I felt some of my self-loathing dissipate. I had

my problems, my weaknesses, and succumbing to them had contributed to the lousy belief that I did not belong anywhere, not in a marriage and not at home with my mother either. But it was comforting
to think that the earth always found a place for us.

I fitted the key in the lock and pushed the door open wide. The
maid had left the bedside lamp on when she came to do turndown
service, and we could see that the coast was clear.

"Thanks for walking with me," I told Gail. "But now I feel bad
you have to go the rest of the way alone."

Gail frowned, thinking. "How about this? I'll call down to reception and ask them to transfer me to your room once I'm back. Ruth
Wachowsky, right?"

"Right," I said. "But I'm here with my friend Martina Cannon.
The reservation is under her name."

"Ruth Wachowsky and Martina Cannon," Gail said, committing
our names to memory as she started back down the hall.

"If I don't hear from you in two minutes, I'm calling the sheriff,"
I warned her.

Gail laughed and quickened her pace. "Start the countdown,
Ruth Wachowsky!"

I waited until the elevator came and Gail climbed on before I
closed and locked my door. I went over to the bed and peeled off my
wet socks while I waited for the phone to ring. My mind wandered
again to Julia Child and something she once said on an episode of
The French Chef, in her "ridiculous" voice that my mother couldn't
stand. "Nothing you ever learn is really wasted," Julia had said with a
chicken neck in one fist, "and will sometime be used." I was thinking
about this when Gail called to let me know she'd gotten back in one
piece.

PAMELA

Tallahassee, 1978

Day 14

I arrived back in Tallahassee as the sun cleaved the Westcott Towers, feeling like I'd gotten twelve hours of sleep instead of two. It was Sunday, and while I had a million things to do to get The House ready for the girls that evening, I was not at all concerned about how I would get them done. Some people need caffeine to get them going, others just need to be able to say *I told you so.* Though I'd known it was The Defendant I'd seen at our front door, I'd been made to doubt myself. I was champing at the bit to confront Sheriff Cruso with what we'd learned in Colorado.

But the rush of being right began to fade as we neared The House, and when Tina parked at the curb to drop me off, I couldn't stop thinking about all the days the place had sat dormant, the extensive number of rooms, the claustrophobic hallways, the closets and nooks and crannies—

"I'm coming in with you," Tina said as we stared out at the blank-faced windows.

I didn't protest.

Tina turned off the engine, and together we walked up the white brick path to the front door, pausing at the mailbox so I could collect the last few days' worth of mail. I wedged the bills and letters of condolence from alumnae and perfect strangers under my arm and entered the new combination code.

The hallway smelled cold and stale. There was a slash of black tape across the threshold where I'd seen him and scratches on the hardwood from the Brillo pad I'd used to scrape up flecks of dried blood.

Tina rubbed her arms. "Let's start by putting on the heat."

———

We pushed the couches in the rec room against the wall and I vacuumed while Tina held up the cord. We laid out the sleeping bags in the shape of a sunburst, then pushed the couches up to the border, creating a wall around the girls who would sleep in the outermost ring. We found cake mix in the cupboards—Tina suggested a sheet cake cut into squares instead of cupcakes. Ruth had made her one once, after she mentioned it was something they did in Texas. Plus, it would come together faster than cupcakes, and we had a lot more work to do.

I had scheduled the new mattresses to arrive on Saturday, back when I thought I'd be returning from Colorado late Friday night. They'd been dumped unceremoniously by the back door; a rodent had chewed through one of the boxes while I was away. At least it hadn't rained.

But before we could take them upstairs, we had to dispose of the soiled mattresses from Eileen and Jill's room. We got the first one down the back staircase in a spectacular tumble, and I wiped my brow. "I'm gonna turn off the heat."

Tina nodded. *Please.*

We filled a bucket with hot soapy water and spent nearly two hours scrubbing at the blood that had congealed in the crevices of the bedframe. We took the cake out of the oven and jiggled it; it needed another twenty minutes. We got one new mattress upstairs and took the cake out again. This time it was ready. We let it cool on the counter while we loaded the other mattress onto our backs and huffed and puffed up the stairs. We made up the beds with the fresh linens, frosted the cake, and hung new curtains in room ten. I looked at the clock and could not believe when I saw it was four in the afternoon. My skin felt slick, and the back of my shirt was stiff with sweat that had dried, then gotten wet and dried again.

"Do you mind," I asked Tina haltingly, "just hanging around while I shower?" I could not imagine doing it alone.

"Not at all," she said.

"I'll be quick," I promised.

"Take the time you need."

In the bathroom, I stood before Denise's cubbyhole. Denise was a beauty junkie who always had the latest shampoo or hand lotion in her shower caddy. I took it into one of the stalls with me. She would hate for any of that to go to waste.

I turned on the shower as hot as it would go, and then I stood under the spray far too long, working Denise's shampoo into my hair, lathering my knees and underarms with Denise's shaving cream. It was something called Crazylegs, and I loved it so much I became a convert. When Johnson & Johnson discontinued it in 1986, it felt like another death.

———

I returned from the shower, pink skin wrapped in a bath towel, to find Tina sitting at my desk, paging through one of Denise's old *Cosmopolitan*s and scratching at her scalp. It was the first time I had ever seen her without something covering her head. I cleared my throat noisily to announce my arrival. Surely she hadn't meant for me to see her without her hat of the day.

But Tina hardly glanced at me before she went back to turning the pages in the magazine. "Ruth found a cure for her acne in one of these things." She ran her finger left to right, under the small print for a shampoo advertisement. "I think her stress eased considerably once she got out from under her mother's roof, and that helped her skin clear up faster than any pill could. Still," she said, sighing, "can't hurt to keep an eye out for some miracle treatment, since no doctor in the world can figure out why it won't grow back." She was speaking about the twin bald patches on either side of her head, like she'd recently had a pair of devil horns surgically removed.

"What happened?" I asked, going over to my bureau and pulling open the drawer where I kept my undergarments. An unkind thought popped into my head—*should I ask Tina to leave while I get dressed?* The woman who had stayed and helped me ready The House, who'd stood guard while I showered, who was sitting there completely unarmed and exposed to me. Like some sort of bigot exposure therapy, I dropped my towel and went about my business the way I would with any other woman in the room.

"I pulled it out, actually," Tina said. "The day Ruth didn't come home. I was so out of my mind I just grabbed my hair in my fists, and I pulled so hard it came out at the roots." She licked the pad of her thumb and flipped the page of the shampoo ad defeatedly. "One doctor said I traumatized the follicle. That it will grow again when it feels *safe* enough." She laughed roughly at that word. *Safe.*

I tugged a sweater over my head and went down the hall without pants, going toward the back of the house until I reached Denise's room, where I ducked under a thatch of black tape. I hoped they were there, what I was looking for, but if not, I knew where to buy them.

"This is a multivitamin Denise used to take," I said to Tina when I came back into the room. "To help her hair and nails grow. She really needed it after her last breakup with Roger. She got so thin. Thinner than she got on any of the crazy diets she was always trying—not that she needed them, but she weighed herself multiple times a day and would panic if she gained as much as an ounce. It stressed her out so much, her hair started to fall out. She found this woman here, some sort of holistic person, who gave her this. I don't know how it works, but it does. Denise had the best hair in the whole sorority." I tossed the bottle underhand to Tina, who caught it in the cradle of her arms.

"Have you ever heard of anorexia?" Tina asked, examining the label on the bottle.

"The thing where women starve themselves?" I said in a dubious voice, shimmying a pair of jeans up my legs. "That wasn't Denise," I said naively. "She was just really careful about what she ate."

Tina pressed her lips together, saying no more. Many years and Lifetime movies about the subject later, when eating disorders were so ubiquitous that my own daughter briefly battled one, I'd realize Tina had stopped herself from explaining to me that Denise was suffering from one too. That she'd spared me from thinking about Denise in any more pain than she'd already been in at the end of her life. Tina twisted the top off the bottle and spilled some of the thick white tablets into her palm, examining them more closely. "Thank you," she said. "I'll definitely give these a try."

"No," I insisted. "Thank you. I never would have gotten all of this done on my own." I reached for a hairbrush on the vanity near where Tina sat, and we made eye contact in the mirror. "And I want to say I'm sorry, Tina. For the things I said at the hotel. What I implied about your character. You've got it in spades."

Tina smiled at me in the mirror. "I'll have you know this is a very satisfying moment for me. I live to prove people wrong."

I raised my eyebrows agreeably. "I know exactly what you mean." We shared a laugh. I started for the door as I dragged my brush through my wet hair. "I don't want to keep you any longer."

"You're sure?"

"The girls are supposed to arrive around five. I'll survive the next fifteen minutes on my own."

Tina nodded. *All right then.* I walked her down the stairs and to the front door.

"Call me if you need anything," Tina said.

"I'll let you know when I hear from Carl," I told her.

Tina and I nodded at each other in this professional way that didn't suit the new bounds of our relationship. Which was what, exactly? Not friendship. What we had was sturdier than that, able to sustain a sort of acrimony that friendship could not.

It was more like sisterhood, I realized, than anything I'd experienced under this roof. Because I hadn't chosen Tina, hadn't vetted her like I had members of this chapter, and yet we were fated to go through life together connected by spilled blood. I stepped forward and hugged her. Tina's hands dangled lifelessly at her sides at first. Later she would tell me she often left places in a rush, trying to spare other women that awkward beat when they wondered if they could hug her without the gesture being misinterpreted. Eventually, I felt her arms hook around me, loosely, as though giving me the option to break free at any time.

———

After Tina left, I went into the kitchen to cut the cake and go through the mail. I didn't even want to think about how many thank-you cards I had to write to all the people who had reached out and offered their thoughts and prayers.

There was a kind note from an alumna in Adrian, Michigan, who told me about the successful pecan sale she had hosted, netting several thousand dollars that she'd donated to her local battered women's shelter under our chapter's name. There was a letter from a man in New Hampshire who had read about what happened to us and, citing a statistical increase in violent crimes against women, suggested we speak to our local precinct about hosting a handgun training session for women. If they didn't have the manpower, he was happy to provide his services. He had an army friend in Pensacola he'd been meaning to visit. Even to that derangement I would eventually reply, thanking him for the generous offer.

I came to the next piece of mail, showing a return address in Fort Lauderdale, directed to the care of Mrs. Pamela Armstrong.

How odd, I thought. Armstrong was Brian's last name. It was like a window into the impending future, and in a flash I saw the next ten years of my life with Brian, in a Florida kitchen, preparing an after-school snack for the kids who were coming through the door and calling out to me at that very moment.

"Hello?" came a tentative voice from the back of the house. My sisters had arrived.

"In the kitchen!" I hollered, slipping a butter knife under the gold-embossed seal and removing the typed letter on official government letterhead. "Dear Mrs. Armstrong," it read. "We regret to inform you—"

"Smells good in here!"

"It's *freezing.* Let's get the heat on!"

"Look at this!" Whoever said that had discovered the snuggery of sleeping bags in the rec room.

The heat kicked on with a clang, and a Pavlovian sweat beaded my upper lip. I was still flushed from my hot shower, and the document in my hands had taken on the degree of tinder. The victims' assistance committee had reviewed our claim and found us "ineligible for financial restitution due to a sexual relationship exclusion in the eligibility requirements, foreclosing recovery for claimants found to contribute to their own injuries." They sent along their deepest sympathies for our terrible ordeal, but it was their elected duty to protect the program. The rules were the rules.

RUTH

Issaquah

Winter 1974

t's unbelievable," Tina was still saying once we'd landed back in Seattle and gotten into her Cadillac. "How could she just disappear into thin air like that?" I had filled her in on my conversation with Gail in the elevator.

"It's what happened to the University of Washington student earlier this year," I recalled. "The one who read the ski reports. She went into her room, and in the morning she wasn't in her bed, and no one has seen her since."

Tina and I drove along in mournful contemplation, thinking about the impossibility and the possibility of something like that happening to us.

"You know," Tina said bashfully as she exited the highway and braked for the stop sign at the bottom of the off-ramp, "you're always welcome to come stay with me for a while. I would be grateful to you, really. Being in that big house all alone? I'm feeling spooked." She saw my mouth tighten and insisted, "You'd be doing me a huge favor, Ruth. I know it's a lot to ask, but I just figured I'd put it out there."

She was doing that rich-person thing again, begging me to take pity on her by accepting all her charities. The clothes, the trip, a six-bedroom mansion in which to crash. Yet there I was, wearing her clothes, having returned from her trip. It was a very effective ploy.

"Thank you," I told her, and I did mean it, "but my mom really needs my help right now."

Tina took her time turning onto my street, in case I changed my mind mid–tire rotation. Quietly, she asked, "With what?"

The question threw me. I had to rack my brain for a satisfying answer, and all I could come up with was "Stuff around the house."

"I see," Tina said in a tone that conveyed the opposite of seeing.

"Cleaning. Cooking. Paying bills," I added, beefing up my role. "My dad used to do all that for her. She'd be a wreck on her own."

"My mom was pretty depressed when I left home too," Tina said. "I mean, when I really left. Like never-coming-back left. But you know what?" She pulled into my driveway, and we sat facing the small rambler I called home. The headlights of the Cadillac illuminated the stains on the aluminum siding that I'd been meaning to scrub off all winter.

"What?" I asked finally, because Tina had turned to look at me, waiting for me to engage.

"She's fine, Ruth. She survived it."

For a moment we tracked the silhouette of my mother in a window, puttering around the kitchen.

"She'll be okay too," Tina said.

———

"I'm back!" I shouted, and held my breath. My mother would have heard the car in the driveway and the front door close behind me, but I had learned long ago to announce myself when I entered the house. I was good at gauging my mother's mood based on the tenor of her response, and I preferred to step into her arena prepared.

"In here," came my mother's barely audible reply. She was angry with me, but she didn't have any reason to be, meaning she would have to find one. I walked into the kitchen knowing it would end brutally.

I found her on her hands and knees, the refrigerator door open, wiping the cold shelves down with wet tissue paper and leaving little wadded pellets behind. There was a half-eaten brown apple on the counter, and I knew I was done for. I couldn't believe I'd forgotten to throw away that apple half before I left for the weekend. I had no appetite in the morning, but if I took my Acnotabs on an empty stomach, I got queasy. On Friday, before I left, I'd saved the other half for Saturday morning out of habit.

My mother carped, "There were fruit flies everywhere, Ruth."

"It won't happen again," I assured her as I disposed of the rotted produce, then decided I better take out the trash for good measure.

"Don't go anywhere yet," my mother said as I tied off the top of the garbage bag. She climbed to her feet, wincing painfully when she bore the entirety of her weight on one knee. "Sit down. Something I want to talk to you about."

I propped the garbage bag against the refrigerator door and lowered myself into a chair gingerly, as though it were lined with rows of invisible tacks. My mother sat down across from me and sort of reeled back when she realized I wasn't wearing my own clothes.

"Where did that sweater come from?" she asked.

"Tina let me borrow it," I said. I saw the disapproving tug at the corner of her mouth and quickly concocted a fib. "I spilled something on myself."

"You didn't pack anything else?"

"Nothing that would work for what we were doing."

My mother laughed in a way that filled me with dread. "I didn't realize it was a *fancy* weekend." She picked up her mug of tea and took a sip, smacking her lips with displeasure when she tasted it. She'd steeped the tea bag in boiling water, I bet. Burned the leaves.

"Do you want to hear something wild?" I offered up. I told her about the missing woman before she could answer one way or another.

I could tell my mother was intrigued by the story. She listened with a blasé expression, but her lips were twitching with curiosity.

There were questions she was dying to ask, but she had too much pride, so I provided as many details as I could to sate her.

"I'll have to keep an eye out on the news for it," she said when I finished, and I relaxed for the first time since I had entered the house. I was sure she just wanted to talk to me about my father's garden ceremony, about convincing CJ to attend so that she didn't have to explain our divorce to all his old colleagues at Issaquah Catholic. But instead, she folded her pudgy, childlike hands on the table and bowed her head, as though what she had to say wouldn't be easy for either of us to hear. "I spoke to Dr. Burnet this morning."

My mouth went dry. "About what?"

"Oh," my mother said with a weary sigh. *Where to begin?* "I've been concerned. About how much time you're spending with that woman. A grown woman inviting another woman away for the weekend? It's queer, Ruth. I felt funny the whole time you were gone, and finally, I couldn't take it anymore. I wanted to know if Dr. Burnet thought I had a right to be concerned."

I sank down lower in my seat.

"We both agreed it might be in your best interest to start seeing him again."

My voice came out quavering and small. "You want me to go back to Eastern State?"

"Dr. Burnet wants you to. Never mind what I want. He's the doctor."

I nodded, indulging her, though it was just a matter of semantics. "Can I have a few days to think about it?"

My mother placed her palms flat on the table and hoisted herself up with an involuntary grunt. "I think you'd better." She shuffled into the den, and a few moments later, I heard the TV go on. I sat for a long time, slumped down in my chair, watching the fruit flies halo the garbage bag, thinking about the women's ward at Eastern State, the sound of the orderly locking my door before I fell asleep at night.

Eventually, I hauled myself to my feet as well. I seriously considered leaving the bag of garbage to decay in the kitchen but decided I could spare my mother one last kindness.

———

My bike was rusty from being left out in the damp, and it took me nearly an hour to pedal to Tina's house, the bottle of Acnotabs rattling like a tambourine in my coat pocket. Those and the journal Frances had given me were the only things I took. There was nothing else I could carry; nothing else I would miss.

Tina opened the door, a flag-sized bedspread draped over her shoulders and pooling around her bare feet like a medieval cape. Her blond hair was pulled back into a ponytail, and the dark slashes above her eyes were raised in alarm. She opened the door wider for me, and I stepped inside, where it was homey and warm. Sweat instantly broke out on my upper lip and I lifted a shoulder to wipe it away.

"Sorry," I said, suddenly losing my nerve. "You mentioned, if I wanted, that I could stay here. But I don't have to. I just got home, and I realized I couldn't be there one more second."

"The offer stands," Tina said in this sterile way that stung. The hall in the foyer was cavernous but narrow. We were standing with our backs against opposing walls, and still there wasn't much space between us. The blanket had slipped off one of Tina's shoulders, and she was looking at me in this reverent, hopeful way, like I was the porcelain doll she'd wanted for her birthday, but now that she had me, she could see how easily I'd damage. I'd been looked at like that once before, by CJ, and it had terrified me then too, though not for the reason it did now.

"I don't want to take advantage of your generosity," I backpedaled, staking the perimeter of the conversation. This was about formalizing a living arrangement and nothing outside of that. "It would just be for a little while. Until I get a job and get back on my feet."

Tina tightened the blanket around her shoulders. I'd said the wrong thing. The coward's thing. "Ruth," she said, the same way you might say the word *stop. That's enough now.* "If that's what you want, it's completely fine."

Her signals were all over the place, giving me whiplash. More out of frustration than boldness, I retorted, "It isn't what I want, and I don't think it's what you do either."

Tina tipped her head back against the wall and gazed at me through hooded eyes, amusedly. She was driving me nuts. "Do you know what you're getting into here?"

The house was silent, hearing, all ours. "Unfortunately, I do."

Tina sighed. "I really need you to, though. I can't have you on my conscience along with everything else."

My heart was riding my collarbone. *You do it,* Tina seemed to be saying, *and after that, I'm not responsible for what happens, for what you feel.* Tina was taller than I was and, with her head tipped back, even more difficult to reach without her explicit cooperation. I took a step forward, balancing on my tippy-toes. Tina let me kiss her for a few moments, let me absolve her of any responsibility, and then, as though I had recited the password to the fortress correctly, she opened each end of the blanket and closed it around us, fastening us safely inside.

PAMELA

Tallahassee, 1978

Day 15

knocked on the door of Brian's house, neighborly at first, then made a fist and banged until the bone of my wrist turned red and one of the Freddy Fraternity Boys roused himself from sleep.

"Pamela?" Brian's brother was standing at the door in his underwear and half-tied robe, digging a crusty out of a corner of one eye. "You girls okay?"

I averted my eyes from his small, pale potbelly. "Everything's fine. I need to speak to Brian."

"You want me to wake him?" he asked through a horrid-smelling yawn.

"Please."

He stepped back from the door, inviting me in. It was just after seven in the morning, and I'd been showered and dressed for hours. I'd drastically overestimated my ability to sleep on the floor with thirty-four other women, under the same roof where, a little over two weeks ago, we'd been a house of thirty-nine. Even with all of us heaped together in a protective pack, I'd been hyperaware of every bump in the night, hyperaware of acting like I wasn't hyperaware, putting on a brave face for the girls.

It's just the wind, I'd said to the sister who stirred at one a.m. To the one who bolted upright at two, it was the old bones of The

House. At three, it was the sprinklers in the neighbor's front yard. At four, it was the paperboy, who really needed to oil the wheels on his bicycle, and by then there was no going back to sleep, not when it was an acceptable hour for people to be up and about their days. I went into the kitchen and put on the coffee and began drafting letters to our repeat donors, inviting them to a luncheon at The House. I was going to need to recoup the monies I'd borrowed from the dues account for the damages incurred at The House, assuming victims' assistance would soon cover the deduction. Just thinking about the language of the rejection letter made the tips of my ears turn pink with shame. I had no idea what a sexual relationship exemption entailed, or how it was that we had contributed to our own injuries, but I wanted to crawl into the earth and disappear, picturing a panel of esteemed figures in the community—picturing my future father-in-law—reviewing our case and determining that there was something unsavory and inappropriate about it, about *us*. Sitting there at the kitchen table as the sun cracked the night sky, I was furious with myself for subjecting the girls to this kind of scrutiny. I had let them down. Worse, I'd let *Denise* down.

Brian came jogging down the stairs, wearing light gray sweatpants and a dark gray sweatshirt with his orange fraternity coat of arms on the left chest. "What in the hell is going on?" he asked with crazy eyes and crazier hair.

I passed him the rejection letter from the victims' assistance committee. Brian took it from me and scanned it, standing, then sank down on the third step and read it again.

"What happened?" I asked, my voice much too chipper. I sounded like someone trying to remain calm who was one minor inconvenience away from an atomic meltdown.

Brian tongued at the white film in the corners of his mouth, removing it with his thumb and index finger, wiping that on his sweatpants. I stared at the slime on his knee and experienced a fearsome urge to be alone forever.

"Maybe because of Roger?" Brian offered dimly.

"It's definitely because of Roger," I snapped. "Otherwise there would be no need to apply the sexual exemption to our situation. They're saying he did this, and because Denise used to date him, she somehow brought this on herself."

"I know you're disappointed, Pamela—"

"Furious, actually—"

"Think of it from their point of view! No one's been arrested! All they have to go on is your account. And I'm not trying to upset you, but you did say you thought it was Roger. And now you're considering pressing charges against him—"

"I did press charges."

Brian did a double take. "When did that happen?"

"Yesterday. I called Sheriff Cruso last night."

I'll let the prosecutor know right away, Pamela, Sheriff Cruso had said over the phone. He'd yawned loudly, then laughed, hearing himself. *I'll be honest. I had trouble sleeping last night, thinking about letting this guy out on the street tomorrow. You made the right call.*

I still don't think he killed Denise and Robbie, I'd been quick to say, before we started braiding each other's hair. I wanted desperately to tell him about the trip to Colorado, but Tina and I had talked it over and realized that Carl's story would be more likely to sway Sheriff Cruso if he believed that another person had come to the same conclusion we had, independent of our influence.

Brian nodded firmly. "Good. I think that was your only option, Pamela. But it's not going to help your case here." He waved the rejection letter in case it wasn't clear what he meant by that.

I closed my eyes and pictured the uniform vacuum lines in my carpet that I'd made that morning when I couldn't get back to sleep, willing the orderly image to lower my blood pressure before I said anything I regretted.

"They're only trying to protect the fund for the people who actually need it," Brian said. "And it's hard, because there are a lot of women out there who willingly put themselves in dangerous situations."

"I wish you had communicated this to me before I applied." I opened my eyes to find I was still incapable of focusing on anything but the slobber on Brian's knee. "I could have spared us the humiliation."

From his position on the lower step, Brian reached for my hand, giving it a downward tug. He wanted me to sit next to him. "Who's humiliated? The only people who know about this are me and the people on the panel."

"But I know about it," I said quietly, allowing him to pull me into his lap.

Brian bounced me on his knee as if trying to cheer up a brooding child. "Want me to talk to my dad? Maybe I can get him to reconsider. At the very least, let me pay you back for whatever you're out of pocket."

It was under two thousand dollars. I would easily raise that with a luncheon among our regular donors. "I'd rather you didn't," I said. "I would like to be done with this."

Brian's knee stilled, and he slipped his hand under my hair, lifting it up and over my shoulder so that my face was exposed. "I really admire how you've handled this," he said. The right thing to do was lean in and return the kiss he was clearly angling to deliver. Denise once did this impression of me when someone tried to hug me, or cuddle up, or sit too close. Her thin shoulders shot up, her neck disappearing, and her eyes went big and horrified. *You want to touch me?* She was right that getting too physically close to anyone repelled me. I was afraid of what they might say and how they might smell. I'd had sex with Brian before, but it was always after a date when we'd both been properly perfumed and minted. We'd never spent the night together, and I was aghast to learn what his mouth tasted like in the morning. I parted my lips and accepted the dry slug of his tongue, realizing you have two choices in life. You either wake up to someone's fusty kiss or you wake up alone. Pick your poison.

Later that week, I was up in my room, working through the thank-you notes, when someone shouted my name from the first floor, telling me I had a visitor.

I hurried downstairs to find Carl on my doorstep, a proper beard where I'd last seen thirtysome-hour scruff. He'd been gone six days, and it looked as if he'd come straight from the airport to my front stoop. He broke into a toothy, lopsided grin when he saw me descending the stairs, his whole face taking on a clandestine slant that indicated we shared a secret. I was blushing furiously by the time I met him at the door.

"You're back." I hoped I didn't sound too worshipping.

Carl leaned down, his long eyelashes fluttering sleepily. "Is there somewhere we can talk privately?"

I spun on my heel, gesturing over my shoulder for Carl to follow me, using the short walk to the formal sitting room to bring my cool palms to my hot cheeks. It was lunchtime on a Friday, the sun high and white in the sky, and the girls were ferrying lifeblood through the veins of The House again, bustling to and from class, meetings, practices, appointments. In the daytime, you could almost believe none of it had happened, and maybe that's why the nights hit us as hard as they did. The House was a pressure cooker, but at least during the day we were up and about, back doors and side doors and front doors swinging open and shut. At night, the deadbolts bolted and the drapes drawn, the reality of our situation was detained, compressing in on us with whistling force.

I pulled the double French doors closed. One of my sisters passed by on her way to band practice, her flute in its wooden carrier that I always worried might nick the walls, and she slowed her pace, peering into the narrowing entryway to see who had warranted a meeting in the formal room. I gave her a quick *nothing to worry about* smile just before shutting her out.

Carl let his duffel bag slide off his shoulder and lie in a heap at his feet.

"Here," I said, reaching for it, "let me take that for you."

Carl did a funny karate chop to my wrist, stopping me. He dropped down, butt on his heels, and unzipped the bag. I don't know why, but I followed, plopping onto the carpet across from him. Because I wanted to. Because I was feeling cute.

Carl retrieved a yellow file folder, and instinctively, I grabbed for it. Carl held it high, out of my grasp. "So impatient, Pamela."

"Carl!" I laughed.

"You won't even know what you're looking at if I don't explain it to you first."

I folded my hands reservedly in my lap. "Fine."

"Seattle wasn't all that happy when I showed up asking questions, but I wore them down. Especially after I mentioned making a FOIA request. Do you know what that is?"

I shook my head. Carl explained that the Freedom of Information Act was amended in the aftermath of Watergate, in response to the public call for more transparency from the government. "Technically," Carl said, "the materials Seattle took from Colorado are now federal property, since they crossed state lines. They have to share them with me if I make this request, by law. Seattle knew that, and so they made me a deal."

I stared at the file folder in Carl's hand, too keyed up to breathe.

"They made me a copy of the container list, which catalogs every item in The Defendant's possession during the time he was incarcerated in Colorado." At last, Carl offered me the folder. With trembling hands, I opened it. "Let me know when you see it."

I went down the list with my fingernail, cataloging what I was reading line by line. Interrogation tape number one, interrogation tape numbers two, three, and four—

"After he was captured," Carl explained, "he would only speak to Seattle PD, remember? These are the recordings of those conversations."

"I want to know what they talked about!"

Carl laughed. "Don't we all?"

"So this is what we are going to ask about in the FOIA request?"

Carl shook his head regrettably. "You can only request physical files. Anything video or audio is protected." This would change eventually, but not until 1996, and by then it would be too late. Carl nudged my knee. "Keep reading, though." There was a third-edition criminal law textbook, a few family photographs, deodorant, and . . . I stopped. Tears of relief sprang to my eyes. "Carl," I whispered.

"A 1977 brochure for Florida State University," Carl said without having to look. "He'd had designs on this place for an entire year before he got here."

I wondered where we were and what we were doing when he decided on us. I understood in a new way why premeditation carried a stiffer sentence than crimes that occurred in the heat of the moment. It was a unique kind of violation to think that when you were curled up on the couch, watching *As the World Turns* with your best friend, someone was plotting your demise. I found I was having difficulty swallowing. The more I tried, the tighter my throat became.

"What does this mean for us?" I asked Carl in a strained voice.

"It means I'm going straight from here to get this story down. Four thousand words on the Colorado cover-up that led to a completely preventable double homicide right here in our backyard."

I dragged the heel of my hand beneath my chin, flicking tears onto the copy of the container list. "Oh, God, sorry," I said, using the hem of my sweater to dab the page dry. "I'm just so relieved. They'll have to listen to me now."

Carl nodded with this adoring smile on his face. "It's going to be okay, Pamela."

"Thanks to you," I said. I went to hand him back the document, and he leaned forward slightly. In the heat of the moment, I scooted closer and kissed him.

———

Carl's editor at the *Tallahassee Democrat* wanted the story ready to go. Though we were technically in the golden era of the American serial killer, that would have been news to most of us in 1978. The term had been coined earlier in the decade, but *serial killer* was not yet part of our colloquial true-crime-junkie parlance. There have always been serial killers—in the sixteenth century, they were put on trial as werewolves. There are women serial killers who amass their victims by manipulating others to do their dirty work, and Black serial killers whom we rarely hear about not because they are Black but because their victims are. After a boom of buzzy, media-driven notoriety for The Defendant, the Night Stalker, the Hillside Strangler, and the Golden State Killer, there was enough awareness around the idea that a deranged killer could be masquerading as the friendly usher at your church that anyone imprinted with that dark pathology was forced to tap into a different victim pool in order to keep hunting without getting caught. We don't hear about serial killers much anymore because they target sex workers, people who get into a stranger's car as a means of survival and whose disappearances are less likely to raise alarm bells.

Denise and all the others in Washington, Utah, and Colorado just so happened to be part of a particular victim pool, at a particular moment of comprehension in the field of criminal and social sciences, at a particular moment of media interest. But that flashpoint in history, as most flashpoints tend to be, is detectable only now, with the benefit of hindsight.

So: what Carl's editor thought had promise was not a story about an assailant who was still classified by dull governmental nomenclature but a story about a cover-up. We were post-Watergate, and headlines about corruption and calls for transparency sold big at the newsstand. However, his editor said, we couldn't go around making litigious claims. He would run the story if and when The Defendant was arrested and charged. To say we were all disappointed and frustrated was an understatement, but Carl did take a copy of the container list to Sheriff Cruso, who asked if he could hold on to it. This, the slightest sign of interest, buoyed me for a few days. Then nothing came of it, and I began to envision a life in which the case was never solved, not because there weren't any leads but because of

pure human arrogance. Hopelessness turned to vengeance. I imagined ghoulish scenarios where Sheriff Cruso's wife became The
Defendant's next victim, where he came to me a broken man, ruing
the day he decided to focus on Roger instead of listening to me. My
mind had become a bleak and unrecognizable place.

One week passed indeterminably, then half of the other. At The
House, we moved from the floor of the rec room and into our beds,
figuring that we were scared no matter where we closed our eyes, so
we might as well be comfortable. Denise's roommate that quarter
was a girl named Rosemary Frint, who had been away on a ski trip
the night Denise was killed. She was matter-of-fact about returning
to room eight—all her clothes were there, and she liked the prox-
imity to the bathroom—but I would have felt like a captain abandoning ship if I'd let her sleep in there alone. I offered my balcony
bedroom to Robbie's roommate, who was less keen on returning to
her old accommodations, and I slept in Denise's bed with the new
linens, where, if I lay on my right side, I could be eye to eye with her
print of Dalí's *The Persistence of Memory*. Denise had been staggered
to learn that I lived only thirty minutes outside of New York City
and I'd never gone to see the real thing hanging in the Museum of
Modern Art. The first time she came to visit me, we took the train
in and went straight to the fifth floor, where the original still hangs
in the Alfred H. Barr, Jr. Galleries. I was surprised by the diminu-
tiveness of the piece—the world-famous work was just a couple of
inches wider than a page in the legal pads I used for note-taking in
class. Denise broke down the composition element by element for
me, tourists and schoolchildren gravitating, like she was an erudite
museum guide.

The landscape, she told me, was what Dalí saw outside the window of his single-room shack in Portlligat, a small fishing settlement
in Spain. We were looking at the Mediterranean Sea and the Serra
de Rodes mountain range, rendered hyper-realistically in order to
ground the surreal story taking place on the shore. Over the years, I
would think about that contrast in relation to the mundane realism

that filled my day-to-day life while the story around me continued to unfold in horrific and inexplicable ways.

On Thursday, February 9, shortly before nine in the morning, I was forty minutes into a lecture on proposed reform efforts to the Florida grand jury at the same time a seventh grader named Kimberly Leach was giggling through a set of fifty jumping jacks in gym class at Lake City Junior High, about an hour and a half east of Tallahassee. Remembering that she had forgotten her prized denim purse in her homeroom class, she asked for permission to run back and retrieve it before the light rain turned heavy.

While I was scribbling down the difference between *accusatorial* and *inquisitorial,* Kimberly was rushing back to gym class with her purse tucked under her arm. While I was punctuating *elect more responsible prosecutors* with a question mark, Kimberly was turning to see who had called out to her to slow down before she slipped on the wet pavement. I likely raised my hand to answer the professor's question about what organized-crime figureheads feared the most about grand juries (the promise of immunity from witnesses) at the same time Kimberly screamed. One of the teachers heard it from the second-floor ladies' room, but she had started her period and was trying to get herself cleaned up and sorted. By the time she'd flushed and buckled her belt and gotten over to the window, there was nothing to see, and she thought perhaps it was just one of the middle schoolers dappy about the upcoming Valentine's Day dance. Next door, they were gluing paper lace to paper hearts, threading them to make a party banner for the gym's entrance, where the next day, Kimberly's classmates would scuff up the floors dancing in their dress shoes.

The Persistence of Memory is most famous for its depiction of melting clocks, Denise told the crowd that day in the MoMA. Timepieces are meant to be sturdy, solid, orienting us in the world in a reliable, man-made way. *But look, Pamela,* she said, gesturing, *see how Dalí's clocks are soft and pliant?* Time is illogical, *subjective,* was the interpretation. *What feels like forever for one may feel like a blink of an eye for another,* Denise said, laughing in this sort of astonished way.

It astonishes me too, that while I sat there in Eppes Hall, internally groaning for the professor to wrap it up—by a certain point, he was only echoing the arguments from the reading—Kimberly must have been wishing for a stay as The Defendant slowed to a stop alongside a rural dirt road deep within the Suwannee River State Park. He would have been terrifying to her from the moment she laid eyes on him. Gone were the head-to-toe tennis whites, the plummy voice, and the handicapped act, the pleas to compliant young women for help, which we'd been conditioned since birth to answer the same way he'd been conditioned since birth to expect a woman to take care of him. By the time he snatched his final and youngest victim, he was operating in a desperate and brazen state. I think often about the forces that allowed his abominable last act to occur, how, if not for the corrupt everyday men in the Colorado legislature insisting on The Defendant's extradition for reasons other than justice, Kimberly Leach would be fifty-seven years old today. An age so young it is one year younger than Sandra Bullock.

At last the lecture came to a close, and then I was hurrying back to The House to meet the Coke delivery man, who had not received a copy of the new key and would not ever again. My trust in even those who deserved it had eroded. I had ten minutes to get there and back across campus for economic growth policy at Dodd Hall. I wanted time to slow down at the same time Kimberly was probably wishing it would speed up. When her body was finally found, the pathologist determined she had sustained a massive injury to her pelvic region before she died.

I imagine that as I hoofed it back across campus, checking the watch on my wrist, Kimberly and I were at last in sync with our experience of time. Feeling like there wasn't nearly enough for all the things we had to do.

———

It would take another eight days for the casual two-knuckled rap on the door. Lunchtime on a Friday. I said a muffled hello to Detec-

tive Pickell and Sheriff Cruso through a peanut butter mouth. Their
faces were pleasant but bordering on impatient.

"We left word for you," Cruso said.

I chewed, chewed, forced myself to swallow the last bite of my
sandwich. "I was just eating a quick lunch. I didn't have time to
check the board."

"We have some follow-up questions," Cruso said.

I glanced at Pickell, who nodded. Follow-up questions.

I went to get my coat, heart beating loud and slow, the dramatic
death march that sounded whenever I thought I might have done
something wrong. I assumed they'd heard about me going to Colorado, sticking my nose into official police business. I was cold with
dread as I followed them out to their car.

In the back of their big tan sedan, I told Pickell that we were doing
okay when he asked how we were getting on at The House. The rest of
the drive passed in taut silence. Yes. I was definitely in trouble.

Pickell led me to the same small room where he and Sheriff
Cruso had conducted our first interview. Sheriff Cruso returned
with two coffees and one sugar packet to split between the two of
us. He'd remembered that we took our coffee the same, and I hoped
that meant he had some affection for me, that he'd show me some
mercy.

"Do you know what a photographic lineup is, Pamela?"

I gaped at Sheriff Cruso. I was prelaw and I watched television.
Of course I knew what a lineup was. I also knew that a lineup occurred only after a suspect had been arrested. I tried to temper my
excitement. Roger could be that suspect. Then again, would they really bring me there to pick out someone I knew as well as I did Roger?

"I do," I answered as nonchalantly as I could.

Sheriff Cruso signaled Pickell, who produced a three-ring
binder. He set it on the table while Sheriff Cruso explained why I
was there and what he needed me to do.

Inside were twenty-nine photographs of Caucasian men in their late twenties and early thirties, stored in plastic-slip pages and numbered in charcoal pencil. I was instructed to go through each page carefully to see if I recognized the man I'd seen at the front door in the early-morning hours of January 15. It was like a man proposing without getting down on one knee. This was such a huge moment, but it all felt so unceremonious.

Around suspect nineteen, panic set in. The Defendant's face was nowhere to be found.

"There is no rush," Sheriff Cruso said, sensing my anxiety.

"No one is trying to trick you," Pickell added. I believed him that they weren't trying, but still I felt tricked.

"Can I start from the beginning again?" I asked. The pages were running out, the left side of the binder heavier than the right. Maybe he had been there and I'd missed him.

"Take as long as you need," Cruso said.

I flipped back to the beginning, went through the first half again. I hadn't missed him. I was sure of it. I proceeded past suspect nineteen. Near the last page, my heart boomed with relief and recognition.

"This one," I declared confidently. I placed a fingernail beneath suspect number twenty-seven. It was The Defendant, wearing a black turtleneck, sporting a costumey handlebar mustache.

Sheriff Cruso's demeanor gave no indication as to whether I'd chosen correctly or not. "Do you feel this is definitely the person you saw, or do you feel this is a striking resemblance?" He used his fingers to cover up The Defendant's hair and neck so that only his face was visible.

A spike of fear, of not wanting to close down my options so quickly. But I answered firmly, "That is definitely the person I saw."

"Please read the photograph's number out loud for me."

"Twenty-seven," I said, too loud.

"This concludes the photographic lineup. Time is two-oh-eight p.m., Friday, February seventeenth, 1978." Sheriff Cruso switched off the recorder.

"Has there been an arrest?" I asked. "I haven't seen anything on the news."

"Miss Schumacher," Sheriff Cruso admonished with a teasing smile. I should know he wasn't at liberty to disclose that kind of information, not even to me, The Eyewitness. He stood and held open the door. "Thank you for your time. Hopefully, Leon County won't need any more of it."

But Leon County would—a lot more of it. The next day, Saturday, I woke to find The Defendant smiling in handcuffs on the front page of the *Tallahassee Democrat*, wearing a pretentious alpine-style sweater on his way into circuit court in Pensacola, the westernmost city of the Panhandle. The bizarre tale of his capture had started at one thirty a.m. on Wednesday, six days after Kimberly Leach went missing and approximately one month after Denise and Robbie were killed and Jill, Eileen, and the student in the off-campus apartment on Dunwoody were nearly bludgeoned to death. The article described how a Pensacola patrolman stopped a man in a Volkswagen that had been reported stolen in Tallahassee earlier this month. How the man attempted to run from the car after a high-speed chase.

At the city jail, the prisoner gave his name as Kenneth Raymond Misner, twenty-nine, of Tallahassee. Though he carried Misner's identification papers and a number of stolen credit cards, the real Kenneth Misner, a former FSU track star, soon came forward.

By Friday morning, detectives had developed a hunch that their prisoner was The Defendant. Two hours later, FBI agents arrived with Wanted posters and fingerprints. Two hours after that, Pickell and Sheriff Cruso had shown up at my door.

References were made to the fact that The Defendant was indeed in Tallahassee during the month of January, when the FSU slayings took place; and that some of the other crimes The Defendant was sought for also involved blunt weapons, sexual assault, and strangulation.

One of the investigators said there was evidence that The Defendant had rented a room in an apartment complex in Tallahassee, known among FSU grad students as The Oak. They were combing through it for evidence now. I sat down hard, my kneecaps turned to taffy. Read that again. *The Oak.* The hairs at the base of my skull were bristled, painful quills.

The Oak was two blocks away. All this time, he had been my neighbor.

RUTH

Issaquah

Spring 1974

ne thing you did that always made me angry.

CJ and I started sneaking around after we kissed at my brother's wedding. At first it was only letters and trinket gifts, addressed to me at Eastern State, where I'd returned the day after the ceremony. No matter that CJ was married to another woman—Dr. Burnet was as proud as a father giving away his own daughter at the altar. Here was proof that I'd never been a lesbian to begin with, that I'd only been acting out my anger at my father for failing to protect me from my overbearing mother. *Textbook*, Dr. Burnet declared.

With Dr. Burnet's blessing, I was discharged a few months shy of my eighteenth birthday. I was too embarrassed to return to school, to spend the year I'd missed lying about where I'd been. Instead, I got a job as a cashier at a pharmacy, and on my lunch breaks, CJ would come by in his Grand Prix and make drugged-sounding promises to me in the back seat before ejaculating. He was going to leave his mess of a wife as soon as I turned eighteen, and then we would start a family and be together forever. CJ and the wife were barely speaking at that point, sleeping in separate rooms on the nights she didn't pass out drunk in the driveway, but he was concerned about what his parents would think, what his wife's parents would think, if he initiated a divorce to be with a seventeen-year-old girl. Neither of us worried about my family. My mother was acting like she'd had a biopsy and the result had come back benign. Relieved. Grateful. She had a whole new lease on life.

I was in no rush for CJ to leave his wife. The idea of it left me ridden with anxiety about the future. Would he propose right away? Did I really want to say yes? To CJ? We'd known each other since we were kids, and I cared about him like a brother, maybe even more than my own brother, who had betrayed me without thinking twice about it. I found the sex thrilling at first. The way CJ gripped my chin in his hand and forced me to look at him, the way my name trembled on his lips—like he was checking to make sure I was still beneath him. I wanted to do it again and again, to bask in his uncertainty that he could really have me. In my family, everything revolved around the emotional temperature of my mother. No one had ever treated me like I was the silver ball of mercury in the thermometer's glass chamber.

So why, then, did I start awake in the middle of the night, heart flapping in the trap of my chest, at the thought of marrying this man who adored me so much? I didn't need a psychiatrist to tell me it was because of Rebecca.

Growing up, Rebecca was my best friend, a skinned-kneed, scraggly-haired runt of a girl. But sometime around the fifth grade, we were playing two-hand tag with my brother and a bunch of the neighborhood kids when I noticed that she had spawned breasts. Heavy ones that bounced around in her sweater when she ran. The same boys who used to charge us with no mercy, who used to laugh when we climbed to our feet, chewing dirt, suddenly started going easy on her, handling her with the gentle hands Rebecca would later remind me to use while holding her newborn. More and more, Rebecca emerged from the game the last one standing, the boys too smitten to touch her.

My brother, who for so long wanted nothing to do with the two of us when we were in the house, started finding excuses to drop by my bedroom when Rebecca was over, and Rebecca, in turn, stopped wanting to play with the door locked. We were getting too old to play like that anyway, she told me. It was babyish; unhygienic.

Soon we were painting our nails and listening to Bob Dylan records with my bedroom door open. I liked the Beatles, but Rebecca said the Beatles were for little girls, which we weren't anymore. Before long, it wasn't even my room Rebecca was spending time in. My brother was fifteen, Rebecca thirteen, the first time he called her his girlfriend. Yet still the two of us didn't stop until we were made to stop.

I can no longer remember whose idea it was, but when we reached high school, we started meeting at the old clergy house after school. We'd talk for a few minutes about our day, which teacher was hassling us, and then one of us would lie back and pull down her wool tights, let her legs fall open for the other. We coached each other through it, in an uninhibited and plainspoken manner, as though reading the steps to a recipe—knuckles first, softly, then the thumb, firmer, then firmer still, now with the heel of the hand. We kept time. Whoever went second got as long as the one who went first. We were fair like that.

Dr. Burnet called what we did *exploring*, something all children did, and something that, due to our respective emotional difficulties, the two of us had simply failed to grow out of.

It's a comforting ritual left over from childhood, Dr. Burnet was always telling me. *Like sucking your thumb or sleeping with a stuffed animal.* When I would nod with half-hearted agreement, he would remind me that Rebecca and I never once kissed. *Lesbians kiss, Ruth.*

Rebecca and I had an unspoken agreement that we wouldn't meet during the spring, which was when my father held class outside on the lawn, teaching the unit about the clergy house's role in the Underground Railroad. It was a warm afternoon in October when my father walked in and found us. He didn't look surprised, which was how I knew he'd always known.

When he came upon us, Rebecca was the one lying back with

her skirt pulled up. This mattered because he saw what *I* was doing to *her*, that I was the aggressor and Rebecca my witless victim. My father shielded his eyes and, in a muted voice, told me to meet him at the car. The drive home was brittle with silence, and when I looked over at him, trying to figure out what I might say to break it, I saw that he had big fat tears dripping off his chin.

I went straight to my room when we got home. I unpacked my books and started on my homework, knowing I would be called downstairs once my father told my mother what he'd found out about me. It was a last gasp at absolution. *Here I am,* I hoped my studiousness telegraphed, *memorizing algebraic variations, being a good girl.*

The volume of my parents' voices downstairs was terrifying and confusing, much too quiet for the severity of my transgressions. My mother yelled when she was angry. She slammed cabinet drawers and pummeled the door with her fist, growling at you to get your butt downstairs or else. This ferocious hush between the two of them seemed to suggest that I'd committed an offense so perverse that their larynxes had to produce a whole new set of sound waves and vibrations. Though at one point, inexplicably, it was my father's voice that pierced the bubble, delivering an anguished apology to my mother: *How many times can I say I'm sorry?*

I waited and waited to be summoned downstairs, but the call never came. The resentful whispering ceased when my brother came home. Dinnertime came and went. The television went on and off. I was too petrified to leave my room, and I went to bed without brushing my teeth, dying for a glass of water, my stomach performing somersaults for food.

In the morning, I rose before the sun was up. I showered, dressed in my school uniform, went downstairs, and downed a glass of water. I was scrambling eggs when my mother came in and asked with a malicious laugh what the hell I thought I was doing.

"You're not going to school today," she informed me.

I pushed the eggs around in the pan. My father and I liked them wet, but we cooked them on high heat when my mother or brother wanted some. They both thought wet eggs were disgusting, even though, during the brief period when my father filled in as the home ec teacher, he'd said that was the true chef's way of cooking them.

"We'll talk about it later," my mother said, not that I had asked.

After school, my father came home with the young priest who taught gym class at Issaquah Catholic. He was grossly out of his depth on our couch, boxed in on one side by my erect and formidable mother and the other by my hangdog father. My mother spoke at a pitch so low I had to hold my body completely still to make out what she was saying. There was a place where I was going to receive psychiatric treatment. Father Grady was nice enough to pull some strings to get me in. I was not to talk about where I was going and why—not even to my brother. *Especially* not to my brother, who would be disgusted to learn what I'd done to his poor innocent girlfriend. Did I understand?

I nodded tearfully. "When do I go?"

"Tomorrow," my mother said.

I whimpered and looked at my father. *Tomorrow?*

"It's not a bad place, Ruthie," he said softly. My mother shot him a savage look around Father Grady's head and he cleared his throat. "But since you are seventeen, in order to be admitted, you need to agree to go voluntarily."

I frowned. "So I don't have to go if I don't want to?"

Father Grady finally spoke. "No. You don't. However, Issaquah Catholic is not an option for you until you've been evaluated by a psychiatric professional."

"Can't I go to the public school?" I asked—no, begged—my father. I saw his features tighten once, then slacken, like it was too much effort to hold the anger he was meant to hold against me.

"Remember what you said last night," my mother cawed at him.

My father closed his eyes a moment, his nose reddening and running. When he looked at me next, it was with a cold detachment that blindsided me. "You are lucky, Ruth, that this is all we are asking of you. We could kick you out of the house. We could call Rebecca's parents. We could never speak to you again."

My lungs felt bruised; it hurt to take anything but the shallowest of breaths.

"Please, Ruth." My father was the one to beg me then, so pitifully I cringed. "Help me out here."

When he submitted to my mother—that was the one thing he did that always made me angry. *Be the man,* I wanted to say. I wanted to humiliate him, to tug, tug, tug on the thread that would unravel the murky suspicions I'd always harbored about him. Why we were so well matched in every aspect, why he seemed to understand me on a level no one else did. *I know what is wrong with you,* I could have said, *because you passed your sickness on to me.*

But I couldn't do it. Not then, at least. I went upstairs and I packed my bags. It was never an option to say no to someone who needed my help.

———

Tina rested my journal in her lap, splayed open to my last line. We were lying in her four-poster bed, our feet intertwined, wearing sheer lace nightgowns. Tina's mimosa-yellow kimono hung on one post, designed by Norman Norell and featured in the 1965 issue of *Vogue.* Every night, the housekeeper set out matching white cotton slippers on either side of the bed as if this were a hotel. Tina lived urbanely, like someone was following her around and writing a profile about her and she didn't want to give them one negative thing to put in print.

"Well, *I'm* proud of you," Tina said.

I rolled my eyes.

"You did the best you could do under those circumstances. You have a very superficial mother, Ruth, who is much more concerned about appearances than your well-being."

I pictured my mother's bowl haircut, her everyday walking shoes with the thick slabs of foam on the soles to protect her knees. I could

not square *her* with such an impeachment. My mother, superficial?
She terrified me, sure, but right then she was likely watching television all alone, minding the electricity bill by keeping a single lamp
on, so unneeded by anyone in our dark, empty house.

"You feel bad for her," Tina observed.

"She's all alone now."

"But it's not your responsibility to make sure she's okay. Nor was
it to help your father out by succumbing to your mother's wishes."

I shrugged. *Sure.*

"Do you know what an empath is?"

I laughed, it was so obvious. "Someone with a lot of empathy?"

"It's when you care so much about others that you take on their
feelings and experience this *compulsory* urge to help them. A lot of
women are like this, and society is all too happy to exploit it." I must
not have looked properly incensed, because Tina began listing, in
an outraged tone, examples of how this quality had sent my life off
the rails. "You ended up marrying someone you didn't even want
to marry to make your parents feel good! You dropped out of high
school to go to a mental institution to appease them!"

I lifted my hands impotently. "I guess I just don't see what you
want me to do about it now."

"I want you to get mad! You should be mad!"

I reached for my journal and snapped it shut. "I did get mad. You
read it yourself."

"And it lasted for approximately one evening, when you were
seventeen years old, and then you just went along with everything
your family wanted you to do."

"You're actually wrong," I said, because she did not yet know
how my father died. "And *now* I'm getting mad." I reached over and
shut off the lamp on the bedside table.

"How am I wrong?" Tina asked in the dark. "What happened?
Why did your nephew say that thing about you hurting your dad's
feelings right before he died? Why did he say everyone hates you?"

I rolled onto my side, giving Tina my back. "Didn't you tell me in Aspen that it's okay to stop when it starts to feel like too much?" I turned my face so that I was speaking to the ceiling, so that the word carried. *"Stop."* It didn't escape me that she was perhaps the only person in my life I'd told to stop anything, and that not only did she listen to me, she didn't make me feel bad about it either.

In the morning, fog shrouded the panoramic views from Tina's bedroom windows, razing the Seattle skyline to the same elevation as Lake Washington. Tina was asleep, and I lay there watching the pink scar on her tan chest rise and fall—Nixon had marked her as his—wondering if I had the courage to wake her up the way she had been waking me up for the last few weeks.

"Sorry," Tina said, her eyes still closed. "About last night. I shouldn't have pushed you on it."

"I have an idea," I said, and she opened her eyes to hear it.

Tina had been hard at work, studying for her jurisprudence exam in August. I had relished having her big, gorgeous kitchen to myself for most of the day, with expensive gadgets and her Ruffoni copper cookware, in making her French press coffee and plating beautiful meals for her on her old wedding china.

When I was CJ's wife, I didn't think anything about making dinner and cleaning up after him. I bought cheap cuts of meat because even though CJ earned a decent living, he was frugal, and he had no palate. I made the things my father made for us at my mother and brother's behest: casseroles and meat loaf with gravy, thick sloppy stuff that clung to CJ's beard and neutered my appetite in more ways than one. But at Tina's, I served fish and vegetables that were not previously frozen. I poured red wine into crystal glasses and lit candles that burned high between us.

I suggested we throw a dinner party.

"We can invite all the girls from the grief group," I said. "And Frances, of course."

Tina reached out and tucked my hair behind my ear with a

closed-lip, conciliatory smile. "I'm not sure all the girls in the grief group would understand." She gestured: me in her bed.

"But Janelle was here," I protested. "You introduced me to Janelle." I thought about Janelle more than I cared to admit. I wondered if Tina thought that people might have an easier time understanding her and Janelle because Janelle was composed and confident, because she wore nice jewelry and didn't have acne pits in her cheeks.

"I wasn't planning to. You arrived early."

"So it's a secret society we're in."

Tina frowned. "Secret society?"

"Of people like you," I said, and realized that wasn't cruel enough to hurt her. "*Women* like you."

Quietly, Tina said, "There's no secret society, Ruth. Just women who care about each other." She sat up and reached for her robe. I reached for her hand.

"I'm sorry." With my thumb, I brushed the thin blue vein that ran the length of her forearm. "I would really like to throw a dinner party, though." Tina shivered, but she didn't lie back down. "We could invite Janelle too."

Tina looked down at me with a gorgeous smirk. And then she was crawling on top of me, straddling me on all fours. "Let's just add CJ and Martha to the list while we're at it," she said. It took all my strength to push her face away when I felt her cool breath on my neck.

"I was just trying to be nice."

"So am I," Tina said. She grabbed my wrists and pinned them to the pillow above my head, nuzzling the stretch of skin between my jaw and my ear. I wondered if Janelle had taught her that, or if Tina had always known what to do. I couldn't decide which version of her made me crazier, the girl who had to be taught or the girl who just knew.

PAMELA

Tallahassee, 1978

Day 35

The Defendant's capture unleashed something into the world. At first, from the epicenter in Tallahassee, I was unaware of the impact. Here, it was completely normal that The Defendant was all we could talk about, that his picture was on the front page of every newspaper and the top news story of the day. He had proclaimed his innocence with a waggish grin. He'd fled Colorado because although he hadn't murdered Caryn Campbell, the media had already convicted him and tarnished his shot at a fair trial. He'd lied about his identity to the police in Pensacola for two days because he'd known they would tie him to the carnage at The House as well as to the disappearance of Kimberly Leach, and he had nothing to do with either one. Women were attacked all the time, by all sorts of men, weren't they?

It wasn't until my mother called and pleaded with me to come home for the weekend that I had any sense of the nationwide strain. My mother did not plead.

"Bring . . ." She paused. I had no doubt she was closing her eyes, knowing she had one shot to get this right. "Brian," she said, by some small miracle.

There weren't any direct flights from Tallahassee to Newark back then, and there still aren't today. It was in the tin hangar of the

Atlanta airfield, a decade before it was transformed into the yawning Hartsfield-Jackson complex, that I first noticed it. The Defendant, everywhere. I went to buy a coffee and a magazine and overheard a customer asking where he could get a newspaper. I read the labels on the empty stalls as the cashier apologized: they had completely sold out earlier that day. No one could get enough of the story about the polite murderer in the robin's-egg-blue suit he'd worn to his arraignment. I saw Carl's byline constantly, and I'd scan the article, eager to read the Colorado cover-up story finally, but it was never about that. *My editor said he needs to be charged, not just arrested,* Carl scoffed in a *Can you believe this guy?* tone. *I have the whole thing written and copyedited and everything.* But within weeks, The Defendant had been charged with first-degree murder for the slayings of Denise and Robbie, and the attempted murders of Jill, Eileen, and the student in the off-campus apartment. He pleaded not guilty. And still Carl's editor wouldn't run the story, saying if it came out now, it would get lost in the swirl of publicity. He wanted to make sure that when the article ran, it made a splash.

Sitting back down at the makeshift gate, I took stock. Everywhere I looked, people were holding up their papers, local and city and national alike, various versions of The Defendant's face staring back at me like some perverted version of masks at a masquerade ball.

"I'm already so sick of this," Brian said, shifting uncomfortably in the too-small chair. Travel was a wholly unpleasant experience for someone with his gangling proportions, and back then we did not dress for comfort. Brian wore a summer blazer and linen loafers, looking like the last of the Southern gentlemen, and he opened doors and carried my bag. Other women were watching us dreamily, and I forced myself to watch back, the way they tell you to look to the stewardesses when you hit a bad patch of turbulence. If they're not worrying, then neither should you.

I always took a taxi home from Newark airport. Denise loved that about coming home with me. She'd pop her hip, fling her thumb into the street, and throw me a minxy look over her shoulder. *Am I doing it right?* I would laugh and pretend like this was a part of my life that dazzled me too. I used to believe that Denise and I told each other everything, but there were certain things neither of us was ready to admit to ourselves back then. How deep it cut that my parents could never be bothered to pick me up from the airport. That was my best-kept secret, even from myself.

On the radio, they were talking about The Defendant. There was a three-way war raging between Colorado, Florida, and Utah. Utah wanted him back behind bars, where he should have been all this time anyway. Colorado was whispering into Florida's ear: *Let us try him for Caryn Campbell's Aspen murder while you guys work out the details on your end.* The radio hosts were saying, *Florida better get their act together, present their evidence before a grand jury sooner than tomorrow.* No one thought it was a good idea for Colorado to have him. They'd proven their incompetence twice over.

"Hell, I'll take him," the driver said. "Give me fifteen minutes with the son of a bitch." I stared at the back of his head in utter disbelief. Was there some sort of script men were instructed to follow in these kinds of situations? It was exactly the language Brian and Mr. McCall had used over dinner at the mansion in Red Hills.

"Sir," Brian appealed. Their eyes met in the rearview mirror, and Brian's slid in my direction. *A lady is present.* My stomach slopped sideways. Motion sickness, perhaps. "Can we listen to some music instead?"

The driver twisted the dial and landed on an old track by the Supremes. *You're nobody till somebody loves you.* He nodded apologetically at Brian in the rearview mirror.

———

Doreen, our housekeeper since before I was born, was the only one home. She was an Irish woman in her midforties with six children, petite and round-faced, like me. My mother was always taking her by the hands and holding up her arms, crucifix-like, saying, *This waist, Doreen.*

Doreen took the bags from Brian as if they weighed nothing and asked if we were hungry. Brian was starved, but I just wanted to shower and to know when my parents would be home.

"Soon," Doreen promised, which was what she used to tell me as a kid. *Soon* could be anywhere from an hour to two days. "Go freshen up and I'll make you a plate." Doreen took Brian's bags to the first-floor guest bedroom, and he followed, saying he couldn't wait for a hot meal.

I'd moved into my older sister's room after she graduated from college and got married. There were eight years between us, and while I didn't have many memories of what my mother was like with her, their relationship intimated a sort of closeness and comfort that had been established early. Some part of me thought I could slip into her place and my mother may not notice. Of course, it didn't work out that way, but I never forgot the trying, how it made me ache with confusion. What was I doing wrong?

I went into my mother's room and shook one of her sleeping pills into my hand. I stepped out of my shoes and hung my coat in her closet, nuzzled alongside her pack of minks. I curled up without getting under the covers, my head at the foot of the bed, and fell fast asleep, thinking about how my parents would find me immediately when they came home.

———

I woke with my pulse gaveling my wrists. Someone was in the bed, touching me. I launched forward, tangling in the blanket by the footboard, wheezing and wild-eyed.

"It's me!" my mother was saying. "Pamela, it's me!"

She came around the back of the bed and hooked her elbows under my armpits, freeing me from the snarl of the comforter. My blouse clung to my back in a feverish sweat.

"What time is it?" I asked her in a drowsy voice.

"Eleven."

"In the morning?" I cried.

"Shh, shh," my mother said. "It's nighttime, and Brian is sleeping." She pointed at the Turkish rug, where, just below, his bedroom was located.

I looked at her properly then. The diamond-shaped peonies in her ears, the matching collar of the necklace. Fifty thousand dollars, her head was worth. She'd been out somewhere. A dinner. A party.

"You weren't supposed to get in until tomorrow," she said, a touch of defensiveness in her tone.

"But I found an earlier flight. I told Doreen to tell you."

"I didn't know," my mother said, stroking my hair. It would not have been fair to call her a liar. Few things were worth remembering, in her world.

For weeks, I'd been a wave cresting, searching for a shore on which to break. I immediately dissolved into my mother's arms. It had been so long since she'd let me hold her that I'd forgotten her smell: Lubriderm and lipstick.

"Come downstairs," my mother said when I finally released her. "Doreen said you missed dinner. You're so *thin*, Pamela." I had noticed that my pants were fitting looser, that sometimes I went to bed wondering why I was so hungry because I'd had a burger for dinner, before realizing that was the night before. Each day seemed impossibly long, the permanence of the situation unbearable, and yet the details of my hours remained a complete blur in my memory. This would happen only one other time in my life. The spring of 2020, during the worst of it. I realized then that those years following Denise's death weren't unlike the shutdowns and the school closures and the unceasing confinement of quarantine. I was held captive by a virus that had been around a long time, that had finally mutated to infect me. Him.

———

I watched my mother set a bowl of soup in front of me, wondering if I was still dreaming. My mother was a very influential woman, platinum blond and buttoned up in a Halston shirtdress, something of a suburban snake charmer. You could go to her, shredded to pieces over some terrible hurt, and come away with hypnotized, drugged eyes, speaking in her same distracted lilt, as though nothing in life was worth so much bother. She was twenty-one when she married my thirty-five-year-old divorced father, and she was still throwing outrageous parties with her young friends where they turned up Elton John on the record player and baked midnight brownies that I brought to the neighbors in the morning, apologizing for the noise on her behalf. *Your mom is a blast,* Denise once said, and I'd burned with embarrassment for the both of us. It took my mother a year to remember that my best friend's name was Denise and not Diane.

"Dad is at work?" I assumed.

My mother was looking around for the table linens but had no idea where they were. She swiped the dish towel off the hook, folded it, and set my spoon on top.

"He's spending the night in the city," she said. "But he made reservations for lunch for all four of us tomorrow."

"Manny Wolf's?" I guessed. Manny Wolf's was a steak house in Midtown that offered enormous portions on white tablecloths. My father had been a regular for decades.

My mother laughed lightly—*where else?* She sat down across from me and popped off one of her heels, then the other, groaning as she kneaded the ball of her foot with her thumbs. She had her ankle balanced on her knee, the sole of her foot turned up, when she said, "Do you remember cutting your foot on the beach in Sanibel Island when you were little?"

I chased a piece of carrot around the bowl. "Sanibel Island? As in Florida?"

"Yes," my mother said with a palpable sense of dread. It was how children sounded when asked if they knew what they did wrong.

When they were caught, red-handed, drawing on the cream-colored sofa with crayons.

I set down my spoon and looked at her, realizing I was in the middle of something. "You said it was my first time in Florida when I went to visit the campus."

My mother turned away from me with a quiet moan. "When you were four years old," she began, "we went to Sanibel Island for a vacation." She frowned, remembering. "The beaches were terribly rocky."

I almost laughed. My mother stayed in some of the nicest hotels in the world, and yet she always had a *comment*. But this wasn't a review. The terribly rocky beach was the inciting incident.

"You cut your foot, and I took you back to the hotel for a bandage," she continued. "You were bleeding quite a bit, and I didn't want to track it onto the hotel carpet. I set you down on a lounge chair by the pool for all of sixty seconds while I ran inside to ask for bandages." She crossed her arms and gave herself one fortifying squeeze. *You can do this.* "When I came back, you were gone."

We stared at each other across the kitchen table. There was a dull ache in my rib cage, like an old injury that throbs in the drop of barometric pressure right before a storm hits.

"What happened to me?" I asked in a mechanical voice.

My mother got up from the table and came back with a bottle of gin and two glasses. She poured each of us a medicinal splash. I actually drank mine. "You were found by a park ranger four days later, wandering some place called the Robinson Preserve?" She turned up a palm—maybe I knew it now, after living in Florida the last few years? But I shook my head. I had never heard of it, though once I got back to Tallahassee, I'd go to the lobby of Tina's hotel and request one of the tourist maps of Florida, where I'd locate the waterfront farmland near the southwest border. Robinson Preserve was five hundred square acres of uninhabited swampland and mudflats.

"It was two hours away from where we were in Sanibel. You should have been covered in bug bites. Dehydrated. Weak. But you were *fine*. Happy, even. Pamela, I—" She stopped. Considered how to say the rest. I was remembering what I looked like as a child when I was happy. I had curly hair at that age. Cut at my chin. Dimples then too. They faded sometime in high school, around the same time the curls grew out, as if the biology of womanhood mandated a disposal of frivolity. My mother had been the one to point out that the dimples had disappeared. *I knew it would happen once you lost the baby fat,* she'd said with relief. I hadn't known dimples were a thing one should hope to lose.

"I accepted," my mother was saying in a somber stranger's voice, "that you were dead on the third day. I'd let you go. I know you've probably felt some distance from me over the years, and while it is no excuse, I think a part of me has always been afraid to get too close to you again. I'd already lost you once." One black mascara tear escaped an eye. My mother wiped it away expertly, without leaving so much as a smudge.

"Why wasn't I covered in bug bites?" I felt a distinct lack of fear. Like I had been watching a scary movie all my life, suspended in the anticipation of encountering the monster, a disquiet far worse than any kelp-strung swamp creature could engender. I was in the next part of the movie now, the part where I knew what I was up against, what I had to do to survive.

A tremble of my mother's lips, almost a pitying smile for me. No satisfying answer could be supplied. "That's the mystery, Pamela. There's no way you could have gotten to where you were on foot. Someone took you. But when we asked you what happened, if anyone hurt you, you would just point to the wound on your foot and say *ouch.* You had been hurt by someone, I'm sure of it, but your mind seemed to have confused the source."

That night I would sit on the floor of my bathroom, where the light was overhead and the floor a luminous hospital white, and examine every inch of my bare feet, searching for a trace of the shell-shaped scar. When I detected a pink wrinkle in my right instep, I would flounder for the toilet and throw up the gin.

"Then," my mother said somewhat angrily, "you were absolutely hell-bent on attending Florida State."

I had the sensation of lying on a cold slab, split down the middle, organs taking turns on the pathologist's stainless-steel worktable. So this was what it felt like to be autopsied alive.

"I hated the idea of you being back there, but the place had this viselike grip on you. You would not be dissuaded." My mother had made woo-woo remarks like that in the past, but I'd always written it off as part of her shtick. The universe and its mysterious ways made for a convenient scapegoat for a woman like Marion Young, a woman who was always talking about going with the flow, as though her actions and choices did not impart a tidal force of consequence.

I could think of nothing to say. A part of me wanted to deny it. No one person was destined to suffer this much misfortune! But how could I deny something that rang this true? *I don't know you well enough to know what happened to you young,* Tina had said to me, so sure something *had* happened, and I realized in a spangled explosion of awareness that she and I shared something few people could understand. The particular trace pain of the unknowing, like an undercurrent that swept us through life, stronger at times than our own free will. I may never know exactly what I endured those four days my mother thought I was dead, but I knew I had suffered, and that wasn't for nothing. It returned a modicum of control, a sense of agency over my choices in life, and it committed me to giving that to Tina too. My unknowing featured impassable borders, but hers did not. The answer to what happened to Ruth was sitting in a jail cell in Leon County.

For the time being, there was only one thing I could say to my mother. The truth is something people will go to great lengths to keep for themselves. It shouldn't feel like a gift when you get it, but it is. I looked her in the eyes, and I thanked her for giving it to me.

The next morning, I found Doreen in the kitchen, preparing the tray that came out only when someone in the family was sick.

"It's that head cold going around," Doreen told me. "Your dad is still expecting you and Brian for lunch." She saw my face and moved fast to give me a distraction. "Slice up that lemon, won't you?" I reached for the cutting board, crestfallen. I had been nervous to see my mother that morning too. A shuttered line of connection had opened between us, and it was bound to be nebulous and uncomfortable for a bit. But still I'd showered and dressed and come down to the kitchen to put the clumsy morning after behind us, to move forward honestly. I hacked at the lemon, feeling more motherless than ever.

When I'd looked out the window that morning, it was overcast in a way that made me think it was cold. But an hour later, walking the Penn Station train platform between the fountains of engine exhaust, I felt slick and grimy in my winter coat.

"New York really is such an ugly city," Brian remarked as we waited in the taxi line on Seventh Avenue. He scowled at the spartan hub built upon the rubble of the magnificent old terminal. No one had realized how beautiful it was until it was gone.

"Tallahassee's new Capitol Building isn't any better," I reminded him. Though, in fairness, the community down there had banded together to save the original structure, a sprawling white mansion with candy-striped awnings, an acre of marble for flooring.

Brian turned his scowl up to the sky. "At least you can see the sun. And pretty soon we'll be smelling the ocean on the way to class." Shorebird College of Law was located on the Gulf Coast, some inlet that supposedly drew more bull sharks than anywhere else in the state. *Those are the docile kind, right?* I'd asked Brian. But that was the lemon shark. Bull sharks were responsible for over eighty percent of fatal attacks on humans.

"The weather isn't cooperating today," I quibbled.

Brian laughed. "Does it ever here?"

You should see the Fifth Avenue tulips on Easter Sunday, I would have said if the bellman hadn't been whistling irritably for us to get into the taxi. I loved that they still wore the old uniforms that the Vanderbilts had designed, with the spiffy waistcoat and the red-and-black brimless cap.

In the taxi on the way to meet my dad, Brian continued to lodge complaints. It smelled like trash, didn't it? Could I roll up my window? "This traffic!" he cried when we sat at the same Lexington light for three cycles.

I peeled off my coat and concentrated on breathing in through my nose and out through my mouth. When we finally made it to Third Avenue, I took out my wallet and thrust a ten-dollar bill at the driver. We had only six blocks to go, but I needed air.

Dad was the in-house counsel for a big bank, boisterous and brilliant; he wore a rotation of pretty paisley-printed bow ties and dark suits. *I'm serious only if you make me—but you don't wanna make me* seemed to be his legal strategy. Once, when my nephew was a baby, I'd overheard him when he thought no one was listening, cooing something about how he was rich and one day my nephew would be rich too. My nephew had giggled and shrieked in delight.

Thankfully, the air-conditioning was on at Manny Wolf's. Dad was already sitting at his regular booth, the one beneath the autographed picture of Dean Martin smoking in the basement meat locker, surrounded by hanging carcasses brindled with fat.

"Here she is," Dad sang out as he stood. He clasped me by the shoulders and made a show of looking me over, as though to confirm for himself that I was intact and all right. I was almost positive it was to hide the fact that there were tears in his eyes, and I felt an immediate sense of grounding. Like I belonged to someone, somewhere. My father and I had never been particularly close, but something had shifted after he found out I'd gotten into Columbia Law. He started to talk to me like a peer then. In the latter half of my life, he would become my best friend.

"Nice to see you, sir." Brian was nearly a foot taller than my father, but next to him he always appeared diminished and nervous. Like an elephant afraid of a spider.

"Monsieur Armstrong," Dad replied archly. My father was a first-generation Irish immigrant from Woodside who spoke with long o's and w's, just like Ed Koch. Southern niceties sparked suspicion.

We sat and I sipped my ice water. It tasted like home, pure and clean. Brian asked for a Budweiser, which they did not have, so he settled for a whiskey and soda.

"Sorry to hear your mother isn't feeling well," Dad said.

"You two were up late," Brian said. "Gabbing away in the kitchen."

Alarm coursed through me. "You heard us?"

"A word here and there," Brian said. I stared at him, wanting to ask which words, but then the waiter came over with menus and a recommendation for the oysters, arrived on ice from Montauk that morning.

"So," my father said after we'd decided on a dozen for the table, "I'm hearing Farmer is on board."

Millard Farmer was a hotshot civil rights attorney from Atlanta who spent much of his career representing Black people in high-profile capital punishment cases and making sure everyone knew he represented Black people in high-profile capital punishment cases. The Defendant had written to him, asking if he would join his team of defenders in Leon County. Farmer had readily agreed.

"What I don't understand," Brian said, "is how come he even needs Farmer if he's planning on representing himself again?"

"It's a complex litigation," I answered.

"I'd love to hear your thinking on it, sir," Brian said, straight across the table, as though I hadn't spoken at all.

Dad turned up a palm, coolly. Could be any number of reasons. "A case with stakes this high requires a team. The witness list will be long. No chance one person could handle all those depositions, documents, transcripts. In short"—he grinned in his own hotshot way—"it's a complex litigation." He tucked his napkin into his collar. The oysters had arrived.

"What if Farmer is the one to depose me?" I worried. This was the thought that had been keeping me up at night, ever since I learned about this infamous addition to The Defendant's legal team. It would be so easy to destroy my credibility, based on the scintilla of a second when I thought I'd seen Roger at the front door. It was the jugular I would go for if I were the one to depose me.

"You and I will prepare for that," Dad said portentously, "together."

"Hold on, though," Brian said, his hand raised like a traffic cop's. "What if *he's* the attorney who deposes you?"

I had a flash, what I realize now was a premonition, of The Defendant sitting across from me in a spiffy oatmeal-colored suit. As quickly as I saw myself at that table, I dismissed it. That would be outlandish. The court would never allow it.

"I believe one must pass the bar before one can be called an attorney," Dad intoned.

"Fine. What if he's the *law student* who deposes you," Brian amended.

Though that was an unearned rank as well. The Defendant had applied widely to a number of reputable programs, but his admission scores were so poor that the only place that would take him was a night school called Tacoma Narrows, located in a shared office building in downtown Tacoma. He fell behind almost immediately, stopped attending classes, and the next quarter scrubbed all mention of his time there on his application to the University of Utah, where he got one year under his belt before he was arrested and charged with the kidnapping and attempted murder of Anne Biers. That was three years ago. He'd been a convict for twice as long as he'd been a law student.

"I'd almost prefer if it *was* The Defendant who deposed you," Dad said, not joking in the least. "I very much doubt Shorebird Law turns out the best and the brightest of the legal profession."

I busied myself, squeezing lemon all over the oysters, giving Brian a moment to recover. He was flushed a girlish pink.

"No, Dad," I said, passing the platter his way and gesturing for him to dig in first. "Shorebird is the name of the school Brian and I are attending in the fall. The Defendant was at a place called Tacoma Narrows."

My father smeared an oyster with horseradish, seemingly oblivious to the offense he had just caused. But I knew he was not. My father took great pains to appear laid-back, but that was a tactic too, one that belied his meticulous diction. His comment had been a deliberate, targeted attack on Brian, meant to remind him—his daughter had gotten into Columbia Law, but his daughter's boyfriend had not.

"It's those aquatic-sounding names." Dad brought the wide end of the shell to his lower lip, tipped, and chewed before swallowing. "Tough to keep straight." He pushed the platter in Brian's direction, a peace offering.

"Thank you, sir," Brian said quietly.

My father waved the waiter over, ordered another round of drinks, then insisted we all have the filet, though I knew Brian preferred the strip.

"Dad," I said when the waiter had gone, "I'd love to pick your brain about something."

Dad brought a fork to the side of his head, pretending to twirl his thinning blond hair. Pick away. I gave him the half laugh he was after.

I'd taken a debate and rhetoric class my junior year; learned about something called process values. In a rule of law–based society, you could make a winnable argument based on these values. Even when a legal outcome might not appear obvious, fair, or logical, you could at least show that the process to get there was. I clasped my hands in my lap, made my voice sonorous. "Don't you think," I started, "that if the state is going to use citizens' tax dollars to extradite somebody, charge them, and prosecute them, then that should happen? The person should not be allowed to escape. Our system recognizes that as a criminal offense in and of itself."

"Not every country penalizes escape," Dad pointed out.

I nodded eagerly. I liked when we did this. Built a case together.

"But ours does. And part of that penalization involves increasing security around an escaped prisoner if and when he's recaptured, usually by moving the inmate to a higher-security facility."

"Sure," Dad said. "If a higher-security system isn't available, measures like round-the-clock surveillance can be implemented by the judge."

Our entrees arrived, and I readied the rest of my argument while the waiter fanned out the identical plates. My father had been a civil attorney for fifteen years before making the move to in-house counsel. He would have only cursory knowledge of criminal law, so the fact that he had retained knowledge like this boded well. The clearest argument is always the one that relies on ordinary people's latent understanding of our system.

"The Defendant was remanded—appropriately—to a level-three facility in Utah after he was convicted of kidnapping Anne Biers," I continued once the waiter had gone. "The Colorado DA came in and extradited him to a level-one facility in Aspen, which is the least restrictive—"

"Can you pass the breadbasket, Pamela?"

I passed Brian the breadbasket and tried to remember what I was saying. "Level one is considered minimum security. Someone who's been convicted of aggravated kidnapping and charged with first-degree murder really should be somewhere more restrictive. At the very least, he should not be permitted to roam free, unshackled and unsupervised. Which is how he escaped the first time. You would think Colorado would have learned from that, put tougher restrictions in place. Instead, they remanded him to yet another level-one facility and failed to follow the judge's ruling that he should have round-the-clock—"

"And the butter?"

I passed Brian the butter. "Surveillance," I finished. Then, "I think I have enough to make a claim."

My father split his baked potato down the middle and let the steam pour out. "Which would be?"

"Negligent infliction of emotional distress against the Colorado Department of Corrections. Witnesses and bystanders can sue for emotional anguish if they witness something horrible. I'd say I qualify."

My father raised his eyebrows.

"This all should have ended in Colorado. Two adults and a child are dead because of their negligence. When a girl in The House violates the organization's standards, it's my job to hold her accountable. Why would this be any different? Plus, a lawsuit gives me the opportunity to request the evidence that the prison guard told me about, anything that could connect The Defendant to crimes in other states. There are families who are desperate for answers about what happened to their loved ones. I could help give them some solace." I stopped. Poked at the verdant pile of spinach on my plate. Waited to hear what my father thought.

"That's a tough case to win," he said at last. "A lot of steps to prove."

Brian nodded in vehement agreement. He was eating only the charred perimeter of the meat, leaving behind a pink puck at the center. I knew he preferred his well-done. "That's what I said too," he said pompously.

I turned to him, my patience whittled down to something speared and dangerous. "Actually, that's not what you said at all. You said to sit back and let the police do their job, because they've done such crack detective work up until now. Oh, and what else? That Tina had brainwashed me."

"Someone managed to brainwash Pamela Schumacher?" My father forked a piece of steak into his mouth with a laugh. He'd believe that when he saw it.

Brian went from pink to a scalding red. "Just so you are aware, sir—"

"Bill."

"Bill, sir. I'm just a little concerned about how much interest this woman has taken in your daughter. She was in a lesbian relationship with one of the victims. Supposed victims, that is."

My father glanced between Brian and me, chewing. "Are you in a lesbian relationship with this woman, Pamela?"

"No, Dad," I said. "I'm not."

"Then I'm not concerned. You know what does concern me, Brian?"

Brian stared at him insolently.

"That is the best cut of meat north of Fourteenth Street. Eat up."

For some reason, I turned right out of the restaurant. Right was uptown, away from Penn Station. Brian trailed me in a stewing silence, unaware for the first few blocks. "Hey," he said, pawing at my arm, trying to get me to stop. "We're going the wrong way."

But I wasn't, I realized with razored clarity. I was planning to grab the crosstown bus at 66th Street, then an uptown train to 116th Street, where the sanctity of the Columbia campus waited for me.

"I want to go to Columbia," I said, shaking him off me.

Brian peered up the street. "Isn't that a long walk from here?"

"I mean for school," I said. "Next year." I turned and faced him. Pedestrians were barreling toward us like goats with their heads lowered, muttering obscenities when they were forced to weave around us. I put my palms on Brian's chest, gently but firmly, and maneuvered us closer to the curb.

"I think that's a great idea," Brian said, all soft and supportive. "Let's do our first year at Shorebird. Then we reapply to Columbia. They will see it as a commitment, to reapply, and maybe this time your father can put in a word for me too."

I looked up at him, agog. "What are you talking about? Who would Dad put a word in *with*? He went to Rutgers."

"Right, but . . ." Brian made a face, one that begged me not to make him say it.

"But *what*?"

"They know who he is."

"Dad's successful, sure, but this is New York. Trust me, he's not on anyone's radar."

Brian smirked. "If you say so."

I was filled with rampant loathing for him. "I have a four-point-two GPA. I'm the president of the top sorority on campus, and I'm one of three women congressional pages out of thirty. I scored in the ninety-fifth percentile on the admissions—"

"Jesus!" Brian shouted. "I know!"

I kept my voice calm. "Actually," I said, "you don't know. I made a point of not telling you my score. Because I didn't want you to feel bad."

We stared at the pavement, both of us oddly shy about what was happening. We knew lots of couples who split up and got back together, rinse and repeat, but that had never been us. We did not know how the other would act, would be, in this scenario. I was standing at the curb with a perfect stranger.

A man walking by spit something green and gelatinous onto the pavement. In the street, a horn blasted, then another, like wolves howling to their pack members, communicating the location of a predator.

"This is where you want to spend the next three years of your life?" Brian gestured incredulously.

It felt like all of Third Avenue was impatiently cheering me on. What had taken me so long to get here? And now that I had, could I hurry the fuck up?

I could not tell him *yes* fast enough.

RUTH

Issaquah

Summer 1974

||| prepared for the dinner party the way I had my driver's exam, studying the July issue of *Good Housekeeping* like it was the Washington DMV handbook, and then I got behind the wheel and practiced with about eighteen whole chickens until I nailed the temperature and roasting time. I'd serve the protein alongside buttered purple carrots and small potatoes, a fresh green salad sprinkled with California walnuts. If you couldn't find them from California, the magazine said, imported would do fine. But I wasn't one to cut corners.

Nature's Mart was a clay-red structure, about half the size of the grocery store in Clyde Hill, that carried all manner of mysterious "health food" ingredients. They hadn't yet removed the Easter Bunny from the roof or the clever sale sign for eggs. Before my nephew, Allen, became so cruel, we used to dye eggs in the bathtub and hide them around the house for the younger kids in the neighborhood. I wondered if he was disappointed that I wasn't around for Easter this year, or if he even remembered that he used to like me. I grabbed a basket from the stand and asked the cashier which aisle for the nuts. He had a long gray beard and a turban around his head. "Aisle three, dear," he said, and I don't know why, but something about the way he called me "dear" made me want to cry.

Who knew there were so many nuts! Of course I knew about cashews and peanuts, but not Brazil and pumpkin. I found three varieties of walnuts on the bottom shelf, and I crouched down to read the labels. I was trying to determine which walnuts were from California and which were imported when someone spoke my name. I looked up and saw my sister-in-law. She was bouncing the new baby girl on her hip, the one for whom she made her own baby food, and pushing a cart filled with organic vegetables and fruits. For all the healthy eating she'd been doing, she didn't look too well. Rebecca had dark rings under her eyes and frizzy, grown-out roots. When I stood, she took me in from head to toe, my leather shoes that matched my leather purse, the freshwater pearls in my ears, and she shifted the baby to the other hip, positioning her in such a way that she covered a stain on her shapeless old shirt.

"Ruth," she said with a thin smile. "I almost didn't recognize you."

———

Tina put the herbs in the refrigerator and said ominously, "So now we're thirteen."

I took the herbs *out* of the refrigerator and arranged them in a cup of cold water like the cashier recommended I do as soon as I got home. "You should have seen her face when I mentioned the party. It was like . . ." I saw that strand of hair, the one that was always stuck to her lips. "Unadulterated longing."

Tina went around me to the bin where she stored her mail. She shuffled through a few things, then extended an envelope my way. "This came for you," she said.

I saw my mother's name and address in the upper-left-hand corner. I ripped it open and inhaled sharply. It was the invitation to my father's garden-naming ceremony. At the bottom, there was a handwritten note: *Your dad would want you there.*

Tina hoisted herself onto the countertop and bit into an apple, waiting for me to explain why I was struggling to breathe.

"It's the thing I told you about," I said, showing her. "The garden ceremony for my dad."

"Don't go," Tina said simply. She set the invitation on the countertop without even reading it.

Something flared in me at her dismissiveness. "You didn't even look at it."

"Why did you look at it? It's just going to make you want to go."

"I do want to go."

"Why?"

"Because someone should be there who really loved him."

"There are other ways to honor your father," Tina said.

I opened the bag of California walnuts and bit into one. I couldn't understand what made them so special. They tasted the way I knew walnuts to taste. Crunchy and bland.

Tina had this ice-blue silk sheath dress with darker blue feathers at the wrists. I thought I had managed to conceal my admiration for it—it was a gorgeous, silly thing that people wore in magazines, not anywhere near Washington State—but she suggested I wear it to host the dinner party. I reminded her I was roasting a chicken and there would be grease as I pulled it over my head. We stood next to each other before her full-length mirror and stared.

"You look like a snow queen out of a Tolkien story," Tina said.

On the hanger, the dress didn't appear half as iridescent as it looked against my white skin and black hair, eyes bluer than they had any right to be. I was tempted to put it back on the hanger. I didn't trust that I could look that good for longer than five minutes. But then the doorbell rang downstairs, and it was too late to change.

I felt ridiculous when I opened the door to find Frances in tan slacks and a turtleneck sweater, standing alongside the six-foot-tall woman with the waist-length gray hair whom I now knew to be Irene, Frances's partner.

"I'm going to change," I said, and everyone begged me not to.

"Wait," Tina said, "hold on." She ran upstairs and Frances, Irene, and I waited without speaking, as though we were playing freeze tag and she'd thumped us on our backs. When Tina came back down-stairs, she'd changed out of her minidress and knee-high boots and into a silver satin floor-length gown. She looked like she was going to a Hollywood awards ceremony and like she was poised to win. "After all," she said regally, "we are the hostesses."

"You both look divine," Frances said.

I relaxed a little as the other girls trickled in. They had all gotten dressed up too. They couldn't get over my feather sleeves, the shade of blue on my skin, my *skin*. Fingers grazed my cheek, I heard the word *porcelain*, and I could not believe this was at last my life.

We took our drinks to the living room, where I'd set out a plat-ter of hors d'oeuvres. Toasted ovals of bread with olive spread, raw salmon on cucumbers, dates wrapped in bacon. My mother would have gagged if I'd served any of this to her.

"Don't fill up," Tina said, her smile proud. "Ruth's roast chicken is the best you've ever tasted."

"It smells heavenly!"

"I should go check," I said, standing.

_____

I ran a knife between the bird's body and thigh and tilted the roasting pan, watching the juices run pink. When the doorbell rang, I knew it was Rebecca. I'd counted the guests in the living room before I'd come into the kitchen. We were short one.

"I've got it!" Tina called. I could hear her satin dress sweeping the tiles of the floor. The groan of the medieval wooden door. Tina's hello, my sister-in-law's apology, Tina telling her it was nothing to apologize for. We could make room. For a panicked moment, I thought she'd come with my brother. But then they walked into the kitchen, and I saw it was just the baby barnacled to her hip. That piece of hair got all tangled up in her tongue as she greeted me.

"I kept trying to leave, but she wouldn't stop screaming unless I held her," Rebecca said.

"Can I try?" Tina opened her arms.

Rebecca looked her over critically. "I wouldn't want to ruin your nice dress."

"Oh, that's okay." Tina was speaking baby. "Who cares about a stupid-woopid dress?"

The baby stared at Tina with an aloof expression, sucking two of her fingers. Reluctantly, Rebecca handed her over. No one screamed. Rebecca was at a loss for what to do with her arms now that they were free.

Tina burrowed her face into the baby's neck and inhaled. "We should put you on a platter and serve you up for dinner." The baby frowned, as if considering the idea, and put her pink little hands on Tina's lips. *No, thank you.*

Rebecca peered over the counter to see me basting the chicken. "Did you get the chicken from Nature's Mart?"

"Pascale's," I answered a little haughtily. Pascale's was the Italian butcher on Third. The chicken had cost six dollars more than the one at the grocery store.

"The chicken from Nature's Mart gets fed a corn diet," Rebecca said. "It's healthier for them than wheat pellets."

Briefly, I wished for my mother, who would have met the look I cast at her. Motherhood had made Rebecca an insufferable know-it-all.

"In Italy the chickens are fed wheat, and it's the best chicken I've ever had," Tina said. She'd gotten the baby to coo and laugh by pretending to eat her nose.

"Well, of course, in Italy." Rebecca laughed, her snobbery bested for once. I felt her eyes roving all over me. My dress. My hair. My face. I sensed outrage at what she saw, and maybe a little bit of betrayal. I'd told her the attire was festive, and she was wearing the black wool dress she'd worn to my father's funeral.

"Come meet everyone," I said to Rebecca, and showed her the way to the living room.

———

Rebecca seemed to relax next to the fire with some gin. The other women were empathetic to her situation, full of advice about how they'd gotten their babies to stop being so clingy. Rebecca listened to them and didn't interject with any of her success stories about Allen. She didn't mention Allen at all. Everyone assumed the baby was her first, and she allowed it. She finally tucked her hair behind her ears and even laughed at a joke Frances told, though I saw the way she looked at Irene sitting so close to Frances on the couch. Her disapproval was radiating off her in waves.

We moved to the dining room for dinner. Before we sat down, Frances insisted on taking a picture of Tina and me, holding my prized roast chicken. The other women piled behind her in the doorway, exclaiming over what a great picture we took together. Frances promised to send us a copy as soon as she had the chance to get the film developed.

Everyone raved about the meal. They wanted to know how I got my potatoes so crisp, whether I stuffed the cavity of the chicken with butter. The women took turns passing the baby so that Rebecca had a chance to enjoy her meal. The bones on her plate were picked clean by the time my niece made it back around the table.

"You could do this professionally, Ruth," one of the women said. Down the formal stretch of the burlwood table, Tina and I met eyes. We'd been talking about my goal to enroll in culinary school, but first I had to complete my GED.

Tina raised her glass with an impish smile. "Actually," she said, "Ruth is going to culinary school to do just that."

I realized Frances was grinning too. "That's the plan eventually," I said before the women got too excited for me. "But I have to go back and get my GED first."

Tina gave a small shake of her head. "I spoke to the school. They're willing to waive the requirement in exchange for a summer of work in a restaurant kitchen."

Frances said, "And we have a friend who could use the help." Irene nodded, and Rebecca's jaw clenched at the use of *we*.

The women asked a million questions. How many years was culinary school? Did I want to work in a restaurant, or catering, maybe? Someone's cousin had found success in catering weddings. Maybe I could even open a restaurant of my own one day!

The final course was a lemon tart with a thin layer of chocolate between the pastry and the filling. The women moaned in ecstasy, but I noticed that the baby was drifting off in Rebecca's arms and that she hadn't been able to touch her piece.

"You can put her in our room," Tina said to Rebecca. I registered the seriousness of the words *our room*, but it didn't seem as though anyone else did. Everyone was too full, too tipsy, too happy for me.

"It's a big house," I said as humbly as I could. "I'll show you."

Rebecca and I removed the cushions from the love seat, the one by the bay windows that seemed to cut Mount Rainier off at its snowy head, and constructed an infant-sized nook on the floor. Rebecca rocked back on her heels and took in her surroundings. In the bedroom she shared with my brother, there was not even space for a bureau, and they stored their clothes in a linen closet in the hallway.

Rebecca's eyes dipped over an indent in a pillow. The bed was made, but Tina had jumped on top of the covers and put her hands behind her head to watch me try on clothes for the party. Remembering her like that—watching—I wished everyone would go that very second.

"Do you sleep in here too?"

My heart met my throat, with bold intentions at first. She had to know the answer; asking implied I had some reason to explain myself. To *her*, of all people. I raised my chin and said, "I do."

I was prepared for disgust, but to my complete surprise, Rebecca put her hand on my wrist tenderly. "You know, Ruth? If you're trying to punish your family for the way they've treated you . . . I wouldn't blame you one bit." She sank into a cross-legged position with a heavy exhale. "I should have thanked you a long time ago. I was so scared the first few months after you went away. I kept waiting for someone to tell your brother about us. For someone to tell my parents. But no one ever did. I got off scot-free. But you"—her eyes glistened with tears—"you suffered, and I'm sorry."

I was so moved I couldn't speak for a moment. "Thank you," I managed finally.

"But Ruth," Rebecca said, tougher now. "This behavior with Tina? Psychologically, it will damage you."

"I no longer believe that's true," I said calmly, and I felt an immediate and welcome weightlessness, realizing I really didn't believe it.

"Oh, Ruth!" Rebecca cried, exasperated. "I'm on your side. I am. And maybe some of your family would be too if you didn't always have to make such an ordeal out of everything. Look what you're doing now! Sleeping in the same bed as another woman! Wearing her fancy clothes and acting like the lady of the manor. Too good for a normal life. All over what? And at the end of the day, you had good parents. They loved you and they gave you a nice life and they were trying to do their best by you. You know I always defended you when your mother called you selfish, but sometimes I think she might be right."

Her voice was dripping with sanctimony, and the baby started to fuss. Rebecca threw the thrashing bundle over her shoulder, and I brought my hands to cover my mouth as her big head snapped back on her little neck. My niece looked dazed a moment before stretching her mouth around an earsplitting yowl. "That's enough!" Rebecca yelled at her, loud enough to make me, a twenty-five-year-old woman, cower.

Rebecca turned the wrong way out of the door, and I sat there waiting for her to realize her mistake when she got to the powder room at the end of the hall. The baby lit up each room Rebecca stalked into; she finally gave up and came back the other way, muttering something about the house being ugly *and* a maze. Downstairs, I heard the women trying to convince her to stay, but whatever Rebecca said back to them, it was at the same decibel my parents had used the night they found out about us. I only felt her leave. The bespoke hulk of a door socked the frame, and the ground shifted and resettled along new fault lines beneath my knees.

PAMELA

New York City, 1979

Day 445

I was nearing the end of my first year at Columbia Law, a single woman with a bold and unfortunate haircut. After breaking up with Brian last year, I decided I was tired of looking like an apple-cheeked schoolgirl. I wanted something more grown up to mark this next chapter in my life. My mother's hairdresser tried to talk me out of a shag—that round Irish chin—but I told him, regrettably, that it was only hair and it would grow back. Tina mailed me a few hats from her extensive collection that she was needing less and less thanks to the sorcery of Denise's multivitamin, and I hid in the back of lecture halls, too self-conscious to put myself out there to anyone. I certainly couldn't bring myself to speak to him—the man I would one day marry, sitting four rows in front of me in Civil Procedure.

I would not see him on campus again after that first year. My husband is a careful thinker, someone who likes to mull, to talk things over, before he arrives at a solution to a problem, and he felt law school penalized this quality. The summer after his first year, he interned at a talent agency, reviewing contracts for the theater department, and never left. Today he represents Tony-winning performers and directors; he has producing credits on some of the longest-running shows on Broadway. If you read the playbills closely enough, you'll see my name under *special thanks to*, for all the times

I've come home from my own family law practice to advise him on acquiring rights or box office compensation clauses.

In 1987, one year into my thirties, I returned to Tallahassee for the funeral of Catherine McCall, the alumna who had invited us into her home the night after the attack. I had just stepped off the plane when I heard someone say my name with that sort of cautious up-speak people use when they are sure they are mistaken, you can't possibly be who they think you are, but maybe? I turned to see the guy from my civil procedure class, who was not traditionally hand-some, as Brian had been, but somehow his prominent features—crooked nose and full lips, dark, deep-set eyes—came together in a way that had always made me blush beneath the brim of Tina's donated hat.

"I couldn't tell if that was you," he said. He brought a hand up, wheeling the crown of his head. *Your hair.* (*It's normal.*)

I had taken to wearing it in a shoulder-length blunt cut that I knew suited me well. I hooked it behind my ear with a self-effacing smile. "That was a tough year for me."

We laughed and started down the small terminal, which in a few years would be leveled in a deadly tornado, then built back up, stron-ger and shinier than before.

"What are—" we both started, then laughed again. I gestured at him. *You go.*

"I'm here for a funeral, unfortunately. How about you?"

I felt my heart race. "Not for Catherine McCall, by any chance?"

David stopped walking and turned to stare at me, thunderstruck. My husband's name is David. "Yes, actually. She's my great-aunt."

That weekend, in the house where I was once as much a stranger to myself as I was to the man I thought I would marry, I got to know the one I did.

———

But before that charmed reunion could happen, before my father walked me down the aisle asking if I'd heard the one about the divorce lawyer who gets married (something about the wedding qualifying as a billable hour), and after the difficult pregnancy that resulted in the daughter who made me go easier on my mother, I still had the trial to get through. And The Defendant seemed hell-bent on dragging it out as long as legally possible.

I was descending Columbia's Low Library steps, on one of those crisp East Coast April days that feels more like fall than spring, when I passed another first-year who lived on my hall. "Oh, Pamela!" she cried without slowing down. "There's a message for you back at the dorm. The guy said it was important."

I pivoted on the spot, shielding the sun from my eyes in what looked like a salute. "Do you remember his name?" I called up to her.

"Pearl something!" she yelled before the Ionic-style columns absorbed her.

When I arrived at the dorm, the hair at the back of my neck was damp with sweat. I knew of only one man with the last name Pearl. He didn't call about important matters; his calls were a matter of life or death.

"This is Pamela Schumacher," I said to the receptionist at the state attorney's office in Tallahassee.

"One moment, please."

I bounced on my toes anxiously while I waited for the prosecutor to come to the phone. Henry Pearl and I had yet to meet in person, but that would soon change, since we'd officially entered the discovery phase of The Defendant's trial.

"Afternoon, Pamela," Mr. Pearl said in a brusque voice that made my throat go dry.

"The message said it was important."

"I have good news and bad news. Which do you want—"

"Bad."

Mr. Pearl coughed and cleared his throat. "I received notice of your deposition. It's scheduled in two weeks' time at the Leon County Jail, which can mean only one thing."

The Defendant would be the one to depose me. That was the only thing it could mean—because traditionally, depositions take place in a courthouse or law office by licensed attorneys who do not harbor a penchant for bludgeoning dozens of women to death.

It felt like the old brick dormitory on Amsterdam Avenue was swaying. I put my hand to the wall, feeling the pulse of its pipes, the vibrations of the new album from the Cars. A guy upstairs listened to it on repeat every day that spring quarter. "Does that mean Farmer's out?"

"That is the good news," Mr. Pearl said more buoyantly.

The famed Millard Farmer of Atlanta had a federal charge of contempt on his record. He'd had to file a special request to represent The Defendant in an out-of-state trial, and Mr. Pearl was calling to tell me that the judge had denied it. The Defendant would go on to accept and reject the same team of public defenders right up until the first day of the pretrial. People talk about him representing himself like he was the only one on his side of the counsel table. But if that had been the case, I would have had nothing to worry about. He would have drowned in his own ignorant hubris.

"Listen," Mr. Pearl said, "whatever you're hearing about The Defendant's capabilities as an attorney, they've been grossly exaggerated. I watched the same display as your journalist friend, and frankly"—he laughed cynically—"I'm wondering if we attended the same hearing."

The Defendant Making Judicial Gains had been Carl's headline in the *Tallahassee Democrat,* to which I must have been the only New Yorker who subscribed. Carl was in the courtroom to cover The Defendant's request for a delay to the trial, better lighting in his cell, and more hours of exercise. The Defendant was photographed with one ass cheek on the counsel table, wearing a tan suit and glancing down at his notes while he made his argument. Carl wrote that he "appeared relaxed and confident in his own defense—asking articulate, well-contemplated legal questions in a calm, deliberate voice."

The "fit young man," Carl noted, had "succeeded in putting the prosecution on the defense."

I'd called Carl while I was still reading his article, teetering between tears and rage. I'd succumbed to both when he didn't answer, slamming the phone into the receiver again and again like a caricature of a scorned woman. For months, Carl had fed me countless excuses about why the Colorado story still hadn't run, and then he'd stopped answering my calls and letters entirely.

"I'm going to meet you in Florida," Tina said when I hung up with Mr. Pearl and called her to tell her about the upcoming deposition. Tina had moved back to Seattle after I graduated from FSU, around the time the second capital indictment was handed down for the murder of twelve-year-old Kimberly Leach. My father kept reminding me: even if they couldn't nail him for Denise's and Robbie's murders—the evidence in our case was almost entirely circumstantial—the state would get him for what he'd done to Kimberly Leach, for which they had hair and fibers and even soil from the national park where she was killed, found in the stolen van he was driving.

"What for?" I asked Tina, forcing a smile for a cluster of my hallmates as they emerged into the lobby. One of them saw me and mouthed, Lunch? I pointed to the mouthpiece and shook my head. I had to take this call. She shrugged. Caught up with the others. I watched them go, a sharp pang in my chest. I was eight months into my first year at Columbia Law, and I had not gone on a single date. If anyone asked whether I'd made any new friends, I could say yes. Technically, my father was a new friend to me. I was mired in this bullshit, and he was the only one willing to discuss it with me ad nauseam. I was angry then. Angry that over a year had passed since I'd held my dying best friend in my arms and insisted she wake up and get dressed, and that there was still no end in sight.

"We're going to knock on Carl's door!" Tina cried as though the answer were obvious. "Tell him to stop writing this drivel and poisoning people's minds. Remind him that he told you the guy who did this to Denise should burn."

He won't get out of Florida alive, my father kept assuring me. But when he fried, I wanted it to be for what he'd done under my roof.

————————

The state of Florida paid for my travel, accommodations, and three days of meals. It cost them more to fund a face-to-face with the man who'd raped my best friend with a hair spray bottle than it would have to cover the damages he'd inflicted on The House. In the end, alumnae took care of the cost, but it's outrageous that they had to, simply because Denise had once been intimate with a man briefly suspected of harming her.

Tina got a room next to mine, but she ended up using it only to shower. Back then most hotel rooms featured two beds, and we stayed up late into the night, the digital clock on the nightstand between us illuminating the time in that old phosphorous green, talking until we fell asleep.

The first morning back in Tallahassee, we woke early, arriving on Carl's doorstep before he would leave for work. Tina knocked, looked over at me, and asked, "Ready?" I was nodding when Carl opened the door.

"Pamela," Carl said, the blood draining from his face. I am known to have that effect on people. "What are you . . . How do you know where I live?"

I gave him a strange look. "You gave me your address so we could write. Though only one of us seems to be doing that these days."

"Right." Carl patted his hair into place, damp from the shower. "It's been a busy time. Sorry about that."

"I'm in town for the deposition," I said. "Thought I'd pop by, see how the Colorado story was coming along."

"Can we come in for a moment?" Tina asked.

Carl glanced over his shoulder in a clandestine manner. "Well, the place is a mess."

"We don't judge," Tina said. *Speak for yourself*, I thought.

"Uh, sure. Just give me a minute." Carl closed the door in our faces.

I turned to Tina. The hair that was growing back was inscrutably textured—not straight, like it was everywhere else, but not exactly curly either. Crimped, I'd realize when the style became a trend in the next decade. For the rest of her life, Tina would sport two unruly stripes on either side of her head, like an electrocuted skunk.

"He doesn't seem guilty at all," she said, deadpan.

"Not in the least," I agreed.

We waited on the front stoop for several minutes, made to feel like traveling evangelicals, lifting our hands and waving sheepishly at a neighbor who ambled by on a morning walk with her dog. It was one of those archetypally perfect family dogs, a yellow smiling thing, and I watched as it took a hard left into Carl's yard, where it hunched up and deposited a runny shit next to the azalea bushes. I was about to tell the neighbor not to worry about cleaning it up when a woman driving a white convertible turned into Carl's driveway and climbed out of the car. The neighbor and the driver exchanged greetings and exclaimed over the dog together, who awaooed and pawed at the driver's thighs as though he had missed her terribly.

The woman crossed the lawn, picking animal hair out of her clothing and smiling. "Hello?" she said to us curiously. She was older than Carl by about ten years, pretty in a faded kind of way, or maybe that was just my competitive side talking.

"We're friends of Carl's," Tina explained curtly.

The woman wiped her shoes on the welcome mat and opened the door, calling, "Carl! You have guests." She held the door for us. Tina hooked her arm through mine and took me inside with her just as Carl came jogging down the stairs. The house was cramped but lovingly maintained, and though the couch cushions needed fluffing and there were several pairs of shoes heaped in a pile next to the coat rack, the place was hardly a mess, even by my standards.

"Oh, okay. Yeah." Carl was flustered. "Hey, Lynette," he said to the woman as they passed each other on the stairs. The whole exchange was befuddling to me. Their dynamic did not seem romantic in the least, and yet they had to live together; otherwise, she wouldn't feel comfortable going upstairs on her own. Roommates, maybe. His sister?

"There's coffee made," Carl said, clearly wanting to avoid the subject of Lynette. I had so many questions for him that I knew I had to pick my battles, and Lynette was not one worth fighting.

"That would be great," Tina said. We followed him into the kitchen, sun-warmed via a sliding glass door that would be so easy to shatter. I stared at that glass door, quietly seething at the discrepancy in our threat levels, that Carl could write the fawning twaddle he did only because his was tuned so low.

"Milk? Sugar?" Carl asked, stalling before the open refrigerator.

"Sugar," I said.

"Black," said Tina.

Carl placed a dented box of white sugar on the kitchen table and poured us each a mug. Cold. On top of being a turncoat, he was a lousy host. This was the thing that undid me.

"What's going on, Carl?" I asked bluntly. "You're avoiding my calls. You stopped answering my letters. And what you're writing about him—I thought journalists were supposed to be unbiased."

Carl returned the carafe to the coffeemaker and faced me slowly. "Do you not see, Pamela"—he was speaking in this pandering tone that made me want to throw my cold coffee in his face—"the irony in saying that to me when you're so clearly biased?"

"You wrote that he was working his way through law school," I pandered right back. I didn't need to scream and shout; I didn't even need to raise my voice, the facts were that loud. "But working where?" I made my eyes big—this wasn't a rhetorical question. I wanted him to give me an answer.

"I'd have to check my notes," he said.

Tina groaned like someone had made a corny joke.

"I'll save you the trouble," I said. "He was collecting unemployment checks, Carl. And stealing antique rugs from nice hotels on the side."

Carl shrugged in a pouty way that eradicated everything I'd once found attractive about him.

"You also said he's personable and bright," I continued acerbically, "with a girlfriend and many friends who believe he is innocent. But his girlfriend was the one who called the tip line on him." I paused, in case he had a response to this, knowing he would not. His face was baby pink by the time I got to the inarguable kicker: "If this is the route you're going to go, painting him as some kind of legal shark, at least have a word with your photo editor. It's disrespectful to be sitting on the counsel table while addressing the judge."

Tina added disdainfully, "I called your editor, Carl. He said you pulled the Colorado piece yourself. Some bullshit like there not being much to the story after all."

Carl didn't deny it, confirming everything.

"Excuse me," he retorted, "are you with me in the courtroom, seeing what I see every day? Have you spoken to any of his friends and family? Have you spoken to—" He broke off huffily. "Forget it. I don't have to explain myself to you."

I gasped. "Are you speaking to him?" That's what he was about to say, I was certain of it.

"We've exchanged a few letters," Carl admitted.

Tina stared at him like he was the most repugnant person she'd ever shared oxygen with.

"You said the person who did what he did to Denise deserved to burn," I reminded him, hot tears blurring my vision. I had trusted him, and I was ashamed of how little it had taken. Green eyes. One fair article in the paper about Denise. Carl ducked his head, sweeping breakfast crumbs into his hand and dusting them into the trash can. Then he wiped down the counter with a dampened dish towel for good measure. I knew a thing or two about cleaning to avoid facing oneself.

"He used a *hair spray* bottle on her!" I roared, only because Carl had made it clear he was not amenable to reality, to the truth. I wanted everyone to know—Lynette upstairs, the woman out on the street walking that good dog, the neighbors to the left and to the right—that Carl was devoid of dignity, of humanity.

Carl cowered behind the kitchen counter, saying sorely, "This case is getting national attention. And it's all going down right here in my backyard. I have interest from a publisher for a book. I . . . This is what people want to hear about, Pamela."

I saw, so clearly, the copy of *Helter Skelter* in Carl's bag, placed mistakenly in my room during that trip to Colorado. It had become a sensation, thanks to the prosecutor-turned-author's firsthand access to the case. The cold coffee churned in my stomach. He'd been planning this all along.

That woman—Lynette—was standing at the threshold to the kitchen. She saw my agonized expression, saw the worried way Tina was looking at me, and her face softened sympathetically. "I am so sorry," she said, sounding like she meant it. "Um, Carl. He's asking for you. Normally, I would tell him you left for work already, but he can hear all the voices, and he's getting agitated."

"I'll be right up, Lynette," Carl said stiffly. Lynette retreated up the stairs while Carl stood unmoving, his head hung and hair in his eyes. "My dad. He's not well. So I've got his care to worry about, the house, all our bills. I'm sorry," he said, holding my gaze finally, as though having a sick father justified what he'd done to us. "Really, I am. But people are fascinated with him. What would you have me do?"

"You can go to hell," Tina said ruthlessly. She grabbed my arm and pulled me out of there.

———————

In the car, Tina watched as I stabbed at the ignition with the key. I finally landed one of the blows, then nearly took out Carl's mailbox when I hit the gas in reverse. "Fuck you!" I exploded at the gearshift.

"Get out," Tina said. "You shouldn't be driving right now."

I released my seat belt, and we passed each other around the front of the car. Tina turned the key, put the car back in reverse, and bulldozed Carl's mailbox cleanly to the ground before driving off at a leisurely Sunday speed.

One day soon, Carl would secure the exclusive interview with The Defendant he so unilaterally sought, and in a few short years, he would publish a briefly bestselling true-crime novel that was adapted into one decent television movie of the week and one very bad straight-to-videotape production. There were other, better books turned into movies with other, better actors. Occasionally over the years, I would catch Carl on some obscure hour of a morning talk show, hawking a rerelease of his book that supposedly contained explosive new material. Carl always seemed like the guy the booker scheduled because they couldn't get the guy who wrote the block-buster. Still, Tina and I read and watched everything Carl did, hoping for some sort of update on the Lake Sammamish disappearances. But Carl couldn't answer for it. No one could. Eventually, her hopes dashed one too many times, Tina called a moratorium on all things Carl and Lake Sammamish. There would be no knowing for her, and she needed to find a way to accept that so she could grieve it and carve out some semblance of a life for herself.

So when the missive landed in my mailbox—*You may not remember me, but I have never forgotten you*—I kept it from Tina. It was embargoed content until I could tell her it was time to hope again.

February 12, 2021

Dear Pamela,

You may not remember me, but I have never forgotten you, nor the night, forty-three years ago, when I called you at The House to offer what little assistance I could. I would not be surprised if your brain overwrote my memory, as that's what healthy brains do in traumatic and stressful situations. I know this because I work in the science of memory disorders.

I am writing with what may be important information or what may be the confusions of a man suffering from neurodegenerative demise.

In 2017, the journalist Carl Wallace came to me in the early stages of dementia. The disease has progressed considerably since then, and, as you may know, a common response to memory impairment is paranoia. Carl has taken to accusing me, with increasing aggression, of being you. He believes you are posing as his doctor in a plot to steal his research. He alternates between threatening to kill me and fits of terror, sure that I am the one planning on killing him. At the start of our treatment, I did share with him that I was an alumna of the sorority house that he wrote about in his book. I believe that's how he came to conflate me with you.

When a patient is confused, it's best not to correct them, as it can only exacerbate their disorientation. As Carl's delusion has manifested over these last few months, more of the story has come to light. How much of it is rooted in reality I can't say for sure, but in case any of this means anything to you, here goes:

In the eighties, when Carl was in the final stages of editing his book, the government forced him to hand over some of the recordings he made with The Defendant at the Florida State Prison allegedly containing the Lake Sammamish confession. Officials were still hoping to bring charges against The Defendant and did not want this information publicized, as it may have jeopar-

dized the investigation. Obviously, this never came to fruition. I have not been able to ascertain all the details of what is allegedly on these tapes. I don't know the right questions to ask, but you might.

I feel, as you do, that the families of the other victims should know what happened to their loved ones, and I know you are still in touch with some of them. I'd urge you to get down here quickly and speak to Carl yourself before his memory declines irrevocably. I've written to you because I don't want an electronic record of this—I'm not technically violating HIPAA here, but I find myself in an ethical gray zone.

I would say I hope you are well, but I know you are because you are so good about submitting your chapter notes to the community magazine every year. You inspire me.

Your sister on purpose,
Dr. Linda Donnelly, class of '67

RUTH

Issaquah

Summer 1974

The night before my father's garden-naming ceremony, my mother called. "Rebecca said she had a nice time at your party. It was thoughtful of you to invite her, Ruth, and I know your brother appreciated it too.

"She's been awfully lonely for a while now," my mother continued, carving me up with the skilled blade of a butcher. She knew how the word *lonely* hacked at my heart, making me think of my father and how he must have felt right before he died.

When my father was in college, he worked a couple of shifts a week as a bartender in the Georgian Room at the Olympic Hotel. One night near closing time, a patron came in and sat down at the empty bar. My father was always exhausted by last call—working nights as a full-time student took its toll. He poured the customer a finger of rye and hoped he would down it quickly, but the guy wanted conversation, about the beers on draft and then about the Scotches on the shelf. He wanted to know which team my father was rooting for in the World Series—the Cardinals or the Browns, and if my father thought it was as wild as he did that both were from St. Louis. My father thought he was hiding it well, his weariness, his disinterest, but after a few minutes of stunted conversation, the customer lapsed into silence and focused on finishing his drink. He dropped a few bills on the bar, and as he stood to go, he said that he traveled a lot for his job, that he hadn't been home in a while and was just hoping for a few minutes of friendly conversation.

I must have been no older than Allen when my father told me this story, which means I have thought about that man and his hurt feelings for nearly two decades. The haunted look on my father's face as he recalled that night taught me a formative lesson. Other people's pain mattered more than my own discomfort.

"I hate hearing that," I said. From the kitchen table, where we had been trying to figure out what was missing from my bouillabaisse, Tina mouthed, *Hearing what?* I turned away from her. It wasn't fair, but I blamed her for the regret in my mother's voice in that moment.

"I know you've been angry with me," my mother said, humbled, "and you've certainly given me some time to think." Her glum laugh loosened something in me.

"Mom," I croaked.

"No, listen, Ruth. I don't want you to be upset. It's good that you've moved out. That you're not tied to CJ like poor Martha will be for the rest of her life. I am glad—" It sounded as if the line had gone dead, but I knew that was her just doing her best. There is supposedly some universal biological response that new mothers have to their crying infants, something that activates the primal protective regions of the brain. Rebecca probably told me about it. I was certain something similar happened in me when I heard my own parents cry.

"I'll be heartbroken if you're not there tomorrow," my mother finished in a voice of pure surrender.

"What about CJ?" I couldn't stand to pretend like we were still married, not now. Not after Tina.

"Martha forbade it."

I weighed my options now that this condition had been removed from the scales. Tina and I had talked about going, about not going, about going, every night for the last week. Tina said by not going, I was refusing to participate in my family's cover-up of my so-called crimes. I took an important first step, not like I had any idea where I was going next.

"I'm sorry, Mom," I said. "I don't think it's going to work for me."

"You don't think it's going to work for you," my mother repeated tonelessly. "Well, then," she said with what I imagined was a lethal smile. "Goodbye, Ruth."

"Bye," I said, though she'd already hung up on me.

I turned to find Tina stirring the cold dregs of the bouillabaisse broth with her spoon, smiling to herself with raised eyebrows, like she was expecting a thank-you from me.

"That must have felt great, huh?" She laughed in a way that assumed the answer went without saying and began clearing our plates, humming the new Fleetwood Mac song and swaying her hips.

I gave her a capitulating smile and pitched in, though a queasy awareness was building in me. If this was what *great* was supposed to feel like, I was doomed.

PAMELA

Tallahassee, 1979

Day 467

The morning of the deposition, I woke jittery and tearful, repentant for every wrong thing I'd ever done in my life. It must be the way people feel when going into risky surgery. *This will either save me or kill me, and it can't kill me, because I don't know that I was a good enough person to get into heaven.* I lay staring up at the popcorn ceiling, paralyzed by every violent and degrading possibility the day held, until Tina said she was going to her hotel room to shower and recommended I do the same. I pulled myself into a seated position, where I sat immobilized for a long time. Eventually, I summoned the strength to drag the phone into my lap.

"You are the kind of witness who keeps a defense attorney up at night," Dad said from his office on Park Avenue, where, on his first day, they gave him a choice of view—the East River or the Hudson. "Let's look at the data, okay?"

I licked away the tears on my lips. "Okay."

"Your story has remained consistent, no matter the environment."

I gripped the phone tighter, nodding to myself. This was true.

"Your character is unimpeachable, which means your testimony will be viewed as unimpeachable too."

"How do you know?"

There was a surprised, proud-father laugh. Dad was the one who'd taught me that the most effective response to any argument is the question *How do you know?* Shift the burden of proof to your opponent and force them to back up their position with mountains of evidence.

"All right," he obliged. "You're an Ivy League law student who graduated summa cum laude. Your senior year, you led your sorority chapter to complete more service hours than any other Panhellenic organization in the South. And remind me of The House's cumulative GPA again?"

"High enough to drive the opposing counsel to murder," I replied with acid in my veins.

"Mmmm," Dad said in a teasing, adversarial way. "And yet, how do you know?"

I snorted. "That he's an idiot or that he's a killer?"

"Both."

"The DA unearthed his academic transcripts. His grades were in the bottom fifth percentile at Tacoma Narrows, and he only got in to the University of Utah because his application was embellished and falsified."

"And?" Dad said over the creak of his office chair. I imagined him stretching and taking in the Hudson at the window. No less brown than the East River, but if you looked north, the cherry trees in Central Park were telling you it was spring. "How do you know he's the one who killed Robbie and Denise?"

"Because I saw him with my own two eyes."

———

Henry Pearl met me in the parking lot at the Leon County Jail. He was younger than I'd pictured over the phone, with a blond mustache and a peaches-and-cream complexion that was splotchy in the Florida humidity. He thanked me loudly for being on time, almost as if he wanted someone else to hear. A quick survey of my surroundings revealed a young woman smoking on the curb wearing heavy tortoiseshell sunglasses that would leave purplish indents on either side of her nose for the next few hours. She had black, ironed-straight hair and a tiny hourglass figure buttoned up snugly in a plaid suit. This was Veronica Ramira, thirty-two, the sole strategic female on The Defendant's defense team. I despised her and wanted her to like me on the spot.

"Hello, Henry," she said, pronouncing his name *Enri*. Later, in her closing remarks, Veronica would tell the twelve jurors that she arrived in Miami as part of the first wave of Cubans after the revolution, a twelve-year-old girl who barely spoke English, with parents who no longer had a cent to their name. When she spoke about the pain of being persecuted for something for which you bore no responsibility, her hand lightly resting on The Defendant's shoulder, her voice carried considerable weight.

We walked past her into the jail and ended up waiting nearly an hour to be called back into the interrogation room. The Defendant did not like to be told what to do and when to do it and once jammed his jail cell keyhole with toilet paper so the guards couldn't get in when they arrived to escort him to his arraignment. For this he was called cunning and clever, though I had a dog who also tore up toilet paper when he didn't get enough attention.

The Defendant came into the dreary cement-walled interrogation room shuffling papers and sighing and apologizing, as though he'd had to rush across town from another important meeting to make this one. Quite the performance from a man who had taken a supervised shower that morning.

He sat down and avoided eye contact until the guard removed the shackles from around his wrists. Only then did he flash me an empathetic, mischievous smile, a smile that said neither of us belonged here, and wasn't this just a monumental drag on the pair of us? Two fine upstanding citizens with nice looks and respectable backgrounds. Then he was touching temples with Veronica Ramira, murmuring and indicating an underlined passage in one of his documents. "I recall," she said to him. There were greetings on either side of the table that were far too pleasant for my taste. The bailiff brought in the Bible, and the court reporter swore to the certification of the proceedings.

"Do you understand what it is we're doing today?" The Defendant asked me slowly, *chivalrously*, as though he was happy to spell things out for the sorority bimbo across from him. He was wearing the oatmeal-colored suit from my premonition, and I was overcome with a powerful sense of reassurance. I'd seen him coming.

"I've sat in on a few depositions for one of my classes at Columbia," I answered with a lofty lift of my chin.

The Defendant's face fractured terrifyingly with smile lines. "Then you should know it's best to answer with a simple yes or no."

"At Columbia, they teach you to frame the answers in favorable terms." I shrugged, unperturbed. Must be an Ivy League thing. "But yes, I understand the nature of today's proceedings."

"Thank you," he said. Absentmindedly, he rolled his notes into a tube and, while we spoke, choked it with small hands, eyes drifting to my throat.

"Please state your address for me." His arousal, that the power of the state gave him the authority to ask this of me, was unmissable— he adjusted himself in his seat, rubbed his lips together wetly.

"One-one-two-four Amsterdam Avenue. New York, New York."

"What is your occupation?"

"I'm a student at Columbia Law School."

"But it's only your first year, correct?" The Defendant was quick to clarify. Veronica Ramira scribbled something, shielded it with her hand, and pushed it toward her client. I knew what she'd written without needing to read it. *Name.* The Defendant was so eager to find out where I lived, to minimize my qualifications, that he'd forgotten to ask my name, which is how you're taught to begin proceedings at any law school worth its salt.

"I am a first-year student at Columbia Law," I said. *Columbia, Columbia, Columbia. Ask me again about my occupation, you verifiable loser.* This was all I could batter him with; this was *my* oak club.

"Please state your name for the record."

"Pamela Schumacher."

"All right," The Defendant said, unrolling the papers standing in for my elitist-bitch neck, "I'm going to ask you some general questions about the timeline of that morning. After you saw an intruder at the front door, what did you do?"

It was the obvious place to start. "I went upstairs to talk to Denise Andora." I steeled myself for the follow-up question—*why her, of all people?* Which would force me to acknowledge my initial, mazed logic. That it was Roger I'd seen ducking out after Denise had smuggled him upstairs.

"Did you encounter someone else before you got to her bedroom?"

"Oh, uh," I stumbled. Were we really going to gloss over the weakest part of my testimony? "Yes. I did."

"Who was that?"

"Jill Hoffman."

"And what was Jill Hoffman doing?"

"She was coming out of her room and heading for the bathroom."

"Did she have her back to you, or was she coming toward you?"

"She had her back toward me," I said, more confused than ever. What did *that* matter?

"Did you call out to her?"

"Yes."

"What happened then?"

"She turned around, and I could see that there was some blood on her face and hands."

"Some blood?"

I looked to Mr. Pearl, aghast.

"Please clarify that question for my client," Mr. Pearl instructed.

"In your statement to the police"—The Defendant shuffled his notes like a deck of cards—"you described it as 'more blood than I'd ever seen in my life.'" But the page in his hand was upside down. Inwardly, I recoiled. The barnyard animal sitting much too close to me had memorized that part.

"For someone like me," I replied priggishly, "who spends most of her time in the library, yes, it was certainly more blood than I've ever seen in my life."

"Please answer the question."

Blithely, "Was there one?"

"Was it a lot of blood or only some blood?"

"It was a lot."

There was a purse of his lips, like an air kiss. In that moment I understood. This was all he wanted: to relive it. There was no trap-door beneath my feet, at least none The Defendant had the pull cord to. He had summoned me here to tweeze the goriest bits from my memory. I could not believe anyone could call him intelligent, or even take him seriously. His act was so transparent, his character so fundamentally hollow, that it should have been an affront to the court, a place that was venerated and inviolable to me.

"What did you do after you saw that Jill was covered in a lot of blood?" he continued to no objection. There was none to make. This was all legal. Unbelievably legal.

"I ran down the hallway to wake up the other girls."

"Did you go into Denise Andora's room then?"

Her name, in his mouth, sounded all wrong. Denise Patrick Andora was a denomination that warranted a reverent inflection. Salvador Dalí had sent her mother a condolence card after she died. *When you fry,* I willed my pleasant features to express, *your mother will have to grieve in societal exile.*

"Yes," I said. "I went to check on *Denise Andora* then. I loved her. So many people did." In death penalty cases, copies of court transcripts must be saved forever, and I wanted a permanent record of this unsparing truth, for Denise. "I was worried because she wasn't out in the hallway with the other girls."

"Can you describe her physical state when you found her?" There was a quick dart of his lizard tongue, dabbing his thin lips.

"Her eyes were closed, and I thought she was sleeping."

"Did you notice anything out of place in her room?"

"The window was shut, and she had the covers pulled up. Denise ran hot, so that was unusual for her."

"Anything else?"

"I don't understand your question," I said stubbornly.

"From your police statement"—The Defendant smacked his lips together lasciviously—" 'The nozzle of the hair mist bottle was covered in blood and sort of dark brown gunk and hair.' Do you recall saying that to Detective Pickell?"

I zipped up my knees, pelvis torching with sympathy pains. "I do."

"Can you describe the hair mist bottle?"

"What does he mean?" I asked Veronica Ramira, whispering a little. I could see in her face that I'd shocked her, but I was realizing that about the only time The Defendant didn't scare me was when I was in the same room he was. When I could confirm the exact location of his whereabouts with my own two eyes, and there were guards with guns who would put a bullet in his middling brain if he so much as breathed wrong. If I wanted to make him feel like scum on the bottom of my shoe, this would be my only chance.

"What is your understanding now as to why the nozzle of the Clairol hair mist bottle was covered in those elements?" The Defendant hastened to ask before Veronica Ramira could get involved.

I bit my tongue as Veronica Ramira leaned across her client, head bent to block his face, and whispered something. For a moment I thought she was resigning as counsel, having remembered she was a woman.

"I apologize," she said to me. "I need to use the ladies' room."

We took a break, and when we came back into the concrete room, Veronica Ramira took over the interview and destroyed my unimpeachable testimony in ten brisk minutes.

"Going back to the conversation you had with Bernadette Daly in the early-morning hours of January fifteenth," she began, "do you recall telling her that you thought you saw Roger Yul at the front door?"

"I said that was an initial reaction when I first saw someone, because Roger was around a lot, and because they are both on the small side." I enjoyed suggesting to his face that The Defendant was a small man.

"And Roger Yul was Denise's steady boyfriend?"

"He was. But not by then. They'd broken up before the break."

"Did anyone else at the sorority ever date him?"

Panic roused with a guard dog's growl. Veronica Ramira, unlike The Defendant, had actually graduated from law school and passed the bar. She wasn't here for cheap thrills; she was here to win her case. "Yes. Bernadette Daly."

"How long did they date?"

"I believe it was just the one time they went out."

"And what did they do, that time they went out?"

Sweat beaded at my bra line, but I kept my face placid. "She said they went to see a movie."

"What about after the movie, in his car?" Veronica Ramira put a slight emphasis on *car*. She knew. "Did Bernadette talk to you about something that happened in Roger's *car*?"

My head roared with blood. Carl and Tina were the only two people on earth who knew what Roger did to Bernadette. And if Carl was trying to win The Defendant's affections, wouldn't this be exactly the sort of information he would offer up to The Defendant, as proof that there was someone else capable of the attack on The House?

"In confidence," I said, bristling, "she did."

"We are way past worrying about the bonds of sisterhood at the sorority house," Veronica Ramira said in this infuriating *hate to break it to you* tone, as though I were the reason we were here, airing all our private and personal matters. "What did Bernadette say happened with Roger?"

I supposed I had no right to be furious with Carl for leaking this to the defense. It was like leaving the trash out and blaming the racoons for getting into it. Carl Wallace was just doing what every member of the rodent-faced press did back then.

"She said that Roger pushed her head into his lap."

"To perform oral sex, isn't that correct?"

My neck flushed violently. "Yes."

"Did Bernadette say how she felt about that?"

It was like being strapped into a speeding vehicle with my hands tied to the wheel and a brick on the gas pedal. I could see the point of impact drawing nearer, and yet I could not turn or slow down. The impact would be unavoidable and deadly.

"She said she was scared and that she didn't want to," I answered helplessly.

"What was she scared of?"

"She couldn't breathe. She was scared Roger would accidentally kill her."

"Did you also have a frightening experience with Roger in January 1978, approximately one week after Robbie and Denise were killed?"

"Yes."

"What happened there?"

"He jumped behind the wheel of the car when I was in the passenger seat and drove off without my consent."

"And for that, you pressed charges against him, didn't you?"

"Yes."

"Aggravated kidnapping charges. Of which he was convicted last fall, correct?"

"Correct."

"You had the choice not to press charges, and yet you did. How come?"

The answer was the base of the tree, coming at me one hundred miles an hour. "Because I thought he was dangerous and should be behind bars."

"I have nothing further." Veronica Ramira turned to The Defendant, who in just a few short months would be described by the *New York Times* as a "terrific-looking man with light brown hair and blue eyes, rather Kennedyesque." That was on the heels of the *Miami Herald* asking *Is Quiet, Bright Student a Mass Killer?* Though any flashes of brilliance in that bleak room emanated directly from Veronica Ramira, no one wanted to remember it that way.

"I have no more questions," The Defendant concluded with a parasitic smile, looking tremendously self-satisfied for doing fuck all but attach himself to a woman who was good at her job.

PAMELA

Tallahassee, 2021

Day 15,826

Eileen once told me it felt like getting a tooth pulled. Pressure where there should be pain, adrenaline the body's natural novocaine. That is the danger zone that few come back from, doctors told her later. Pain is your body's way of saying something is wrong and you still have time to do something about it. But pressure. That is palliative care.

I wake with inhuman strength, clawing blindly until I feel skin scrape and curl beneath my short fingernails. The pressure sweeps open like a stage curtain, revealing pain. I open my eyes with the profound gratitude that follows a hyperrealistic nightmare. If I am in pain, I still have a chance.

The room makes complete sense at first and then none at all. I am reminded of the nurse's office at my daughter's old middle school. The little cot against the wall, the apple juices next to the stacks of clean gauze, the filing cabinet with the glass jar containing an assortment of lollipops in an array of primary colors. It is a place to administer medical attention but not the lifesaving kind.

There is a whistling intake of breath through teeth, and I look over to see a woman in her early seventies with cascades of silver waves swabbing dampened cotton pads over what look like cat scratches all up and down her arms.

"Hi," the woman says, continuing to tend to her injuries.

"I am—" *So sorry,* I am about to say, but something iron-from-the-fire-hot jabs at me. I run my tongue over my bottom lip and feel the telltale ridge of stitches.

"I can wear sleeves," the woman says, assuming I was about to apologize. She smiles quickly at me and touches her own lip, indicating. "It's only two stitches. I was able to do it here. But I do want to get you to Tallahassee Memorial for a more thorough checkup."

"He came after me," I say slowly, remembering not so much Carl's face but the cut of his figure in the khaki safari hat as he came toward me, the way that ridiculous hat stayed on his head even as we fell to our knees in the grass. I plant my hands on either side of my thighs and draw myself up to a seated position with a sore-sounding groan. My neck feels tender and tight. He had his hands around my throat, but I remember thinking that I could still breathe, that it takes several minutes to kill someone by strangling, and that help would arrive soon enough, so there was no need to panic. I was calm when I passed out from lack of oxygen.

"There was no fecal incontinence, which means the injuries are likely surface."

I raise my eyebrows. "I like giving the good news last too."

Dr. Linda Donnelly sincerely laughs at that. We have never met in person, but it has to be her. She is the right age, and she's wearing a gold charm bracelet on her slashed-up arm that features a ruby-eyed owl, the most flaunted of our sorority's symbols.

"Do I have to go to the hospital?" I ask.

"I'd feel a whole lot better if you did."

"Will you allow me to talk to him again tomorrow if I go?" Somewhere in the room, a cell phone begins to rattle.

"You must understand how difficult this was for me," Dr. Donnelly says as she goes over to the infirmary door, where my purse hangs from a coat hook. "To write to you. I could be accused of breaking my HIPAA oath—credibly." Dr. Donnelly hands me my trilling, seizing phone. "You put your husband as your emergency contact, but his assistant couldn't get ahold of him, so she gave me your daughter's number."

I hurry to hit the green button with the pad of my thumb. "Hi, sweetheart," I say soothingly, for her.

"Mom? Are you okay? You're in *Florida*?" Allison sounds hurt that she didn't know this, and my chest swells with a little bit of warmth and a lot of guilt. I tell my daughter most things, the boomerang effect of having a mother who shut me out. But I know that I made just as many mistakes. I raised a worrier, and while I have a lot of remorse over that, I also have compassion for my own mother in a way I didn't before I became one myself, so there is a strange fairness, an empathetic balancing of the scales, that comes out in other ways, and that is good for the world at large. Or at least that's what I tell myself.

"It was very last-minute," I tell her.

"Did something happen?" Allison asks in a smushed voice. She has her phone balanced against her shoulder, and I can hear the smattering of her keyboard. Allison designs graphic props for film and television, often hand-making objects for productions so they are accurate to the time period in which the story is set. She is fascinated with period pieces—she doesn't like to work in anything contemporary, and sometimes I feel bad about this too, especially when she refers to herself as an old soul. Old souls are just people who had to fend for themselves ahead of their time. I've spent most of my life fuming over the Colorado officials who, had they just done their jobs, could have prevented The Defendant's last murderous spree. But who am I to point the finger when I had a job to do too?

"Everyone is okay," I assure her. "There is someone down here who may know something about what happened to Ruth. I came down to talk to him."

The typing stops abruptly. Breathlessly, Allison says, "Really?"

"Please don't mention anything to Tina," I say. "I don't want to get her hopes up if it turns out to be a false alarm." When Allison was in middle school, she used to spend the summers with her godmother at her house on Vashon Island; Tina was also on her summer break. Since 2000, Tina's class at the University of Washington has been known to fill up within minutes of going live on registration day. The name sounds like the title of a soupy self-help book, which it is, and which Tina always addresses on the first day of "Finding Possibility in Impossible Grief," from the wood-paneled stage of Kane Hall. *You can roll your eyes,* she's been telling a sea of rubbernecking college students since 2000, when the university's new president invited her to create the curriculum. *I know I did when my publisher first suggested the title.*

The students are drawn to the course for an insider's account of her time hunting their hometown serial killer, on the campus where he once briefly matriculated as a psychology student himself, but many come up to her on the last day of the semester, asking her in tight, shy voices if it's all right to give her a hug.

Over the years, Tina worked with her mentor, Frances, to adapt the concept of complex grief into its current iteration—impossible grief applies to cases where the grief-processing mechanism has been obstructed, like a clog in a drain. Family members of people who were in the towers the day they fell, who were never given remains to bury. Women who were assaulted by a classmate, a boyfriend, a friend, who are told by almost everyone that what they experienced does not qualify as assault. Impossible grief is grief that does not adhere to a social contract of justice or human rituals that have existed since the dawn of time. A death with no body, a violation by someone who is not seen as the transgressor. A woman whose relationship wasn't recognized as legitimate at the time she lost her partner. Tina teaches people how to snare the obstruction so that grief can make its way through the proper channels unencumbered. It's always running in your veins, but better that than a life-threatening clot.

"Tina has wanted this for close to half a century," Allison says headily.

I am looking at Dr. Donnelly when I say, "I don't want you to get your hopes up either. I'm doing my best to get to the bottom of things, though."

We hang up, and Dr. Donnelly reaches for her umbrella. Out the window, it is still sunny, but bruised clouds are barreling in. She offers me her arm, and I stand with her assistance.

"If the hospital clears you," she says as we make our way carefully to the parking lot, "we will try again tomorrow. I'd hate for this to be for nothing. It takes a lot for me to break the rules—I'm certain you understand."

I do. More than anyone. I thank her profusely as we get into her car and head for the same hospital where Denise was legally declared dead, something that close to half a century later, still cannot be said of Ruth.

RUTH

Issaquah

Summer 1974

You could not spin the dial on the radio station without hearing about the gathering heat wave poised to detonate Seattle on Sunday, July 14. Tina and I had been planning on spending the day at Lake Sammamish all week, and we weren't the only ones. We had to go to three different hardware stores to find one that wasn't sold out of coolers. Summer is the most beautiful time of year in Seattle, but temperatures tend to be mild. Bona fide beach days were rare, and that one would fall over the weekend was rarer still. We woke early, and I set to work making lunch while Tina packed the car with lawn chairs and towels and sunscreen.

Tina found me in the closet, wearing her black bikini and staring at a pristine navy shift that I could picture her wearing to a luncheon at a place where they served ice water in wineglasses. Her palms were smeared with white sun lotion. "The top popped off. You want some?"

I shook my head.

"Are you sure? You're so pale." She laughed.

I thought about lying to her, telling her I wasn't feeling well, to go on and enjoy the day without me. Then sneaking off. But just the word. *Sneaking*. I could not do that to Tina. "I think I want to go to my father's ceremony after all."

Tina looked at me, startled. "No, Ruth. We talked about this. I know it's hard, but it will be a huge step backward for you to go and participate in this charade now that you know what a charade it is."

I gave her a one-shouldered shrug. "It's the one-year anniversary of his death. I should be with my family."

"We don't have to go to the beach." Tina's voice turned soft. "We can go to his gravesite right now, if you'd prefer. Just you and me."

I gazed at the closet's green carpet, the same intense shade as a tennis court, and volleyed back. "You didn't hear my mother on the phone last night. She knows she was wrong. She just wants us to be together today."

Tina stepped forward and got in my eyeline. "Is it about being together or showing people you're together?"

"If I'm being honest," I answered, "probably a little bit of both."

"You're not being honest, though," Tina protested. "Because if it was just about being together, she would not expect you to show up today and hide who you really are! The same way your father hid who he really was! That's the coward's way!" By then, Tina knew the story of how my father died.

My eyes flashed at the word *coward*. "Fuck you."

Tina nodded as though I'd gotten the answer to some unasked question right. "That's good. You're mad. You should be mad, but not at me. You can be mad at your father and still love him. Hell, you can be mad at your mother and still love her. But they're the ones you need to get mad at." Tina's hands were flying around as she spoke, and I removed the navy shift from its hanger, folding it against my body protectively, not wanting to see it splattered with lotion.

"Fine," I said, my voice nasty. "I'll just never talk to my family again, if that's what you want."

"That is *not* what I want, Ruth. I want you to have a relationship with them on your own terms. One that doesn't only feel good to them but to you too."

I gaped at her. "You think what we have right now feels good to me?" I began to unbutton the back of the dress. "My whole family is getting ready to attend a celebration on the one-year anniversary of my father's death, and I am the only one not going. My mother is despondent."

"She is an adult, and she will be okay!" Tina cried as I stepped into the dress. She lowered her voice, changing tack. "Listen, Ruth. This is not easy. I went through it with my own parents and—"

"And you never speak!" I laughed meanly. "You have no family. I don't want that. I don't want to be like you."

Tina held up her hands as I barged past her, considerately, so as not to get any lotion on the dress. I didn't say anything more to her after that, but in the driveway, I did listen while she told me that she understood why I had to do this, and she knew it would get easier in time—that all this just took time—that she loved me, and if I changed my mind, I knew where to find her. She got behind the wheel of her rich-lady Cadillac, and I swung my leg over the seat of my rusted old bike, and at the end of the driveway she made a left, toward the water, and I went right.

PAMELA

Miami, 1979

Day 540

The trial started Monday, July 9, 1979, a scorcher of a day in Miami. The walk from the hotel to the rain-stained terra-cotta Justice Building took only five minutes, but that was enough for Tina and me to arrive with matching sweat patches on our lower backs. In the brick-laid Met Square, the jungle of media and spectators slowed us, everyone passing at the pace of treacle through the single entrance door. The Defendant would go on to blast the "bloodthirsty and virulent press" that assaulted his mother on these same stairs, butchering the word *virulent* so badly that the court reporter recorded it as *variant*. But it was perhaps the only point on which we agreed. They couldn't have offered some of us a side door?

Patiently, I shuffled forward with the crowd, trying not to tear the shopping bags I carried in each hand, pastries, fruit, and yogurt in one, thermos of coffee in the other. I was essentially hidden in plain sight among the other young women who had parted their hair down the middle and put on their Sunday best that morning. There was no way to tell which of us was there to ogle the Kennedy of Killers and which to testify against the booger-eating alcoholic who had picked up a heroin habit on the inside.

"This is a case study waiting to be written," Tina said, eyeing a girl who could not be older than sixteen, hopping bunny-like on the balls of her feet and craning her neck as though she were at a Beatles concert, hoping to catch the eye of Paul.

"If they only knew what we knew," I said.

"They do," Tina said darkly. It continues to be Tina's professional theory that most, if not all, of the young women who populated the hundred-seat Miami courtroom, giggling every time they caught a glimpse of the man they described to reporters as "fascinating," "impressive," and "possessing a rare kind of magnetism," had experienced some form of sexual abuse in their pasts. Victims are always drawn to those men who remind them of their abusers. Not that the media ever took the time to explore the phenomenon of the courtroom groupies beyond asking a few bubblegum-smacking teenagers if they were there because they thought The Defendant was cute.

The worn marbled lobby was obscenely cold, a surround sound of striking heels. By day's end, my sweat would freeze to a crackly film that I could scratch off with a fingernail. I hadn't yet met the lone female professor in law school who would teach me to layer warmly even in the swamp of summer because the thermostat in government and office buildings is set to accommodate men in wool suits, men with higher metabolic rates all year round. *You can't concentrate when you're cold,* this unicorn would not tell me for another eight months. So I spent all day blowing into my hands and worrying the jurors might mistake my discomfort for the nerves of someone who was lying.

"Pamela!" It was Bernadette, waving. "Over here!" She was standing halfway up the central stairwell.

Tina and I turned to each other like steadies departing on the train platform during wartime. "I'm going to get in there and find a seat," she said with an end-of-the-movie finality.

I didn't dare say a word. I sensed the voice that would come out of me—childlike and lost—would demolish me. I just stared down at the fabric of my blue dress that I'd ironed and starched last night and again this morning and nodded with my lips smashed together.

"It's normal to be nervous," Tina said. "That doesn't mean you don't get up on the stand and do a good job."

It was more than nerves, though. It was a fatalistic feeling about the world in which we tried to make our way. I once had a doctor tell me there are a certain number of catastrophically bad things that, statistically speaking, must happen every year to a certain number of people—rare diseases, freak accidents, and, yes, serial killer attacks. Little grains of tragedy carried by the wind. I could make peace with the idea that one of those currents happened to catch my corner of the world. But a brush with the improbable Defendant had amplified something about my everyday terrain that was proving harder to accept. Which was that guys like Roger did not arrive into our lives on the curve of some unfavorable wind. They were already rooted and ubiquitous.

Some nights I lay in bed sleepless and full of apathy, realizing that The Defendant could have gone anywhere in the country, done this to any other group of women, and the defense could likely raise reasonable doubt by pointing a finger at the Roger who already resided among them. Rogers were everywhere, reasonable-doubt scapegoats waiting in the wings for a case like this. There was not so much as a hair of forensic evidence linking The Defendant to the scene at The House. This was a capital punishment case, and a man's life—a normal-looking, normal-seeming man's life—hung in the balance.

"You've already done the hard part," Tina said, referring to my pretrial testimony, which The Defendant's team had moved to strike, calling me a "well-intentioned but unreliable witness." I had pretended not to notice the way Mr. Pearl's posture sagged with relief when Judge Lambert had ruled I could testify for the jury. Without my eyewitness account, all we had was junk science known as bite-mark analysis. Robbie had been bitten on her left breast and buttocks, and an odontologist was prepared to testify that only five sets of teeth in the whole world could have made those marks, of which The Defendant's was one. The defense would call it guesswork, and they would be right. So right that, in the years since, many states have banned bite-mark analysis in criminal trials.

Bernadette called my name again, and I hurried to meet her on the stairs, shopping bags bouncing and rustling against my outer thighs. From up there, I could see everything and everyone beneath us, including Carl, sharing a bench with some colleagues, press badges hanging around their necks. They were sipping from Dixie cups and ribbing one another while they waited for the lobby to clear out before taking their place in the roped-off media section. Carl had been at the courthouse every day for the pretrial, and he would be there every day of the six-week trial that would have taken five if not for The Defendant's colicky tantrums and spectacles. I was clenching my jaw in the way that made my neck string with veins, seeing Carl joke around like he was killing time before his favorite band took the stage.

"Now," Bernadette said, surveying the scene at our feet. "Where do you suppose we go?"

I looked back down at the bench to see that while Carl's colleagues were still there, Carl had gone. He'd seen me, I knew.

Bernadette flagged down a police officer, who took us to another police officer, who took us to the chambers of a judge whose secretary found the bailiff, who showed us to the witness room on the second floor. Eileen was already there, along with another young woman with strawberry-blond hair pulled off her face in a clashing peach headband, the hearing aid in her left ear strategically on display for the jurors. It was Sally Donoghue, the FSU senior who'd been asleep in her off-campus apartment on Dunwoody Street when The Defendant crawled through the kitchen window and landed six blows to her head before the neighbors came to her rescue. That morning, she was still walking with a cane.

"I brought goodies," I said. "Sally, can I make you a plate? We have fruit, muffins, yogurt."

"Oh, bless you," Eileen said. She was helping me unpack the shopping bag and had come across the real creamer. "The coffee here is putrid."

The trial revealed to me things I knew and things I did not. Eileen had lost teeth, I knew, but I learned the approximate number was nine. I knew her jaw had to be wired shut, but I didn't know how long (seven weeks, plus another six, after the doctors discovered it wasn't healing correctly and had no choice but to rebreak it). I knew Jill didn't remember the attack, but I didn't know that her first memory occurred in the back of the ambulance, when the EMTs were trying to cut off her pajama top and she came to pleading with them not to. I had no idea that her finger was nearly severed in half, and because of that, she had lost an opal ring given to her by her grandmother. To this day, that ring has never been recovered.

These were not things that the girls would have talked about unless they were compelled to under oath. They wouldn't have wanted people to pity them or think they were complaining. Nobody liked a complainer, and we wanted so much for people to think well of us.

A grisly day of tearful testimony, Carl's story would read the next morning, *but still no word from the state's only eyewitness.*

I waited around all day as the witnesses were led into the courtroom by the bailiff, one by one, until it was just me, acid-mouthed from drinking too much of the putrid courthouse coffee.

"Won't you sit, Pamela?" Eileen begged four hours in. "You're making me nervous."

But I couldn't risk wrinkling my dress. The judge was allowing cameras in the courtroom, and it seemed a matter of life or death that no one caught the star witness without so much as a hair out of place.

In the end it didn't matter, because court was adjourned and the bailiff was telling me it was time to go home, reminding me not to read the papers or watch the news until I had testified. Tina would collect all the headlines from that week and save them for me to read, something I wouldn't do until well after the trial ended, out of some bizarre sense of superstition.

I walked through the lobby on tiptoe, straining my eyes to locate Mr. Pearl. Why hadn't I been called to the stand? I was scheduled to fly back to New York the following morning. Did I need to change my flight? I was externing at a firm in Midtown that summer, and I'd used all of my excused absences to make the trip for the trial.

"Pamela!" Mr. Pearl had found me first. I turned to see him hurrying toward me at a forward-leaning angle, as if walking uphill, his briefcase latched but corners of paper sticking out of the seams. I focused on those shards of papers, a pit in my stomach. He had closed it in a hurry.

"You need to go back to your hotel room," he said the moment he was within earshot, "and not watch the news or read anything, and just wait to hear from me. Can you do that?" He put one hand on my shoulder in a consoling gesture.

"Yes, but—"

"I have to get to Judge Lambert's chambers. Right now. But I need you to do that for me. Okay?"

I nodded. *Okay.* "But my flight is tomorrow and—"

"Don't change it for now."

Panic constricted my lungs. *Don't* change it? "But if I don't change my flight, I won't be able to give my testimony."

Mr. Pearl squeezed my shoulder harder, not comfortingly but out of frustration. "Please, just—I'll explain as soon as I can."

I watched him go, my shoulder throbbing.

———

I did the five-minute walk back to my hotel in three and a half. I kept picturing the phone in my room ringing before I could get there and taking wild risks—darting out into the street despite the traffic officer's open hand. "Watch it, lady!" he shouted over the furious percussion I left in my wake.

About the only time the hotel lobby was quiet was in the late afternoon, after court adjourned. The lookie-loos were mostly locals and members of the press dispatched to the ninth floor, the makeshift site of their serpentine media center, to edit down their coverage in time for the evening news. So I noticed the woman right away. She was plump, with a practical wash-and-go haircut, sitting on one of the lobby couches with her hands folded in her lap, her thumbs going round and round, managing to look impatient and nervous all at once. When I came flying through the doors, she stood and intercepted my path.

"*Excuse* me," she said in this entitled way, as though I'd stepped on her foot and needed to apologize at once. I'd ignored the hand signals of a traffic cop, body-swerved moving vehicles on a busy city street, but here was finally an obstacle to thwart me. This was the confusing, potent presence of Shirley Wachowsky. Ruth's mother.

RUTH

Issaquah

July 14, 1974

I t was fifteen fiery miles from Tina's house in Clyde Hill to Issaquah Catholic, the wintry conifers gone still in the heat, too spent to sway. By the time I arrived, I had wet rings under my arms, one shade darker than Tina's navy shift. Rebecca gave me a spacious hug, leaving plenty of room for the Holy Spirit between our pelvises, and informed me I was clammy. My brother achieved an even more distant, one-armed embrace, smashing my niece between us. She grabbed my finger in her sticky hand and examined it with orbed eyes, mesmerized by what she'd found. Allen stared at my clear skin and my Italian leather sandals suspiciously before taking off to play with some cousins in the circular pattern of the grass, cut for us first thing that morning, my mother announced self-importantly. The purple hydrangeas in my father's garden had bloomed a feminine shade of pink; this seemed to be his way of foiling her color scheme from up above. She had dressed like a giant grape, hoping to match him, but now she just looked like a giant grape.

"I took the liberty of copying down a few lines of Scripture that might be nice for you to say," my mother said, pressing a wilted sheet of paper into my hand. She didn't usually speak like this—*Scripture*—but Sister Dennis and Father Evans were standing right there, looking itchy in their wool habits and stiff collars. What would they say if I told them we didn't even keep a Bible in the house? That my mother must have gone to the library or asked a neighbor to borrow their copy? That, as a very last resort, she would have gone to church?

"Ruth," a familiar voice said. I turned and saw my ex-husband, who wasn't supposed to be there, his belly rejecting the buttons on a bad suit. "Wow. You look like you stepped out of a fashion magazine," he said. I hugged CJ tight with sincere relief. Although he was the world's least stealth philanderer, he had always made me feel less alone in the presence of my family. More than that, he was the very personification of what Tina was trying to drill into my head: that today was not about being together as a family but about my mother performing togetherness for others and maybe even for herself. I imagined my being there did allow her to keep that small voice at bay, the one that spoke to her in the solitude of the night, torturing her with the truth. Our family was irrevocably broken.

"I thought Martha forbade you from coming," I said to CJ, and I was amazed that I could sound so sweet and compliant when, inside my head, a one-woman rebellion was forming.

"Is that Martha Denson, you mean?" Father Evans asked. Martha had also attended Issaquah Catholic. My ex-husband's first wife was a senior when I was a freshman, and my ex-husband's third wife was a freshman when I was a senior. CJ could write a hit country song.

"We should probably take our seats while they are still in the shade," my mother suggested before Father Evans could ask any more perfectly reasonable and inconvenient questions. Everyone began to disperse. It took my mother a minute to realize I was walking back the way I'd come.

"Ruth!" she called after me, laughing a little, as though I'd accidentally gotten turned around.

I stopped for her, though I recognized it was only a courtesy. There would be no convincing me to stay. Something ethereal and serene descended upon me, and it didn't feel so much decided as divined by God: *Time to go, Ruth.*

"I only came because I didn't think CJ would be here," I said without anger or blame. My mother had lied to me to get me to come. This was who she was and would likely always be. It was my responsibility to accept that. In a dizzying flash, I saw Tina in Frances's kitchen the first night we met, her fingernails in Nixon's black fur. *You think you're going to come here and you're going to get advice, and then if you just follow that advice, it will get better. Instead, what you learn is how to take responsibility for it.* It was a sensational moment of lucidity, one that begged to be shared with the person who prophesied it.

"I didn't think he would be!" My mother was flailing, desperate to reclaim her hold on me. "I guess he finally took a stand against her." She smiled and rolled her eyes—*that ole battle-ax Martha*. But this act had finally worn thin, and my expression was bored and disengaged. It must have been terrifying for my mother to realize she had so completely lost me, and for that I did feel compassion. "Please don't make a fuss, Ruth," she added, her voice verging on panicked. "You're here. And you look . . ." She flopped her arms in my direction, at a loss for words. Not because I looked beautiful beyond description but because my mother never paid me compliments, and it must have been like sifting through a drawer of sharp knives for a blanket. Her mind wasn't where you looked to find something soft and warm. "So put together," she ended up saying. "It would be a shame for it to go to waste."

But it wouldn't go to waste—Tina would see me. Tina, who wouldn't struggle to tell me I looked beautiful, whose mind was not barbed but curved in the way of a prescription lens, focusing the light and rendering things clearly. "I'm sorry, Mom," I said, taking a small step away from her, "but this doesn't feel good to me."

My mother appeared genuinely dumbfounded. "Good for you? It's not meant to feel good for you. Your father is dead."

"I don't mean that. I mean *pretending*. That I'm still married. That we are one big happy family when we aren't."

My mother wore her comfortable victimized sneer, as broken in as a favorite pair of jeans. It had always frightened me that she could find anything amusing about her disappointment. As if she spent her days waiting for life to let her down like she expected it would, then shared a dark laugh with herself. She had been smart to prepare for the worst.

It was the same sneer I'd seen the morning my father died in a car crash on the way to the place where we stood now, after suffering a minor heart attack on the heels of the argument the three of us had around the breakfast table. I'd stayed the night after CJ and I had our final, explosive fight about a bobby pin he didn't even realize he had stuck to his collar when he came home too late again, and in the morning I'd informed them that CJ and I were not going to work things out this time, that I was going to ask for a divorce because I was a homosexual, and they both knew I was because my father was one too.

"I knew you would do this," my mother declared with a sick sort of triumph. Her face was ruddy, pin-cushioned with beads of sweat. "I said to myself—maybe it's better Ruth doesn't come. Because I knew you would only make it about yourself. But I extended an olive branch, and now here I am, doing exactly what I knew I would spend the day doing. Comforting you, when I'm the one who needs comforting."

I was grateful to her for giving me such a hammy display of her cruelty, which up until that point she had doled out discerningly, at a rate meant to keep me coming back for more. She had made it so easy—not just easy, but *pleasurable*—to walk away from her. I got on my bike, and I rode to the water, where the breeze was, and Tina too.

PAMELA

Miami, 1979

Day 540

In the hotel room, the phone rang at the same time the door opened.

"I have to answer," I found myself saying, impossibly, to Ruth's mother and to Tina. Neither acknowledged me. The two of them were staring each other down like longtime rivals in the ring.

"Pamela?" Mr. Pearl said. "Do you think it's possible you can move your flight?"

I felt like I could breathe again. I was still going to testify. "Of course," I said through my long exhale. "What day should I leave?"

There was an awkward pause. "Good question," Mr. Pearl said with a laugh that made me queasy. It was the laugh of someone who had battled an irrational toddler all day and had lost the will to live. "Judge Lambert wants to meet with you in his chambers tomorrow morning. And then he will decide whether or not you can remain on the witness list."

I wanted to sit down, my feet were blistered and aching from standing all day, but I also didn't want to have to iron my dress again. It wasn't computing. That it might not matter. Because I might not testify. "And *then* he'll decide? What is going on, Henry?" I didn't think I'd ever called Mr. Pearl Henry before.

"The defense filed another motion to strike your testimony

today. Based on evidence that it was influenced by your relationship with Martina Cannon. The prosecutor provided a sworn statement from the mother of one of the missing Lake Sammamish girls."

I stared at the author of this statement, right there in my hotel room, her back up against the wall as if Tina had physically threatened her, though Tina was only standing by the door with her arms crossed and her foot tapping impatiently. I spoke calmly through my mounting hysteria. "What does this statement say?"

"The mother believes her daughter ran away due to her psychological troubles. Apparently, she was committed for a period of time, and there was talk of sending her back to the facility. Her belief is that Martina Cannon manipulated and took advantage of her daughter, and Ms. Cannon's insistence that Ruth was killed that day is really just a refusal to accept that Ruth realized the way they were carrying on was wrong and ran off."

"And yet," I said in a bladed voice, "I don't see what this has to do with me."

"It doesn't. It shouldn't. The judge just needs to speak to you and make sure you are of sound mind and that you haven't in any way been manipulated by Martina. You haven't, have you?"

"No!" I cried.

"That's what I figured, but I needed to ask."

"What happens if he decides I have been? Influenced, that is." I glanced at Tina, whose foot stilled above the carpet at that word. *Influenced.*

"Look," Mr. Pearl said sternly, but then he didn't follow up with anything for some time. *Look where? At what?* I nearly screamed. "In cases like these . . ." He trailed off, less sure-footed. My heart sank. He was going to say some version of what my father had been saying to me for months. I could feel it. "Where there are serialized killings . . ." My knees buckled, and before I knew it, I was sitting on the edge of the bed. To hell with it. I'd iron the dress again. Or maybe I wouldn't even have to. I brought a hand to my mouth, leveled by the thought that some technicality would keep me from telling everyone the truth, from winning this for Denise. "You rarely get a conviction for all the victims," Mr. Pearl said in a sad jumble of justifications. "But because there are so many of them, the silver lining is that in some of the cases, at least there is strong forensic evidence, and that's how you nail these guys."

"Like how they got Al Capone on tax evasion charges," I said drolly.

Mr. Pearl groaned. "I am doing everything in my power to win this case for Denise and Robbie and all you girls. But if Judge Lambert decides to strike your testimony, there is strong forensic evidence in the Kimberly Leach case. He won't get out of Florida alive, I promise you that."

I closed my eyes. I'd wanted him to say it. But now he had, and I wished for the moment back, to maintain even a fraying thread of hope. Without my testimony, The Defendant would win. I did not know that *I* would get out of Florida alive if I couldn't testify.

"Eight forty-five sharp tomorrow. Okay?"

I'd be there at eight thirty.

Ruth's mother spoke before the phone's headset met the base. "This young woman deserves the truth," she said to Tina, the most blatant attempt at magnanimity as I'd ever seen. "You may not be able to accept it. But that doesn't give you the right to go around peddling your delusions to people in vulnerable situations."

"Do you know the psychiatric definition of a delusion, Shirley?" Tina raised her dark eyebrows expectantly and waited to see if Shirley felt like taking a stab. "No? Okay, well"—Tina leaned back against the door and said through a yawn designed to infuriate—"it's a false sustained belief despite incontrovertible evidence to the contrary." She patted her mouth. "Sorry. You're so textbook it's boring."

Shirley gasped. "You are a wicked person." With me, she pleaded and pointed. "That is a wicked person right there."

Tina did not bat an eye. "There were eyewitnesses who put Ruth at Lake Sammamish that day, talking to a man who fits The Defendant's description. Even more damning . . ." Tina threw her arms up to the ceiling, like Shirley was never going to believe this one, and Shirley turned one cheek against the wall as though Tina had back-handed her, though they were as far apart as the square footage of the hotel room would allow. "Ruth was happy, and you don't run away from a life that makes you happy."

Shirley peeled her face off the wall. "How come her body was never found, then?" She laced her fingers in a beggar's prayer and shook them at me. *Please. Let this sink in.* "It's been five years. They found the body of the other girl who went missing that day. But not Ruth's. That's not strange to you?" Shirley threw me a reproachful look—*have some sense,* it seemed to say.

"Because no one's looking for her!" Tina thundered. "That other girl's mother was on every news outlet that would have her. She showed up at the police station every day for three months. She was a goddamn dog with a bone!" Tina banged a fist on the wall and cried out in frustration. "But *you.* The only thing you've been relentless about is making sure no one looks for her! If the mother of a missing girl is telling the detective assigned to her daughter's dis-appearance that, actually, nothing suspicious is going on here, they believe *you.*"

"They do," Shirley said, and she did this sickening little shimmy, pleased as punch with herself, "because I am a mother. And what are you? You have nothing."

At this, Tina stumbled, injured, *reduced.* I felt a protective fire ig-nite within me, as though Tina were not just my sister but my younger one. In grief, the world treated me like I had seniority anyway, be-cause there was nothing about mine that others found unsavory.

"I don't think you're delusional at all," I said to Shirley. "I think you would much rather everyone believe your daughter ran away. Because if her name is connected to all *this,* people might start dig-ging. And they might find out that she was living her life in a way that you find shameful. So you would rather never know what happened to her, or learn where your *own daughter* is buried, than risk people finding out that she wasn't 'perfect.' What kind of mother is that?"

Shirley blinked at me, speechless, and burst into tears. Or at least she pretended to, bringing her hands to her face and making all the requisite boo-hoo noises. She did this long enough to realize I wasn't going to take back what I'd said, to comfort her and tell her I didn't mean it, that she was a mother and therefore sacrosanct. When I did nothing but let her blubber on, she dropped her hands and focused her dry, flinty eyes on me. "I'd like to leave now," she said with a courageous wobble to her voice, as though we were keeping her there against her will when she was the one to seek me out.

Tina opened the door for her, swept her arm in an exaggerated half circle. *You can see yourself out.* "Well!" Shirley tutted. She straightened her blouse and regarded me in a way that let me know how profoundly disappointed she was in me. "For once, a reporter was telling the truth. You are completely under her spell. Good luck to you, young lady." She rocketed out the door, her face a livid shade of purple.

Tina and I stared at each other for a long time after Shirley left, incredulous but also not. There should be a word for that. How very little people can surprise you. I suppose the word is *jaded*, but that's not what I am. Because on the other side of this is someone like Tina, who taught me not to be surprised that people can be so good you will miss a week of work, drive through the night, and put yourself in harm's way for them. Some people are your black swan event.

PAMELA

Tallahassee, 2021

Day 15,826

Carl is wearing a T-shirt that says *Make Orwell Fiction Again*, and despite everything he did to us, I am unbearably sad, picturing him designing the item on Redbubble from one of the community desktops in the Internet room at the assisted-living facility where he now resides.

"When I arrived in Seattle," Carl said, referring to the day we parted ways in Aspen, "I spoke to as many people as would speak to me about the case. And I heard a rumor." He held up a single finger, Holmes-like. "Actually, it was more of a theory."

It is one o'clock on a Thursday, and Carl is cogent. His best hour is immediately after lunch. Sundowning is setting in earlier and earlier, and it's taking Carl longer to shake off the morning fog, as evidenced by our first encounter during the previously safe hour of eleven a.m. I was released from Tallahassee Memorial with no sign of a concussion or internal bleeding, and the stitches in my lip will dissolve in two weeks. My injury pales in comparison to the brain bleed one of the aides suffered recently after Carl threw a chair at his head. That was when Dr. Donnelly started requiring Carl's visitors to sign a waiver.

"What was the theory?" I ask benignly, interested but not desperate. The moments that Carl comes up for air are infrequent, and they can turn on a dime, as I experienced firsthand. If Carl detects anything threatening or impatient in my tone, the Carl who has information that he's concealed from us for four decades will go, and I may never see him again.

"The theory," Carl projects in this strange speaker's voice, as though he is not talking to me but, rather, giving a talk, of which he did many in the decades after his book was published, "had to do with the interrogation tapes that Seattle made when they came to Utah to interview him after his first escape."

Carl means Colorado, not Utah, but Dr. Donnelly advised me not to correct him. I nod, urging him on. "I remember seeing the interrogation tapes on the container list you showed me." *On the day I kissed you,* I do not add but cannot stop myself from remembering with a wave of fresh shame.

Carl snaps his fingers and points at me. *Exactly.* He sips the coffee a staff member made him. Iced, so no one ends up with third-degree burns. "There was a theory," he continues, "that he confessed on those tapes."

"Why would he confess?" I wonder indifferently, though my heart is about to beat through my skin.

"Oh," Carl muses, as though it could be any number of things. He is building anticipation, enjoying my audience. I am in agony. Finally, "Utah [Colorado] had the death penalty, but Washington did not. And you know. After that first escape, he was in a bad way. He'd spent a week trying to survive in the mountains without shelter or food or sleep. His strategy was to bait the Seattle detectives, give them something that would make them want to muscle in and extradite him. Save him from the Caryn Campbell trial, which he was almost certain to lose after the escape attempt. Guilty people don't try to escape. He knew the prosecution would use that against him if the Caryn Campbell case went to trial, and it would end with his neck in a noose."

I raise my eyebrows. Murmur, "That makes a lot of sense." And it does. Carl doesn't say anything for a spell, and I look over to see that he's staring angrily at the door to the visitors' lounge. There is no one there. It's just us in the khaki-painted room with the red-striped club chairs and the tan couch with the matching red-striped pillows. This is what's called luxury senior living, though the facility looks like a four-star hotel built in the early aughts and left untouched ever since. But then—

"Seattle PD didn't like that," Carl says, and the memory attached to this statement revives his mood. He turns his focus back to me, beaming as he remembers his hard-bitten journalist days. "The pressure from the public to get him back from Florida was already so intense. Seattle was just trying to keep a lid on things long enough that they could hand down their own indictments, and all of that takes time, if they wanted to get it right, that is. Not rush things just for the sake of saying they did something, like the other jurisdictions did. But I'm not letting it go, and they realize they have to give me something." Carl's pupils have dilated; his cheeks look like mine after a morning workout—flushed with accomplishment. "One of the detectives suggests I go out and talk to the mother of one of their victims. That mother—" Carl whistles with wide eyes. *What a piece of work.* "She tells me she doesn't even think her daughter is a victim." He makes a disbelieving expression. He is sharing all of this with me in the present tense, as if he is on Shirley's doorstep right this moment. "It's obvious she's covering for something. But then—" Carl cuts out abruptly, like someone's pulled his plug.

I can't help myself. "But then *what*?"

Carl brings his fists up to his ears, like he can't bear the judgment in my voice. "They catch him. And everyone wants to talk to him, get his story." He blinks at me, childlike and full of regret. He has hardly any eyebrows left, but his eyes are still that mineral shade of green.

"How did you get it out of him?" I prod gently.

Carl cups his hands around his mouth and confesses in a whisper, "I wrote to him. I said"—he scrutinizes the empty doorway again—"I had evidence to support his innocence in one of the crimes he was accused of, and he put me on the visitors' list right away. And from there, we developed a sort of friendship, and . . ." Carl is back to speaking in the past, as though he needs distance from the person who did this. His eyes are flicking to the door and back to me, to the door and back to me. "*Please*," he begs me, and he cowers in abject terror.

I angle my shoulders to the side and slightly away from him, assuming an unthreatening stance, as Dr. Donnelly advised if I felt like he was starting to go.

"If I tell you where to find it," Carl says in a frightened whisper, "can you get her to leave me alone?" By *her*, I assume he means me.

In an ideal world, Carl would be an undiminished man who could withstand a blistering castigation from me, something I used to dream about giving him when I was younger and hamstrung by my own inexperience. But that's an urge that, over time, has diminished for me as the years reordered the rungs on my priority ladder. Carl's comeuppance moved lower and lower until it was succeeded by something more sophisticated than vengeance.

"She won't bother you anymore," I promise him, and I don't even have to feign kindness. Tina told him to go to hell, and all these years later, that's exactly where he is.

PAMELA

Miami, 1979

Day 541

J udge Lambert was copying something out of the case file when his secretary escorted me into his chambers, five minutes past our scheduled meeting time.

"Good morning, Your Honor," I said, bowing my head and standing a respectful distance from his vast desk, the way I do now when someone enters their pin at the ATM. Mr. Pearl warned me not to sit until I was invited to, to which I shot back, *I know that.* Though I didn't, not really. That wasn't standard courtroom etiquette, that was just Judge Lambert.

Judge Lambert did not acknowledge me. His secretary gave me a maternal smile, as though to infuse the place with some human warmth, before shutting the door quietly behind her, cowing slightly at a squeak emitted from the hinge pins. It was the expression I would one day make while trying to get out of my daughter's room noiselessly after hours of rocking her to sleep.

I stood there for a good minute, watching Judge Lambert annotate key phrases from yesterday's late-breaking motion. I'd expected his office to look like some old English tavern—low ceiling and reddish walnut walls, scarred leather furniture, brown drink on a brass tray—but the room had a mumsy feel to it, the furniture upholstered in metallic brocade, yellowed sets of French botanicals framed on the walls. Judge Lambert closed the case file and looked up at me, performatively startling. "You're so quiet I didn't even know you were here," he said with a vibrational chuckle. "Please, sit. You're making me nervous." It was the second time in twenty-four hours someone had said as much to me.

"Thank you, Your Honor," I said, and as I sank into the stiff cushion of the rose-patterned chair, I thought about that weaving hanging on Denise's bedroom wall in Jacksonville. The very one Carl had been admiring the day I first met him. It was a scrap from a Navajo wearing blanket, and you could tell that the woman who made it had done so under duress, Denise once explained to me. *See the radio pattern of the lines?* She'd pointed them out, rising and falling hard and horizontally, creating a chaotic diamond series. The shapes only started to appear in the mid–nineteenth century, when Hispanic families in the Southwest captured and enslaved Navajo women and children. The textiles were valuable, and the women were forced to create them for their captive family's profit. In a show of defiance, they invented a new loom sequencing meant to communicate that these weavings were not made by choice.

I would show respect for Judge Lambert in his chambers not because I respected him but because I had no choice but to get on the stand.

"It appears," he said in jokey castigation, "you've been keeping some questionable company." He wagged his finger at me, tsking. What a grand old time he was having while I sat there clinging to the crumbling edges of my sanity. "Filling your head with all kinds of fabrications, if I am to believe the affidavit."

I stared at him with doe eyes.

"Miss Schumacher," he said, suddenly impatient. "Am I to believe it?"

"Absolutely not, Your Honor."

"Absolutely not?" His eyebrows jolted upward. "Nothing in life is absolute, Miss Schumacher."

"No, Your Honor," I agreed quickly.

He reclined, soft broad hands draped across his hard old-man belly, the Florida flag on one side of his silvering sideburns, Stars and Stripes on the other, looking so much like a human toad that I half expected him to ribbit at me. "Tell me how you came to be acquainted with Martina Cannon."

"I met her at the hospital, Your Honor. Tallahassee Memorial. The Monday morning following the attack."

"And how did that meeting go?"

"How do you mean, Your Honor?"

He turned one hand over on his gut irritably. "What did you talk about? When did you learn that she was from Seattle and that she was connected to an alleged missing girl out there?"

"That day." I realized my short answer could be construed as defensive. "She gave me a ride home and told me who she was and that she believed the person responsible for what happened at my sorority house was the same person responsible for her friend's disappearance."

"Is that the first time you heard The Defendant's name?"

Woefully, I admitted, "Yes, Your Honor."

"That right?" Judge Lambert murmured to himself, as though surprised to learn that there was something to this affidavit after all. He sat in contemplative silence a few moments while I felt like I was being burned alive.

"If I may say one last thing, Your Honor," I said, and winced a little, sure I was about to be scolded for speaking before being spoken to. To my surprise, Judge Lambert only regarded me with an open and curious expression. "I think, if you have a chance to review my initial statement to the police, you'll see that I was insistent about the fact that the man I saw at the front door was a stranger. I know I said that at first I thought it was Roger, but then I also said it was only a fleeting thought. And that immediately I came to my senses and realized I'd never seen this person before. And I was consistent in this statement to everyone I spoke to over the next thirtysome hours, well before I met Martina Cannon. My sisters, my boyfriend, even the alumna who hosted us at her house that evening. And then, even though Sheriff Cruso focused on Roger those first few weeks, I stuck to my guns. I insisted that it was not Roger I saw, though it would have made my life so much easier if I'd just caved to the pressure. And I think what I'm trying to say," I said, flushing a bit because Judge Lambert's eyes had glazed over by then—*Judges appreciate brevity in testimony,* a law school professor had recently cautioned—"is that I am not someone who is easily influenced."

Judge Lambert trilled his lips in deliberation. "I'll need a chance to review those statements. Speak to these people face-to-face. You'll give the names of these corroborating witnesses to Mr. Pearl then."

That hand again, this time with a fluttering of fingers. *Too-da-loo,* he might as well have said.

"Thank you, Your Honor," I said in this pathetic, groveling way that haunts me still.

PAMELA

Miami, 1979

Day 542

In my hotel room, I went soft, looking out the window. There was a billboard for *Our Winning Season*, Dennis Quaid blotting out the view to the ocean, and for the first two days I took this as a good omen. But by day three, I realized members of the defense were also staying in this hotel, and who was to say it wasn't *their* good omen? I started closing the drapes then.

It wasn't that I wasn't allowed to leave. I could go anywhere I pleased so long as I didn't mind missing a call from Mr. Pearl with an update. Once I did try and go for a walk, right around the time when court started, figuring it was unlikely the phone would ring then. But about half a block away, I remembered that The Defendant's preferred method of showing contempt was through chronic lateness, and I turned around and sprinted back. I was so paranoid of doing anything that may taint my credibility in the eyes of Judge Lambert that I wouldn't even let Tina bring me coffee in the morning before she left for court. *Not even if I leave it outside the door?* she asked through the closed door. *Please, just go away!* I hissed, worried someone from the press might overhear this exchange and write that the eyewitness whose testimony may have been influenced was conversing with the woman who was alleged to have influenced it.

Going soft is different than going out of your mind. In the seven days I spent in that Miami hotel room waiting for Judge Lambert's ruling, I didn't lose my grip on reality, but certain convictions began to rot like a bad back molar. It was with the same dull ache of an infected tooth that I began to question things I had previously labeled unquestionable.

That summer, I was externing at a big firm in the mergers and acquisitions department, unable to admit to myself that it wasn't just that I hated my stink-faced supervisor, who took pleasure in reminding all the externs that we were being paid not for our brilliance but for our availability, that this was the sort of job that didn't just affect your personal life; it would *be* your personal life. What I hated, what left me with an empty, almost nihilistic feeling, was the idea of a career spent representing companies and not actual human beings. Most people who went into corporate law, like my father, were drawn to the impersonality of it. The last thing they wanted to do was deal with a client in a crisis, someone going through a divorce, a custody battle, a bankruptcy. When I was growing up, my father always laughed about how god-awful that sounded, and I always vehemently agreed because I needed this, this one thing we had in common. But sitting in that darkened hotel room, forced to consider what it would feel like if the phone rang with the news that Judge Lambert had struck my testimony, all but ensuring the jury would find The Defendant not guilty, I was also forced to consider what that would feel like for Mrs. Andora, for Robbie's parents, for Jill and Eileen and Sally, to have to see his smug smiling face in the paper, fist raised in triumph. How would I live with myself, should it go down like that? And I knew the answer wasn't by making sure big wealthy firms remained in compliance with the law so that they could continue to be big and wealthy.

On day four, when I called that snot-voiced supervisor to tell him I was still in Miami, waiting to find out if and when I would testify, he informed me a little too eagerly that I had ventured into unexcused-absences territory. On orientation day, we were warned that we could be terminated for missing more than three days of work.

"There is nothing I can do," I told this supervisor, whose name I can no longer recall but whose squinty and constipated face I can.

"In real life," he was saying—hilariously, as though he knew more about the inconveniences of real life than I did—"our client doesn't care about your circumstances, outstanding as they may be. In real life, you've just lost your client."

The thought was so clear, it was almost as though someone had spoken it into my ear: *I don't give one flying fuck*. "It's possible this could go on awhile," I said without inflection. It had been exhausting, trying to keep up this pretense that I cared, with everything else going on. My stamina was in rags. "I don't want to let down the firm any more than I already have. I'll draft my resignation letter today."

Stuttering, the supervisor said, "Let's not be rash here."

"Thank you so much for bearing with me on this," I said graciously. "I apologize for any trouble I've caused. Take care."

I hung up quickly, in case Mr. Pearl was trying to reach me.

PAMELA

Miami, 1979

Day 548

O n the stand, when Mr. Pearl asked if the man I'd seen at the front door was in the courtroom, I answered, "Yes. He is."

Then, as I was raising my right arm to identify him for the jurors, I found I was rising to my feet, the compulsion to stand as instinctual as the night in The House when I ran toward him rather than away. We were about the same distance from each other as we were then. Thirteen feet, two inches. Only this time, he gazed back at me, legitimately bored, one elbow on the counsel table and his face supported in a sprawled-open hand. I was one hour into my testimony, and I had another to go, and he would not be the one to question me. The way his team had to manage him, by calling inconsequential witnesses to the stand just so he had someone to question without torpedoing his defense, would later remind me of a toddler given one of those play cell phones because that's what all the adults have and he is *not* a baby.

"Relax, now." The directive came from the most prominent bench. Though he'd ruled to allow my testimony, I despised Judge Lambert with every fiber of my being, the way he addressed me as *ma'am* and The Defendant as *young man*, then later as *cowboy, compadre, partner*. I was twenty-three years old to The Defendant's thirty-two. I had earned top marks in my first year of law school. *I* was the young woman, the compadre, closer to his equal than The Defendant, but you never would have known it by the way the judge spoke to him.

I sat back down on my own time, brushing the lap of my dress smooth.

"What were you doing," Mr. Pearl continued, "right before you came downstairs and saw The Defendant?"

"I was sleeping."

"How had you spent the night previously?"

"I was working out the volunteering schedule for some of our spring charity events. After that, I finished up some reading for an econ class."

"Busy evening. And did you see Denise at all?"

"Yes. She stopped by my room because she wanted to borrow one of my coats, and to see if I wanted to attend a party with her."

"And what did you tell her?"

"I told her I couldn't because I had too much work to do."

"How did she react?"

"She was disappointed, and she tried to get me to change my mind."

"What did she say?"

"She told me that it was our senior spring and that I deserved to have a little fun." I angled my knees so that I was speaking directly to the jurors. Mr. Pearl had told me to try and seek out the juror who wore cat's-eye glasses and a silver cross around her neck. She was a nurse and a single mother, a woman likely to be sympathetic to the account of another woman up to her ears with deadlines and responsibilities. "She told me it was just one party, and that I had my whole life to be Pam Perfect."

"That's what she called you—Pam Perfect?"

"Yes. It was a nickname she had for me. After the cooking spray commercial. You know the one that promises to help you save money, calories, and time?" The women jurors were smiling among themselves, nodding. "In the end, they always show the dish and it looks delicious and they say it came out PAM Perfect."

"And why did she call you Pam Perfect?"

Veronica Ramira objected to that. It called for speculation.

"How did you feel about Denise's nickname for you?"

"I laughed about it with her, but secretly, I was a little embarrassed by it," I said. "Perfect is not something anyone wants to be."

"Isn't it?" Mr. Pearl asked with a furrowed brow.

"Not by the standards of college students, no. That's the time in your life you're supposed to be having fun. And I wasn't doing any of that. I put a lot of pressure on myself to do everything by the book. I still do." The single mother was watching me intently.

"Is it fair to say that you felt the nickname was well suited to you?"

"Yes. That's why deep down it embarrassed me. I couldn't defend myself when Denise called me Pam Perfect, because I knew it was true."

When it came time for the cross-examination, Veronica Ramira reviewed her notes for a moment before rising. She had her hair clipped back with a barrette on either side, giving her a girlish, youthful effect. I knew that was intentional, an optical illusion for the jury—just as easily as one young woman could accuse her client of a horrific act, another could believe in his innocence. It was a clever touch on her part. Not that she ever got any credit for it.

"Good afternoon, Miss Schumacher," she began pleasantly.

"Hello," I replied. We smiled hatefully at one another.

"I want to start on Saturday night, January fourteenth," Veronica said, sauntering around the counsel table with her hands folded comfortably at her belly button. "The evening before the attack. What time did you fall asleep?"

"I don't know exactly, but some of the girls came into my room and said they were going to get hot fudge cake from Jerry's, which closed at midnight. I remember they said they would make it just in time. Jerry's is about a ten-minute walk from The House, so I'd estimate that was about eleven forty or eleven forty-five. I'd fallen asleep by the time they got home, though."

"And how do you know that?"

"Because later, one of my sorority sisters said she came upstairs to tell me the cake was here but she found me asleep and decided to just let me be."

"So at the absolute latest, you fell asleep at twelve fifteen in the morning."

"Yes." I nodded. "That sounds right."

"And you say you were awoken a few minutes shy of three in the morning, correct?"

"That is correct."

"Two hours and forty-five minutes is a significant amount of time to be asleep, would you agree?"

"Practically a full night for me," I said, and some of the female jurors laughed.

Veronica Ramira was unrattled. Worrying, frankly. She had something up her sleeve; she must. "I don't know about you, but I'm pretty groggy when I wake up from a deep sleep."

I said nothing. There was no question.

"Did you feel groggy?"

"A little, at first. But when I came out in the hallway and saw that the chandelier was still lit, I snapped out of it. I'm a total neat freak, and when things are out of place, I get very focused on correcting them. I was determined to figure out why the timer wasn't working. That cleared away the cobwebs."

"Is that part of being Pam Perfect?" When one of the male jurors snickered, four female jurors swung their heads, boxing him in with severe, reprimanding expressions. His smile turned limping and apologetic.

"If Denise were here," I replied, "and I really wish she could be"—my voice caught as I thought how very much Denise would wish it too—"she'd tell you yes." I batted away my tears and stole a glance at Mr. Pearl. *A little emotion is all right,* he'd told me, *but Judge Lambert doesn't have patience for hysterics.* Mr. Pearl gave me an almost imperceptible tip of his chin. *Just enough.*

"And what happened then?"

I went through it for the final time. The *I Love Lucy* rerun. The dirty plates in the rec room. The draft coming in from the back door. The thud. The reptilian impulse to run him down.

"And you believed it was Roger Yul you saw at the front door, isn't that correct?"

"Only for a split second, and then I looked closer and realized it was a stranger."

"The chandelier was on, though." Veronica Ramira tipped her face up to the harsh track lighting in the ceiling of the courtroom, purpling the hollows of her eyes. "Would you say it was as bright in the foyer as it is in here?"

"Close enough," I said.

"And yet," Veronica Ramira said, unblinking, "you still thought you saw Roger."

"Only for a second," I repeated with a certain measure of relief, thinking her strategy at last had been revealed. If this was all she had, I could handle it. "And then I got my bearings and realized I did not recognize the person after all."

Veronica Ramira followed up swiftly: "What was your relationship to Roger Yul?"

The low-level fluttering in my stomach intensified, but I answered quickly too, not wanting to be seen as stalling. "He was a friend. He was a member at the same fraternity as my boyfriend, and he and Denise dated on and off for years."

"So you spent a lot of time with him?"

"Roger was in the mix. We found ourselves in the same place, hanging around the same people, fairly often."

"But never alone?"

Here was where I faltered. "N-no. Of course not. We didn't spend time alone."

Veronica Ramira said dubiously, "You've never been alone with Roger before?"

"I'm sure there were times . . . over the years. When someone went to use the bathroom, maybe, and yes, we were alone for a few minutes."

"During one of these times," Veronica Ramira said, "did you and Roger kiss?"

The witness box is precisely designed to be the second-highest prominence in the courtroom, lower than the judge but higher than the jury, meant to convey the importance of the person providing the testimony. An unintentional consequence of this layout is that it provides clear sight lines for the witness—you can see every spectator in the room. In that moment, my eye fell on Mrs. Andora, who looked like she'd just had a religious revelation. I knew what she was thinking—that was why the last breakup was as bad as it was. That was why Denise ended up in the hospital for dehydration.

Veronica Ramira's voice cut like a knife. "I asked if you and Roger kissed, Miss Schumacher."

I needed to see how bad this was, so I was looking at Mr. Pearl when I answered, "He made a move on me once." Oh, it was bad.

"Did you kiss?"

"*He* kissed *me*. And I pushed him off right away. He was very drunk, and I don't think he even remembered doing it the next day."

Veronica Ramira smirked as though this was exactly the kind of blame off-loading she expected from a girl who kissed her best friend's boyfriend. "And it was after that when Denise and he broke up, in the December before the attack, correct?"

"That's correct. Because I told her what he did. And she was mortified and made me promise not to tell anyone." I hadn't, not the detectives and not Mr. Pearl, figuring it didn't matter, because only two people in the world knew about the kiss, and one of us was dead. I'd assumed Roger had been too drunk to remember, not just because he came at me with the motor functioning of the walking dead, but because when Denise broke up with him in December, she had asked him if he knew why she was ending things for good this time. He had begged her to tell him, and Denise had refused, thinking it would be a harsher punishment for his imagination to run wild. I wouldn't ever find out how it got back to The Defendant and his team, but at some point, Roger must have come clean. Told someone that he'd played dumb to Denise when, really, he remembered everything.

"I'm sure she was mortified," Veronica Ramira agreed. "Her best friend and her boyfriend. It must have hurt her a lot."

I flashed hot at the suggestion that anyone but Veronica Ramira's client had hurt Denise. "I would never hurt Denise. I loved her."

"But Denise was upset with you."

"Denise was upset. But not at me."

"I thought you said . . ." Veronica Ramira turned her back on me a moment to rustle around with her notes on the counsel table. The Defendant pushed a few pages forward, and I could tell by the way his eyes flicked upward and the smile that appeared on his face that Veronica Ramira had smiled at him first. "Thank you, counsel," she said to him before turning back around with her memory refreshed and the gloves off. "You made an early statement to Sheriff Cruso that there had been a bit of a strain between you and Denise at the time she died."

A sickly bead of sweat escaped the band of my bra, rolled with a bowler's aim down the knobby lane of my spine. It could not have been more than sixty-six man-made degrees in the courtroom, and I was freezing. "I did say that," I admitted. "But that had to do with me being president. Sometimes she thought I was bossy."

"And I'm sure kissing her boyfriend didn't help matters."

"She didn't see it like that, because that's not what happened."

One of the male jurors was smiling in this small, nauseating way. Two women pecking at each other. That's how he heard us. I wanted a shower. I wanted to get off that stand and take my cold, sweaty dress straight to the dry cleaner.

"And a few weeks later, you think you see her boyfriend, whom you kissed, at the front door, and then your story changes to protect him. Is that what happened?"

Before I could tell her that she had inserted her own interpretation into the question, Mr. Pearl objected on those very grounds. "Argumentative, Your Honor."

"Sustained," Judge Lambert drawled.

Veronica Ramira shrugged as though she'd been prepared to take the hit. "Thank you, Pamela. I have nothing further."

"Adjourn until one p.m. for lunch," Judge Lambert said, and struck the sound block cleanly with the gavel.

There was that churchlike congregational rising, the swishing of pants legs, the popping of sedentary bones, while Judge Lambert gathered up the hem of his robe and descended the bench from the back with stiff knees, disappearing into his private, secure corridor. Courtrooms are always designed so the judge does not cross public areas to access the bench, but rarely with that consideration in mind for witnesses. This meant that the insect-like shuttering of the cameras captured the ill-timed moment when I nearly intersected with The Defendant as he stood for the lunch hour. The press had spilled so much ink over his tactical brilliance that I was bordering on indoctrination myself, and I gritted my back molars in anticipation of him smiling at me in that courtly way of his, bowing to open the partition's gate with a sweeping curve to his arm—"After you, ma'am." *Handsome attorney displays chivalry for the homely coed who accused him of murder,* Carl could have captioned the image.

Instead, The Defendant, realizing we were on a collision course, did something I'd seen boys do a thousand times before. I say *boys,* not *men,* because it was with the bumbling awkwardness of a pimpled teenager that he suddenly did not know what to do with his hands, where to look with his small, piggy eyes. This was the man characterized by the press as a deadly Casanova, the likes of which women had never before encountered, and he was flustered by the mere presence of someone of the opposite sex. He turned his back to me and set his hands on top of the wooden partition separating counsel from the public, saying something to his mother, who had a rough graying bob and often dressed like a fifties housewife in a full poodle skirt and shrunken cardigan. She was looking right at me, and while her son had shown his rather mundane hand, hers was the face I would continue to see long after the trial ended, the one that would derail my life, briefly, then set me on course.

PAMELA

Issaquah, 2021

Day 15,858

In 1996, when the Freedom of Information Act was amended to include audio and video files as documents the public could access, I requested the recording of The Defendant's rumored Lake Sammamish confession, the one Carl had told me about from the carpet of my sorority house. It took months for me to hear back that the request could not be completed because no such file existed. As proof, or maybe a consolation prize, government officials sent copies of The Defendant's meandering conversations with the Seattle detectives who came to Aspen to question him in the days following his first escape.

I listened until the tape ran out, just to be sure. Indeed, there was no confession, but there was another admission that proved meaningful to me involving the identity of The Defendant's father.

The story had long gone that The Defendant's mother had gotten pregnant at sixteen, the consequence of a short-lived love affair with the heir to a department store in Philadelphia who died in a car crash. With no husband in the picture, his mother was forced to remain under her parents' roof. For the first few years of his life, The Defendant enjoyed a bucolic upbringing in his grandparents' Philadelphia home before moving across the country to live with relatives in Seattle.

But a darker telling emerged on the tape I listened to in 1996. One in which The Defendant railed against his mother, a weak woman who failed to protect him from the brutal beatings at the belt of his grandfather, who didn't even bother to lock her bedroom door at night, which is when he forced depravity on his adolescent daughter. When pressed to say more, The Defendant refused.

There is little that can be done to substantiate the rumor that The Defendant was a product of incest, but there are enough links in the logic chain for me to believe it to my marrow. In 1996, this was the push I needed to leave the family law firm I'd worked at for a decade and a half to start my own practice, dedicated exclusively to mediation. Mediation may be a near-ubiquitous option now, but in the eighties and early nineties it was an experimental alternative to divorce litigation that child welfare experts were hoping would not only increase satisfaction around dispute resolution but also reduce the workload of the court system. Columbia, my alma mater, offered a pilot training program that I enrolled in out of curiosity, then ended up taking to with an evangelist's fervor. It was the first time I'd heard anyone propose an approach to the law that centered the well-being of women and children. Mediation aimed to keep families out of the courts, preserve civility, and promote their ability to work together in the future, families with women who wore the same disquieting expression as The Defendant's mother did on the day I testified in court. I even notice echoes of my past life as the president of the southernmost chapter of my sorority house in what I do, the challenges and rewards of presiding over thirty-eight brilliant, bullheaded women who were supposed to support one another like blood. But mostly, I continue to be drawn to mediation because I know better than anyone that All-American Sex Killers are not born, that they come from broken and battered homes, human systems that fail them well before they reach the penal ones, and then they go out into a world that tells them that women are deserving depositories for their impotence and rage.

Kids who are raised in hostile environments are seven times more likely to become violent perpetrators as adults, and I've been given the unique opportunity to disrupt that pattern. For the small curve in the road where I get to stand, holding my traffic sign that indicates a better way, I have no choice but to feel belligerent gratitude.

I remind myself of this, all these years later, when the response from an old law school friend at the Justice Department who fast-tracked my FOIA request lands like a coldcock. The reason the original request could not be completed back in 1996 was not because the file didn't exist; it was because the file didn't exist where I'd told them to look—in the records taken by the Seattle detectives who visited The Defendant in his Aspen jail cell after his first escape. I had no idea at the time about the second confession Carl had obtained, that in the midnineties, the recording was still part of an active investigation into the Lake Sammamish case and not eligible for public release. Nor did I know that when they closed the case and the file should have become available, someone else got their hands on it and requested all copies be destroyed—a woman by the name of Rebecca Wachowsky from Issaquah, Washington.

Rebecca is still married to Ruth's brother. Their two children are grown now—Allen's kids go to UDub, Rebecca tells me when she finds me taking the chronological tour of their lives as displayed by the pictures on the mantel. Little League games and dance recitals, prom dresses and graduation gowns, weddings and babies for both.

"Mine is thirty next month," I tell Rebecca, accepting the glass of lemon water she's offered me. It scours my throat, the liquid acidic from a rind she let soak too long. I have told her I am an attorney representing a family member of one of The Defendant's long-ago victims, working through a checklist of evidentiary items that the state has not been able to locate. There was an affidavit in my purse in case she did not invite me in, but she did, warmly, telling me that when Ruth's mother died in 2001, she had discovered a notice from the Federal Bureau of Prisons in a pile of old mail, alerting her to the release of her daughter's belongings from evidence and laying out instructions on how to request the items. Rebecca continued to clean out the rest of the house, assuming she would find a box of Ruth's things somewhere, but it was only after all the shelves in all the closets were down to sawdust that she realized her mother-in-law had likely never done anything but read the notice and cast it aside.

"Shirley had difficulty acknowledging things that were . . . unpleasant," Rebecca tells me as she leads me down the carpeted basement stairs. "After Ruth died, we rarely spoke her name again. It was so sad, like she never existed in the first place. I couldn't stand the idea of her things just sitting in storage somewhere, so I was the one to put in the request." She hits the light switch, revealing a basement that is half TV room, half junkyard of decorative Bed Bath & Beyond storage boxes.

"I knew right away that some other poor girl's things got mixed up with Ruth's," Rebecca says. "I always wondered who they belonged to."

Rebecca sits on the flat gray carpet and removes the lid of a faux-leather bin with a hexagonal design. I think I own the same one.

She begins to separate the items she doesn't recognize as Ruth's from the ones she does: a halter top with yellow flowers, a white plastic barrette, a paperback with the cover torn off. The first line reads, *Beneath the suede brim of his cowboy hat, his gaze was piercing blue.* She bows her head over the box, eyes flicking back and forth, and goes to close it back up.

I take a step forward, arm outstretched as if to say, *Halt right there.* "Would you mind if I looked through myself? In case you missed anything."

Rebecca's smile is protective and vaguely threatening. "That's it. That's everything that wasn't Ruth's. You can have it. Hopefully, the family recognizes it. Who are they, if you don't mind me asking?"

There is a beat when I wonder if I should push harder to rummage through that box before coming clean. But she asked point-blank, and I'd have a hard time regaining her trust if she looked back on this moment and realized I didn't answer honestly when she gave me the chance.

"Martina Cannon," I answer.

Rebecca's cautiously friendly face turns panicked. She wraps all her limbs around the box, anchoring it to her person in a wrestler's hold. "Get out of my house before I call the cops on you." She is reaching for menacing but it's a stretch. She is far too afraid of losing Ruth.

I reach into my purse and extract the folder containing the affidavit. "If you do, they'll only be obligated to enforce this." Rebecca refuses to release the storage box long enough to take the file from me, so I lay out the broad strokes. "This is a sworn document from Miss Cannon, listing the items she is entitled to inherit as the registered domestic partner of Ruth Wachowsky."

At that, Rebecca rips the document from my hands, leaving me with matching paper cuts. I hiss under my breath as her eyes go immediately to the items listed. She snorts rudely. "Well, I don't have what she's after."

"If you'll keep reading," I say, "I think you'll find that there is no use lying about that."

Rebecca scans the language frantically. I know the moment she locates it—undeniable proof that the assets in question were released to her—because her whole body goes slack. It is the response from my old law school friend confirming the identity of the person who requested Carl's recording after the Lake Sammamish case was closed, as well as a copy of the release form, denying public access to the file, as was the family's legal right to make in a case where there was no conviction. The confession tape is distinctively human, hereditarily one of a kind. There are no copies made, no more chances after this.

"We intend to keep the recording only long enough to have a copy made for my client," I tell her. "She is willing to return the original to you."

Rebecca lets the pages of the affidavit float to the ground. She folds her body over the storage box, resting her cheek on its hard angles as if it's a pillow. She is taking deep, noisy yoga breaths, whimpering a little on the exhale.

"You have our word that we will return the original to you," I assure her.

"Well, I don't *want* it." Rebecca weeps petulantly. "Not once she has it too." She looks up at me, snot-nosed and furious. "I knew Ruth since we were three years old. *I* knew her."

"Our goal is to stay out of the courts with this," I say in the curated tone I use in highly emotional mediations several days a week, "but the only way to do that, and to ensure your husband does not find out about your relationship with his sister, is if you are willing to cooperate."

"I'm giving it to you," Rebecca snarls. "Okay? It's just—" She is holding on to that box like it is a raft in the middle of the Atlantic. "It's like there's never been any room for how *I* feel. The only time I don't have to hide how much I miss her is when I'm down here." She gestures. *Here,* this basement where Allen's old Atari still sits on the cabinet with the chipped corners, all the remnants of the life she never really wanted packed up and put away, no longer sparking joy, if they ever did in the first place. I am blazing with contempt for Rebecca. *You had your chance,* I think, *to make room for yourself, but you were too much of a coward.*

And I might have been too, were it not for Tina. There is no doubt in my mind that I would have become a lawyer even if The Defendant had blundered into a different sorority house that night, but it would have been a passionless practice, something I did to try and connect with my father because I had no real connection with myself. Instead, I have lived the last forty-three years with purpose, not in spite of what happened in the early-morning hours of January 15, 1978, but because of it.

It is only fair that I take from Rebecca what rightfully belongs to the person who helped me live so well with my pain.

Rebecca lives in one of those neighborhoods with an active Next-door community, people who get dogs just to have an excuse to patrol the neighborhood a few times a day and post about it on-line. *God, I sound paranoid,* Tina said with forced, nervous laughter. Before she dropped me off at Rebecca's curb, she pointed out the nearby convenience store where she would wait for me. She was worried about Rebecca spotting her and doing something crazy, like ripping out the reel with her teeth.

When I approach the QuikTrip parking lot, Tina is sitting in the driver's seat with her hands folded in her lap and her eyes closed. For a moment, I am sure she is dead, that the ping-ponging worry over which way this will go has triggered a massive heart event. I rap a knuckle on her window lightly, not wanting to give her one of those if she is in fact only meditating.

Tina's shoulders draw up with an exhale, so I know she's alive, even though she's too scared to open her eyes. I start nodding so that *yes* is the first thing she sees. *Yes,* I got it. *Yes,* it's over.

She finally looks at me through the driver's-side window and nods back stoically. It's when I go around the back of the car that she makes the sound. It's something that comes through her two front teeth, vicious and devoted, a sound that's been trapped inside her since the Carter administration, older than Tickle Me Elmo and Snapple iced tea. I climb in next to her, crying because one of my greatest fears in life was that she might never be free of it, and now she is and and in my own way, so am I.

RUTH

Issaquah

July 14, 1974

Seattle's evening news anchors had placed a bet live on air about the size of the crowds expected at Lake Sammamish on Sunday. The woman with the dyed red hair said no way they'd top thirty thousand, and as I coasted past the park's painted wood sign, I thought about how she would have to pay up on Monday.

Cars were parked so close together that whole families had to exit the vehicles through the hatchbacks. There was a banner welcoming the Seattle Police Department to its annual summer picnic, another advertising twenty-five-cent pints from a local brewery, live music, free ice cream. Dogs chased flying Frisbees; in the distance, sailboats lazily punctured the horizon. Tina could be anywhere, but I decided to start with Tibbetts Beach, by the softball field. It tended to be quieter over there, drawing groups of high school burnouts and, by extension, fewer children, but on that day, there was no logic to the crowd. The burnouts were passing joints next to toddlers playing with their buckets and pails. No one complained and no one threatened to call the police; everyone was just happy to have found a spot.

At Sunset Beach, I was so hot and uncomfortable I couldn't take it anymore. I dropped my bike and stripped off the navy shift dress; underneath I wore Tina's black bikini. A group of teenage girls agreed to watch my things while I took a dip.

The lake was warm and oily with tanning lotion, but I walked out deeper and deeper, until the moss-green water disguised my own limbs from me, and then I held my nose and dunked my head. Underwater, I laughed in wonder. There is nothing in the world like knowing you did exactly the right thing. I would reenact it all for Tina when I found her. How I finally stood up to my mother and, in doing so, had honored my father's memory more than I ever could have sitting silent and sweating in his memorial garden while people got up and lied about who he was. Tina would hang on every word, and she might even beg me to tell it again.

I returned to the shore, wringing out my long hair, and the high school girls offered me a towel when they saw me drying off with Tina's shift dress. I felt them staring at my body the way I used to stare at beautiful women when I was a little girl, wondering if I would ever grow up to look like that.

I thanked them and spread the towel on the grass, lying on my back, letting the sun decide what to do with me for once. I was twenty-five and had rarely spent time in a bathing suit. Bathing suits were for pools and beaches, and pools and beaches were for women who didn't need makeup. And yet somehow I was one of those women now! I traced my fingers in the grass, imagining how Tina would look at my tawny thighs later.

A cold shadow fell over me. "Pardon me, miss?"

I opened my eyes, expecting to see someone much older. No one my age used the expression *pardon me* without rolling their eyes at themselves. But the guy seemed around my age, dressed in an all-white tennis outfit that set off his nice tan. His hair was neatly combed to the side, and his left arm was cradled close to his body in a sling. He wasn't half bad-looking.

"Could I ask your help with something?" He smiled a little sheepishly.

I sat up on command.

"I'm supposed to be meeting some friends here to help me load my sailboat onto my car, but I can't find them anywhere." The man squinted into the swarm of people, one last attempt to pick them out. "I'd do it myself, but . . ." He smiled down at his bum arm.

Next to me, the chatter had died down. I could sense the high school girls leaning in, listening for their entertainment but also curious about how men and women met in the real world. Something like amused solidarity emanated from a housewife on my right, both of us old enough to recognize the line for what it was.

I patted my towel. "Why don't you sit down and we'll talk about it a moment. Where's the boat?"

The man crouched carefully, flinching as he rested his injured arm on his knee. "It's right here in Issaquah at my parents' house. Not far at all."

"I know. I grew up in Issaquah."

"Whereabouts?"

"Over by the glade. But I'm closer to the university now."

"You're by one of my favorite bars."

"Dante's," we said at the same time.

"My friends just played the venue," he said. "Last Saturday. The Lily Pads?"

I shrugged. Hadn't heard of them.

"They've got a great sound. Folksy, but you can still dance to it. You should really go see them next time they're in town. We could go together."

I glanced at the housewife. She smiled knowingly as she smeared sunscreen over the face of one of her squirming children. She was wearing a modest one-piece that started at her clavicle and ended a few inches above her knees. I could imagine that she was thinking she had been my age not that long ago.

"Maybe," I said, not wanting to hurt his feelings but not wanting to get his hopes up either.

"I could drop you at home after we wrestle this thing into the trunk," he offered. "Or you're welcome to come sailing with me and my friends once I find them."

"Why can't your parents help you?"

"My father just had surgery on his back. My mother"—he brought a finger to his lips and lowered his voice, like what he was about to say wasn't nice—"she's not a very fit woman."

"I see," I said in a clipped voice. "So you sought out the fittest-looking woman on the beach."

"I suppose I sought out the cleverest," he replied suavely. There was something aristocratic about the way he spoke, about his slight build and his starched white shorts. I wanted to tell the high school girls that men were not normally this well-mannered when they bothered you, that in fact this one struck me as so odd that I couldn't picture him with a girlfriend, or even with the group of friends who were supposed to meet him here. I felt bad for him all of a sudden. I wondered if his friends had stood him up. He seemed like that guy in the group, the tagalong.

"What's your name?" I asked him.

His eyes crinkled as he told me. "What's yours?"

"Ruth."

"Ruth." The man extended his good arm. He gave my hand one firm tug, held sustained eye contact.

I pointed. "How'd you do that to your arm?"

"Racquetball."

I laughed at him. I couldn't help it. I didn't know anyone who wore white shorts like that, who played tennis, sure, but *racquetball*? For a moment, I wondered if it was all an act. This was the kind of pretense I thought existed only on the East Coast.

He bowed his head, appropriately cowed. "I learned so that I could play with my boss. Guess I wasn't very good."

"What do you do?"

"I'm a lawyer. Well, I'm studying to be. I've got two years to go. I'm a summer associate at a law firm downtown right now."

"What law firm?"

"Baskins-Cole?"

"Oh yeah. I think I saw an ad for them in the paper before."

"We're mostly corporate law." He shrugged as though this might explain, if I hadn't heard of them.

I brushed the grass back and forth with the palm of my hand, staring out at the sun dimpling the skin on the lake. The housewife was now moderating an argument between two of her children over who got the last Popsicle stick.

"I was supposed to meet my friends right here," the man said a bit sadly, "by the picnic tables at Sunset Beach." He looked around once more, in case they'd shown up while we were talking. "Probably they just ditched me." He laughed, but he didn't seem to be joking. I felt a pang for him. He was the effeminate type, a guy who probably had a hard time making male friends. My brother would have made high school horrible for him. CJ too. I thought of the traveling businessman who came into my father's bar all those years ago, far from home and just looking for a few minutes of conversation.

"You better introduce me to your parents," I said, standing and tugging the navy dress down over my damp bathing suit. There was still something about him that irked me, and I didn't want to be too nice to him in case I gave him the wrong idea. I wanted him to understand I was coming along because he needed my help and because he seemed a little rejected, because that Sunday there had been a galactic explosion of sunlight and freedom, because life has a way of staggering its mileposts, and I was certain I had a ways to go until I got to the next one.

———

I admitted to myself that something was wrong with him in the car, but through some lethal interaction between denial and decorum, I kept the conversation going at a sparkling cadence.

I prattled on about culinary school and helping my friend Tina pass her jurisprudence exam. I saw a hint of something cold in him when I mentioned the exam—resentment, though that couldn't be right. He was a summer associate at Baskins-Cole, and that seemed a hierarchical impossibility.

We exited I-90 and made a left at a stoplight, climbing into the mountains. We hadn't been able to get the trunk shut with my bike inside, but he promised to drive slowly. When he'd said his parents lived in Issaquah, I had pictured a street like mine. The homes on top of one another and kids playing in the yard, fathers mowing the grass in their weekend moccasins. It wasn't that this wasn't Issaquah, it was just that a lot of the houses up here were second homes for wealthy Utah families.

"Do your folks live here year-round?" I asked.

"They do now," he said, flashing a smile at me as if to say that was a great question. "They sold their place out east after my dad retired."

He was from the East Coast. I'd known it. "Where on the East Coast?"

"Philadelphia," he said, turning into the driveway of a spacious alpine-style home with a green roof and shutters, tucked invisibly into the woodlands. It was quiet and secluded, but there was a gleaming black Chevy parked in the driveway, recently washed, and there were lights on inside.

"Dad's car." He indicated with a jut of his sharp chin. "Does that assuage any lingering concerns?" His laugh was self-deprecating.

I blinked at him, a little unsure if I should correct him or not. *"Assuage,"* I said.

He put the car into park and turned to look at me in genuine distress. "What did I say?"

"You pronounced it *ah-soge,* but I'm pretty sure it's *ah-swaje.*"

He tried to laugh it off, but I could tell he was embarrassed. "I've been saying it wrong all my life. That's just great." He opened the door. "The boat's in the garage."

I hesitated. "You said you'd introduce me to your parents."

He gazed up at the house, rocking back on his heels. There was a light on upstairs and one in the back of the house, looking down on the lake. "Looks like Dad is up finally. He's been sleeping late because of his pain pills. That's Mom in the kitchen for sure." He wiggled his eyebrows mischievously. "She's making pot roast tonight. I tell her she should eat more fish, but you're welcome to stay if you're hungry."

I opened the door and stepped onto the gravel driveway. "I wouldn't want to impose," I said, though on some level I understood I was participating in a charade that was designed to keep me calm and cooperative. I knew there was a darker motive behind the dinner invitation; but still I expected to walk into that house and find his mother browning onions and carrots on the stove.

The house was very beautiful and tasteful; I could see how a person like him had come from a place like this, and that set me at ease too, just being able to make sense of him, because I had found his old-world mannerisms odd, almost as though he were from another decade, or acting in a movie about people from another decade. He was just born rich, I realized, making my way into the back of the house. Not even Tina was born rich. It seemed to stand that a person like that might act a little strangely. It's not like there were very many of them in this world.

The home was decorated like a vacation rental or a luxury winter resort. Animal antlers in varying sizes hung above the old brick fireplace. The furniture was dark brown leather, with flannel pillows and blankets thrown about. It was all very plush, very cozy, but as much as it sickened me to admit, the rooms had an abandoned feel. On any other gloomy day I might not have noticed, but that Sunday sunlight blazed a trail of dust through the living room. I looked at the pictures of his parents on the doily-covered side table and started to tremble. They were normal-looking and covered in a fine layer of grime.

I could hear him in the kitchen talking to his mother about me. "I couldn't find those guys anywhere but I found someone nice enough to help with the sailboat. Boy, it's a scene down there."

I followed his voice into the kitchen, fixing my hair for his mother, tugging down the hem of Tina's navy dress.

"Here she is now," he said as I stepped into the kitchen. There was a grin in his voice but not on his face. His arm was bent at a ninety-degree angle, elbow flush against his rib cage, the gun in his hand level with his hip and sort of cocked to the side so that I was half waiting for him to say, *Hey! Look at what I found here!* in his queer British dialect. He wasn't aiming it so much as he was showing it to me.

I must have looked so brainless, glancing around the kitchen for his mother. Left, then right, like I was getting ready to cross the street. He had been talking to her. Perhaps she was in the pantry getting the flour? Pot roast called for a roux. I would soon be tossing around words like that with people like me, people who wouldn't look at me like I had two heads. *Roux. Au poivre.*

"Get undressed," he said. I'd heard people describe rapists and murderers before. How their eyes went black and they saw pure evil. But the man I saw before me was the man I'd seen at the lake, in the car. I'd seen this man all along. I'd seen him and I'd gone with him anyway, because he'd asked for my help, and I'd already denied it to my mother that day. I'd have been a real bitch to tell someone *no* for the second time in twenty-four hours.

"You're not going to use that," I told him, an especially insane thing to say and exactly why I said it. I thought I could get him to comprehend the gap between what he was doing and who he was, because it was an insane gulf, a death swim. He was a law student in tennis whites who had broken his arm playing racquetball with his . . .

I hadn't noticed it at first, but when I did, icy terror packed my chest. The sling hung around his neck, sweat-wrinkled and abhorrent as a used condom. Whatever was broken in this man was not a bone in his arm.

———

There were times, with CJ, that I'd been disgusted too, that I hadn't wanted our skin to touch, that I had to grit my teeth and will him to be finished with me. At least I didn't have to pretend to enjoy this, I thought. At least.

———

After, he gagged me with a mildewed dish towel and bound me to a chair between the front windows, using the same twisted dark rope we would have used to tie close the trunk of his car once we'd loaded in the boat. The rotted rag plugged the laugh in my throat. *Oh, Ruth,* I said kindly to myself, *there is no boat.*

I was facing the lake water I could still smell in my hair, thousands of feet below. It was as if he wanted me to enjoy the view. The door closed behind him and the car engine caught; the sound of gravel giving it to rubber. He was leaving. I sobbed because it was over and it hadn't been that bad, right?

I twisted my wrists in the ropes, soundlessly at first. The scream that had collected in me had reach; I had to make sure he was far away before I used it. I tried rotating, shimmying, sawing, bouncing in the seat of the chair, but the ropes were so tight I could not even blister my skin. I screamed and screamed until my chin was slobbered with saliva and my vision spotted, black holes burning through the edges.

I came to with another burst of relief, the kind that must come after a long-dreaded surgery. *It's over. Behind me. I can get on with life now.* The lake's horizon severed the sun in half like a woman in a magician's box, gutting it orange. The kitchen was dark and the air clammy. I looked down and saw goose bumps flecking my bronzed knees. It had been so long since I'd had a tan.

I thought again that what had happened wasn't so bad, in the grand scheme of things. This sort of thing happened to women all the time and they still fell in love, had careers, babies, if they wanted those. I hadn't been disfigured or lost some seminal ability, like my sense of smell or taste. I hadn't lost the person I loved. I thought of

Tina, and relief turned to a gratitude so pure and intense that I wondered if I'd been drugged with something.

I heard the woman's voice then. The sweetness in it lifted me higher. *It's way nicer than you said!* Even after I processed her words, even after I heard his response, with that peculiar, malignant affect, a sort of euphoria stayed with me to the end.

My back was against the wall, the driveway behind me, the front door to my right. I had no way of seeing either of them through the window. I thought about Tina, the way she sat on the kitchen counter swinging her feet and pinching off pieces of cheese while I was cooking, so that I always had to shred more as I went, and I thought about the culinary school where I would learn to properly chiffonade leafy herbs, and I marveled at the pointlessness of it all, at the timing, which did feel pointed in its own way. Why not a year ago, when there was nothing to take from me? It was like he had scoured the beach for the woman most flush with life.

The girl outside said "Hey!" in this funny, outraged way, and then the two of them came squeezing through the door on my right like some sort of black-and-white comedy duo my father used to laugh at on TV. She was younger than I was by a few years, young enough to look invincible and hassled and unafraid, even with a gun muzzle imprinting her cheek. I wanted to shelter in her adolescent hubris for as long as I had left, but it was obliterated the moment she saw the mangled grief on my face.

———

"Let's just say it was chaos." The Defendant chuckled. "With all three of us there. Total chaos."

Tina's face is earthly in the setting Seattle light. We are sitting in teak chairs on her back stone patio at her home on Vashon Island, Patagonia fleeces zipped up under our chins. The Cascade Mountains are reflected in the looking glass of the sound, and we are one foot in both worlds. The one where we have to imagine how it ended for Ruth and the one where we don't.

———

People die of all sorts of things. Cancer, car accidents, old age. This girl, whose name I would never know, whose parents I could never tell—she died of fight. I *saw* it happen. She was pummeling his head, his neck, left fist, then right. The final swing seemed to connect to some unseen socket. There was an exploding-star jolt; an outage that sounded like electricity itself. The disruption in magnetic fields trembled the house and sent him flying off her. He landed in a crashing heap, tangled up in his own limbs, and dozed off for a moment. I hoped for a concussion, for a brain bleed, his death, and though I didn't get that, I suppose I got the next best thing.

I saw it all over him as he staggered to his feet, kissing his singed knuckles, as he came toward me with her spit sheening his face. She had scared the ever-loving shit out of him. He was as mortal as me, made small by whatever else was out there, whatever had given her white-hot light at the end.

I did not have long, but I did have enough time to return to the kitchen with Tina, smelling of basil and burned butter. You're never supposed to turn your back on butter you're trying to brown, but I'd had to grate more cheese—Tina and her sticky fingers—and I hadn't noticed the blackening foam until it was too late to salvage. I was rinsing out the pan and I was chiding Tina and I was laughing when it happened. *Look what you made me do!*

"I'm so sorry," Tina says, pressing her nose to the back of her hand while the tears fall and fall. "God, I'm sorry, Ruth."

The Court: Is there anything now you want to say to the Court?

The Defendant: There sure is. Did you think you could get away without me saying something?

The Court: Oh, no. If I thought I could, I wouldn't have asked.

The Defendant: I'd like to talk about the choice of counsel, but only briefly. I remember when I brought the issue up a week or so ago about me representing myself. The Court said, "Well, if you were a brain surgeon you wouldn't operate on yourself."

And I started thinking of that analogy in its real perspective and I said, "Well, think about the education a brain surgeon has. There are some brain surgeons I would rather have represent me in a criminal trial than some attorneys."

Because, let's take the medical profession. Four years of medical school, plus six, seven, eight years of residency before they can go out on their own. Think about it.

We have attorneys doing brain surgery after three years. Sort of in a symbolic sense. There's nothing that prevents a newly graduated law student from representing a person in a capital trial. And I think this is a shortcoming of the legal profession.

It's like some incredible Greek tragedy. Must have been written sometime. There must be one of those ancient Greek plays that portrays the three faces of man. And I don't know how the court can reconcile those three roles, because I think they are mutually inclusive. And I think the court, in spite of its experience and wisdom, is just a man.

And I will tell the court that I am really not able to accept the verdict because although the verdict found in part that those crimes had been committed, they erred in finding who committed them. And as a consequence, I cannot accept the sentence, even though one will be imposed. . . . It is a sentence of someone else who is not standing here today.

—THE DEFENDANT'S CLOSING REMARKS, 1979

PAMELA

New Jersey, 2019

Day 14,997

Not too long ago, I was waiting in line at the Summit Starbucks when I heard Judge Lambert's distinctive drawl from behind. I ran my tongue over my teeth, used a knuckle to paste down the unruly hairs in the arches of my eyebrows, before realizing it didn't matter if I was wearing lipstick where it shouldn't be because the man who deserved my nastiest bitch smile had been dead a decade.

"I think it's more toward the end," a girl's voice said, and there were the craggy, telltale signs of a video, stopping and starting, patches of the wisecracks Judge Lambert managed to work into his final remarks even as he sentenced a man to die by electric chair.

"Of this court as to count two of the indictment—"

"You went too far."

"No, I didn't. It's after the sentencing."

"It's at the forty-seven-minute mark," a third voice chimed in. "I'm a total creep for knowing that, but I'm in so deep."

"Dude, who isn't?" said the girl wearing a navy Drew University sweatshirt. I had by then feigned a glance at the line to the bathroom, located behind them. There was a new documentary out, expensively done, and so many people had watched it, myself included, that I was worried the banner with The Defendant's face might never disappear from the homepage on my television screen.

"There!" cried the interloper, just as I reached the register. Absurdly, I placed an order for a Venti Chai Latte while Judge Lambert famously told The Defendant that someday soon a current of electricity would pass through his body until he was pronounced dead by the warden, and that he should, even more absurdly, take care of himself.

"Thank you, Your Honor," The Defendant replied, a degraded quality to his voice, what happens when you take a new video of an old video and throw it up on YouTube. I inserted my credit card into the chip reader, a technology that, just like Judge Lambert's empathy for me and my deceased sorority sisters, did not exist in July of 1979.

"I say that to you sincerely," Judge Lambert reiterated in a paternal tone. "Take care of yourself. It's a tragedy for this court to see such a total waste of humanity that I've experienced in this court."

I entered a custom tip amount. One dollar, every time, because twenty percent of my order is eighty-one cents and that is a worse tip than no tip at all.

"You are a bright young man," Judge Lambert continued solemnly. One of the girls muttered "ass-munch" and was loudly shushed by her friend. "You'd have made a good lawyer, and I'd have loved to have you practice in front of me. But you went another way, partner. Take care of yourself. I don't have any animosity, and I want you to understand that."

"Ew. 'Partner'?"

"Nice for him that he doesn't have any animosity. What about the families of all the girls he killed? Do we even know their names? Or anything about them?"

"Of course we don't. Meanwhile how many movies do we already have about him? And this time he's played by Zac Efron?"

"He wasn't even that hot. Those beady little eyes." There was a vibration of lips, and I knew the girl behind me had shivered the way you do when something or someone gives you the heebie-jeebies.

I wanted to turn around and tell the girls to watch what had pre-

ceded Judge Lambert's tender farewell speech. I wanted to tell them
how The Defendant asked and was granted permission to address
the court, and how he had shrilly protested his innocence for thirty-
four minutes (I kept time). If you had placed him on a street corner
in dirty rags, people would hurry past with their heads bent, strenu-
ously avoiding eye contact with the madman, and yet to *that* asinine
performance the judge responded soft-heartedly, knighting The
Defendant some kind of savant. I wanted to tell these girls that they
were still being manipulated, because the documentary filmmaker
had omitted The Defendant's gobbledygook from the episode, or
perhaps he had just not dug deep enough to find it, or worse, didn't
understand why his thinly veiled idiocy mattered to the story. What
was worth their ire was not an old man in an old video clip grieving
for the ruined future of a potential protégé, it's that there was never
anything to grieve. The Defendant flaunted his true nature with au-
dacious displays of ineptitude time and time again, and I wanted to
tell these girls, I wanted to tell everyone in that Starbucks, that they
should be irate that effort and money had gone into dusting off the
story and telling it again for a new generation, only for the filmmaker
to wear the same blinders as the men who wrote the headlines forty
years ago.

"What's the name?" the barista asked me, black Sharpie poised
an inch from the cardboard cup.

"Pamela," I said, and stepped aside. The girls ordered a bunch
of iced things with extra foam, though it was February and barely
forty degrees outside. They couldn't have been any older than Denise, forever twenty-one. My daughter used to beg me to take her
shopping at that store but I could never bring myself to go inside
because of the name.

It's my daughter who pointed out that while there have been
documentaries before, what's different about the latest addition
to the canon was not its faint art-house aesthetic—it's the social
media of it all, the women on Twitter and Instagram who are so
unitedly over this shit they got handcuffs on the Oscar-winning

movie producer and a grabby senator out of Congress in the middle of his term. It's a climate that assigns more value to my side of the story too. Not that I responded to any of the interview requests, not even the ones from the good people at the good places. The risk was still too great that the media might buy and sell my story for parts, treat it as a garment to be tailored to The Defendant's specific measurements.

But as I listened to those girls pick out the polite chauvinism in that tinny clip, I wondered if maybe it was time to fish my name out of the footnotes; unstitch the lie of him.

PAMELA

Tina parks on the shoulder of the road, by an unremarkable Issaquah hillside.

We set off along the old dirt logging track, fern variety packs strapped to our chests. Overhead, the branches are mottled with tear-shaped buds, signs of spring after a gray, rainy winter in the Seattle area. The conditions have created the ideal soil environment for the plants to thrive, according to the manager of the nursery section at Lowe's.

At the first lookout point, I ask if we can stop and take a breather. Tina has changed over the years, and not in the obvious ways most of us do—white hairs in weird places, a skepticism for the current noise on the radio. She's become a hard-core mountain biker, her body gristly and tanned around the shape of her spandex. She's one of those people who knocks out the advanced biking trail at dawn and unwinds at dusk with a cigarette and two fingers of bourbon.

"Good?" Tina asks.

"Sure," I gasp, wondering what the hell my spinning classes are doing for me.

We come upon a dozen roses, too pink to be from Tina, wilting in roughly the spot where Ruth was left in July 1974. Tina and I don't acknowledge them, but I have to assume Rebecca has been here.

I drop my backpack and drag open the zipper. Inside are two folding shovels, root stimulant, garden shears, a can of smoked Blue Diamond almonds, and not enough water.

"I'll start here," I say, indicating one of several copper markers planted seemingly at random in the glade.

Tina works a hand into a mannish canvas glove and sets herself up at another marker in this haphazard but precise design.

———

When the news of the Lake Sammamish disappearances first hit the papers in 1974, Tina received a call from a woman named Gail Strafford, who at the time headed up the Forensic Anthropology Department at the University of Tennessee. She had met Ruth at the medical conference in Aspen and relayed for Tina the conversation they'd had outside her hotel room door—about Gail's field of work, which was being used to help narrow down the timeline of Caryn Campbell's death. Gail was stricken to hear that Ruth had gone missing less than five months later, that foul play was suspected in her disappearance too. If there was ever anything she could do to help, Tina should not hesitate to reach out.

Gail Strafford is retired now, but she sent a team here, to this slight hillside in Issaquah, and over the last few weeks, they have conducted extensive testing on the area where The Defendant confessed to dumping Ruth's remains. They succeeded in zoning a medium-sized radius where the ground showed dynamic changes to the nutrient profile of the local ecosystem. They tagged locations and told us to plant any sort of hardy, shade-loving fern. In six months, they'll come back and assess the reflectance of the plant's foliage, which has been found to take on a reddish cast from soil containing human remains, even in places where a body decomposed decades ago.

———

For the next few hours, the two of us dig shallow holes, loosen the roots on a half dozen cinnamon ferns, pack them tight with native

soil, spritz with root stimulant, ration our bottled water, and start
again.

We site the last plant in the direction of the fading sun, and Tina
leans hard on her shovel and closes her eyes. Her lips are moving
silently around words I recognize. *I carry you like my own personal
Time Machine, as I put on my lipstick, smile, and head out to the party.*

It's a line by one of her favorite poets, a woman named Donna
Carnes, whose husband went out for a sail in San Francisco Bay and
has not been seen since. I love it too. How many parties have I gone
to over the years, and laughed, and had a good time, while still managing to hold Denise close?

Something shifted for me after we got that guilty verdict. It was
a bit like going to the chiropractor for a stiff back and regaining full
range of motion. Long before my mother told me about the four
days I went missing in the Florida swamplands, I'd sensed there
was a part of me that was mislaid. I'd gone on a pilgrimage to Florida State to find it, not understanding why I needed to be there,
only that I did. I'd cleaned and straightened and organized in an
attempt to bring order to my surroundings because inside, I was
in turmoil. I'd stayed home on nights when I should have gone out
because kicking up my heels and having a few beers at a party did
not feel fun for me the way it did for others my age. This was the
wellspring of shame—the feeling that I was different, that I was
somehow *wrong*. In the days and weeks after the trial ended, that
conviction softened, then sloughed in phases, as life revealed to me
that I'd been exactly who and where I needed to be, that I was the
only person on the face of the earth who could have sent Denise's
killer to the electric chair.

Denise's short life had meaning. She helped to fuse the parts of
me with jagged edges, pieces that ergonomically should not fit together but somehow do. It was an alignment, a relief from pain that
would have been chronic, and it was Denise's lasting gift to me.

The sky is brushed pink and lavender as we pack up, roll our heads on our stiff necks, and head back down the hillside, pants ruined at the knees.

The hope is that when we come back in the fall, one of the ferns will flag Ruth's final resting place. But I can do better than hope. I have faith, because nature is the very best example of integration. Things grow differently when they're damaged, showing us how to occupy strange new ground to bloom red instead of green. We can be found, brighter than before.

ACKNOWLEDGMENTS

First and foremost, my profound gratitude to Kathy Kleiner for responding to my email in 2019 and generously sharing your story. I am blown away by your indomitable spirit, courage, and mostly, your capacity for joy. From one survivor to another, I see you, and you inspire me.

Thank you, Pauline Boss, a pioneer whom I have never met but whose book *The Myth of Closure* served as inspiration for Tina's work with "complicated grief." To anyone going through a hard time or struggling with past or generational trauma, I highly recommend this small but mighty read, which helped me find meaning in something I'd long considered meaningless and gave me a newfound sense of agency in my life.

Thank you, Marysue Rucci, my incomparable editor, who pushed me to the point of (nearly!) breaking. This book needed it, and so did I. Everything I write from here on out will be better because of the standard you held me to on this one.

Alyssa Reuben—friend, confidante, and extraordinary literary agent—I would not have this life without you. Thank you for the nudges, the gentle and the not-so-gentle ones, and for always telling it like it is so that when you tell me something good, I know I can believe you.

To the whole team at Marysue Rucci Books: Jessica Preeg, Richard Rhorer, Andy Jiaming Tang—thank you for the friendship and the support. Elizabeth Breeden, thank you for being you. I would follow you into a fire.

Bruna Papandrea, Erik Feig, Jeanne Snow, Casey Haver, Julia Hammer, Samie Kim Falvey—thank you for getting the band back together on this one. Let's make something great.

Big thanks to Alice Gammill, my Pamela Schumacher-esque assistant, who dots every *i* and crosses every *t*, loves on my big fat bulldog like a second mother, and who procured hundreds of pages of transcripts and case files from the Florida Archives at the height of the pandemic—a painstaking and nearly impossible task that you never gave up on. I could not have told this story without you.

Michelle Weiner, Joe Mann, Cait Hoyt, and Olivia Blaustein, thank you for the wise advice, the nimble negotiating, and for continuing to make all my Hollywood dreams come true.

Christine Cuddy, you make sure all our bases are covered always. With you I have the security to be creative—thank you.

The team at Sunshine Sachs: Kimberly Christman, Keleigh Thomas Morgan, and Hannah Edelman. You three are worth every penny. Grateful for what you see in me.

Briana Dunning is the most talented hair stylist in Los Angeles and I have to thank her not only for a killer cut but for all her native Floridian wisdom. She is the one who taught me the saying that in Florida, the further north you go, the more southern it gets, which helped orient my understanding of the Panhandle. And to my Seattle shepherd, Bethany Heitman, thank you for dispelling me of the notion that Seattle is the rainiest city in the country just before the pages went to press.

Thank you to Tori Telfer, whose powerful 2019 profile of Kathy Kleiner in *Rolling Stone* got some of the wheels turning in my head, and who didn't hesitate to share resources when I cold-emailed her. You remind me of how lucky I am to be a part of this writing community.

On the subject of luck, I have a bit of it thanks to you, the reader. Thank you for preordering, purchasing, reserving at your local library, and for your messages and Instagram tags. Without you, there is no this. I hope number three was worth the wait.

ABOUT THE AUTHOR

JESSICA KNOLL is the *New York Times* bestselling author of *The Favorite Sister* and *Luckiest Girl Alive*—now a major motion picture from Netflix starring Mila Kunis. She has been a senior editor at *Cosmopolitan* and the articles editor at *Self*. She grew up in the suburbs of Philadelphia and graduated from the Shipley School in Bryn Mawr, Pennsylvania, and from Hobart and William Smith Colleges in Geneva, New York. She lives in Los Angeles with her husband, daughter, and their bulldog, Franklin.

BRIGHT YOUNG WOMEN

JESSICA KNOLL

DISCUSSION QUESTIONS

1. Do you consider yourself a fan of true crime? Why or why not? If yes, what kinds of content do you consume and what about it draws your interest? Do you share this interest with anyone else in your life?

2. The characters refer to the killer exclusively as "The Defendant" throughout the whole story, never once giving him a real name. Why do you think Jessica Knoll chose to do this? How did it impact your understanding of the novel?

3. Consider the ways in which the media and newspapers play a role throughout the novel. What kind of power do journalists or headlines have? Have you seen similar examples from this time period or from modern day? Discuss where you find news or opinions. Have you ever considered what kind of partialities are embedded in the media you consume?

4. Pamela hoped she would be "remembered as a fair and impartial leader." How would you describe Pamela as a leader? Have you ever found yourself acting as a leader amid an extreme situation? How did it make you feel? Can you imagine how you or someone you admire would react to being in Pamela's position?

5. Consider how gender is involved in Pamela's recollections of being labeled "a handful." What about Pamela's actions or personality might lead to this kind of description? Have you ever

experienced being labeled based on an assumption or expectation related to your identity?

6. Think about what Mrs. McCall tells Pamela regarding black swan events: "A highly improbable event but also one that, upon closer examination, was predictable.... The point is that nothing can be predicted, really, and so you want to be sure to expose yourself to luck too. Things can go catastrophically wrong, but they can also go so right as to be profoundly transformative." Do you think this was helpful advice for Pamela in the moment? What would you consider black swan events, both personally and on a larger scale?

7. Ruth seems to struggle with the memory of her father, thinking, "My father, whom I loved more than anything in this world, had made me very angry right before he died." What kind of tension did Ruth have with her father, and with her parents? Have you experienced a combination of love and frustration with a family member or parent? How did you come to terms with the situation?

8. Pamela notes The Defendant's crimes were, in part, a result of "a series of national ineptitudes and a parsimonious attitude toward crimes against women" and law enforcement that "would rather we remember a dull man as brilliant than take a good hard look at the role they played." Do you agree with this position? Does this perspective make you consider notorious criminals in a new light?

9. At the Aspen convention, Tina tells Ruth that men will never accept a woman as "one of them," even when they're clearly occupying space as equals. Have you ever felt a lack of acceptance in a space you knew you were qualified to occupy? Who or what made you feel that way?

10. Pamela describes being thankful for her mother telling her the story of her first trip to Florida, as the painful truth "shouldn't feel like a gift when you get it, but it is." Have you ever experienced a difficult truth as a gift?

11. Tina shares her mixed feelings about others commenting on her grief, especially the external representation of it, such as losing weight and not wearing makeup. Is there a "right" way to grieve? What other markers do you think of as part of the grieving process, and what about them stand out to you? Have you ever felt a responsibility to portray grief or pain in a specific manner so others might better appreciate your experience?

12. Consider the lesson Ruth remembers from her father's story about the lonely man at the bar, concluding that "other people's pain mattered more than my own discomfort." How does this statement make you feel? How does this lesson play out in other areas of Ruth's life? Are there other characters in the novel who seem to embody this perspective?

13. In Ruth's first visit to the therapy group, Frances asks the women about their support systems, saying "a good support system included people who were willing to listen to you and who would not judge you for anything you were feeling, even if your feelings were provocative." Who or what is a part of your own support system? Where do you see examples of support or a lack thereof in other areas of the book?

14. *Bright Young Women* is fiction, but it was inspired by true crimes against women. Have you read any other novels that are inspired by historical events or incorporate historical events? How does Jessica Knoll take well-known events and recast them in a new light?

15. Do you agree with Pamela's characterization of The Defendant as "an ordinary misogynist"? What role does misogyny play in the characters' lives? Does misogyny only impact women?

16. In speaking to a patient, Tina says, "Anger in women is treated as a character disorder, as a problem to be solved, when oftentimes it is entirely appropriate, given the circumstances that trigger it." What do you think about the patient's response that she "[doesn't] want to be seen as an angry woman"? Do you see anger as a healthy emotion? In what circumstances is anger an appropriate response?

ENHANCE YOUR GROUP ACTIVITIES

- "The Violence Against Women Act (VAWA) is a federal law that, in part, provides housing protections for people applying for or living in units subsidized by the federal government and who have experienced domestic violence, dating violence, sexual assault, or stalking, to help keep them safe and reduce their likelihood of experiencing homelessness" (hud.gov). Knowing your rights is incredibly important. Research VAWA, its history, what provisions are named, who does the work to provide resources, and what women are entitled to under this act.

- Many women who are victims of violent and/or sexual crimes wish to take legal action against their assailant but end up not being able to pursue this type of justice as a result of the cost. The Rape, Abuse & Incest National Network (RAINN) provides victim services to an average of 800+ people every day, including legal aid, policy improvement, and the facilitation of medical equipment. Consider getting involved by visiting rainn.org and exploring their list of options.

- Cooking is one of Ruth's passions, one she shared with her father before he passed away. Look up a recipe and try making one of the dishes Ruth has in the book, such as pignoli cookies or barbecued meatballs. Do you have any cooking lessons that you keep in mind, such as Ruth's father's advice to always finish a dish with something green?

- Jessica Knoll's debut novel, *Luckiest Girl Alive*, also explores violence (societal and physical) against women and the public interpretation of events. Ask if anyone in the group has read *Luckiest Girl Alive*, and what parallels or differences there are between the two novels. Consider hosting a viewing of the 2022 film adaption (written and executive produced by Jessica Knoll!) of *Luckiest Girl Alive* starring Mila Kunis. How do the characters compare with those in *Bright Young Women*? If you were to cast an onscreen version of *Bright Young Women*, which actors would you choose to play which roles?